LADY of DOOM and DEVOTION

EVA CHASE

RITES OF POSSESSION - BOOK 4

Lady of Doom and Devotion

Book 4 in the Rites of Possession series

This is a work of fiction. Any resemblance to actual persons, living or dead, or actual events is purely coincidental.

First Digital Edition, 2024

Cover design: Sanja Balan (Sanja's Covers)

Map design: Fictive Designs

Page Edge Designs: Painted Wings Publishing

Chapter Illustrations: Bojan Serafimovski

Ebook ISBN: 978-1-998752-82-9

Paperback ISBN: 978-1-998752-83-6

Hardcover ISBN: 978-1-998752-84-3

SILANA
BRYF
STARSIL RIVER
THE PINCH
ZULINA—
VELDUNY
ICAR
COUNTRY BORDERS
PROVINCES
COUNTIES
ROYAL RESIDENCES
FORTS

EEN
COTEA
PIMA
NIKODI
EPPUN PROVINCE
COLIZ
TEMPLE OF
TRANQUIL SKIES
SELCE
TUPNO
IBLIN
SEAFELL CHANNEL
FLORIAN
REGICA
ABERNI PROVINCE
THE
HAVEN
MAJOR
PAWLEM'S FORT
MIPONE
SUNBLOWN
SEA

ONE

Ivy

The room where I'm being held prisoner smells like stale perfume and blood. The latter I assume comes from the crusted red-brown smears that streak across the gilded wallpaper.

This mansion must be the residence of some noble—or used to be before my captors took it over. A couple of the men in soldier uniforms are digging through a wardrobe carved from fine marlwood, matching the elaborate frame of the four-poster bed. Shards of crystal that might have once been fancy perfume bottles litter the thick rug.

Along with the smeared blood and the broken crystal, someone has slashed into the cushions on the chairs so the stuffing spills out like fluffy guts. There's a darker ruddy splotch in the middle of the bedsheets that I don't want to look at too closely.

Beyond the broad picture window, all I can see is the nearby stone wall and a sprawl of empty fields beyond it. The house's shadow stretches long in the late-afternoon sunlight.

I'm guessing this is one of the country estates I've heard and read about, a summer home where some exalted family could retreat when they tired of city politics.

It doesn't look as if anyone's been having a relaxing time here recently.

The men toss several dresses that they retrieved from the wardrobe onto the floor. Their leader peers down at them.

Lothar, the king's secondary magical advisor and apparent head of the conspiracy to murder that king, shifts his tall, lopsided frame with a thoughtful air. I still haven't gotten used to the asymmetry of his body, one arm missing all the way to the shoulder in one of the most extreme dedication sacrifices I've ever seen.

That is, one of the most extreme outside of the poor accomplices he and his supporters have had carved up to the barest edge of survival. Great God help us all, how much power can this man wield when he combines his gift with those of his victims?

I have no idea what his gift even is. So far I haven't seen it in action, haven't felt the tingle of magic coursing off him.

He points at a confection of sleek pewter-gray silk. "That one. Fine but not too eye-catching. Have our 'guest' put it on."

His thick baritone takes on a sneering edge with the word "guest." We both know he's not offering any hospitality to me.

But my arms move all the same. My hands lift to yank off the plain woolen dress I was wearing when he stole me away from my companions this morning.

The wound on my side where one of Lothar's underlings stabbed me last night aches beneath its bandage. With all my might, I scream silently at my muscles to resist.

I can't so much as clench my jaw, let alone hold my body back.

The woman standing next to Lothar has me in the iron grip of her gift, partly fueled by the sacrificial accomplice slumped against the nearby wall beneath a shroud. Sweat gleams on Zaneta's forehead beneath her parted dun-brown bangs and her slim fingers twist at her sides, but her control has shown no sign of ebbing.

At her silent demand, I shuck off the trousers I was using as an underskirt as well. Apparently the scourge sorcerers don't care about my humble underclothes, because she has me pick up the silk dress without adjusting those.

I don't have to get fully naked in front of a bunch of hostile strangers. One tiny blessing in a heap of shit.

Lothar holds up his hand, and Zaneta follows his unspoken command to stop me. He frowns at the grayed ribbon wrapped around my upper arm. "What's that for?"

My puppet master propels an answer out of me. I don't see any need to lie about this, but I stay brief. "A memento."

The leader of the Order of the Wild lets out a scoffing chuckle. "I'm not indulging your sentimentality, fiend."

He tugs off the scrap of fabric—my last remaining fragment of my little sister. A cry of protest snags in my throat, unable to burst out.

Watching me with a look of challenge as if daring me to flex my magic at him, Lothar holds the ribbon to a lantern lit on a side table. My objection crawls through my chest, digging claws into my innards, but I can't move an inch. Can't stir so much as a spurt of my power.

Normally in a situation as threatening as this, my chaotic magic would be wrenching at me to set it free, to let it blast apart all these villains. And in this particular case, I think I might let it, consequences be damned.

But Zaneta's control over me is keeping my magic locked away inside me too. Actually, that's probably what's causing her the most strain. The restless energy wobbles around my heart like it's set at a slow simmer, but I can't whip it out of me.

Flames lick up the ribbon, blackening it in an instant. Lothar drops it into an empty wash basin just before the fire reaches his fingers. More smoke wisps up as the fabric crumbles away into ash.

My throat feels as if it's clamped shut. I can barely breathe.

It's all right. It was only a bit of cloth.

He can't touch my memories of Linzi. He can't destroy what she meant to me.

There's a whole lot more he could destroy, though.

Lothar motions to Zaneta, and she compels me to pull on the gown. I can't take any pleasure from the smoothness of the silk sliding over my skin. It only makes me think of the last time I wore dresses like this regularly—when I was pretending to be noble myself at the royal college.

When I had a countess-to-be's ghost lodged in my head, guiding me through the treacherous noble world. When I had men with me who became allies and then friends and then so much more than I'd ever dared to hope for.

All of that is gone now, as lost as my sister's ribbon. All thanks to Lothar and his sadistic schemes.

My head remains silent. Julita's spirit leapt out of me last night to help defend me from her vicious brother.

She'll have passed on into the embrace of her godlen now.

I have no idea whether the godlen who's watched over *me* is paying any attention to my current predicament. It'd be awfully nice for Kosmel to get on with showing me an escape route if he has any mind to.

And my men… The four men who've become not just my lovers but a tightly knit family like I thought I'd never have again…

It's been several hours since I last saw them. My last words to them, propelled from my throat by this scourge sorcerer's magic, were mocking them for trusting me.

Gods only know what they believe happened. Whether they'll see me as anything but an enemy even if they manage to find me.

Fresh tears prick behind my eyes. I will them back as I tighten the lacing on the dress.

Lothar would only laugh at my weeping. I don't want to give him the satisfaction, no matter how much anguish burns in my chest.

When my hands drop back to my sides, Lothar looks me over with one of his hard smirks. Revulsion crawls over my skin that has nothing to do with his uneven frame.

This man must be a psychopath above anything we've encountered before in our quest against scourge sorcerers. He's built a country-wide conspiracy while pretending to serve the family he wants to see slaughtered.

A country-wide conspiracy that powers itself with the total mutilation of orphaned twelve-year-olds.

His "Order of the Wild" claims to be following the true desires of the gods. The people he's egging on have insisted that their mad, violent practices will bring even the All-Giver back after centuries since the Great God abandoned our realms.

I'm not sure yet whether this man actually believes the stories he's spread or whether it's all a tactic for some other purpose.

The magic advisor motions to one of the soldiers who sorted through the dresses. The stranger steps closer to run a comb through my tangled hair. I can't even wince, let alone recoil from his touch.

While I endure the primping, a slim man with a sallow face appears in the doorway. He can't be more than a few years older than my twenty years, and his slight figure is nearly swallowed up by the layers of embroidered silk and velvet he's dressed himself in. You'd think he was suited up for a ball.

He peers at me, his stance stiffening, and darts a glance toward Lothar. "I heard you brought one of the *riven* here."

A mix of horror and revulsion colors his tone. The typical reaction of most people to my cursed magic, but it makes my stomach lurch all the same.

Lothar speaks with the same chilly authority as before. "You have nothing to worry about. She's utterly under our control."

There's a gloating note to that last sentence. I'd grit my teeth if I could move them.

The foppish man shudders and flicks his hand down his front in a hasty gesture of the divinities, as if calling on the gods to protect him from me. "When you asked for the use of the estate, I didn't realize—"

Lothar's tone hardens. "You committed yourself to our cause. Are you starting to doubt my judgment after all?"

Somehow the other man—the heir to this estate?—turns even paler. "No—no, of course not. All I can offer to the All-Giver and the Order of the Wild."

He scurries off, maybe hoping that if I do end up exploding with evil magic, he'll be far enough away to escape the onslaught.

Was he really master of this estate already? Or did he turn on his parents the way I've heard other noble heirs did with the Order's backing?

When the man with the comb steps away from me, Lothar glances over at a second duo of sorcerer and shrouded accomplice waiting at the other side of the room. The sorcerer is leaning against the vanity, studying a gleaming metal object they retrieved from my pocket when they were checking me over for weapons.

The locket that can be used as a signal to my men. If the sorcerer presses his thumb to the pane on the inside, they'll know where to find me.

But the stout man has only peeked inside and otherwise has been murmuring fragments of the odd language the scourge sorcerers use while examining the exterior.

"Have you untangled the magic on it?" Lothar asks.

The sorcerer shakes his head. "It's definitely been blessed, but it's not giving me any impressions of specifically how. That must mean it's not currently active. I can't pick up on any magic emanating off it right now."

"Keep it in that containment box of yours, then. We don't want to risk it creating some disruptive effect when we're not prepared."

The lopsided man turns back to me. "I don't suppose you'd tell me the truth about what it's for if I let you speak."

I simply glare back at him, wishing my hatred could sear into him the way my magic currently can't.

Lothar hums to himself. "Tie her hair back. The style doesn't need to be ornate. We'll cover it with the hood of her cloak regardless."

Zaneta wets her lips. "Are we going tonight?"

"The more time we delay, the more chance Konram has to adjust his plans. Gods only know what he's made of recent events." He glances toward her accomplice. "We won't be able to bring the blessed one right into the palace. He'll be too obvious. You can continue channeling power from a bit of a distance, I assume."

His sorcerer bobs her head. "Yes, Master Lothar. But it'll take all my concentration."

"That's perfectly fine." Lothar's smirk crawls back across his face as his gaze meets mine. "Our riven sorcerer will finally do something worthwhile with that wild magic of hers. She can take care of the rest."

A chill sweeps through my body. I flail against the invisible hold on me with a renewed surge of defiance, but I still can't budge a single muscle.

What is he going to do with me?

What is he going to *make* me do?

I don't know whether Lothar can read my horror in my stiffened expression or if my response is easy to guess. He steps closer to me, his pale brown eyes gleaming with a manic light.

"You don't like this? Such a pity. You're lucky you had as many years of freedom as you did. Your kind is an abomination—a blight on the realms. Born with so much power you never had to give up so much as a tuft of hair for… You should be grateful I'm letting you be such an important part of our revolution."

Is he sour about how much he sacrificed for whatever gift he's got? It's not as if anyone forced the choice on him.

And he doesn't even bother to use his own magic much, considering the way he's ordering his underlings to handle all the sorcery.

What exactly is he so bitter about?

I can only imagine the caustic remarks Julita would have made about the royal advisor—and imagining them makes my gut twist with the loss.

Somehow she always found something to say that bolstered my spirits, no matter how dire a situation we found ourselves in. I got used to having that bit of company—of friendship—as ephemeral as her ghost was.

It's better for her that she's moved on. She deserves some peace. And I have plenty of practice surviving on my own.

I never thought I'd find myself in a position where I didn't want to.

Lothar snaps his fingers at the men in the soldier uniforms. "Prepare the carriage. I want to be riding out within the hour."

Zaneta sucks in a breath. "What would you have me do with her once we reach the palace?"

The magic advisor lets out a cool chuckle. "If all goes well, I'll be able to get us right to the royal family through my authority alone. Stay ready to intervene on my command if needed. We'll gather them all in the audience room."

His gaze pierces me, even colder than before. "The moment we step into the room and she can see them, have her crack every one of their pretty royal skulls."

Two

Ivy

Lothar keeps the carriage curtains drawn. I know when we've reached the city of Regica because he stops to step out briefly and speak to the guard at the gate.

We're crammed tightly onto the cushioned benches within, my sorcerer puppet master sitting close enough that our elbows knock together when the wheels hit a bump. But I'm not sure I'd rather have her shrouded sacrificial accomplice or the riven-hating, lopsided magic advisor pressed up against me instead.

It's bad enough feeling Lothar's haughty gaze evaluating me from the opposite bench as the carriage rattles onward.

Zaneta may be able to keep my magic locked down, but she can't control every automatic bodily reaction. My heart has been hammering since Lothar revealed his instructions for me, and my stomach churns harder with every passing minute.

I guess she can stop me from outright vomiting.

Although I wouldn't mind puking my guts all over the man in charge right now.

Maybe then he wouldn't be able to waltz right into Regica's royal residence and arrange his murderous audience with the king.

The Order of the Wild member steering the carriage guides us through the city streets with occasional turns. It feels like a long time before the vehicle halts again.

My pulse stutters, but Lothar turns to the sacrificial accomplice rather than me. "You'll be staying safely out of sight as you continue to help. Our friends will look after you while you offer your talent to Zaneta."

"It's my pleasure to serve the All-Giver," the accomplice mumbles.

After they've stepped out of the carriage, I attempt to flex my muscles. Searching for any weak point in Zaneta's hold over my body.

How well can she draw on the accomplice's magic from a distance, even a short one? It's got to be harder, and she already looked as if the effort was wearing on her.

For now, it still isn't straining her enough for me to resist her magic. The only difference I can feel is a sharper jitter of my own power within my chest, as if it senses some tiny loosening of our invisible prison that I can't exploit yet.

I have to keep trying. I have to stop myself from giving in to her demands before we reach the royal family.

I've spent months putting my life and my sanity on the line to protect King Konram and his family's reign over Silana. Fighting to ensure that the scourge sorcerers don't gain the upper hand and impose their brutal brand of leadership over the entire country.

He was just about to pardon me. He finally believed I wasn't a monster.

Gods smite me, I don't want to be one. I don't want to

see the world we'll be left with if the royal family falls to these villains.

Although by the time Lothar's done with me, my mind might not be sound enough for me to even care. My grip on reality was already starting to fracture every time I called on more of my magic.

All too soon, Lothar climbs back into the carriage. He doesn't say anything as the horse tugs us forward, but we've got to be near the palace already. He'd want the accomplice as close by as possible.

My assumption is confirmed when the wheels rasp to another stop no more than a minute later. Lothar nods to Zaneta. "Let us see our purpose through."

My skin crawls at the import of those words.

My limbs shift, pushing me to my feet. I climb out of the carriage in contradiction to every personal intention.

But as I wrench at my body, willing it to refuse, a faint quiver runs down my arm. When the sorcerer directs my hand to drop to my side, my fingers twitch toward my thigh in a soft tap.

Hope jolts through my veins. That was my act—I'm almost sure about it.

I try to wiggle my fingers again, but now that my arm is still, they won't budge. I can't turn my head, can barely adjust my gaze beyond staring straight in front of me.

There was a tiny opening. I have to find another one.

We're standing in front of a high wall of polished stone. A gilded but heavy wooden door fills the gate.

Lothar walks up to the Melchiorek crest carved into the doorframe. Flanking him, Zaneta directs me to tug my hood farther forward to shadow my face.

As I lift my hand, I manage to flex my fingers again. But as soon as they reach my hood, they close around the fabric, ignoring any command I'm giving them.

I can't stop myself from lowering my arm, so I put all my will into propelling it a little faster. Would I be able to make a jab with my elbow?

The joint bends slightly with a brief twitch. Hmm.

Lothar has pressed a token against the crest and murmurs words I can't make out. The gate swings open to admit us.

Several guards in royal sapphire-blue uniforms stand on the other side of the gate. King Konram has clearly ramped up security after seeing absolute proof of the Order of the Wild's intentions.

Just last night, a horde of hundreds of Order members marched within a couple of hours of this city, intending to kill him.

It's only because of me and my men—and a risky plan that required manipulating the Darium soldiers on the other side of the Seafell Channel—that the scourge sorcerer army never made it here. I can hardly celebrate that victory if I let myself become the king's murderer in the aftermath, though.

I wrench at my neck in an effort to turn my head toward the guards, strain at my face to make some expression they'll take as a warning.

None of my efforts produce any result. I just keep walking straight ahead, following Lothar alongside my puppet master.

When I managed to move by my own will before, it was when I was merely extending the motion the scourge sorcerer had already forced rather than pushing against her control. It would make sense if it's easier to slip in a little of my own intention when I'm leaning into her commands.

Cautiously, not wanting her to realize I'm testing the limits of her hold, I focus on flicking the toe of my boot against the hem of my dress. After a few steps, I succeed in giving it a soft tap.

That's something. A small fragment of control I can reclaim.

Now how can I use it to prevent this assassination attempt? If I overplay my hand and fail, Zaneta will tighten her grip on me even more.

I'll only get one chance.

The Regica palace towers over us—not quite as grandly imposing as the palace I'm used to in the capital city of Florian, but an impressive work of architecture all the same. The marble walls gleam, and carved figures of Creaden, the godlen of leadership, peer down from either side of the main doors.

Four guards are stationed at the top of the broad steps leading up to those doors. One holds up her hand at the sight of us.

"Advisor Lothar," she says. "The king is expecting you— but he isn't allowing any unvetted parties into the palace. You'll need to continue from here alone."

Lothar frowns. "These are my assistants. I've vetted them myself. They have key information to impart for the meeting I've arranged with King Konram."

The guard shakes her head. "I'm sorry, Advisor Lothar. Considering recent events, he's put in place a policy that only people he's specifically approved of may enter. I'm sure you can discuss that with him during your meeting."

The magic advisor sighs as if this is all a ridiculous precaution. Never mind that Konram's wariness may save his life tonight.

Unless Lothar can use his gift to force the issue.

Please, let this murderous mission end here. I'm too keyed up for any real hope to penetrate my queasiness, but I pray silently with all my might.

The lopsided man offers the lead guard a smile that makes me want to shudder. "Surely you can at least admit them into the outer halls. It's a rather chilly evening. I'd imagine King Konram will approve of their presence as soon as I've spoken to him."

The guard shows no signs of budging. "If they're cold, they can wait for approval in the carriage, Advisor. I have to follow my orders."

"I'm sorry to hear that," Lothar says with a tone full of acid, and makes a sharp motion toward Zaneta.

I don't even have time to cry out in protest, as unspoken as that cry would be in my present state. The scourge sorcerer's magic yanks at my body—and has me propelling my own power forward in an instant.

Against every particle of my will, I hurl lances of my magic at all four guards at once. The supernatural force slams through their skulls.

My magic shatters their minds before they can raise any protest either.

Four bodies crumple outside the palace doors. With another jerk of Zaneta's control, I'm dissolving those bodies into dust that whips away in a gust of wind.

My magic reverberates eagerly from my chest, but the rest of me is screaming in vain. The bottom of my stomach has completely hollowed out.

I just eviscerated four innocent people—four people who were only trying to protect the leader of the realm. I tore apart their corpses so no one will even realize what happened to them.

Gods only know what consequences echoed out in exchange for those acts.

And this is only the beginning of what Lothar wants from me.

He's already shoved open the palace door. "Make sure no one sees enough to raise the alarm," he snaps at Zaneta under his breath.

He marches down the main hall draped with tapestries and hung with gold-framed paintings. My feet stride after him over the intricately woven rug.

My thoughts scramble in my frantic attempts to figure out how to defy him. I might be able to throw myself faster forward, right into him.

But I have no weapons, and Zaneta is containing my magic again. What would bumping against the magic advisor accomplish other than pissing him off and making her even more cautious?

Maybe when Zaneta pushes my magic out of me again, I can launch at least a little of it toward my captors instead?

I won't have much time to find out. Lothar wants me to destroy the royal family the second we reach them.

I have no idea how deep into the palace the audience room lies. Lothar veers down a side hall, picking up his pace even more, and Zaneta forces me to match it.

Lanterns flicker on the walls, casting their golden glow through the opulent passage. Then voices echo off the vaulted ceilings from somewhere in the distance—an urgent shout.

My heart leaps with the thought that our intrusion has already been discovered. But Lothar and his underling don't react.

My gut knots tighter with sickly understanding.

The shout wasn't a real sound. That was my mind acting up, inventing hallucinations. Cracking more as my magic tears at my sanity.

And there's nothing I can do about it.

Nothing *yet*. With every step, we must be getting farther away from the sacrificial accomplice Zaneta is drawing strength from. I test the boundaries of her control and find I can swing my arms just a little with my strides.

Somehow I don't think a swish of my sleeves is going to save me or King Konram.

I reach toward the power coiled inside me. It's whirling in my chest with a sense of anticipation after being called on once already.

If I can crack Zaneta's control over my magic—if I can shatter her concentration for long enough to break free—

Two guards hustle toward us from farther down the hall. One of them hesitates, looking us over. "Advisor Lothar, I don't think—"

Lothar doesn't even need to gesture this time. Zaneta knows what her orders are—and my body jerks to follow them with the squeeze of her magic around me.

Two more spears of power spring from my hands. Both of the guards collapse, their eyes rolling up, their forms totally limp.

Lothar points to a side room, and Zaneta has me heave the corpses inside. I grapple with my power, willing it to careen farther to the side, to smack into her, but it stays melded to the strict course she's given it.

I still can't deviate too far from her control. She'd need to be right in the way of where she's having me direct my magic, and it's unlikely she'll be that careless.

Lothar lets out a hiss of his breath through his teeth. "Come on. Before anyone else can interfere."

We hurry to another corner and turn toward a door carved with crowns and leafy branches. Zaneta has me cut down the two guards stationed outside before they can so much as speak.

Another scream builds at the base of my throat, but I can't even look away from their lifeless bodies.

As we hurtle onward, she compels me to disengage the door's lock with my magic. More power balls behind my sternum, ready to shove the door wide so I can spring inside and smash through every person waiting beyond it.

No. I can't let this happen. I *can't.*

My pulse thunders in my ears. My thoughts flail in my head.

And as we reach the door, I see my opening.

In the same moment as my first blast of magic hits the door to fling it open, Zaneta throws me forward alongside it. She wants me to charge inside before the royal family has time to react.

So I fling myself even faster in the direction she's already pushed me.

I hurl myself into the edge of the opening door, managing to duck my head just slightly at the same time. My forehead slams into the hard wooden corner with all the force I can bring to bear.

Pain explodes through my skull for a fleeting second. Then my mind spirals into darkness.

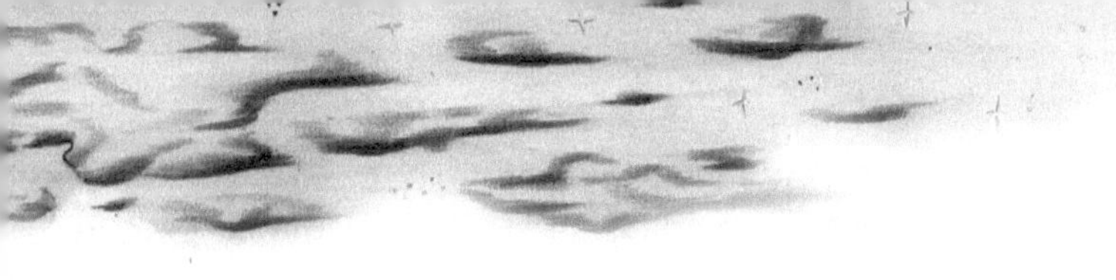

THREE

Stavros

As we wander the city streets, I keep the stump of my left wrist hidden in my pocket. The empty prosthetic base still strapped to it feels unnervingly light.

With fifteen years behind me since I sacrificed my hand in my dedication ceremony to Sabrelle, I can't say I miss it at all. After all this time, the metal and wooden contraptions that've taken its place are even more familiar than the flesh I gave up.

But going completely without leaves me at too obvious a disadvantage.

Unfortunately, the metal combat prosthetic that's the only option I have available is far too identifiable, making it a disadvantage in itself. It's too large for me to easily conceal it in a pocket and too inhuman to escape notice.

And I'm not entirely sure whether I'm prowling Regica as a returning hero or a wanted criminal.

A glow streaks through the thickening night from various

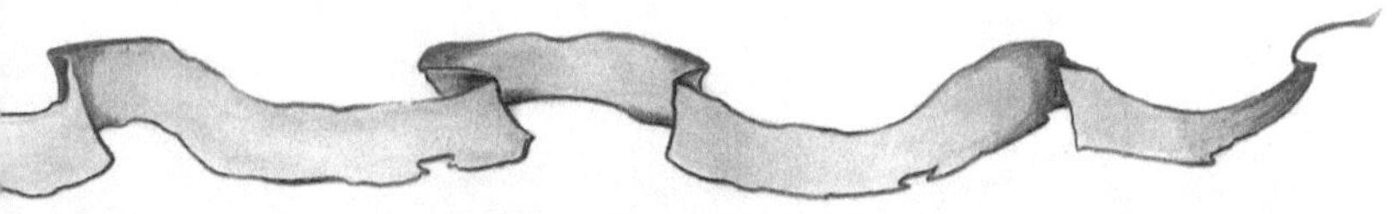

pub and restaurant windows. When a cluster of jovial patrons emerges from one of the pubs, the four of us draw to a stop not far away as if we're pausing to debate our destination.

Rheave studies them for a moment and murmurs beneath a burst of their raucous laughter. "They don't look very important."

The daimon in human form tends to state the truth baldly—a quality I've come to appreciate in many circumstances.

I dip my head in acknowledgment. "They don't. But you never know who might have seen or overheard something odd they'll decide to mention to their friends."

Alek shifts restlessly on his feet. Between the shadow of his cloak's hood and the thin scarf he's wrapped across his lower face to hide his scars, I can't make out the scholar's expression, but I can guess what he's thinking.

We have to take whatever slim chances we can get of dredging up information, because we've gone all day without discovering anything at all.

With every peal of the temple bells on the hour, the dread in my gut has expanded. I've fought unpredictable enemies before but never any as baffling as this.

The pub-goers exchange a few crude comments about one of the barmaids complete with gestures of demonstration and then make noises of commiseration while one complains about his harsh boss at the bathhouse. They amble off leaving us just as uncertain as before.

Casimir grimaces and rakes his fingers through his tawny hair, an unusually tense gesture from the normally serene courtesan. "Whatever happened to Ivy and Hessild, it might not have anything to do with Regica. What if we've come to the wrong place?"

Alek speaks up in his flat, matter-of-fact tone. "The only

thing we can say for sure about the scourge sorcerers is that they wanted to destroy the royal family. The royal family is here. At least, they were here as of last night."

He glances toward me with a question in his brown eyes.

I peer down the street toward the palace's high towers several blocks away. A few windows gleam with lantern light, blurring after a moment with my damaged vision.

My thoughts slide back to last night. "The Order of the Wild's army posed an obvious threat, but as far as we can tell, none of their forces breached even the city walls. In a scenario like that, it'd be unwise for King Konram to leave a secure position and put himself in a potentially precarious one on the road."

"Especially when his advisors are being murdered with magic on those roads," Rheave says helpfully. His dark brown curls sway with the cock of his head.

My stomach clenches at the reminder.

We left Hessild Korinya, the king's primary magic advisor, and her two soldier escorts lying on the road where they died. It felt disrespectful to abandon their bodies like that, but any attempt at rites we offered them could be seen as a sign that we had a hand in their death.

We can hope that leaving them undisturbed will increase the chances that the king's people can determine what—and who—killed them. And that it wasn't the fugitives she'd been sent to retrieve for his pardon.

I left a note tucked beneath her arm, saying that the scourge sorcerers had struck and that we'd ridden off to pursue them. But of course, that's only part of the truth.

The battle that's torn at me since this morning surges up again.

I should go to the king and inform him directly of what happened. Warn him that there's an even greater threat than we realized, one working by methods more subtle than we could anticipate.

But if we go to him without any answers and without the woman he most hesitated to pardon, I don't need my gift of glimpsing the future to predict the outcome.

He'll assume Ivy is to blame and resume his call for her execution.

In my silence, the curiosity in Rheave's smooth face dims. His brow furrows before he speaks more hesitantly than before. "What if it wasn't the scourge sorcerers who attacked? We know that Ivy would never have purposefully hurt those people, but her magic didn't always let her think right. It wouldn't be her fault."

Casimir shakes his head emphatically. "Ivy hadn't used her magic at all in over a day. It wouldn't make sense for the madness to come over her all of a sudden like that, so much stronger than before. And she never spoke to us mockingly even in the worst past times."

Our lover's parting words echo up from my memories. *I got what I needed, and now we're done. Did you really think I cared about you? You're ridiculous, all of you.*

It didn't sound remotely like the woman I've spent nearly every waking minute with for weeks. The cracks of insanity that'd wriggled into her mind made her paranoid and jumpy, not sneering.

Every particle of my body rejects the possibility that those claims came from Ivy, regardless of her state. Even the laugh she let out sounded forced.

A group of scourge sorcerers who weren't part of the march must have launched a new attack—striking down Hessild and then wrenching Ivy away from us.

Unfortunately, they covered their tracks so well that I couldn't manage to follow her. I ran back to my mount as quickly as I could to give chase, but by the time I launched the stallion into motion, it was as if the woman I love had vanished.

My hand drops to the pocket at my hip. The locket all of us except Rheave carry matching copies of hasn't given off the pulse of its magical signal all day.

If Ivy regained control of the situation, she'd come back to us or signal us to come to her, wouldn't she? Which means she's still trapped… or she's no longer capable of reaching out at all.

The knot in my gut squeezes tighter, but I can't deny logic. Regardless of the power the scourge sorcerers can summon from the accomplices they've had mutilated, nothing can rival Ivy's boundless riven magic.

They could very well have wanted to simply eliminate her to ensure she couldn't interfere with their plans any further. Perhaps I couldn't find her… because she was already gone.

My hand balls at my side. I lift it to tap down my front in the gesture of the divinities.

If that's the case, those miscreants will pay beyond any punishment I already hoped to inflict on them. But Sabrelle give me strength, let it not be true. Let her still be alive.

Let us find her.

I square my shoulders, girding myself. "Let's wander a little closer to the palace. Now that it's dark, we don't have to worry quite as much about being recognized."

Alek nods. "Nothing appears to have gone wrong here yet. We should take that as a good sign. Ivy may have escaped already and simply be waiting until it's safe to reach out to us. She knows how to extricate herself from a dangerous scenario."

As we head toward the palace, Rheave's strides take on a renewed energy. "Yes. Our little vine doesn't let anyone stop her. The next time we see her, she might have totally destroyed the Order of the Wild all on her own."

I wish I could summon the same optimism. Tension stays coiled tight around my innards.

It is true that there've been no disturbances in the city. If any fighting had broken out, we'd have noticed—

A distant thump brings my head snapping around. A squeak of a cry reaches my ears, followed by a thunder of pounding footsteps.

My pulse skips a beat. I jerk my hand toward my companions, already swiveling to track the sounds. "This way!"

The commotion is coming from the general direction of the palace, but not straight ahead. I dash down the street and take a right turn with the other men at my heels.

Whatever's going on might not have anything to do with the scourge sorcerers, but we need to know for sure.

There's another thump and a gasp sharp enough to carry past the nearby buildings. I sprint faster, my heart thudding in my chest.

Could that be Ivy fleeing her captors?

We dodge a cart and skid to a stop at the edge of one of the city's broader roads.

Six figures are racing through the darkness, hurtling toward us. Heavy velvet cloaks flap around the three being chased, the form in the middle gripping the other two's arms as if urging them on.

Less than a block behind them and closing the distance with every step, three palace guards charge in pursuit. Their expressions are set with stern determination.

My legs lock up with the uncertainty about who the actual victims here are.

Rheave makes an urgent noise in his throat. "The soldiers —they're all captured daimon."

At the same moment, the wind ripples over one of the fleeing figure's hoods. As I twitch my gaze to track the movement, the fabric flaps back enough to reveal dark hair framing a pale face I recognize in an instant.

Not the woman I was looking for, but a girl who it appears needs my protection even more in this moment.

I don't know why Princess Klaudia is running away from the guards who would normally be defending her or who she's with, but the captured daimon are the scourge sorcerers' tools. I doubt their intentions are good.

"We take the guards down," I bark at the others, and leap into the street.

I miss my prosthetic hand more than ever, but my sword slides from its sheath with a reassuring hiss. I barrel past King Konram's daughter and her companions straight toward their pursuers.

A flash of startled confusion crosses one of the guards' faces just before I slam my sword into his chest. The moment the blade penetrates his heart, his body hardens into the clay it started as.

As he thuds to the cobblestones with a crack of the fired clay, a lightning-like bolt of energy careens through the air and smacks into the woman next to him. She reels backward, the side of her head charred by Rheave's supernatural attack.

Before she can regain her balance, I've slit her throat and spun toward the third pursuer.

He tries to dodge me, lunging after the princess. In the same moment as I drive my sword into his side, an arrow smacks into his temple.

I'm not sure which weapon causes his ultimate end. Like the other two, he stiffens into clay and collapses.

I whirl in the direction the princess was running. My friends were racing over to help me in the confrontation, Rheave with his bow and another arrow in hand, the other two gripping their knives. With the fall of the last body, we turn to consider the three figures in their fancy cloaks who've hesitated in a tight huddle by the doorway of a darkened shop.

Princess Klaudia's voice wavers from beneath her hood. "General Stavros?"

I lost my military position more than a year ago with the injury that damaged my sight, but I'm not of any mind to correct her now. The fact that she recognized *me* may be the only reason she hasn't kept running.

I lower my sword and hold up the stump of my wrist in a gesture of surrender. "I only wanted to ensure they wouldn't hurt you. What's happened, Princess Klaudia?"

The only answer I get is a muffled sob as she presses her hand to her mouth. The girl is only sixteen—gods only know what she's been through to bring her to this point.

Stepping closer, I make out her brother's face beneath one of the other hoods. Prince Jacos is even younger, and his skin has turned sallow despite the blotches of exertion from their run.

The figure in the middle who was clutching them lifts her head to meet my gaze. In the second before my vision fogs again, I find myself staring at one of my former students— Petra, her name is.

Her dark eyes hold mine so solemnly my stomach hollows out.

She's a distant relative of the queen's—not even from the Melchiorek line. Why would King Konram have evacuated her along with the immediate royal family?

Why is she with her cousins and not the king himself or any of their actual protectors?

When she speaks, her clear voice holds steady other than a brief quiver of emotion she can't totally suppress. "Ster. Stavros, we need your help. King Konram and Queen Ishild are dead."

FOUR

My head throbs harder with every stumbling step. Liquid trickles down the side of my face—a metallic flavor seeps between my lips.

Blood; it must be blood.

Everything but the ache feels so far away.

A hand is clamped around my upper arm, yanking me faster. I just want to stop and lie down, make the pounding in my skull stop, but my legs keep lurching onward.

A voice grates out from beside me. "Can't you get her running?"

Another voice, wobbly: "I'm sorry, Master Lothar. I'm doing my best. It's harder when she's injured."

My drooping head sways. The surface I'm staggering over blurs and wavers before my unfocused eyes.

"Wretched riven sorcerer," the man hauling me along snarls. "Not even good enough to get a job this simple done. You don't deserve one fucking shred of that magic."

We burst out a door into a gust of cool air. Droplets of blood splat onto the pale cobblestones in my wake.

My mind recoils from the sight. There was more blood—blood all over marble tiles—blood splattered across a golden crown—

My stomach flips over. Was that me? Did I slaughter someone in that vast audience room despite my best attempt at resistance?

Lothar—yes, that's who's jerking me along so forcefully—he's angry. I made things more difficult for him.

But that doesn't mean he didn't get the basics of what he wanted in the end.

Yells and clangs ring out and fade in rippling waves. I can't tell if any of them are real and not just hallucinations.

I stumble, and a sharper pulse of pain jabs through my skull to shatter my few coherent thoughts. I reel in a wave of dizziness.

My sense of the world around me completely fizzles out. I fade in and out of awareness.

I'm slumped against the wall of a jostling carriage—

Lothar is snapping something at his companions—

Someone presses something against my temple, maybe intending to bandage my wound but so roughly I'd flinch if the magic controlling me would allow it—

Then we're spilling out into the dark chill of the night, our feet thumping onto a packed dirt lane. Lothar yanks me on toward a looming stone house.

As we march inside, I catch enough glimpses through the muddled haze to recognize that it's the same summer estate home he brought me to before. There's a stumble behind me.

"What's the matter now?" Lothar demands.

Zaneta's voice has become outright ragged. "I—I'm doing my best, but the strain—Keeping her totally in my hold for so long is draining me—"

The magic advisor spits out a few curse words and shoves me through a doorway. "Fine. I suppose you should get some rest before we mop up this mess."

He raises his voice. "Biani! Where's the lossum you picked up for us?"

The term penetrates the ache in my head. Lossum—that's a common sedative.

Despite my careening thoughts, a fragment of understanding clicks into place. Drugging the riven is the typical strategy for ensuring they can't use their powers.

They're going to knock me out so Zaneta can rest without worrying about what I'll do.

I'm going to be free from her scourge sorcery... but not conscious to take advantage of that fact.

Her hold must be weakening more. If I can wrench myself away now—

But I'm drained too, and I can't gather my focus through the pain still radiating from my forehead. All I manage is to suck in a deeper breath, and then my body is tossing itself onto its back on a low bed.

A vial lifts to my face. Bitter liquid coats my tongue.

My head lolls as I try to summon the control to gag and spit it out, but I simply roll onto my side.

An even thicker, darker haze rolls over me, and I don't know anything at all.

Well, my wayward rogue, you do have a knack for getting yourself into the most contorted sorts of trouble, don't you?

The voice echoes through the fog I'm floating in as if from all around me.

I know it. I've heard it before.

It's important.

I open my mouth, but I can't find the wherewithal to respond. My mind is so fuzzy…

You need to wake up, the voice says. *Now!*

The last word hits me like a punch, and the eyes I didn't know were closed pop open.

The room around me is hazy too, just a hint of the dawn's glow seeping through a window beyond the foot of the bed. I'm lying on my side on top of the covers—no one bothered to so much as drape a blanket over me. My limbs feel cold and achy.

My head throbs too, but with a duller pulsing than the previous sharp pangs.

I have the urge to shift and stretch, but at the same moment a large figure adjusts his position where he's leaning against a side table near the door. A bulky man with his mouth set in a bored scowl.

He's going to realize I woke up—he's going to hurt me. I have to hit him first, before—

I yank back my mind from those frantic thoughts. The quavering panic of them is horribly familiar.

I used a lot of magic last night. Possibly more than I know.

Now I'm having delusions of danger again.

Of course, I *am* in a lot of danger. But it's not as immediate as my scattered sanity would have me believe.

The man is gazing toward the window, not toward me. I dip my eyelids so I'll still look asleep if he glances my way.

Yes, I could knock him down with my magic. It's already unfurling around my racing heart with my newly recovered consciousness.

But my guard is far from the only threat I'm facing. I have to be smart.

I study the man for a few moments through my eyelashes. I think I saw him around the house after Lothar brought me here the first time. One of his stooges, maybe a captured daimon.

Inside my mouth, I curl my tongue assessingly. The movement comes easily without any force obstructing it.

I'm still wearing my boots. I wiggle my toes inside them, where the man can't see.

A jolt of hope shoots through my chest. The scourge sorcerer's magic isn't clamped around my body any longer. Zaneta must still be sleeping.

I can move myself through my own will.

More memories float up in fragments. Lothar brought me back here—he drugged me so that my puppet master could sleep.

But I've woken up sooner than he must have expected.

Because of the voice in my dream.

It was Kosmel. The trickster godlen hasn't completely abandoned me after all.

How much time do I have before I lose the small advantage he's given me?

My magic shoots farther through my abdomen, burning hotter with each passing second. These assholes kidnapped me, forced me to do their bidding—

Great God help me, I don't know what I actually did last night. The deaths I do remember are awful enough.

A wallop of guilt and anguish hits me right in the sternum. I close my eyes tighter against the swell of emotion and clench my jaw.

I can't get distracted by regret right now. What matters most is getting away from these monsters so they can't turn *me* into even more of a fiend to serve their sick purposes.

After that... then I can worry about the crimes I've committed.

I don't think the drug has completely worn off yet. When

I try to focus on a plan, my thoughts drift sluggishly through my head.

I have to deal with my guard... get out of this room... tackle whatever's waiting on the other side.

My magic squirms right up to my throat. I could hurl it out of me, smash through this entire building and everyone in it—

A starker smack of horror shatters the image that formed in my mind. I swallow thickly and clamp down on my power as tightly as I know how, picturing a vine wrapping close around me.

I can't let the delusional panic take over. I was already going mad before Lothar took me prisoner. Gods only know how much the magic he made me use last night has addled my mind on top of it.

How much can I risk using to free myself? If the riven insanity takes over completely, I'll be an even greater threat to the country than the conspirators I'm freeing myself from.

Everything I could do feels wrong.

The weight of the decisions ahead presses down on me. For a second, I can't breathe.

I'm injured and weaponless and partly drugged, up against an unknown number of enemies.

But I have to get out of here. I can't let myself be the scourge sorcerers' tool for one more minute.

Whatever happens after... I'll make sure I'm prepared. I'll do whatever I need to do to ensure I don't harm the kingdom any other way.

I peer surreptitiously around the room. I can't see anything except the bed, the side table, and a low dresser near the window. Not a single object I could use to stab or even bludgeon.

I suppose I could try to smother my guard with the

pillow under my head, but somehow I don't think he'd sit quietly long enough for me to pull that off.

The moment I move, he might raise the alarm. And I doubt I can move all that fast in my current state.

There's nothing for it. I have to rely on my magic this one final time.

At least since I'm in control and I have time to think, I can choose the backlash.

I focus on his neck and the brass handle on the table's drawer. When I'm sure of my concentration, I let one thin stream of magic fly out toward the guard.

It rams into his throat and clenches his windpipe so swiftly he doesn't have time to make a sound before I've crushed his source of breath. The drawer handle bulges, expanding to balance out what I constricted.

With his eyes bulging with terror and lack of oxygen, the big man slumps toward the floor. I whip out another sliver of magic to erase the sound of him hitting the boards—and project it to the farthest distance I can see beyond the window.

The man sprawls on the floor and stiffens into clay. The daimon that was trapped inside that sculpted body will be flying free.

My guilt lifts at seeing I didn't really take a life, but only slightly. This is just the first step in my escape.

I ease upright, hesitating when my head spins. When I touch my temple, I find a hasty bandage fixed there with a thinner swath of fabric.

The cloth is crusted with blood, but I can't find any wetness on my face now. The bleeding appears to have stopped.

I crouch beside the clay man, but it looks as if Lothar didn't even bother to arm my guard. Maybe the scourge sorcerers figured it would be too dangerous to have any weapon in the room with me, assuming the captured daimon would defend the rest of them by shouting an alarm and battering me with brute strength.

An impression of hollers and pounding footsteps rushes over me. I freeze—and the sounds dwindle rather than rising.

Just another little whiff of insanity. Wonderful.

And it could get so much worse.

I stare down at the fired clay figure, but I can't see how to do this next part without any magic either. It'll only take a tiny effort, though.

Wielding my power like a blade, I slice a chunk of clay about the size and shape of a knife out of the man's torso. The point of the clay shard should be sharp enough to cut flesh.

And if I've succeeded in sealing a little of the torn flesh on my head to balance out the consequences, so much the better.

Gripping my makeshift blade, I ease to the door and press my ear to the crack. The only sound that reaches me is the slow rasp of a sleeping breath.

Ever so carefully, I nudge the door open.

It's as if the scourge sorcerers set up this scene to perfectly cater to me. Zaneta lies sleeping on a mattress that's been placed on the floor of the outer room, just a few paces from the door.

Presumably Lothar had her stay there in case she needed to leap to subdue me. But it means that she's within easy reach.

My fingers curl tighter around the clay shard. My muscles balk at the idea of murdering a person so defenseless, no matter what else she's done to me.

She's under Lothar's sway. Who knows how he's manipulated *her*?

But she called me to them from miles away when she first

brought me under her spell. I'm not safe as long as she's alive, and that means neither is anyone else I care about.

A distant bugling of a rooster from some neighboring farm stirs me into action. I'll do it fast and as painlessly as possible, but shit and smitings, I have to do it.

I spring forward and drive the shard of clay into her neck.

Zaneta's body shudders. Her eyes pop open.

A sputter of blood passes over her lips, but her expression slackens just seconds later.

I press my lips against the urge to vomit and yank myself away from her. My magic roils in my chest with a fiercer shudder, but I hold it in.

If I see Lothar, I'll destroy him too. But otherwise, I simply have to get away.

My gaze darts through the room and snags on the box I saw one of the other scourge sorcerers stick my locket in. One small blessing.

With a quick dash, I undo the lid's clasp and retrieve my trinket. Clasping the locket in one hand and my clay blade in the other, I hurry to the next doorway.

The house is quiet. It isn't until I've slunk almost to the ground floor when I hear any voices—a murmuring from down the hall.

"When did Master Lothar say he'd return?"

"I don't think he mentioned."

I grit my teeth. The conspiracy's mastermind isn't here for me to end him like I did two of his underlings.

I prick my ears to check for any other signs of human presence around and bolt for the front door.

As I race across the yard outside, my head jumbles with a renewed aching.

There's a stretch of woods in the distance. If I can get to them, I have some hope of disappearing amid the trees.

Of course, I don't know what kind of tracking magic Lothar and his followers might be capable of...

A soft but urgent nicker catches my attention. I pause at the wall and spot several horses wandering in a corral by a nearby stable.

One of them looks particularly familiar.

Relief swells inside me so abruptly I almost choke on it. I run to the corral, let the gate swing wide, and reach up to hug Toast's neck when he trots over to me.

Lothar obviously isn't one to waste potential resources. He held on to the horse he stole with me, thank the gods.

"It's time we got out of here, boy," I murmur, shoving the clay blade beneath the corded belt of my dress.

With the help of the wooden fence, I heft myself onto the stallion's back. Gripping his mane, I tap him with my heels to send him galloping toward the woods.

We flee through the stretch of forest, hurtle across a few fields, and dive into a denser woodland. The sun is high in the sky, my stallion panting, and my head pounding like someone's trying to chisel into my skull when I finally decide we've come far enough.

I don't know where to go from here. I don't know who to turn to. But I really have only one option.

Or rather, two options. I've still got my makeshift blade if the madness rushes over me and there's nothing to do but end myself.

Suppressing a wince at that thought, I slide down from Toast's back and sit against a tree. I rest the blade on the ground next to me within easy reach.

With growing trepidation, I flick open the locket and press my thumb to the surface within.

Then I tip back my head against the tree trunk, my stomach roiling, and wait for the horror of the past day to either end... or get even worse.

FIVE

Ivy

I might have spent the night conked out, but I don't think the sedative made for a very satisfying rest. I'm still exhausted.

Somewhere in the midst of my waiting, with Toast grazing peacefully nearby and beams of sunlight slanting through the bare branches to warm the air around me, I drift off into an uneasy sleep.

Which I only realize when I snap back to wakefulness at the crinkling of the forest's underbrush somewhere nearby.

As my eyes pop open, my hands is already groping for my clay blade. My fingers close around the handle-like end, I push onto my feet in a crouch—

And a voice carries to me, so familiar it cracks open my heart: "Here's our lady thief."

There's no mistaking the relieved affection in his tone. I whirl toward the voice, and Stavros barrels through the woods to catch me in his arms.

The former general squeezes me tight against his massive

frame, and I can't help clinging to him in turn. Tears burn behind my eyes. I have to swallow a sob.

I'm back with one of the men I love. He still trusts me so much he ran straight to me.

Of course, that could change once he finds out exactly what I've been doing during the past day.

That final thought sours my joy with a knotting of my stomach. But I keep gripping Stavros's arms as he eases back from me, his eyes with their blending of blue and brown feverishly bright beneath his dark red hair. He gives that little tick of his head that tells me he's focusing his vision on me more intently.

"What happened?" he demands, his voice darkening with a promise of retribution. He lifts his hand to the edge of the blood-crusted bandage on my forehead. "Are you all right? How did you get away?"

Not "Who took you?" but maybe that part of the story is easy to guess. Who but the scourge sorcerers could have compelled one of the riven?

"I'm all right now," I say. Before I can pull more answers together, another figure steps forward, with a smile on his gorgeous face that could warm me even in a blizzard.

Casimir sets his hand on my shoulder. "Before you get into the interrogation, Stav, let me offer my own welcome."

The courtesan tugs me into a tender embrace that's nonetheless just as emphatic as Stavros's. I burrow my head against the crook of his neck, breathing in his honeyed sandalwood scent and wishing I could stay right here without having to say another word.

There is at least one question *I* need to ask, though. I don't hear anyone else approaching.

I lift my head, my throat constricting. "Where are Alek and Rheave? Did something—"

Casimir shakes his head before I can get any farther into

my anxious speculation. "They're both perfectly fine, other than being out of their heads with worry for you. Which will be resolved as soon as we get you back to them."

Stavros grins crookedly. "Have no doubts that they wanted to come with us. Rheave looked about ready to send one of his lightning bolts straight through me so he could take my place. But we couldn't leave the royal children undefended."

My heart leaps. "The royal children? Princess Klaudia and Prince Jacos are all right?"

That means I didn't carry out all of Lothar's murderous plan. But if the prince and princess are relying on my men for protection, then King Konram and Queen Ishild...

The hope that sparked inside me blinks out. Stavros must see the change in my face, because he brushes his fingers over my hair and speaks before I need to ask more.

"They're as well as they can be, considering what Lothar did to their parents."

He knows about Lothar. Well, the prince and princess were there in the audience room—they would have told him.

My mouth opens, but for a few seconds I can't push the words past the tension in my throat. "He wanted *me* to kill them all. One of the other scourge sorcerers, a woman who's been controlling at least some of the daimon, was holding me with her magic so completely that at first I couldn't even move a finger unless she commanded it. But she had to leave the sacrificial accomplice she was drawing power from behind when we came to the palace—her control weakened a little—I tried to make sure they couldn't use me..."

My hand rises to my bandage.

Casimir lets out a rough sound as if he's the one who's been wounded. "We'll have a medic look after that as soon as we can arrange it. You did everything you could—you shouldn't have been put through that horrible ordeal in the first place."

Renewed queasiness is building in my gut. The ordeal was even more horrible for people other than me.

"But I didn't manage— Lothar still attacked the king—?"

Stavros pulls me closer and presses a kiss to my unharmed temple. Then he bows lower and captures my lips with every bit of the heat and tenderness he's brought in the past.

When he eases back, his voice has thickened. "The kingdom is in disarray, and we have a lot of work ahead of us, but neither of those things are your fault. I think you should hear exactly what happened from those who witnessed it—the people your efforts did save."

I swallow hard. Yes. If I hadn't knocked myself into a stupor, Zaneta would have forced me to slaughter every member of the royal family.

She and Lothar must have attacked the king and queen while I was unconscious, but they didn't have the power on their own to destroy the entire royal family all at once.

Guilt remains lodged like a stone in my stomach. "The scourge sorcerers wouldn't have been able to get into the palace at all if it wasn't for me. I killed some of the guards…"

"Because Lothar forced you to," Casimir says, stroking his fingers up and down my back in a soothing caress. "You're no more responsible for that than Rheave is for the damage they've compelled him to inflict."

And yet it's so much easier to forgive the daimon-man than it is myself.

Stavros gives me a gentle shake. "You haven't answered my first question yet. How did you get away from them?"

I gather myself and explain about the sedative and Kosmel's voice in my dream, waking up and killing the daimon guard and Zaneta.

Casimir's deep blue eyes brighten at that part. "Then she can't bring you under her control again."

I nod. "And it was hard for her to keep up her influence, so I'm not sure if any of the other scourge sorcerers could manage it. But that doesn't mean—we'll still need to be careful. If I start acting strangely again—"

"We'll recognize what's going on and react much faster," Stavros finishes for me.

That wasn't what I was going to insist on, but I can't summon much enthusiasm for arguing with him about when he should murder me.

I do arch an eyebrow at him. "You came right to me here without having any idea whether I was in my right mind or if it was a trap."

The former general snorts and motions at the shard of clay I dropped by my feet. "It seemed incredibly unlikely that your captors would have sent you to assassinate us without even a proper weapon."

Trust him to have paid that much attention to what blade I was holding. And I guess he has a point.

I exhale in a shaky rush. "All right. What do we do now?"

Stavros glances at Toast, who's been watching our exchange with an air of mild disdain. "Get on your horse and follow us back to where we left ours nearby. We've temporarily taken shelter in one of the military's hidden supply stores, just a couple of hours' ride from here."

Looking around with my non-military-trained eyes, I wouldn't have a clue the patch of forest we've entered contains anything other than trees, birds, and the other obvious components of a woodland. But Stavros directs his stallion through the brush without a moment's hesitation.

He stops and dismounts at a spot where the layer of leaves and dirt on the ground looks a little more stirred up than elsewhere. With a sweep of his arm, he uncovers the slab of stone that he removes to reveal the round steel hatch underneath.

The metal surface is etched with the crest of the Melchiorek family—and scorched around the edges.

The last time we broke into one of these underground storage rooms, Rheave had to shatter the magic sealing it with his daimon power. It looks like he used a similar tactic here.

The seal must be permanently broken. Stavros gives a quick pattern of knocks, presumably designed to let those below know it's him and not an unwelcome intruder, and then hefts the hatch upward without any resistance.

"We've got—" he starts to call down.

Before he can get out one more word, a well-built form with a topping of chocolate-brown curls launches up the ladder and springs at me.

Rheave catches me in his muscular arms and spins me around with his face pressed close to my hair. A rush of exhilaration sweeps through me as I hug him back.

"My little vine," the daimon-man mutters with a rasp in his normally clear voice. "They tore you away from me."

Casimir lets out a soft chuckle. "Be careful with her. She's injured, you know."

Rheave growls in consternation and pulls back to look at me, letting my feet return to the ground. As he takes in the bandage on my forehead, his lips draw back to bare his teeth. "Those bullies. When I get my hands on them…"

A swell of affection fills my chest. It's only recently that I've accepted that my own intense fondness for Rheave goes beyond friendship, but there's never been any denying how devoted he is to me.

I set my hand against his cheek. "I'm all right, especially now that I'm back with all of you. It's good to see you too."

The daimon-man makes a sound that's almost pained. For a second, I think he's going to dive in to kiss me, but then something flickers in his eerie sea-green eyes. His expression tightens as his grip on my arms loosens.

Maybe he's only concerned that he'll hurt me with his enthusiasm. I don't have much time to ask about it, because Alek has just scrambled out of the underground room after him.

I'm just as delighted to be reunited with the scholar as my other men. As I turn toward him, my mouth stretching with an eager smile, he pulls me in against his lean frame.

He doesn't hesitate to kiss me, as soundly as he knows how. "I knew they wouldn't be able to hold you for long."

All at once, I choke up again. "I wish they hadn't been able to at all."

Rheave grunts dismissively. "The scourge sorcery can control thousands of daimon all at once. How could any one person fight it off?"

When he puts it that way, the idea that I should have somehow broken Zaneta's control does seem a little ridiculous. But that doesn't stop me from hating what she put me through.

Stavros beckons me over to the hatch. "Let's have the rest of this conversation down below where we can't be spotted by anyone on patrol. I'd imagine Lothar has sent quite a lot of his available forces to search for both you and the royals he lost."

He descends the ladder first, and I follow with trepidation creeping through my nerves. I'm about to face the two teenagers I nearly murdered, whether I had any say over my actions at that point or not.

When my feet hit the packed earth floor and I turn to peer through the lantern glow, my pulse hitches in surprise. Princess Klaudia and Prince Jacos are waiting there, sitting huddled together on one of the chests. Their dark brown hair and deep-set eyes remind me enough of their father's to send another jolt of guilt through me.

But they're not alone. Standing next to them is Petra, the distant niece of Queen Ishild's who I wasn't sure I'd ever see again after we left the college.

The royal siblings tense at the sight of me with a visible recoil. Princess Klaudia grasps Petra's arm. "Are you sure—"

"It's all right," Petra says in a soft voice. "I promise you, Ivy wouldn't be here if we couldn't trust her."

I gape at her for a moment before finding my words. They tumble out of me more abruptly than I'd have preferred. "What are *you* doing here?"

The king and queen must have dozens of minor relatives. I have no idea why they'd have drawn Petra in close enough for her to have followed them to Regica.

She did make some effort to chat with me while we were both at the royal college, enough that I wondered if she was spying for King Konram. I never had that suspicion confirmed, though.

Come to think of it, she was with them during the attack on the Florian royal residence as well.

Did she come along because she was close at hand, and they wanted to protect every part of their family they could reach?

Stavros steps to the side as the other men descend after us and tips his head to Petra. "I think you'd better tell Ivy everything you told us. She's completely out of the scourge sorcerers' influence now. She killed the one who was controlling her."

Petra clasps her olive-brown hands together in front of her. Her sleek black hair is pulled back from her face, but only in a loose bun, not one of the elaborate courtly styles. As elegant as her features are, the distant royal never followed fashion trends much even at the college.

"I've deceived you," she says, her melodic voice not quite as steady as usual, "as I've deceived almost everyone for the past seven years… It was supposed to bring some security in a situation like this… But I suppose none of us could really have been prepared for this kind of attack…"

As my brow knits in confusion, she gives her curvy body a little shake as if to get herself back on track. Her chin comes up, and in her stance as in her looks I can see an echo of Queen Ishild.

"You're aware of King Konram's original heir," she goes on. "Prince Dunstam."

It's not a question, but her pause makes me feel I should answer anyway. "Yes. He supposedly died of a sudden illness just before his twelfth birthday."

My hands clench at my sides. "Did Lothar have something to do with that after all? I suggested to King Konram that the scourge sorcerers might—"

Petra raises her hand to stop me. "In this particular crime, the traitors to the Crown had no involvement. Because there was no crime. There wasn't even a death."

She pauses, and the corner of her lips quirks upward with a hint of wryness. "A little more than seven years ago, I stopped being Prince Dunstam and became Princess Petra."

I stare at her for a moment before her full meaning sinks in.

She does look rather a lot like Queen Ishild for a distant niece, doesn't she? And something about her way of speaking has always reminded me of King Konram.

I try to recall Prince Dunstam's face from the scattered times I saw him as a child. He was a year younger than me, an occasional presence in parades and celebrations—and on the palace balcony during the riven executions.

I'm not surprised I didn't see it, even if it makes sense now that she's told me.

"That's the gift you asked your godlen for. To change your sex." My gaze drops to the two missing fingers on her right hand—little and ring—then rises again. "And more than that. Your hair color—your face…"

Petra's mouth curves into an actual smile, though it still looks more sad than anything else. "Exactly. Certain parts of my body never felt quite right when I was growing up. I was meant to be a woman, and Ardone transformed my outer self to match what's inside. I… might have been a little vain as well. I asked her to take inspiration from my mother more than my father. The features I originally inherited from him weren't very comely."

The revelation helps so many pieces fit together that a laugh tumbles out of me. *That's* why she's been so close with King Konram and Queen Ishild—they're her parents. That's why she was so invested in the rumors the conspirators were spreading to discredit the royal family.

But—

"Why did you pretend to be someone else altogether?" I have to ask. "You could have announced the change after your dedication ceremony, and everyone would have adjusted with a little time."

Asking for a dedication gift that's a one-time but permanent change rather than an ongoing talent isn't common, but it's not seen as strange either. And when it does happen, it's often for the same reason Petra gave.

I heard of kids who'd made a similar switch during my

days of listening in on gossip on the streets of Florian. Most of the time the talk involved a lot of tongue clucking and people saying it was too bad they'd had to wait so long when it'd been so obvious they'd want the change since they were much smaller.

Petra looks down at her hands. "That was my father's idea. He's always been so concerned about our safety."

She glances back at her siblings and then meets my eyes again. "I discussed my intent with my parents before the dedication ceremony. Father suggested that we could concoct a story about me dying, and I could mingle with noble society under a different identity once my appearance was changed. I could learn more about the people I'd be ruling over without them censoring themselves in front of me, and I should be safe from assassination attempts or our enemies trying to use me to hurt him. Then, once I'd finished my education and he was ready to have me start officially training in as his heir, we'd reveal the truth in a big celebration."

"I didn't like it," Princess Klaudia mumbles, and swipes at her eyes. They're ruddy from a lot of recently shed tears, understandably. "It meant we could hardly see you and talk with you at all."

Petra grimaces and steps back to slip her arm around her sister's shoulder. "I know. I'm so sorry I wasn't there more, Klaudia. There were times when I wondered if all the subterfuge was really worth it, but once I'd committed..."

She sighs and lifts her head toward the rest of us. "It's over now regardless. My parents are gone, so it's up to me to see that Silana doesn't fall to the scourge sorcerers."

Stavros said all but the exact words, but my body stiffens anyway. "Your parents—"

"Are dead." Her voice flattens with the words—with the emotion I have to think she's suppressing.

Her gaze homes in on my bandage. "I have to thank you for fighting against our enemies as hard as you did. We all might have died back in Florian, and we certainly would have in Regica if not for you. But Lothar took us by such surprise as it was—as soon as he saw what you did, he leapt at my father—"

She falters, and Prince Jacos shivers beneath his cloak. He peers at me with his mouth set at an anxious slant—and a little flinch when I raise my hand.

I freeze, my heart lurching painfully at the reminder of everything my presence must remind *him* of. Everything my vicious magic made possible.

I'm not going to force Petra to go on. I can imagine the scene well enough from hearing Lothar's plotting, from the flashes of memory of blood and pained gasps.

"I'm sorry I wasn't able to stop them completely," I say hoarsely.

Klaudia turns her head away as if she can't bear to look at me.

Petra glances at her sister and then back at me. "It isn't your fault. That awful man…" She cuts herself off with a hiss of breath. "I tried to tell our father that you weren't a threat, you know. Even back at the college, I could tell you were honestly on our side. But he always leaned a little too far toward caution."

A heavy silence falls over the underground room. I drag in a breath thick with loamy odors. "Where do we go from here? As soon as we announce you as the Melchiorek heir, all of the Order of the Wild's forces will be after you."

"I know." Petra lifts her chin. "I'll have to gather all the support I can as quickly as I can. Any help you'll offer, I'm immensely grateful for. But our first step is clear. I need to return to Florian to gather the proof of who I am to make sure those who would support me believe it at all."

The defiance in her voice steadies my own resolve. There isn't any question in my mind of what I owe to the family I nearly eviscerated.

I square my shoulders and hold her gaze. "I'll be right there with you, no matter what the scourge sorcerers send our way."

SIX

Rheave

The horses' hooves clop across the forest floor at an even rhythm that I'd delight in if I didn't have so much distracting me from the simple pleasure.

Even when I'm not looking at her, every inch of my skin quivers with the awareness of Ivy's presence. I do look at her quite a bit, because some part of me needs the extra confirmation that she's really here.

My hands tighten around the reins, but I resist the impulse to urge my horse closer to hers. I'm already riding within a few feet of her as we pick our way through the forest. There are spaces two horses can't squeeze through side by side.

If we hadn't managed to borrow a couple more mounts from a farm we passed for the royal heirs to ride on, I might have shared Toast with her like we did from time to time on our journey before. I could have kept one arm wrapped around her waist as we rode, had her slim body pressed up

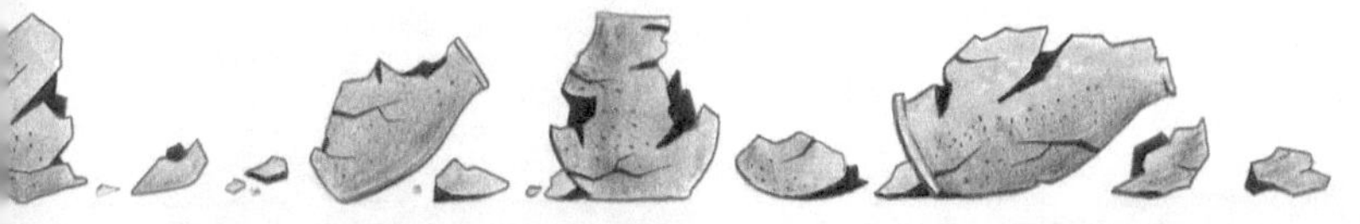

against mine and my chin tucked over her shoulder as if there was no way I could ever lose her again.

Of course, that would have worn Toast out much more quickly.

I can't suppress a pang of regret all the same.

We pass through a clearing, and I nudge my gelding to keep pace. Ivy's pale reddish-blond hair catches a glimmer of moonlight that looks almost like a flare of magic—and a different sort of pang lances right through the middle of me.

For an instant, my body seems to squeeze tight around me, cold and hard as the cooled clay before the scourge sorcerers brought my prison to life. My lungs ache with my next breath.

If something else happens to her—if I did lose her again—

I don't know how I *will* continue to live.

I've been injured in this body. I've felt shame over actions that harmed my companions to the point that I considered destroying the form of conjured flesh that makes me almost human.

But I've never felt any pain like the agony of the past day, not knowing where Ivy was or what our enemies might be doing to her, not knowing if she was even alive herself after the story we heard from the royal children of how she defied her captors…

Is that the other side of the joy being with her brings me? Like the backlash that balances her magic, my delight in her must come with equal anguish?

Last night, there wasn't anything I could do to cast off the frantic, searing emotions. They radiated all through my body, from the thoughts whirling in my head to the constricting of my throat to the listing of my stomach.

For the first time since I gained control over the body the

scourge sorcerers made, it felt like a prison again. Just remembering the sensations gives me a chill.

I'd never been apart from Ivy for more than a few hours before, and then always by our own designs. I never realized the unsettled feelings that would rise up in her absence could become so much more intense.

Why do humans care so strongly about each other if the sensations can turn so debilitating?

I thought following Ivy wherever she went would ensure my freedom. I thought she was the path to escaping the torment the scourge sorcerers put me through.

But somehow the adoration that's grown in me can lock me up and send me into harsher torments than I felt under our enemies' sway.

That's not her fault, though. It's something in me.

And the only thing worse than knowing how my heart's ties to her imprison me is the thought of having to go through that agony again.

So I keep glancing at her, checking for any sign of distress. I ride close even though it stirs up the unsettling memories, so I'll be near at hand to leap to her defense if necessary.

I simply won't *let* anyone wrench her away from me again, and then we can have nothing but joy.

Ivy peers over at Petra, the woman it seems is now supposed to be queen. She's the only one of us riding with company, I've noted more than once with a twinge of envy—her brother sits in front of her on a large stallion's back, leaning into her arms with a droop of his head as if he's a wilting flower.

The prince's eyes have closed, his wan face gone slack. The royal children have been through plenty of agony of their own in the past day.

At least Ivy returned to me. Their parents are gone forever.

I wasn't born, and I have nothing but revulsion for the people who trapped me with the intention of making me their slave, so I'm not sure what a regular human would feel toward a mother or a father. From the few times she's mentioned them, Ivy's connection to her parents has seemed mostly unpleasant.

But clearly that isn't always the case. Even if I don't understand, I'm sorry these three have had to experience such a permanent loss.

Ivy keeps her voice quiet, I assume to avoid waking the prince. "What exactly will we need to do once we get to Florian? You said there's proof of your claim to the throne?"

Petra's mouth tightens, but she nods. "We expected that Father would be able to announce me and then there'd be no question… But he kept a blood-sworn letter confirming my identity in a secure area of his private quarters. We'll want to retrieve that if possible. I'm not sure what's going on in the Palace of the Crown now."

Princess Klaudia shivers. "All our things—all Mother and Father's things—they can't just *take* our home…"

She trails off with a miserable expression.

"We'll get your home back for you as quickly as we can," Casimir says softly, but his worried expression tells me that he suspects "quickly" is probably not going to be very quick at all.

Petra's tone firms. "Lothar and his followers won't get away with their crimes." She turns back to Ivy. "We can also reach out to the cleric at the Temple of the Crown who oversaw my dedication. She can vouch that I'm next in the royal line."

Ivy lets out a rough chuckle. "That should be simpler than getting into the palace, at least."

"What about all the soldiers?" Klaudia demands abruptly. "Aren't they supposed to be loyal to us, not the traitors? They know Jacos and me, even if they won't be sure of you right away. Why can't we ride to one of the forts and get them to set things right?"

I know the horrible answer to that question. "There are daimon like me mixed in with the soldiers. But unlike me, the scourge sorcerers are still controlling them."

Stavros grimaces. "Yes. The last thing I'd want to do is to lead you to a group of armed men and women with uncertain loyalties. The scourge sorcerers wanted all of you dead, and it wouldn't mean much to them to sacrifice a few of their captured daimon to see it happen. Rheave can identify his fellow spirits, but only when they're very close by. We'll reach out to the military presence near Florian, but we'll have to be very careful about it."

Ivy looks over her shoulder at me, her brow knitting. "But maybe we won't need to worry about the other daimon anymore. Lothar said that the woman who was controlling me had gotten 'practice' by directing the daimon. She's dead now. Doesn't that mean they'll be as free as you are?"

My spirits lift momentarily at the idea that I might never have to worry about those bonds of magic yanking at me again. They sink just as swiftly. "I don't think it can all have been handled by just one scourge sorcerer. There were so many of us. And they didn't need to work their magic on us regularly. The commands would linger for days after they took hold."

Alek has been taking in our conversation in silence. He interjects with his usual scholarly precision. "It must be much easier for them to manipulate people whose bodies they created and whose spirits they already harnessed than a regular person whose body is her own. And Ivy's magic would have required so much more effort to contain. That one sorcerer could have been in charge of hundreds of daimon who haven't felt her renewed influence in a couple of days already."

Petra sighs. "But we can't know how long the previous influence will last or whether other scourge sorcerers will enforce their will again. Ster. Stavros is right. We need to proceed with every possible caution."

She glances down at her sleeping brother. "The consequences of a misstep would be far too great."

We lapse into silence, broken a few minutes later by Casimir's tentative question. "Did you have any idea of Lothar's intentions? Obviously your father still trusted him up to the end, but now that he's revealed himself—did anything show in his words or behavior, looking back, that might help us determine his next steps or how to undermine him?"

"I never liked him," Klaudia mutters. "He always talked like he thought he knew more than anyone else possibly could. And he tried to get the festival for Signy cancelled, because he insisted we shouldn't be celebrating heroes from other countries. But she helped all of us get free from the Darium empire!"

Ivy hums to herself. "He does seem to be obsessed with doing things the 'right' way—his Order of the Wild is built on a vision of how Silana is meant to be and what would bring the All-Giver back."

"He wants to rewind history to before Dariu ever invaded," Alek says. "As if that was any kind of golden age."

Petra frowns. "There were definitely things about him that rubbed me the wrong way, but even now, I can't think of any warning signs we missed. He always acted as if he wanted to support Father completely. But then, I wasn't around him very often after my dedication ceremony. I don't know how much I missed."

Stavros adjusts his grip on his reins, his expression grim. "He's had access to some of the innermost levels of the country's rulership. There won't be much he doesn't know how to manipulate. It's no wonder we've found the conspiracy so difficult to rout out."

Ivy shakes her head. "But people can't really want the kind of world he's been working on creating—all wildness and violence. We know who and what we're really dealing with now. We'll expose him and his practices, and most of Silana will be on our side. It's just a matter of getting the word out."

She looks so determined that I have to fight off another urge to push closer, to hug her to me. It doesn't matter how hard our journey gets—she's always willing to keep up her own fight.

As we emerge from the woods and cross a large stretch of fields, we let the conversation fade. Ivy hasn't risked using her magic to hide us like she did in the past, but we waited until night fell to start our trek, and so far we haven't encountered any patrols. Staying off the official roads must help.

The thought has just passed through my head when my eyes pick up a figure on horseback cantering along a small country lane in the moonlight up ahead.

We draw our horses to a halt, but the man doesn't glance our way. A thin flag whips about in the wind of his passage.

Stavros makes a sound of consternation. "He's flying the banner of a royal messenger—and that looks like an official messenger's uniform. What are the scourge sorcerers up to now?"

Ivy doesn't even hesitate. She nudges Toast back into motion. "We'd better find out. He's alone. We can defend ourselves if we need to."

I tap my heels to my steed's sides to follow her. We're too far off still for the messenger to have noticed us, as focused as he seems to be on his mission.

He appears to be riding toward the nearest town, where a few faint lights glimmer in the distance. Along the way there, several farmhouses stand at a distance from the road.

The nearest of the farmhouses has a candle burning near one of the windows, indicating someone in there is awake. As we close the distance, the messenger slows by the wooden fence along the road. He dismounts to open the gate and leads his horse past it, heading toward the house.

Ivy slows her horse to a walk, watching. She pitches her voice in a whisper. "We need to know what message the scourge sorcerers are spreading across the country. I'll go listen in—I can make sure the messenger doesn't notice me if I'm on foot."

She's barely finished speaking when she hops down from Toast. Stavros sucks in a breath as if to argue, but I slide from my horse first.

"I'll make sure she's all right," I tell him and hurry after her form darting through the night.

The others don't follow, presumably realizing that more people would be more difficult to hide. Ivy spares one glance at me with a hint of frustration, but I'm not hanging back and letting her go alone.

I need to be in arm's reach in case the worst happens again.

She sprints across the remaining fields, keeping her stance low. I copy her pose.

We reach the fence just as the messenger is knocking on the farmhouse door. Ivy nimbly clambers over the boards and lands with barely a sound on the other side. I do my best to mimic her stealth.

We creep through the thicker shadows along the fence

until we near a wagon standing in the yard. Ivy darts over to it so she can get closer to the house, with me at her heels. She presses her finger to her lips, as if I don't already understand that we need to keep quiet.

The door is just squeaking open. A weary looking man peers out at the messenger, jerking straighter as he takes in the royal uniform. "What is it?"

The messenger bobs his head. He must have delivered this announcement dozens of times already, because he speaks at a clipped tone, fast and without any hesitation to the practiced words.

"We're crossing the country to inform the people of Silana that a new age is upon us. The Melchioreks who forced their rule on us and defied the will of the gods have been vanquished. King Konram is dead. A new ruler will rise who will see that the gods favor us again and the All-Giver knows it's time to return. May the Great God shine on all of us who are worthy!"

The farmer stares at the messenger, his mouth dropping open. "I—the king is dead?"

"The false king," the messenger says with an edge of menace even I pick up on. "We must celebrate the chance to see our country returned to its former glory."

Ivy sucks in a strained breath. We both know what he's saying isn't true.

But the farmer doesn't appear to believe he can argue. He stiffens but bobs his head. "Yes. Yes, of course."

The messenger makes a brisk gesture of farewell and hustles back to his horse. As the farmer closes the door with a bewildered air, Ivy tenses next to me.

"We can't let him keep making those claims," she whispers, her hands clenched. "They're making it sound as if King Konram was killed justly through the will of the gods instead of murdered in cold blood by a traitor. And they're spreading their story everywhere they can as quickly as possible before anyone can find out the truth."

Her tone is so fierce that panic jolts through my veins. I can so easily picture her launching herself at the man—tackling him physically and leaving herself open to another injury—or hurling her magic at him and addling her mind, simply to protect the rest of Silana—

Every particle of whatever kind of a soul I have recoils in horror. The man strides up to the gate, gripping his horse's reins, and Ivy leans forward.

Without another thought, I snatch a stick from the ground and whip it forward with a heave of my own power.

My daimon energy crackles across the projectile. It doesn't fly as fast or far as an arrow I launched from a bow, but I don't need it to.

The stick smacks into the messenger's back with a crackle like lightning. He jerks and topples over, his shirt and flesh charred.

I spring forward, hurling another bolt of energy at him the moment I'm closer. His body disintegrates into ash.

A gust of breeze disperses most of the evidence of his death across the yard.

Ivy jogs up behind me and grasps my arm. "What are you doing?"

"You said we couldn't let him spread the message. I made sure he couldn't."

I glance at the horse, who sidesteps with a snort but doesn't outright run. Animals seem to take well to me most of the time. "And now Prince Jacos can have a mount of his own. We needed another horse, didn't we?"

Ivy sputters a dark laugh, muffled by her hand. "Come on, then, before the farmer notices us."

As she grabs the horse's reins, I find myself glancing

toward the distant town. A sense of melancholy drifts over me.

The people of that settlement won't hear the scourge sorcerers' claims right away, but how many other messengers have our enemies sent hurtling across the countryside?

I can't burn all of them up. The poison is spreading too fast for us to stop it.

SEVEN

Ivy

"Not much farther," Petra says as we pause at the corner of one of the city's streets. She draws her cloak tighter around her. "We're almost there."

It's hard to tell from her tone how much she's reassuring me and our other companions and how much herself.

The four of us gather close together, scanning the road ahead. There's an uneasy edge to the atmosphere in the city that I'm not used to, especially when surrounded by the elegant stone buildings of the inner wards. Nobles and other upper crust citizens hustle by with anxiously hasty steps and heads ducked low, attitudes much more common on Florian's fringes.

Even though it's only early evening, many of the shop and restaurant windows along this stretch are dark. No music or laughter trickles from the establishments that have their lanterns lit, as if even the dinnertime chatter has become subdued.

No one gives us a second glance, but I tug my hood

farther forward just in case. Thankfully the wound on my forehead has healed enough that I only need a small bandage now.

What would Julita have made of the unnerving change to the capital city so soon after we left it? It's hard not to wish I could hear one of her arch remarks that would settle my nerves just a little.

Maybe it's better that she never had to see this, though.

Only Casimir and Rheave joined Petra and me on our venture into Florian, since the rest of our party is rather recognizable. And Petra wants to keep her younger siblings out of danger as much as possible. Stavros and Alek stayed back with Klaudia and Jacos, setting up a campsite in a secluded area using supplies we grabbed from the military storage room.

I'd prefer an even smaller group for sneaking through the city that was under lockdown just a month ago in the hopes of dragging me to the gallows, but having the heir to the throne with us makes other types of caution necessary. Rheave can fend off attackers with his magic without worrying about going insane or other backlash. Casimir may be able to use his gift to cajole less hostile parties into helping us.

The most important part of our mission is that we keep Petra—*Queen* Petra, I still have to remind myself—alive.

I don't spot any soldiers or obvious Order of the Wild sentries among the pedestrians. When I glance at Rheave, he shakes his head to indicate he doesn't sense fellow daimon nearby.

I touch Petra's elbow. "I think it's safe to continue."

As we walk down the street, aiming for a steady but casual pace so we don't look as furtive as I feel, Petra shoots me a quick, tight smile. "I guess you're used to navigating the city like this. It mustn't have been easy—all those years you had to stay in hiding to conceal your powers."

A lump rises in my throat at the thought of all the loneliness and fear that taint my past. Not that I'm particularly less afraid at the moment, but at least I'm not facing the challenge alone.

I aim for a light tone to cover how fraught the question actually is. "I hope the pardon your father planned to extend to me will remain in place under your rule?"

Something flickers in Petra's expression, there and then gone so swiftly I can't read the emotion. She reaches over to grip my arm with an emphatic squeeze. "As far as I'm concerned, you were never a real threat. I truly am sorry about how he treated you—how stubborn he was about seeing you as an enemy."

The genuine regret in her tone puts me off balance.

I force myself to shrug. "I guess it was understandable. People with my kind of magic haven't exactly made a great case for ourselves over the centuries. And you weren't sure of me at first either, were you? Even when you didn't know about my magic. You weren't chatting with me at the college only out of friendliness."

I don't say it as an accusation, only a statement of fact, but a hint of a blush colors Petra's tan cheeks. "I'm sorry about that too. You were a relative unknown who'd abruptly joined Ster. Stavros in his investigations. My father wanted to hear what I made of you, whether I thought you had any ulterior motives."

"I don't blame you for that," I assure her. "I'd imagine I'd have done the same in your position."

"Still… Thank you for everything you've done for my family. You've been through more hardship on our behalf than I've had to face even a fraction of. If I can regain the country, you can be sure—"

Her voice falters as we come up on another cross-street. Behind me, Casimir makes a soft pained sound.

What used to be a statue at the center of the crossroads now lies shattered across the cobblestones in chunks of marble. A forearm clutching a broken sword lies near my feet. Beyond it, amid the smaller shards, I identify pieces of a leg, a jaw and neck... and the top of a head with a chipped crown.

I passed this statue more than once on my ventures into the inner wards. It depicted King Konram, erected shortly after he took the throne.

Petra draws in her breath with a rasp. But even as I reach for her, she draws herself a little straighter, her shoulders rigid.

Her voice comes out taut. "They're finding every way they can try to destroy him and our family's legacy."

I grimace. I wasn't King Konram's biggest fan, but I'd take his rule over the scourge sorcerers' any day. "They need to convince everyone that the Melchioreks were the villains so they'll look justified in taking over."

"Statues can be rebuilt," Casimir says gently. "We won't let them win."

Petra nods in a jerk, her stance tensing even more. "I'm just glad Klaudia and Jacos didn't see this."

As we take another turn onto a street that'll take us to the large courtyard at the foot of the Temple of the Crown, my stomach knots. I don't have the most pleasant associations with the country's largest temple.

It's the place where I watched several riven sorcerers walk to the noose and meet their deaths over the years. And the place where *I* nearly died stopping one of the scourge sorcerers from calling a wave of destruction down on the city.

But none of my trepidation could have prepared me for

the sight that greets us when we reach the edge of the courtyard.

Petra stops in her tracks, sounding as if she's stifled a gasp. I grip her shoulder and turn her toward me so we can pretend we're paying attention to each other rather than the scene on the other side of the stretch of cobblestones.

I'd rather look at my future queen than the carnage on display there. Splotches of brownish red linger at the edge of my vision—blood splattered across the temple's marble walls.

Rheave lets out a hushed growl. "Who are those people? Why would anyone have killed them?"

The blood I'm trying to shut out has come from several bodies who've been pinned to the walls by metal posts through their chests. Girding myself, I allow my gaze to veer toward the gruesome display again.

The figures have been savaged as if by wild animals— gouges torn through their clothes and flesh, organs spilling out, necks ripped open. But when I force myself to focus on them, I note the shape and color of their tattered outfits.

Robes of worship.

A surge of horror fills my throat. "They were all clerics and devouts. The ones who worked in the temple, maybe?"

A shiver passes through Casimir's body. "The ones who refused to play along with the scourge sorcerers, most likely. Did they set hunting dogs on them?"

My stomach churns. "Only their followers, I'd bet."

When I was playing at being a new recruit to the Order of the Wild, one of my tests was to race through the woods on all fours and tear apart a live rabbit with my bare hands. The conspirators take the name of their organization very literally.

As if there's anything holy about savaging innocent creatures… or people.

"Yes, look upon those who betrayed their gods!" someone

shouts from the doorway of the temple. "So many of the chosen leaders of our faith cared more about their own satisfaction than that of the All-Giver and the godlen. But the gods have willed that they and the false monarchy who steered our country so wrong should fall and a new age begin."

More of the scourge sorcerers' fucking propaganda. My teeth set on edge.

Will anyone in the city buy into their garbage? No doubt. They found plenty of recruits for their conspiracy, after all.

But far more will shut their mouths and stay out of the conflict not out of faith but out of fear that they'll be ripped to shreds next.

Petra turns her head slowly. She takes in the ruined bodies with only the slightest tremor of her chin.

Her gaze pauses toward the end of the line, and her lips purse in frustration as well as horror. "That's—that's Otyla there. The cleric who handled my dedication ceremony, who could have vouched for me. Of course she'd have resisted… And now she's gone."

The scourge sorcerers have screwed over the royal family even more than they know.

I swallow a curse and squeeze her arm to bring her attention back to me. "Was there anyone else at the temple who was involved—who'd be able to confirm that Prince Dunstam didn't die, only became Princess Petra?"

She shakes her head. "Father kept it as quiet as possible. No one knew except him, Mother, my brother and sister, and Otyla. Although Lothar may have started to suspect after seeing that I was brought along with the rest of the family to Regica."

Her hands ball into fists. "I could have stayed at the

college—kept up the ruse—then I'd have been here when the scourge sorcerers took over…"

Casimir comes up beside her and rests a comforting hand on her shoulder. "Your parents wanted to keep you safe. And if you hadn't been with them, it's possible Klaudia and Jacos wouldn't have escaped Lothar's attack. You can't blame yourself for anything that's happened."

She inhales sharply and gathers herself. "If we can't—"

She's interrupted by a trumpet sound that carries from the balcony high over the temple's doorway. The balcony where her parents and siblings—and she herself, before she became Petra—used to stand to oversee the riven executions.

A bluish glow forms around the figure who's appeared there. His lopsided frame gives him away in an instant.

Lothar is here. He's standing up on the balcony, looking down over us with a typically haughty expression, his formal robes draped across his tall but uneven body.

His voice rings out loud enough that it must echo through the streets all through the inner ward. He's using magic to amplify it.

"Good people of Florian! Please stop and listen to what I have to say. I was once the secondary magical advisor to the Melchiorek family, and now I am the highest authority this country has left."

"Because of his treachery," Petra mutters. Even more color drains from her face as she glares up at him.

"I don't claim any right to rule," Lothar goes on. "But I saw so much wrong in the course of my duties that I feel it is my responsibility to guide our country into its new era. We must find our way back to the true will of the gods and the essence of what makes us alive."

By maiming and killing other living things. Brilliant strategy.

I keep the sarcastic remark to myself, but a tremor shakes

Petra's body. Her hand drops to the dagger she's carrying on the belt of her dress.

There's no way she could cut him down from here. Even I'd have trouble keeping my aim steady across that distance without the help of my magic.

My magic.

Lothar's next words turn tinny and distant through the rush of cold that courses through me. My power wriggles in my chest, sensing my interest.

I could end so much of this catastrophe right now. Lothar stands at the top of the Order of the Wild. He's directed all their madness and violence.

Without him, they might not fall apart instantly, but they'd be deeply shaken. So much easier to break apart and overcome.

He forced me to kill people—he has gallons of blood on his own hands. Would destroying him really be murder or simply self-defense?

The chill comes with a growing certainty. I've tried to follow my conscience and the laws of the land, and where has that gotten us?

The king is dead. The man up there would murder the woman beside me if he realized who she is.

And I'm the only one who can definitely stop him, right here, right now.

The thrum of my magic expands to a roar inside my skull. It trembles through my nerves, but I hold it in with a clench of my jaw.

If I'm going to do this, I still have to be smart about it. The smallest possible effect so no one suspects—so I don't tempt more insanity than I have to.

Thinking of how I dispatched my daimon guard, I train my gaze on Lothar's neck and set my hand against one of the stones of the building we're standing next to. I picture his throat crumpling inward as the stone's surface bulges just enough to compensate.

My heart pounds, and I launch my power forward like one of Rheave's arrows.

It flings out of me, smacks into the figure on the tower—and fizzles out as if it's encountered nothing but air.

I flinch in surprise, and Casimir's head jerks toward me. "What's wrong, Kindness?"

Shame sweeps through me as swiftly as the certainty before it. How can I tell him what I just attempted?

Would the kindest man I've ever met still think I deserve the nickname he gave me?

"I—I tested him a bit with my magic," I say, fighting to keep my voice steady. "He isn't really there. It's an illusion—some kind of magical projection, I think."

Rheave hums to himself and bares his teeth with a fierce smile. "He knows you got away, that you have your mind back. He's afraid of you."

The daimon-man is probably right. Of course Lothar wouldn't take the chance that I could use the magic he was so eager to exploit against him. I should have realized that to begin with.

The effort I put into the jab of power was still expended —and still took some toll. As I turn my head, I think I catch a flicker of sapphire blue—soldiers, maybe daimon, coming to arrest us. I have to—

I blink hard and look again through the stutter of my pulse.

There's no one wearing blue at that corner of the square at all. The closest is a woman staring up at Lothar who's got on a green dress.

I don't entirely have my mind back, no matter what Rheave says.

So when a tingle of magic passes by me a moment later,

my first instinct is to assume it's another hallucination. But I wait, concentrating on the feeling, and it lingers.

I scan the square and adjust my position, taking a small step forward and then to the side to track the direction the magic is coming from.

As I follow my impression of it, a filmy figure swims into view, standing on the other side of the street we emerged from with his narrow face set in a mask of revulsion.

I tug on Petra's arm. "Your father's third magical advisor… What was his name? Tinom something? He's here!"

"What?" She peers in the direction I'm looking. "Where?"

She can't see him. He must be using some kind of distracting spell that I was able to overcome once I knew where to look.

Right. His specialty was illusions, wasn't it?

He definitely doesn't appear pleased with his colleague's speech. I waver and decide to take a gamble.

Better to start adding to our allies than fling my own magic around again.

As I march straight up to the magic advisor, his gaze twitches to me with a flicker of surprise. I fix him with my firmest stare. "Are you on Lothar's side, or are you ready to start saving the kingdom?"

EIGHT

Ivy

Tinom raps his sinewy hand against the wooden dining table. His face has gone ruddy beneath the thin fringe of his gray-and-white hair. "Whatever else we put in place, we *need* that blood-sworn letter."

His voice rings through the sparsely decorated room with so much force I have to restrain a wince. My gaze darts to the narrow window overlooking the city street outside, where another evening is descending into night.

We shouldn't have to worry. Tinom owns this tenement building in one of Florian's wealthier middle-class neighborhoods as part of his family's holdings, and the two apartments on the uppermost floor were vacant when the Order of the Wild swept into the capital. The magic advisor has been hiding out here along with a couple of devouts who escaped the purge at the Temple of the Crown, using his considerable skill with illusions to ensure his former colleague and Lothar's new comrades don't discover his refuge.

But we've taken shelter in apartments we thought were safe before, only to have to run for our lives. Since the moment the king declared me and my men enemies of the kingdom, we've had to constantly be on the move.

The only place we had any security was the hidden sanctuary for the riven, the Haven, where the only other sane riven sorcerer I've met taught me the basics of controlling my power. But that safety came with a different sort of price. We couldn't interact with the outside world at all—and when we decided we needed to stand up to the scourge sorcerers again, Sulla tried to turn the Haven into our prison.

I never thought I'd miss the days of sleeping on Stavros's sofa in his professorial quarters at the royal college, but that time looks strangely peaceful through the lens of my memory.

A flash that could be a flare of magic whips past the window—but no tingle of energy crosses my skin, and no one else reacts. I yank my eyes away from the hallucination, back to what's real around the table.

About twenty of us have squeezed into the now-cramped room. Petra, her siblings, my men, and I are clustered around one end of the table. Tinom sits at the other end, flanked by the two devouts along with several soldiers and a couple of nobles he's sure are loyal to the Melchiorek family.

We've spent most of the past day gathering this group of loyalists. It felt like we were making quite a bit of progress in the moment, but seeing the end result, I can't help thinking back to the army of hundreds Lothar was able to send to cut down the king.

Of course, my men and I left that army in disarray, the most devoted of them cut down in battle themselves. But we only managed it by tricking the Darium soldiers stationed on the other side of the channel into doing most of the work.

We're not going to get away with using that gambit twice.

Petra leans forward where she's sitting, setting her elbows on the table. I can't help being impressed by the increasingly queenly demeanor that's come over her with more supporters to command.

"The letter is the best proof we have of my identity," she says. "But Lothar's people could lie about the results of a test—they could destroy it. We'd need a loyal cleric to confirm its validity who the people also trust."

The baroness next to Tinom lifts her chin at a haughty angle that immediately sets my nerves on edge. I don't think Julita would have liked Baroness Sibelle either. The woman has gone to the effort of sculpting her dark hair into stylish whorls and painting her eyelids as if it matters how fashionable she is while the world is falling apart around her.

Her eyes flicker with a gleam that's a little sly. "We don't need to worry about confirming it yet. Simply showing the letter with its seal will be enough to convince most of the commoners. Look at how easily they've bought into the refuse Lothar and his ilk are selling them."

The devout at her left nods eagerly. "Many are eager for solid ground after the news of King Konram's and Queen Ishild's—that is, your parents'—deaths. They'll want to believe that the Melchiorek line can be continued."

He blushes at his brief stumble. I can't help wondering to what extent any of our allies believe Petra's story without definitive proof.

Tinom might be insisting so urgently as much to convince Petra's latest supporters as wider society. Maybe he even needs to convince himself.

"She has the testimony of her siblings as well," Stavros points out, in a slightly ominous tone that makes me think he's picked up on the same hints of doubt.

Petra shakes her head. "I won't bring Klaudia and Jacos for the initial announcement. It'll be too dangerous."

I frown and motion toward Tinom. "You're a master of illusions. Couldn't we use a similar trick to what Lothar did at the temple last night—project the image of Petra into a public place so she can speak to the people without being physically under threat?"

My skin prickles as several gazes settle on me alongside his. Tinom's is coolly assessing. He knows what I am—he almost ran off last night before Petra dashed over and flashed her family's seal.

I suspect he's still not all that happy to be making plans with a riven sorcerer.

The others, I don't think he's told, maybe because he isn't sure what they'd think of *him* allowing my presence. But I haven't put on my false noble airs like I did at the college. They probably have no idea what to make of me at all.

Tinom pauses before dipping his head in a slow nod. "Yes, of course, projecting illusions would be the obvious solution. Since we wouldn't want to allow any direct interaction at that tentative early stage regardless."

Petra knits her brow as if she isn't pleased with this line of conversation. From getting to know her better over the past several days, I suspect she'd prefer to meet her subjects properly for such an important announcement.

But she can't deny how necessary the precaution would be. "All right. Regardless, we shouldn't set anything into motion until we have objective proof that I'm the heir to the throne. What's the current situation in the Capital Palace?"

She looks at the standing soldiers. They've shed their blue uniforms so they can blend in when we venture outside, but I can see the military training in their postures.

Next to me, Rheave's gaze darts over the assembled figures. He already confirmed that none of them were captured daimon who'd infiltrated the royal military, but I get the impression that he doesn't totally trust them as humans all the same.

I can't say I'd be keen to put my life in their hands either, considering how many of their colleagues have attempted to hunt me down in the past few months.

The man among them who has the highest rank—a major—glances at Stavros as if the former general will be able to answer for him before clearing his throat. "I'm afraid the palace is entirely overrun. The Order of the Wild encouraged total disrespect of the Melchiorek legacy. The initial looting has waned, but many of Lothar's followers have settled within the walls. We couldn't simply walk in and take what we want."

Alek speaks up a little hesitantly. "Are you sure the letter would even still be there? It wouldn't have been found during the looting?"

"My father had a secure hidden cache in his bedroom," Petra says. "It could only be found by someone who knows where it's meant to be, which at the moment is only our family."

She turns to me. "Ivy, I hate to ask more of you, but it appears stealth would be a much more viable option for us than strength. That's your area of expertise. I'm sure Tinom could give you additional protection with a temporary concealment enchantment."

The magic advisor draws his posture up straighter, his shoulders going rigid. "It would be simple enough. But are you sure— To send her alone—"

To leave the riven to her own devices, he must be thinking. As if I haven't had plenty of opportunities to sow ruin before now if I'd wanted to.

Petra cuts a glance toward Tinom that stops whatever concern he was going to express before the rest of the words leave his lips. "There's no one I'd trust more than Ivy with the task." Her attention returns to me. "If you'll take it."

As I stare back at her face so like her mother's, the traces of her father's bearing showing in her calm composure, my throat constricts.

King Konram asked a lot of me before he knew what I was. But he never truly *asked.* It was either direct orders or commands phrased like a question that didn't allow for an argument.

Petra is her father's child, but also her own person. A person I find myself not particularly wanting to let down.

I wet my lips, picturing myself slipping through the halls of the grand palace I've only entered once before—and then in the midst of a daimon battle. Even with the help of a concealment illusion, it'll be dangerous.

I've done dozens of things equally dangerous or more in the past few months, though. What's another for the history books?

My mind is still acting up, yes, but I've been able to recognize the hallucinations before I react. And the longer I can go without turning to my own magic again, the more the effects should fade.

I hope.

It's not as if we have time to waste. The longer Lothar keeps his hold over the country, the more people he'll draw into his brand of madness.

"Of course," I say. "Whatever I can do to see you on the throne and Lothar in his grave."

I'd worry that my death wish for the former magic advisor might be a little too blunt, but a couple of the soldiers snort in amusement and Sibille's lips form a sharp grin. Clearly it's a sentiment we all share.

"Thank you," Petra says like she means it, and pushes to her feet. "It's been several long, hard days for all of us. I think we should get some rest and finish our planning with clear heads. We can aim to send Ivy on her mission tomorrow evening."

She dips her head in a dismissal.

As I push myself to my feet, my legs sway under me. I didn't sleep all that well last night even with proper walls around me.

Images of Lothar standing in the temple and me hurling a murderous lance of magic toward him kept flashing through my mind. That and the way Petra's siblings recoiled when they first saw me in the underground storeroom.

Casimir slips his hand around my arm. "Come on, Kindness. Let's set aside all these responsibilities for a little while."

He guides me down the hall to the room the five of us have taken as our own. It's unfurnished, but we were able to gather enough blankets to form a large sleeping mat that covers about half of the floor.

My other men follow us. As I turn to face them, a swell of emotion rises up in my chest.

I was torn away from them, and I haven't really gotten to appreciate being back with them since we reunited. There've been so many other problems dogging us, other people around that I had to put on a strong front for.

These four men accept my weaknesses as well as my power. There's nothing I'm craving more right now than a reminder of their affection.

I kick off my boots by the door and sink down in the middle of the blanketed area. Then I hold out my hand, beckoning them all over.

I think they can tell from my attitude that I'm looking for comfort rather than passion at this moment. They settle themselves in a ring around me, Casimir by my back, Rheave and Stavros at either side of me, and Alek in front.

Rheave loops his arm around mine while Stavros takes my hand, stroking his thumb over my knuckles. Casimir rubs my back in a gentle motion, careful of my scars.

Alek caresses his fingers over my cheek, tucking a few stray strands of hair behind my ear. "How are you doing, Ivy? I thought we'd been through a lot already, but this…" He shakes his head. "At least it seems we've finally gotten to the core of the conspiracy."

"Yes," I say. We just don't know what to do about it. But I want to spend a little time *not* thinking about Lothar for once. "I'm just glad I'm with all of you again. Whatever happens going forward, having you is the bright spot that helps me through the dark parts."

Stavros lets out a low rumble. "Don't ever doubt that you do the same for us."

Rheave's voice dips low. "When you were gone, when we didn't know what had happened to you…" His voice trails off raggedly, and then he seems to master the emotion that gripped him. "But our little vine is back with us, and that's what matters."

The daimon-man leans in to kiss the side of my neck. He's only just started exploring the bodily pleasures two—or more—people can conjure together, but he's both an eager student and a quick study.

The press of his lips sends a jolt of heat straight to my sex. All at once, my nerves are humming with desire for the other sorts of intimacy we haven't had the privacy or energy for while on the road to Florian.

As usual, Casimir picks up the shift in my mood immediately. He teases his hands down to my waist to undo my belt and then up to work at the lacing on my dress. "I think our woman deserves the full welcome she's had to go so many days without."

Stavros's heated chuckle is all agreement. Alek simply

offers one of his quiet but bright smiles and trails his fingers up my thigh.

Rheave eases back to watch as Casimir peels the dress off me. The daimon-man's eyes widen taking in my partial nakedness, my chemise and the pants that serve as an underdress still in place.

We didn't have much opportunity to undress the first time we came together that intimately.

He hums thoughtfully. "Less clothes makes it easier. No clothes would be even better."

A laugh I didn't expect bubbles out of me. "It does, but normally we work up to that. I wouldn't mind seeing you without that shirt, though."

He obliges without hesitation, pulling off the woolen tunic and tossing it aside.

The makers of his body might have used twisted magic to bring it to life, but they gave him quite a nice form to work with. Taut muscles define the planes of his broad shoulders and his quite literally sculpted chest.

I expect him to reach for me again, but instead he glances around at the other men. "You all know Ivy and what she likes better than I do. I want to see... what you each would do for her, to make her feel as good as possible."

Stavros lets out a soft snort. "Looking to replace us all once you've added to your repertoire?"

Rheave appears to take his question at face value. "Oh, no," he says hastily. "I couldn't be you, just as you couldn't be each other. Or me. But I don't know—I never paid much attention— I think if I had more of an idea of the options, I could make her feel just as good my own way."

I touch his jaw, bringing his gaze back to me. "You're very good already, Rheave. I haven't been disappointed with anything you've offered me."

He aims one of his sunny smiles at me. "Then I can look forward to bringing you even more joy."

Casimir grins. "A sentiment I couldn't approve of more." He nips the crook of my shoulder. "Who would like to provide the first demonstration?"

I suspect the courtesan is holding back so as not to intimidate the others. The carnal arts are the main focus of his training, after all. Just that tiny scrape of his teeth has set my skin alight.

Not one to refuse a challenge, Stavros twists toward me. He tucks his prosthetic under the hem of my chemise, the hooked loop of metal grazing my waist beneath, and his mouth curves into the cocky smirk that used to infuriate me. "I know what special benefits I can bring to the bedroom."

As he uses his prosthetic to drag the thin fabric over my head, I shiver giddily. And then with a headier pleasure as he flicks the metal surface over one bared nipple and the other. A whimper creeps from my throat.

A faint flush has colored Rheave's pale face as he watches, but he doesn't stir from his vantage point.

Stavros catches the waist of my trousers next, and Alek helps him slide them from my legs. As the former general traces his prosthetic down the front of my drawers next, he wraps his other arm around me and claims his first kiss.

As always, the feel of his massive frame enveloping me is overwhelming even without the additional pleasure of his artificial appendage. With the melding of our mouths, warmth floods me.

Not breaking the kiss, Stavros lifts me right onto his lap. The incredible strength contained in that impressive body of his is a turn-on all on its own.

I've been carrying all my weight for a long time. It's a release to be able to trust someone else to support me.

I sling one arm around his neck to pull myself deeper

into the kiss. Stavros tightens his embrace so he can toy with my nipple between his fingers while returning his prosthetic to the dampening place between my thighs.

Rheave was right when he said that he couldn't become any of my other men and none of them could become each other. There's nothing quite like the sense of being so fully encompassed and possessed that the military man offers.

As Stavros pinches my nipple to provoke a flash of bliss, he works his prosthetic right under the fabric of my drawers. When the metal loop strokes over my clit, my fingers dig into his tunic. I moan into his mouth.

He's gained confidence in using that part of himself since our first explorations. He works my sweet spot over until I'm shaking with need and then hooks the prosthetic right up inside me.

His breath scorches my cheek. "Yes, that's what you need."

I can only whimper in agreement.

Our kisses turn wilder as Stavros pumps the metal loop into my channel. He keeps the base rubbing my clit with the perfect amount of pressure. There's nothing I can do but hold on through the waves of delight he's summoning.

He tangles his fingers in my hair and devours my mouth even more forcefully. His thrusts speed up, propelling me over the edge.

My climax sweeps through me with another moan I muffle against his lips. Stavros holds me through my shudders and marks my cheek with a more tender kiss as I come back to earth. "It's always an honor to feel you let go— and let me take you there."

A breathless giggle spills out of me. "You can have that honor whenever you like."

"Very good," Rheave murmurs. When I look at him, his

hands are clenched by his folded legs, but he stays where he is.

To my surprise, Alek makes an impatient sound before I even need to encourage him. "You can't keep her all to yourself, Stav."

With another sweet smile, he draws me away from the taller man. My heart aches with happiness seeing the assurance that's so new on his mottled face.

As I set my palm against the scholar's scarred cheek, he lowers his head to claim a kiss of his own. He leans into it, adjusting the angle of his lips, varying the pressure, flicking his tongue between my lips so I clutch at him even more eagerly.

He eases back with a glint of triumph in his bright brown eyes and looks at Rheave. "I didn't have much experience to call on at first either. But the most important thing isn't what you'd do with any woman, it's learning what will give *this* woman the most pleasure."

I beam at him. "And I've been delighted to become your latest research project."

Alek laughs and guides me down to the floor so my head is resting on Stavros's muscular leg like a firm pillow, the ridges on my back cushioned by the blankets.

As the scholar tracks a path of the places along my neck and shoulders where he's determined his lips and teeth have the most effect, the former general hums approvingly and combs his fingers through my hair. The graze of their tips over my scalp heightens every sensation Alek provokes.

The scholar laps the tip of one breast into his mouth and swirls his tongue around it. When I gasp and grip the thick waves of his hair, he exhales over the sensitized peak in a hot rush. Then he moves to the other side to repeat the effect.

He doesn't linger on my chest long, though, before

working his way down the side of my belly. There, he tugs my drawers down.

"The sweetest spot to study," he murmurs, and lowers his head to my sex.

The swipe of his tongue over my clit has me bucking to meet his mouth. I catch a vaguely strangled sound from Rheave's direction, but my mind has hazed too much with desire for me to linger on that fact.

I rock with Alek's skillful attentions, another wave of ecstasy building in my core. He plunges his fingers inside me and curls them along my channel until he finds the headiest spot within.

As he suckles my clit and pumps his fingers against that blissful place, the sensations sweep through me even faster. Pleasure coils and unfurls and swells, sending a chorus of needy noises out of me.

"Fuck, Alek," I mumble, and clutch his hair harder as the wave finally crashes over me.

My head sags back into Stavros's lap. Alek dapples tender kisses along my inner thigh before sitting up with a satisfied expression that makes me want to kiss him all over again.

Before I can, Casimir is nudging me upright. He turns me around and pulls me against him so my back is flush with his toned torso.

He nibbles at my earlobe before murmuring in a silky tone, "And I know that our woman likes to be pampered *and* lose control."

His hands glide over my body with the gentlest of touches, coaxing every flutter of bliss he can from my nerves. I lean into him with a sigh, giving myself over to his sweet adoration.

The courtesan is right that he's discovered other approaches I find equally thrilling. When his hands reach my thighs, he yanks my hips back against him with a jerk. The force of the motion and the press of his rigid erection against my ass make my heart skip giddily.

His voice comes out in a purred growl that's even more electrifying. "You'll open yourself for me now."

My legs slide farther apart automatically. I'd forgotten just how freeing it feels to let Casimir take charge of me. To know that if I let him, he'll tend to me as only he knows how.

He aligns himself behind me and plunges into my already drenched sex. The rush of being suddenly filled after so much stimulation shocks a cry from my lips. I clench my teeth against it, not wanting to alert the entire apartment to what we're up to.

Casimir works his way even deeper with a few steady thrusts from behind. He lifts one hand to fondle my breast while looking over my shoulder toward Rheave.

The daimon-man is completely flushed now, his hands dug into the folds of the blanket he's sitting on. His eerie blue-green eyes flare with an even starker light than usual.

I can hear the courtesan's smile in his voice. "One thing I know better than anything else is that two or more of us can offer Ivy even more pleasure than just one, if we work together. Would you like to put any of tonight's observations to use right away, my friend?"

Rheave sucks in a shaky breath that turns into a rumble in his chest. His body surges forward, right toward me.

The daimon-man catches my face between his hands and kisses me so hard I could drown in him. I sway between my two lovers, wanting to give myself over to both.

Rheave drops lower, flicking his tongue over the tender flesh just below my belly button and then diving even farther.

Without any sign of concern about Casimir's proximity,

he presses his mouth to the spot just above where the courtesan and I are joined.

Casimir thrusts into me again, and I push against Rheave's mouth. His tongue darts out across my clit, and I grasp his dark curls with a partly stifled moan.

"So good," I rasp. "It feels so fucking good."

Rheave's pleased hum reverberates through my sex. I clutch on to him with one hand and Casimir's arm with the other.

Why didn't Alek's erotic poetry book ever suggest *this* particular combination? Or maybe it did and we simply hadn't gotten to it yet.

Either way, I'm caught between the two men in the most delicious possible way. With every pump of Casimir's cock and caress of Rheave's mouth, I careen higher.

My final orgasm starts with a shudder that resonates right out of the center of me. I crack apart in a blaze of pleasure that knocks the breath from my lungs.

Casimir groans and nips my shoulder when he follows me over. As we sag together, Rheave sits up, licking his lips.

"I look forward to learning all I can," he says in an awed tone.

A breathless giggle escapes me. "I think I'm looking forward to it even more."

At least I have a few good things waiting after all the trials I haven't yet faced. Assuming I survive that long.

NINE

Ivy

The previous time I entered the Capital Palace, I was racing at Stavros's heels, no thought in my head except preventing an impending disaster. I'm not sure the enormity of that act sank in until this moment.

Where I'm perched on the broad stone wall that surrounds the palace, all of the front courtyard sprawls before me. Dark splatters and scorch marks discolor the polished cobblestones and squares of garden.

I can't tell how many of the blotches are from the attack we intercepted weeks ago and how many are more recent. A sour, faintly rotten scent laces the cool winter breeze.

Definitely recent is the refuse scattered across the grounds. A soiled velvet vest lies crumpled here, a torn silk gown there. Broken chunks of marlwood and porcelain litter the terrain as if some looters had second thoughts after running out with one or another treasure and opted to destroy them instead.

I spot at least one brownish lump where a particularly

ornery intruder relieved themselves on the palace's front steps. Through the swelling horror, I wrinkle my nose.

I can almost hear Julita's horrified voice. *Really, have they no limits at all?*

Do the looters not realize that even if they've decided *this* king was false, the point is to find a new ruler they'll want to lead them? And that ruler will prefer to move into a palace that's not shit-stained?

They're not even finished. As I watch, concealed from view by the blessed charm Tinom provided me with that dangles from a fine chain around my neck, a few figures hustle out of the palace. One is dressed like a noblewoman in an ornate embroidered gown, though her hair has fallen loose from its typical courtly style with only a few small curls still pinned up. The two men behind her are well but more plainly dressed—merchants, perhaps.

They're all carrying ill-gotten gains: the woman a bundle that could be clothing or wrapped jewelry, one man a box gilded with gold, the other a stack of fine plates.

My jaw clenches. People like them benefitted the most from the king's rule, and now they're picking apart his legacy like vultures descending on a carcass. And they see themselves as the height of society?

How could they so easily turn on the family they pledged their loyalty to?

The only good thing about the current situation is that someone has propped open one of the double doors. Tinom's charm, the same type he was wearing outside the Temple of the Crown the other night, keeps me from being seen as long as no one knows to look for me, but I can't pass through walls. If people start wondering why doors are swinging around apparently of their own accord, I'll be in trouble.

When the latest looters have hurried out the gate and the courtyard is momentarily still, I slide down the wall and slink across the grounds, carefully dodging the worst of the mess. The charm also only obscures smaller sounds. If I bang into anything and someone looks over, they might spot me through the illusionary magic.

I pass the purpling body of a guard who was clearly not a daimon, partly obscured by a garden shrub. A twinge of sympathy prickles through my chest.

I might have feared the Crown's Watch and their ilk, but that woman was only doing her job. She gave her life in an attempt to protect the king's home, maybe even after she had reason to believe he'd no longer be returning.

As I slip through the door and creep down the main hall, I have to avoid more figures coming in and out of the rooms where they're rummaging through what's left of the furniture and snatching the art still remaining off the walls. The noxious stink thickens. Whiffs like putrid meat reach my nose, along with the tang of urine and a rank note of body odor.

The source of the latter becomes clear in a matter of seconds. In several of the side rooms, the furnishings have remained mostly intact. Packs of men and women in questionable states of cleanliness sleep on the thick rugs or lean against the tables while they chatter in rough voices.

They wear a mix of clothing from cheap cotton to fancy silk, all of it smudged and stained. The fervor burning in many of their eyes reminds me of the Order of the Wild's march.

These must be the scourge sorcerers and their allies, the followers Lothar has installed in the capital to maintain control.

My magic jitters against my ribs, pleading with me to let it wash away the wretched scents. To hurl all these intruders out through the windows in a hail of shattering glass.

I clamp down on it and hurry onward.

When a woman already carrying a set of gold candlesticks under her arm approaches one of the rooms filled with new inhabitants, a man snaps at her. "This spot belongs to the Order of the Wild for now. Grab what you want wherever else."

She scurries off without argument. Whatever the locals have seen of the Order, they don't appear keen to pick fights.

I weave through the halls, following Petra's directions, leaping to the side when a couple of teens come racing out of one of the doorways just ahead of me. More blood stains the floors, but I don't come across any more corpses until I pass a room wafting the worst stench yet.

That door has been shut. I pause and nudge it just a crack open, then recoil in revulsion with a defensive flare of my magic.

Decaying bodies, mostly guards and nobles from what I glimpsed of their clothing, sprawl in heaps beyond the doorway. The Order mustn't have felt like bothering with trying to bury them yet in the hardened winter ground, so they simply dragged them out of the way.

Maybe they like the idea of the rotten scent winding through the palace, reminding everyone who ventures inside of the fate they could meet if they fall out of favor. As if the spirits of the murdered linger on to haunt this place through the stench.

Julita might have found that idea darkly amusing. As I dart up a staircase to the second floor, avoiding a soggy spot in the carpet, I find myself imagining the other arch remarks she'd have made, no doubt alongside an indignant huff.

The people would rather see the palace turned into a refuse heap than be ruled by the Melchioreks? Can they not think past the end of their noses?

Another lump rises in my throat. It's easier not to think about the friend I lost, not to miss her constant presence in my mind—occasionally irritating, but so often rousing and encouraging—when I'm surrounded by other companions. When I'm on my own, the emptiness in my head yawns louder.

Julita never hesitated to stand up to the evils she saw brewing in Florian, even though she had a more direct reason to fear scourge sorcery than the rest of us. She sacrificed what remained of her life to save me from her brother.

She'd have been so horrified to see the wreckage the scourge sorcerers have already left in their wake despite our efforts.

Shoving the grief aside with a few hasty blinks, I turn a corner and pad down a narrower hall. Another left, then a right, and all the way at the end…

I stop in my tracks, my gut dropping. A bulky, square-jawed man in a guard uniform is standing outside the door Petra directed me to—the one that leads into the royal family's private quarters.

He must be with the scourge sorcerers, or they wouldn't have left him alive. I guess it makes sense that Lothar wouldn't want anyone other than his sycophants rummaging through the most personal remains of the king he murdered.

Is the former magic advisor himself staying in those rooms? I shudder at the thought.

It doesn't really matter if anyone is beyond that door if I can't get past it myself, though.

I edge closer, setting my feet silently as I study the guard. Without Rheave's daimon senses, I can't tell for sure, but I suspect this fellow is one of his brethren in animated clay. There's a sort of blankness to his expression that looks like more than human boredom.

I could simply stab him and hope he collapses back into fired clay. But then whoever assigned him to this spot would realize someone must have broken in.

What I really need is to draw him away from his post for long enough for me to slip inside.

I backtrack to the previous hall and glance around. No one else seems to be stationed nearby. He'll probably come running at any nearby disturbance.

I step into one of the rooms where the door stands ajar. Most of the smaller objects have been looted, but a display cabinet stands by the wall, the glass panes of its windows cracked.

They're about to face a lot worse than that.

Gritting my teeth, I grasp the side of the cabinet and heave. With a shove against the wall for extra leverage, I send it crashing to the ground.

And oh boy, does it crash. The frame thumps against the floor hard enough to echo, the glass shatters, and the wood splits open down the back.

I dash back into the hall and duck through a different doorway just before the guard bustles around the corner on stomping feet.

The moment he's stormed into the other room, I bolt all the way to the door he was guarding, dipping my hand into my pocket. I pull out the ring Petra gave me with the Melchiorek crest and press it to the spot beneath the doorknob.

There's no click of the lock, but the door opens at my nudge. Lothar's people must have broken whatever magical protection it had on it.

As soon as I step inside, it's clear someone's been through these rooms. Rather aggressively, too.

Side tables lie overturned. Upholstery has been cut open. All of the paintings have been yanked from the walls, some propped against them, some tossed aside.

I skirt a broken plate and hurry deeper into the apartments, eager to get out of this place as quickly as possible. Stale air trickles into my lungs, containing a lingering trace of a floral perfume that perhaps Queen Ishild liked to wear.

What if Lothar managed to ferret out King Konram's most secret hiding place? I might have risked venturing in here for nothing.

He might already know that Petra is the greatest threat to his Order's authority.

Petra warned me not to take anything from her siblings' rooms, as much as they might appreciate a few tokens from the lives that've been wrenched from them. We don't know to what extent the conspirators have catalogued the contents of these quarters to notice if something's gone missing—or how easily they might be able to track those items.

Still, my gaze veers toward a sitting room I can tell was once Prince Jacos's from the model ships perched in one of the cabinets. I wish I could bring the royal teens a little something they might find comfort in. They didn't have a chance to carry anything with them from the palace in Regica but the clothes on their backs, which are stained and travel-worn now.

But really, what would they care about getting back other than their parents, which I can't accomplish even with my fathomless magic?

So I push onward, through a larger sitting room with forest-green curtains and gold leaves rippling across the wallpaper and into a vast bedchamber that could contain the entire apartment Tinom arranged for us.

A four-poster bed stands in the middle of the space, more forest-green fabric draped around it. A deep gouge has been cut in the mattress, feathers spilling out of it onto the floor.

Lothar knew there might be something hidden in here.

The wardrobe doors and dresser drawers hang open, various kingly outfits of velvet, silk, and wool scattered around them. The mirror on the wardrobe is cracked, as is the porcelain wash basin nearby.

None of that matters as long as the one item I came for has gone undisturbed.

I crouch down and squirm under the bed. Dust tickles my nose, and I rub my face to prevent a sneeze.

Then I take out Petra's ring and slide its face across the floor.

The boards beneath my flattened body feel perfectly smooth. There's no reason for anyone to suspect a secret cache lies beneath them. But toward the headboard on the lefthand side, right where Petra told me to look, a gleam lights up on a circular spot that matches the ring's crest.

I press the ring to that etching, and a small wooden hatch lifts to reveal a square of thicker darkness.

Normally I'd hesitate to shove my hand into a magically hidden space with contents unknown. Today, I'm trusting that Petra wouldn't send me into a trap.

The opening is only about twice as wide as my arm. I reach in and fumble through the empty recess beneath.

Well, it's not entirely empty. Though the first object my fingers encounter isn't a letter but dry leather. What feels like a book.

Interesting. I might as well bring that back too, because I doubt King Konram would have hidden it here unless it was important.

I wriggle the book out and tuck it into the largest pocket on my skirts. Then I grope around in the secret cache again.

There. My hand closes around a piece of folded parchment.

I pull it out and squint at it for just long enough to confirm it's got the blood-sworn sigil sealing it. Tucking that away too, I push the hatch shut.

In an instant, the floor looks as seamless as ever. King Konram outsmarted Lothar in at least one way.

The guard has no doubt returned to the door that leads into this part of the palace, but that's all right. I've already identified my escape route.

I lope back into the sitting room and ease aside the heavy curtains. The pane is shut to keep out the winter chill, but it's designed to open in the summer.

I peer down onto the grounds below, at the back of the palace with a pleasant view of the larger gardens and the hunting forest beyond. When I'm sure no one's wandering around down there at the moment, I pull the window open, clamber out onto the ledge, and slide it shut in my wake.

It's a longer drop than I'd prefer to jump given the choice, but I've done worse. Ignoring the niggling of my magic offering its help, I brace myself, skid partway down the stone side of the palace, and launch myself into a roll that diffuses the worst of the impact.

Then I'm off and running to deliver the key to our true queen's succession into her hands.

TEN

Ivy

The smell of frying dumplings drifts up to my rooftop perch from a stall at the edge of the city square. My mouth starts to water with a pinch of my stomach, but I hold my position.

My job here is to observe the ordinary citizens milling around below me, not to join them.

At least I'm not alone in my current mission. Rheave has hunkered down on the roof tiles next to me. He's wearing one of Tinom's concealing charms too, but when we're touching, I can see and hear him without the illusion interfering.

Right now, he has his fingers looped casually around my wrist as he peers over the busy square. "The city has so many people. How will we be able to talk to them all?"

"We don't need to speak to all of them. As long as we catch the attention of a bunch, they'll chatter about it to everyone they know, and word will spread that way."

The daimon-man's eyebrows leap up. "It's like a kind of magic. Humans are so eager to share things with each other."

Despite the tension coiled in my belly, my lips twitch with a smile. "I guess the sharing helps us understand the world—by finding out what everyone around us makes of it too."

For a long time, I didn't have anyone *I* could really talk to that way. All I could do was listen in from the shadows.

It is easier to feel like I have a place here when I've got people who want me beside them.

Rheave adjusts his quiver against his back. He's brought his bow and plenty of arrows so he can shoot down any captured daimon we spot in the crowd we expect to form.

That'll both ensure they don't interfere and give proof to the story Petra's going to tell.

I glance at the clock tower visible over the tops of the nearby buildings. "Just another few minutes to go."

Rheave shifts on his feet. His hand slips from my wrist briefly and then snatches it again when he ripples out of view as I must have to him. His gaze twitches to me and away.

It still feels like something's a little strange about how he's acted with me since I escaped Lothar. The uneasiness I'm tamping down creeps up through my chest.

"Is everything all right?" I ask him. "Nothing's come up in the past several days that's bothering you?"

The daimon-man lets out a dismissive huff. "Of course not. You're back with us, and that's what matters the most. We'll deal with the rest of the scourge sorcerers like we brought down their march."

His fingers tighten against my skin, but he still keeps his gaze averted. Maybe it's only general daimon oddness… or maybe there's something he doesn't want to tell me.

I was under the control of the same scourge sorcerer—or

at least one with the same gift—as the one who's manipulated him. Does he associate me with that awful magic now?

"You know," I try again, "even people who care a lot about each other sometimes have problems come up that they need to talk through. That's part of having a close relationship with someone—at least for humans. So if you ever are concerned about anything to do with me or my other partners or anyone else we're spending time with, I'd want you to say so."

Rheave scoots a little nearer so he can give the side of my head a brief nuzzle. "I know that, Little Vine. So much talking. But the only thing I'm wondering about right now is what the people down there will be saying when Petra talks."

His voice has lightened enough that I'm not sure if I was just imagining my impression of his discomfort. It could be the lingering madness provoking a more subtle paranoia.

So I smile at him and set my hand over his to give it an affectionate squeeze.

Before I can say anything else, a light flashes overtop a stack of crates at the other end of the square.

The brief flare is an illusion conjured by Tinom, designed to draw people's attention to the main show. It fades into a projected image of Petra as I know she's standing in a building elsewhere in the middle wards.

We picked out the three squares in this section of the city where we thought there'd be the most activity—the most people around to hear our true queen's message. The nobles of the inner wards, Petra and Tinom can reach out to directly. It's the more ordinary people who make up the majority of Florian's citizens who she needs to get on her side against the scourge sorcerers.

Rheave and I are here to take note of reactions in this spot. Alek and Casimir are watching the second square. The third is within viewing distance of the place where Petra is actually standing, where Stavros has been coaching her on the best ways to stir people's loyalties and remind them that our country is worth fighting for.

Petra didn't have her royal crown, but she found herself a violet dress of sweeping silk worthy of a queen. For once, she's swept up her dark hair into the formal, swirling style favored by the court. And her stance is nothing short of regal.

Her clear voice rings through the square, amplified as part of the illusion like Lothar projected his the other night. "People of Florian! I have important news to share with you. You've been lied to about the death of our king."

As planned, those words get everyone's attention quickly enough. Most heads in the square swivel toward the illusion of Petra. Startled murmurs pass between the onlookers.

Petra hurtles onward, unable to hear the response she's getting. She holds up the blood-sworn letter with the sigil showing. "I was there when King Konram was murdered, because he is my father. You may not recognize me, but you should see the resemblance to my mother, Queen Ishild. When I was twelve years old, at my dedication ceremony, I stopped being Prince Dunstam and became Princess Petra. My parents decided to keep my new identity secret from you for my own security, as this blood-sworn document confirms. But it is your security I'm most worried about now."

The warble of voices has risen while she speaks, some people below us sputtering in disbelief, others letting out shocked laughs. I notice more figures are arriving from the streets that lead into the square, others emerging from the shops and eateries along its edges.

"Prince Dunstam *died*!" someone hollers. "This bint could be anyone!"

"She does have Queen Ishild's look to her," a woman murmurs to her companion just beneath my rooftop perch.

Petra lifts her chin, the anger in her expression clear even across this distance. "My father was *murdered*. One of his magic advisors, Lothar Riosemek, stabbed him with a knife and let him bleed out on the floor of his palace in Regica. He would have killed me and my younger sister and brother as well if we hadn't managed to escape. Now this same man is trying to tell you this death was the will of the gods. It was not. It was Lothar's will, so he can impose his ideas on this city and the rest of the country."

"All lies!" a man near the illusion calls out. "She's not even real." He scoops a discarded piece of food off the ground and hurls it through the image.

Another voice rises up from off to his left. "That's right! A real ruler would show herself, let us see this proof. What's she so afraid of, huh? That we'll see right through her? We already can!"

I tense in my crouched position. The hostility in those voices makes my riven power writhe in my chest.

Rheave notches his bow next to me. "Neither of the ones talking are daimon, but I can see a couple moving through the crowd. Should I shoot them now?"

I shake my head. "Not until they start pushing people around or Petra mentions the scourge sorcery."

Whatever's happening in the square nearest her, she must be aware of the sorts of protests people are raising. She holds up her hands in appeal. "I wish I could be with all of you in the flesh, but I wanted to speak to as many of you as possible at once. And I know that as soon as Lothar learns where I am, he'll continue his quest to murder me and all of my family."

"Easy excuses," someone in the crowd sneers, and flings what looks like a battered shoe at her projected form.

I can't tell if the rest of the restless voices below us agree with the skeptical comments or are questioning what Lothar's told them.

Petra keeps going, though the tensing of her lips suggests she's not pleased with whatever she's witnessing from her own vantage point. "Think about what's happened in this city since Lothar and his Order of the Wild marched in. How many murders have been carried out before your eyes? How have they desecrated our most sacred buildings? I can't believe that this is the kind of world you'd want to live in— one full of violence and cruelty.

"And it isn't just simple cruelty. Lothar and his followers are practicing scourge sorcery—the same magic that nearly ended our civilization and drove *away* the All-Giver all those centuries ago. That's how they wield so much power. They're helped by those they convinced as children to sacrifice every part of their body they could spare while remaining alive, leaving them mere shells of human beings. And by daimon, whose spirits they've trapped in bodies made of clay, upsetting the proper balance of life itself."

Rheave doesn't wait for me to give him the go-ahead. The moment the last statement has left Petra's lips, he releases my arm.

Since I still know he's there, I glimpse a wavery image of him pulling back his bowstring. One arrow and then another launch into the air from our rooftop, sped onward by crackles of his daimon magic.

They hit their marks in quick succession. Spurts of black smoke shoot up as the bodies collapse.

I lose sight of the toppling forms amid the now milling crowd, but the yelps of shock tell me they've transformed back into clay.

I duck low behind the jut of a dormer window so my voice won't allow any eyes to seek me out and raise my voice to carry as far as it can. "She's telling the truth! There are fake people walking around with us."

The murmurs swell across the square. Some sound panicked, others angry. They're starting to drown out Petra's voice despite the amplification.

"It's a trick!" someone yells—probably one of the Order members. "This false princess is using her lies to try to undo the progress we've made! She doesn't care about you. She can't even be bothered to come to actually listen to you. Just like all the Melchioreks!"

Not far from my rooftop, several pedestrians jostle against each other. I can't tell what they're squabbling about, but they knock over a cart full of apples.

As the fruit roll past people's feet, several onlookers snatch one up and whip it toward the illusion of Petra.

"Come and really talk to us!" a woman cries out.

A male voice joins her. "Let's see that proof!"

More and more shouts fill the air.

"Who are you really?"

"Why didn't the Great God come back for King Konram?"

"Everything's gone wrong!"

So many of the bodies are jostling together now. The illusion of Petra wavers. "Please, listen," I think she says, and then I lose track of her words completely amid the chaos.

I can't even tell how many of the unsettled civilians want to believe her and how many are upset with her—but there are definitely too many of the latter. The crowd surges toward the crates below her illusion, more objects hurtling through the air toward her image.

I don't know how to stop them or make them see reason. My magic is flailing around in my chest now, desperate to yank all the people below me into order, but I can only imagine how disastrous that effort would turn out.

As I wrap my unpredictable power tight within me, my gaze sweeps over the churning figures. It catches on a boy of maybe seven or eight stumbling where one of the more aggressive onlookers has shouldered past him.

The boy trips and falls onto his knees. I have a flash of an image of his small body swallowed up and trampled by his fellow civilians, and my heart lurches alongside my magic.

I detach my necklace with the concealment charm and shove it in my pocket. "I need to help someone," I gasp out in Rheave's direction, and leap down onto the jutting store sign below before he can answer.

I don't need my riven power for this. With another hop, my feet hit the ground. I throw myself through the weaving bodies, searching for the pale beige of the boy's tunic.

There. He's just yanking his hand away from being stomped on.

I spring across the last short distance and grasp his elbow to haul him upright—and backward into shelter between two abandoned stalls.

The boy spares me a puzzled glance and then darts forward again with a hoarse holler. "The king is gone! We need someone real!"

Gods help me, has Lothar already managed to muddle even the city's children?

I snatch at the boy's arm again to hold him back. "Why are you talking like that? She's real even if you haven't met her properly yet."

He glares back at me with eyes so hostile I restrain a flinch. "If she's got anything to do with the old king, I don't want her."

"Why not?"

The boy snorts as if the answer should be obvious. "What did King Konram do for any of us who didn't matter enough to wear fancy clothes and go to his parties? Where was he when my dad broke his leg last year and some shoddy medic left him with a limp? If the royals can't help us, we've got to fight for ourselves!"

He jerks his arm free and dashes away into the crowd, leaving me staring after him with a sinking sensation in my gut.

ELEVEN

Ivy

I sprawl across the bough of the oak, careful not to disturb the leaves that would rustle no matter how concealed my body is. My head dips to take in the voices below more clearly.

The rough bark grazes my cheek and digs into my hands. It's a familiar sensation, and yet my nerves remain on edge.

I don't know what's wrong with me. This place used to be where I felt most at home in the world, and now I can't shake the sense that I'm an intruder.

Beneath me in the tiny garden that holds a few sparse vegetables and a beehive, Ewalin and Frida have been puttering around and murmuring to each other for the past several minutes. Maybe it's their own attitude that's kept me in the alert. The daughter and mother I've so often visited in the outer wards are clearly nervous about being overheard in a way I never encountered before.

The atmosphere has shifted similarly all through Slaughterwell. This is only the last of a couple dozen

shabby houses I've stopped at in my survey of the neighborhood. The usual strident shouts and bellows of laughter have been replaced by hushed voices and hesitant giggles.

The change in atmosphere isn't the only thing affecting my own mood, though. The days when I used to watch Ewalin and Frida and long to slip into their family alongside them have faded into distant memory.

I do have a family now, as odd as these two women might find it. And I don't know that I'd fit all that well with these two anymore regardless.

"I wish I could have been there to see it myself," Ewalin is saying as she stops to tug up a weed. "Prince Dunstam—or whatever her new name is—come back from the dead?"

Her mother exhales roughly. "I'd think something got mixed with the ale in the local pub if there weren't so many people talking about it. Would a king hold a false funeral out of some idea of keeping his child safe?"

She shakes her head and rests an affectionate hand on Ewalin's hair. "I can't imagine putting myself apart from my daughter for years. But who can say what goes on in the heads of royals?"

Ewalin gives a soft huff as she straightens up. "Better if he'd spent more time worrying about the safety of the rest of us. How many children of Slaughterwell died while he and his Crown's Watch rarely stepped past the middle wards?"

Frida sketches her hand down her front in the gesture of the divinities. Her voice drops even lower. "There's been far too much death all around just now, if you ask me."

Her daughter grimaces. "Yes. But at least this Order is spreading it around a little more fairly instead of it all landing on us and our neighbors. We'll just keep our heads down and see what comes of it."

As they drift back toward the house, a lump fills my

throat. I've caught similar sentiments all across Slaughterwell, but hearing it from these two hits a little harder.

Before this afternoon's ruckus in the square, I thought most of the ordinary folk of Silana would be happy to have real order restored. But I've obviously spent too much time among royals and nobles in the past few months, absorbing their ideals and letting them kindle my good will.

I used to feel the exact same way Ewalin does about King Konram. I roamed through these streets seeing the desperation and suffering and silently ranted about how he neglected his most needy people.

His police force has always been faster to act the richer the victims are. His laws have always favored the elites of the inner wards above even Florian's middle class.

Why should any of the people he placed lower on his priorities jump at the chance to reestablish the Melchiorek reign?

Why should *I*?

The question niggles at me as I shimmy down the tree and slink along the back alley through the chilly dusk.

I don't know Petra all that well. I don't know what kind of a ruler she'd be.

I'm sure she's a better option than handing the country over to scourge sorcery, but is that enough to throw my support so whole-heartedly behind her? Could there be other options I haven't considered in my panic to push back Lothar and his cronies?

I've been thrown from place to place so often since Julita landed in my head, had so many voices in my ear, that I'm not sure of what I think just for myself.

A couple of lanes farther along, I pass by Zuzanna's house. The guttering candle beyond her grubby window makes the shadows waver in the sigils of Elox carved into the building's outer walls.

The guttural coughing that reverberates from within tells me that her son is sick yet again, her appeals to the godlen of healing gone unheard. Or perhaps he simply can't intervene, as Kosmel hesitated to insert himself more than a little into my life.

Someday, I'd like to get the chance to ask the gods a thing or three about exactly how they're meant to fit into our existence.

I veer closer to the window, and Zuzanna's ragged voice carries to my ears. "I'm going to keep trying, sweetie. Maybe if the All-Giver returns, I can ask for the Great God's blessing to shine on you."

An ache closes around my heart. I pull myself away.

I hadn't really thought about it before, but in some ways Lothar and his ilk are just a more ambitious version of the con artists I used to steal from on these streets. Conjuring hope for incredible things in people who are so hungry for every scrap they can get.

Who from the poorest soul to the richest nobleman couldn't imagine how their lives might be better if our highest creator returned? Who has never found any fault in our current rulers, to think we couldn't have an even better one?

King Konram himself set the precedent that we deal with threats by slaughtering them. How many riven sorcerers did he parade in front of the city on their way to the gallows?

A gloom hangs over me as I weave my way back to the tenement building. Going up the stairs, I slip off my concealment charm and tuck it in my pocket so I'll be visible to the people I want to see me.

No one's in the hall that divides the two apartments on the highest floor. I head into the one where my men and I have been staying.

Alek is sitting in one of the plain armchairs in the front

sitting room. I recognize the book propped open between his hands as the aged volume I retrieved from King Konram's secret hiding spot.

He's smiling before he glances up and takes in my expression. A shadow crosses his face. "Is everything all right?"

"Is it any worse than it was before, you mean?" I say with forced wryness. "No, not particularly."

I amble over to claim a quick kiss and rest my hand on his shoulder. "Have you figured out what was so special about that book?"

It's easier to talk about Alek's discoveries than my own, especially with the way his face lights up in scholarly enthusiasm at the topic.

He pages back through the book. "I think the rumors going around the city that the gods were dissatisfied with his family must have bothered King Konram. Princess Klaudia said she remembers hearing him ask the main palace archivist for any books in the royal collection that dated back to before the Great Retribution. This is one of them."

I peer at the book alongside him. "And it says something about what the gods expect from our kings and queens?"

"Not exactly. But there are several details I've never seen before about those kingship trials we've discussed before. I wonder if he was only preparing for what the scourge sorcerers might try to enact or thinking of finding a way to hold his own version, to prove his legitimacy."

I swallow thickly. King Konram won't get the chance for that now. "Why would he have kept it hidden?"

Alek gives a slight shrug. "Hard to say without being able to ask him. It is a very rare and valuable book—I've never seen anything like it. And he might have been worried about sparking ideas he didn't want in other people's heads."

Stavros appears in the doorway that leads to the inner

rooms. He strides over and wraps his arm around me in an embrace that settles just a little of the turmoil churning inside me.

"Petra wanted to speak with you as soon as you returned from your scouting," he says. "I'd like to hear what you observed as well. We clearly need to adjust our strategy."

I'm not sure I'm ready for this conversation—but it has to happen, and soon. Squaring my shoulders, I nod. "All right. Where is she?"

Stavros leads me to the opposite apartment. Tinom nods to us from where he's sitting at the table in the front room with a couple of the nobles who've joined our cause, but I feel his wary gaze follow me as we walk by on our way to the bedrooms.

He tried to insist that the royal children should each have a room to themselves in honor of their status, but Princess Klaudia and Prince Jacos preferred to share so they wouldn't have to spend any time alone. Petra has taken the room across from theirs, though I suspect she spends a lot of time with her siblings all the same.

Right now, we enter after knocking and find the younger princess and prince standing with her at her vanity. She's unfurled a map of the city and its surrounding area there.

At our entrance, all three look up—and Prince Jacos doesn't quite stifle his wince when he catches sight of me. Princess Klaudia's lips purse tighter.

My stomach clenches. They've never spoken against me in my presence, but it's obvious they're still not comfortable with me.

And I can't blame them. It's just a stark reminder that if it wasn't for Petra, it's unlikely I'd be welcome in this resistance movement at all.

Petra gives both of her siblings an affectionate squeeze of their arms and nudges them. "Why don't you go back to your room and give all of this some more thought? We'll discuss it again after I've heard Ivy's report."

Klaudia's stance stiffens for a moment as if she means to protest, but any interest she has in being part of the conversation must be won over by her desire to get farther away from me. She and Jacos hurry out of the room.

Petra sits down at the vanity. Her dark eyes take me in, steady but pensive. "What news do you have?"

The regal tones I heard her bring out during her proclamation in the square have lingered. She's becoming more a queen with every passing hour—and suddenly I'm not certain that's a good thing.

I drag in a breath. My body tenses instinctively, but if I can't be honest with her, there's no point in supporting her at all.

"You may have an uphill battle to winning over most of Florian. I'm not sure you realize—you must have been somewhat isolated from the common folk even as a supposedly more distant royal..."

When I trail off, groping for the right way to phrase what I need to say, Petra's voice softens. "Whatever it is, you can tell me, Ivy. I need to know."

I can't help folding my arms over my chest protectively. "In a lot of ways, your father... neglected the people whose support he didn't need all that much. I saw it myself firsthand many times over. It was particularly bad in the outer wards—the Crown's Watch would look the other way when corrupt merchants exploited the poor families there, because what mattered was who paid the most taxes. Most people who weren't rich or noble born didn't feel they could count on the Melchioreks in times of need."

Some of the color fades beneath Petra's tan skin, but she inclines her head. "I'm sorry to hear that. I know some of those things he simply washed his hands of, leaving decisions to the discretion of people like the leader of the Watch. But he should have paid more attention, and he should have been there when all his people needed him."

Stavros clears his throat. "It's a difficult balance, of course. Royals need to maintain some distance, or they'll be pulled apart by all the demands. He did a lot of good, as many mistakes as he also made." He shoots me an apologetic glance.

I wave my hand dismissively. "I'm not saying he didn't. There have obviously been worse rulers. But, Petra, you need to convince everyone—or a lot of people, at least—that having you in charge would be better for *them* than waiting to see how the scourge sorcerers will rule."

She grimaces. "They're having children carved up to fuel their magic—they slaughtered all those clerics and devouts—"

"They've been keeping the first part well-hidden," I cut in. "And every ruler has killed their enemies. They're convincing people that they're only destroying those who were threats to our country."

Petra's jaw tightens. "I was born for this. I know I can do what's best for Silana—for everyone in it. I can learn from Father's mistakes. If they'll give me a chance…"

She pauses and appears to compose herself again. "I suppose that means we need to come at the problem from two angles. One is exposing the truth about the scourge sorcerers so they'll lose support, and the other is proving that I'm a better option so I'll gain it. I think you may be better equipped to handle the former. For the latter, I'll have to spend some time beyond the inner wards myself, seeing what's become of our kingdom with open eyes."

Stavros stiffens. "You can't wander around the streets on your own. Lothar will have his people—"

Petra holds up her hand to stop him. "I can use one of

Tinom's charms so no one will spot me. I've spent my whole life learning how to keep myself safe, Stavros. It's about time I learned what the rest of my citizens need for their own well-being."

She sounds confident enough that the worst of my doubts melt away. I don't know how well she'll hold up as she faces everything involved in ruling a country, but at least right now, she understands the problem.

She does care, no matter what people believe of her family.

Petra turns to me. "Whatever we find out, however we decide to approach this, we'll need to bring more people onto our side to spread the word before we can hope to convince all of the city, let alone the country. You've lived in Florian your whole life, Ivy, and mingled with every level of society. Do you have any friends you could call on who'd be willing to take that first step of trust?"

Friends? I restrain a laugh, and a flicker of inspiration passes through my mind.

I hesitate before venturing a careful answer. "Not friends, but I am acquainted with some people of influence who'd be very handy allies… if I can persuade them that it's in their best interests to stand up to Lothar and his Order."

If they don't slit my throat for simply daring to ask.

TWELVE

Ivy

Just before we turn the corner to bring us in view of the Frolic Theater, I stop Casimir with a hand on his arm. When the courtesan turns to face me with a gently questioning expression, my heart beats a little faster.

Out of all the men who've become entwined in my life, Casimir has always been the one I least need to fear judgment from. But that sweetness makes me hesitate to expose him to the grittier parts of the world I came from.

"The people in Crow's Close are… pretty rough around the edges," I say. "They're used to having to lie and fight to survive."

Casimir studies my face. As usual, he picks up on the things I haven't quite said. "It won't be anything like my pampered noble life. I know."

I grapple with the words to get across what I most want to convey. "They aren't all bad people. I mean, some of them are, but for a lot—it's just another way to get by, for people who didn't have many options. Or a

sketchy business that isn't really any more immoral than plenty of things merchants supposedly on the right side of the law get away with. You just have to be prepared that they might be hostile about me bringing you in there."

"Because I'm a stranger. It makes sense." Casimir brushes his fingers from my temple over my hair. "It's all right, Kindness. I know this place is part of who you were—who you are. *You* had to skirt the edges of the law. But you did it for good reasons. Nothing I see in that place is going to change how I feel about you."

My throat tightens. Yes, I guess that is what I was most worried about underneath, even if I didn't want to admit it to myself, let alone him.

I take on a more chipper tone. "It does have a few bright spots. The main pub makes the best amber spritz I've ever tasted. Not that we'll have time to stop for a drink on this visit."

Casimir chuckles lightly. "Perhaps another day."

I'm not sure he realizes exactly what he's getting into even after everything I've said, but I don't want to send him into a panic with horror stories either. He'll take a read of the place quickly enough once we get there.

And if he regrets agreeing to accompany me, well, we'll deal with that when it comes.

I lead the way along the Tangleside street to the theater. One of the comedic shows is going on even in the midst of the Order of the Wild's takeover.

I might be imagining it, but the laughter that careens from the inner doorway has a slightly frantic edge to it.

People need their escapes in times of crisis more than ever.

But we're not here to take in the entertainment. I veer sharply and take Casimir down the basement stairs that lead to the hidden passage that connects the theater to Florian's smallest and most secret neighborhood.

The courtesan doesn't remark on the dankness of the basement room or the darkness of the magical passage. He remains silent as we ascend the identical stairs on the opposite end and emerge onto the enclosed street that holds the most established illicit businesses in the city—possibly the entire country.

He's taking it all in, absorbing it and forming his own understanding. That's why I decided I needed him with me for this negotiation, if he was willing to come.

He understands people better than anyone I've ever known. And his gift can tell us what we can give our potential allies that they'd want most.

I had to bully one of the bosses of Crow's Close's main gang into accepting my last proposition. I'm hoping to handle this discussion in a more amicable manner. But charm isn't really one of my strengths.

As we cross the road to the largest building in the Close —gambling hall, temple to Kosmel, and headquarters for the Black Talons gang—I sweep my gaze over the street. Casimir and I have both dressed fairly plainly, with the hoods of our cloaks shadowing our faces. The way I'd normally dress when visiting this den of criminals.

We shouldn't stick out at a glance. But I have no doubt that the people I intend to speak with will pick the courtesan out as an interloper swiftly enough.

We step into the first-floor gambling hall to the spicy smell of fried goldrud root and a sharper whiff of hazebloom smoke. It's late afternoon, too early for the main nighttime crowd, but far enough along in the day that a decent number of avid gamblers have stirred from their beds. About half of the tables scattered across the sprawling room are full, urgent voices and hopeful shouts echoing off the ceiling.

I weave through those tables around the base of the massive silver statue of Kosmel that stands in the center of the building. It only takes a minute to spot the man I'm looking for.

Garom Rochimek is sitting back against one of the empty tables in his usual scruffy disguise. The memory flits through my head of Julita's skeptical remarks when I approached him weeks ago, with a pang that's amusement and grief mixed together.

What would my ghostly noblewoman friend have had to say about the deal we're attempting to make today?

When I'm close enough for Garom to make out my features beneath my hood, his gaze snags on my face. His eyebrows arch slightly beneath the rumpled blond hair of his wig.

Then his gaze slides to Casimir, and his pale eyes narrow.

He pushes himself out of his chair before I've quite reached him, keeping his voice low. "Come for another chat, Ivy, after all the trouble I went to getting you out of this city? You've used up your favors."

I give him a small smile. "I had a good reason to return. And in this particular case, I may be able to do *you* a favor."

"Who's this pretty boy? Don't tell me you've got a boytoy scampering at your heels now."

If the jab bothers Casimir, he doesn't show it. I roll my eyes, having no intention of revealing that I've actually got *four* paramours at the moment. "He's a good friend, and he can confirm everything I'd like to discuss with you. But the details aren't anything I think you'd want spoken about in broader company."

Garom grunts, but he turns and shuffles toward the doorway that leads to the building's back staircase.

As we head up the stairs, I clear my throat. "The proposition I have isn't just for you but for all three of the

Black Talons' leaders. Are Sonia and Hellar around, or should I arrange to come back another time?"

Garom aims another piercing look at me. "What exactly is this about, girl?"

I lift my chin, letting my smile stretch a little farther despite the tension knotting my stomach. "How would you like to have the ear of the future queen?"

Hardened gang boss though he may be, I've managed to shock him. His expression twitches before he checks himself. "Very funny."

"I'm not joking. I spoke with the heir to the Melchiorek line just a couple of hours ago. She doesn't support all of her father's policies, and she's willing to work with you to make your work go more smoothly."

Garom's gift is a knack for separating truth from lies. He'll be able to tell that I'm being honest.

I've managed to strike him speechless for a few seconds. His throat works with a swallow, and then he swings his arm for us to continue following him up the stairs. "Come on, then. I should be able to round up my colleagues if you aren't in a terrible hurry."

Relief trickles through my chest. I really didn't want to have to stew in anticipation for another day—or to give the Black Talons' bosses extra time to scheme amongst themselves.

Garom brings us not to his personal office but to a larger space set up like a sitting room. Several padded armchairs stand in a loose ring that fills most of the space, with side tables between them and a lower table in the middle that looks as if the legs could be heightened if one wanted to play cards at it.

A faint sour scent drifts from the extensive liquor cabinet against one wall. Those walls are thick enough to shut out all the noise from the gambling hall that filters up through the gap around the godlen statue outside.

"Sit," Garom tells us, and pokes his head back into the hall. After a quick muttered conversation with a lackey, he returns and drops into one of the chairs opposite the two Casimir and I have chosen.

He watches Casimir rather than me as he slides off his wig. Wanting to evaluate the unknown party's reaction, I assume.

Because underneath that wig, the gang boss's scalp is shaved and scarred with a chaotic mess of lines where he sacrificed a significant portion of skin—along with who knows what else that I can't see—for his gift. It's a tradition among the Black Talons families, although only known in the sort of circles they usually run in.

To someone unfamiliar with the city's underworld, it'll simply look disturbing.

Casimir's mild expression doesn't flicker at all, but then, I told him in advance what to expect. He tips his head toward the other man. "I appreciate you taking the time to hear us out."

Garom's eyebrows leap up again. "You're one for pretty speech, huh? And what's that in your mouth there?"

I tense, but Casimir obligingly parts his lips again to give a quick view of the jeweled teeth that replaced the eight molars he sacrificed.

Garom looks at me, his voice taking on an edge of a sneer. "You brought some gaudy teeth for your royal offering? What, is he the *princess's* boytoy?"

I harden my gaze. "He's familiar with the inner workings of court and a trusted friend to the future queen as well as me. You can count on him to know more about what's possible than I do. Think of him as her representative in this meeting."

The gang boss simply guffaws at my words, but he doesn't make any more heckling remarks. Casimir's demeanor remains as unruffled as ever.

The door squeaks open, and a statuesque woman strides in. She sets her hands on her hips and studies the three of us with a faintly irritated expression.

I've only seen Sonia Alinnya at a distance before, but everyone in Crow's Close knows she's the matriarch of another of the three Black Talons families. Her scalp is as scarred as Garom's, though she's let the dark hair that can still grow tumble down to her shoulders in its uneven waves, partly hiding the pattern of her sacrifice.

It's hard to tell how many years she has under her belt with the simple but stark cosmetics that sharpen her features, but I know she has children older than me.

"What's this all about?" she demands.

Garom motions her toward the chairs. "Ivy and her friend are going to explain. I think it'll be worth hearing them out."

Sonia grimaces, but she trusts her colleague enough to drop into one of the chairs. She considers her fingernails and then me and Casimir with equal intentness, but she doesn't speak.

I don't see any point in launching into my pitch until the third person who needs to hear it arrives.

Which he does, a few minutes later. The youngest of the three bosses—though he's still got at least a decade on me—saunters into the room with a swipe of his hand through the strip of bleached hair on top of his head.

Hellar took over the Witorek family's part of the Black Talons a couple of years ago after his mother and last remaining parent was offed under typically murky circumstances. I'm not sure whether rival criminals or the

Crown's Watch were responsible, but I suspect he'll be the hardest sell on our proposal.

His scars form a geometric pattern that dapples his pinkish brown skin around the sides and back of his scalp, leaving a narrow crop of hair on top. The fine strands flop over the edge of scarring like wheat drooping in a field.

He drapes himself across one of the armchairs without prompting and considers us with an air of boredom. "What was so urgent you had to disturb my game, Garom?"

The older man lifts his chin toward me and Casimir. "These two have come to speak to us on behalf of the woman who would be queen."

The newcomers know he wouldn't say it if he hadn't judged it to be true. There's no mistaking the interest that sparks in both of their eyes, though Sonia is better at tempering it.

She adjusts her position, taking a skeptical tone. "Oh, really?"

Hellar chuckles, but he's straightened up to give us more of his attention. "And what does the supposed queen want with us?"

I keep my posture straight and my voice steady. "You've obviously heard about Princess Petra and the message she delivered yesterday. Every word of it is true. Advisor Lothar launched a conspiracy against the king, murdered him and Queen Ishild and attempted to do the same to the royal children, and has been encouraging scourge sorcery among his followers."

Hellar twitches his shoulder in a careless shrug. "What's any of that to the Black Talons?"

Sonia's gaze has turned to a glower. "It's not as if we had things so sweet under King Konram. Let the scourge sorcerers tear each other apart. We'll be fine no matter what."

I focus on her. "Are you sure about that? Have you heard

about the kinds of behavior Lothar and his Order of the Wild are encouraging? They want everyone to tap into their baser instincts—they want violence and chaos. What kind of an advantage will any of you have if *everyone* is willing to ignore the law and act out however they want?"

Hellar makes a scoffing sound. "We'll still be the experts."

"But you'll be up against people who can tap into more magic than anyone should be able to. Who are only looking out for their own selfish interests. The moment they want something you do too…" I wave my hand through the air. "It's gone."

Garom leans back in his chair, seeming to watch both me and his colleagues with equal interest. "And how would things be better under another Melchiorek? We've lost good people and good deals in the years of Konram's reign and his father before him. This new queen might be even worse."

I snort. "Do you think *I'd* be backing her if she had it out for everyone who's remotely criminally inclined? She knows about my past. She knows—" I catch myself before I mention my own illicit magic, which this trio doesn't need to find out about. "She knows, and she hasn't judged me for it. She recognizes that things need to change so all of Silana's citizens can make their living as they see fit."

"She says that now," Hellar remarks dryly. "Watch how fast she changes her tune once she gets what she wants from us."

Sonia leans forward. "What exactly *does* she want from us? Why are you here?"

"She asked me to reach out to people in the city who could help her get a foothold against the Order of the Wild," I say. "It's no easy thing with the kind of power they can throw around and how they've been smearing her family. They're killing everyone who opposes them—everyone who'd be her allies. She needs people who know the city and its people, who can speak to those people and tell them what we're really up against, convince them that Lothar and the Order need to be taken down."

Hellar wrinkles his nose. "And her put up in his place."

"She has the training. She's been preparing for this her entire life. And most of the nobles trust the Melchiorek name. It'll be hard for anyone to set the country back in order without their agreement too."

A tingle passes through the air beside me, telling me Casimir has extended his gift. He lets out a soft cough to catch the gang bosses' attention. "Princess Petra isn't asking anything at all of you yet, other than to talk. This is your chance to have a direct influence over the running of the entire country. I've spoken with her too—I can vouch that she wants to negotiate with you."

"And what could she give us that we don't already have?" Sonia asks.

"She can call off the Crown's Watch. Ensure that you maintain a monopoly over certain types of trade. Negotiate lesser punishments." The corner of his mouth quirks upward. "I'm not saying she'll look the other way when it comes to issues like murder, but you could arrange a lot more room to maneuver."

Garom lifts his voice with a twinge of reluctance. "He's telling the truth. He truly believes all that. Of course, the princess herself could be a fabulous liar."

I pounce on the opening. "You could find that out easily enough. We'll arrange a meeting on neutral ground. It's not as if you have anything to fear from her. The only crimes she's interested in tackling right now are her parents' murder and the illegal sorcery being practiced in this city and the rest of the country."

He looks as if he's leaning toward accepting the offer. But

then something shifts in his eyes, and he peers at me with an intensity that sends a shiver through my nerves.

His lips curl with a hint of what I think is revulsion. "Back when you had to make your hasty exit from Florian, word was going around about a riven sorcerer on the loose. The description reminded me of you—pale hair, pale skin, short and slim."

My gut lurches, but I set my face in the blandest expression I can summon. My tone matches. "That's quite a joke. Do I seem insane to you?"

His gaze skims up and down me, and the chill seeps deeper into my body. I didn't exactly answer the question, not in a way he can judge my honesty by.

Are we going to lose our chance at an alliance over my magic without my even using it?

The wretched power takes that moment to yank at me, demanding that I let it loose to force agreement from their throats. As if that would win us anything but animosity and horror.

I must keep my poker face well enough. Though the question doesn't totally fade from Garom's eyes, he shakes his head with a dry laugh. "Your mind is definitely too keen by half."

Casimir steps in with all his usual smoothness, changing the subject back to the most important matter at hand. "You're free to make your own decision, of course. That's what the new queen can offer you more than anything—a chance to make your voice heard. Lothar doesn't care about any interests other than his own."

I suppress the urge to reach over and squeeze his hand in thanks. I was right to bring him with me.

We work together well—as so much more than just lovers.

"That is the impression I've gotten of that armless

asshole, I have to say," Sonia mutters, and my spirits lift a little higher.

Hellar flicks his fingers dismissively, but he doesn't outright argue, which I'll take as enough of a victory. "If we can agree on a reasonable meeting spot, I could consider hearing the princess out. But our friendship won't come cheap."

I pull my lips into another smile. "I never expected it would."

We've won the first round. I didn't know for sure we'd make it even this far.

Now we'll have to find out whether Petra can hold her own against the most powerful criminals in the city—and win them over at the same time.

Thirteen

Casimir

Jolmi swipes a rag across the varnished wood of the bar counter and peers across it at the mismatched group clustered around two large pub tables pushed together. "So this is the city's last hope, hmm?"

There's a teasing note in his tone, thank the gods. I give my former classmate's hand a playful nudge of my elbow, but his words prickle right down to my uneasy stomach.

The thirty or so figures deep in discussion around those tables *are* essentially the only Silanians we've gathered so far who are willing to stand up to the scourge sorcerers. And it still remains to be seen whether they'll manage to stand together rather than dissolve into squabbling.

The three gang bosses with scarred scalps who Ivy and I convinced to attend this meeting look both wary and skeptical in their seats at one end of the tables. The underlings standing guard behind them only add to the ominous vibe.

The handful of nobles and soldiers we've brought on

board wear equally wary expressions as they consider the admitted criminals. As if we don't have bigger things to worry about than what laws they defied in the past now that the man who made those laws has been murdered.

We've picked up a few other allies over the course of the past couple of days: a cleric who escaped the massacre at the Temple of the Crown, sitting alongside the devouts; the husband-and-wife heads of the merchants' guild; two more guards who've remained loyal to the Melchioreks. All of the soldiers, postures rigid as ever even though they're in plain clothes now, have stationed themselves behind Petra and her siblings at the head of the opposite table.

The whole arrangement gives the impression of a hostage negotiation rather than a communal brainstorming session. Tension hangs in the air thickly enough to set the hairs on the back of my neck on end.

How are we going to overcome the most powerful enemies our kingdom has ever faced if we can't even agree to fight them *together*?

This scenario should be in my wheelhouse. I was able to tell Petra what I'd gleaned that the gang bosses most wanted from me—the guarantee that the new queen would hear them out and offer much more freedom than her father did. I've studied every new arrival for any signs of guilt or subterfuge.

I even arranged this meeting spot on neutral ground. Out of all the dedicats to Ardone I trained alongside at Sovereign College and before, Jolmi was the one I was most sure would abhor what the scourge sorcerers are doing to this city... and who owned a space we could easily make use of.

He's shown a relieving sense of caution, arranging the meeting at a time when even his husband won't hear about it. But I can't tell how much he's agreed out of loyalty to the

Crown and how much out of the thrill of watching the hidden heir pull together her resistance.

It's a moment for the history books, no doubt.

I consider him for a long moment, seeing nothing but the eager gleam in his eyes and what appears to be a genuine wish to please as he pours the drinks one of the gang bosses shouts for. Then I turn my attention back to the tables.

Unfortunately, I can't simply run through them all person by person, delving into their desires with my gift. Even imposing my magical talent on two of the gang bosses yesterday left me exhausted.

It seemed most important to take a peek at the one I skipped yesterday, the one Ivy trusts the most, when they arrived this evening. That was rather a waste, since it turns out his wants are quite aligned with his colleagues', but I suppose it was better to confirm that than regret assuming it.

I could probably discern at least a vague sense of one more person's deepest craving tonight without knocking myself to the floor, but even that would be pushing my limits. So I've held my gift in reserve, relying on my non-magical skills to evaluate the group instead.

Our future queen rests her elbows on the tabletop as she leans forward. I have to credit Petra for the fortitude she's shown in the face of recent tragedies.

Her parents prepared her for this role well, even if only from afar for the past seven years. She manages to keep her stance relaxed enough to give a sense of openness while regal enough to hold an air of authority.

"I'm willing to go further than that in exchange for your loyalty to the Crown," she says, her alert gaze fixed on the gang bosses. "If we consider each of your typical areas of business, I'd imagine I can find some for which I could abolish the conflicting laws completely. How would you like to find yourselves at the head of a guild of your own, not only allowed to pursue those avenues unhindered but keeping full control over who else is allowed to engage in them?"

The gang bosses are giving their best impression of nonchalance, but I catch a twitch of a smile at the corner of Garom's mouth and an avidness in the adjustment of Hellar's position. I doubt they anticipated any Melchiorek making them an offer so generous.

Of course, they're not the types to leap at a chance before eyeing it from every angle. Sonia takes a disaffected tone. "And what guarantee would we have of you following through on your promises if we pave your way back to the throne?"

The guards shift restlessly at the sneer in her voice. Tinom, who's seated himself next to Princess Klaudia, can't conceal a frown.

I wish I knew what to say that could bring these disparate groups together in harmony. I've spent years in training to learn how to set any person at ease.

But when so much hangs in the balance with every word that passes around the table... I was meant to be pampering and entertaining political figures, not guiding their policies. And who can say what's reasonable or not when sadistic sorcerers have taken over the country?

Petra, at least, doesn't appear offended by the gangsters' caution. "I can sign a proclamation to the effect with my personal seal along with that of the Melchiorek family. We can make the establishment of the guild a priority during the very early days of our reclamation, so that you'd see it put into practice while I'm still relying on your support. If there are other methods that would reassure you more, I'd be happy to hear them."

The three bosses tilt closer together to murmur amongst themselves. Garom and Sonia push back their chairs and get to their feet. "You've given us a lot to think about. We'll talk about the details on our own and let you know what we think a reasonable deal would be. Then it'll be up to you whether or not you take it."

Tinom's mouth tightens. "We can't afford to wait very long. With every day, the Order of the Wild deepens their influence—"

Petra holds up her hand. "Advisor, I'm sure we're all aware of the urgency of the current situation."

Across from Tinom, Ivy lifts her head to catch Garom's eyes. "I'll come by tomorrow to find out what you've decided and bring word back."

He tips his head in acknowledgment. "Let's see if we can all end up with more than we started with."

He shoots a sharp smile at Petra and strides out of the pub with his colleagues flanking him.

As soon as the door has thumped shut behind the trio, Petra glances around the tables. "We need to think farther abroad as well as just within the city. The Order of the Wild has spread its influence everywhere. Perhaps we can bring in more allies from across the country—or push back in several places at once."

Stavros taps his prosthetic against the tabletop. "There was a fairly effective group of resistors in the city of Pima in Nikodi, assuming they've continued to avoid punishment."

Ivy's face brightens. "Yes, Voleska and Emor pulled together a good group and were already undermining the Order's authority. You can count on them."

Tinom hums thoughtfully. "There's a well-regarded temple of Elox up north, a few hours from Nikodi—the Temple of Tranquil Skies. The cleric who presides over it has always been a key supporter of the Melchiorek rule in that region."

One of the devouts sits up a little straighter. "Oh, yes,

that temple has a long history. I heard they sheltered revolutionaries there all the way back when Silana rose up against the Darium empire."

I'm even less use at evaluating people halfway across the country. As the discussion continues, I fold my hands in my lap against the unfamiliar urge to fidget.

I helped bring the current meeting together. I'll bolster spirits as needed.

No one would expect a courtesan to play all that large a role in overcoming an uprising anyway.

Alek is in the middle of describing another temple he's visited that he thinks might be worth reaching out to when one of Tinom's sentries slips in from the pub's back entrance.

The woman clears her throat to get the group's attention, though she focuses her gaze on her future ruler. "I've got a man you might want to speak with, though I'm not sure it's safe for you to do it directly. He was being chased by some of the Order members—they were yelling about him turning his back on Lothar. We managed to get him away to a temporary hiding spot. It sounds as if he's defected from the scourge sorcerers."

Stavros's eyes flash. "He might have useful information about their operations. If he can be trusted."

The former general looks as if he's about to get to his feet, but I hop to mine first. My spirits have lifted past their temporary gloom.

"I'll go speak to him," I say before anyone else can volunteer. "I don't have much to contribute to this discussion anyway, and I can get a read on what he's really after."

Having Ivy beam at me the way she does would solidify my resolve all on its own. Thankfully, I have the future queen's support as well.

Petra offers me a smile of her own. "Go and see what you

can find out from him—both in what he says and what he does."

The sentry motions for me to follow her, and we hustle out the back of the building the way she came in.

We hurry through the middle-ward streets. The buildings loom closer together here than in the inner wards, but still with a stately grandeur that you won't find very far beyond the old city walls.

The immensity of the task ahead of us starts to creep up over me again. We have to not just oust the usurpers and their murderous magic but unite the different levels of the city to do so.

I'm ashamed that I never thought all that much before about the lives of the citizens on Florian's fringes. Or the peasants in the towns and villages outside the city. I had a hazy idea of their existence and that they deserved to be happy just as nobles and royals do, but when did I make any effort toward putting that principle into practice?

The world my mother trained me to perform for was nothing more than a gilded bubble. The real crime isn't that I've deviated from her wishes so far but that I didn't realize I needed to sooner.

The sentry weaves through streets where the cobblestones become more worn and the buildings droop lower. They're still a far cry from the dirt roads and ramshackle wooden homes in the neighborhood around Crow's Close, but farther from the elite hub of the city all the same.

As we approach a stable, her steps slow for caution. She leads me around back to a shed attached to the building.

From the smell of leather that permeates the space we step into and the tools hung on the walls, I gather this is a workshop for mending saddles and bridles. At the moment, no one's inhabiting it except for a skinny man who looks to be in his mid-twenties, huddled in one corner.

His tawny hair is rumpled. Both grit and a reddish scrape mark his face. He considers the two of us with nervous eyes, looking ready to try to bolt past us if he feels the need.

He definitely feels under threat. From us, from the people he's run from, or both?

A couple of paces away from him, I crouch down, putting us on the same eye level. In the fading light that filters through the shed's small, grimy window, I examine his face and body language for every hint at his emotional state.

I pitch my voice low and soothing. "I hear you've had a rough time of it."

The man shrugs and tucks his arms tighter around his pulled-up knees. He has a shallow cut on his forearm too, a thin line of blood seeping into his sleeve on either side of the severed fabric.

Whatever happened between him and his former associates, it ended violently.

"We'd like to help you if we can," I go on in the same calm tone. "We'd rather not see anyone getting pushed around or beat up from now on."

The man wets his lips. "How do you think you're going to manage that? You don't know…"

He trails off, looking abruptly more anxious than before. His fear appears totally authentic.

"About what the Order of the Wild can do?" I fill in. "Actually, we know exactly what they're capable of. We're well aware of the magic they've been turning to and the lengths they've gone to so they can enhance it and their manpower."

The man makes a scoffing sound. "Then what do you think you can do about it?"

"We have our own strengths. We simply need enough people willing to take that first step to stand up to the Order, and then we can set Silana back to rights. But for now, you could start by telling me your name."

He hesitates again. As he opens his mouth, his arms loosen, his stance relaxing just slightly. "Filip."

I nod. "And why were you being chased by the Order, Filip? Why did they attack you?"

He sucks in a sharp breath. "I was supposed to— I didn't want to do everything they said we should. It sounded amazing at first, but once I actually saw…"

He trails off, his body deflating. Does he still look just anxious or sad as well?

It's not surprising that he'd be incredibly fearful about his former comrades getting their hands on him—and of how those of us who oppose the Order might retaliate for the harm he's helped carry out. But we still have to be careful ourselves.

If they won him over with promises of glory before, he could be swayed in that direction again.

Thankfully, I'm the best possible person to evaluate his priorities.

"Realizing you've made a mistake and refusing to do so again is a brave thing," I say, and extend my gift toward him.

A tingling shoots through my gums where I sacrificed my back molars for this magic. An ache ripples through my skull, but with it comes a current of impressions straight from the man in front of me.

What could I do that would make him happiest in this moment?

I catch fragments of meetings, Lothar looming tall over his followers; a child standing before a cleric; a surge of tingling exhilaration; a rush of fear. Then a bone-deep desperation that yawns open ever wider.

Understanding flows through that final sensation with the usual certainty of my gift. What would make him happiest is for me to believe him and give him a chance to work alongside me. He wants to take action, to prove himself.

The headache from repeated use of my magic jabs deeper through my mind, but a sense of triumphant relief rises up all the same.

I can bring this man back to the rightful queen. I can show him how to overturn the villains he once worked with.

I hold out my hand. "How would you like the chance to not just avoid your mistakes but turn them around?"

FOURTEEN

Ivy

As he studies the sketched diagrams one of Garom's people passed on to us, Alek rubs his hands like he's about to dig into his favorite meal. I can't help smiling at the scholar's enthusiasm, despite the dangerous mission ahead of us.

It reminds me of way back in my early days at the royal college, when he and I worked together to sneak into the college library's accounting room so I could steal Ster. Torstem's financial records. I never would have guessed during our initial meeting that Alek would be the first to join me in a criminal scheme.

But he does love putting his mind to a problem, no matter how legally questionable.

Now, he taps one point on the map where it's spread on the dining table. "Here's the access spot closest to this building. You enter there and follow this path…" He draws his finger across the passages marked like a diagram laid over the city streets. "Straight ahead until the third tunnel on the

left, then the second on the right, then the first turn to the left. There's another access spot a short distance down that one. It'll let you out just a block from the guardhouse."

Stavros studies the map with a tick of his head to clear his vision. "Are you sure we can open up those access spots without significant difficulty?"

Alek nods. "A jolt of Rheave's magic should melt off the lock. The openings are covered by a simple grate that's heavy but not very intensively secured." The scholar glances up at us with an apologetic wince. "Most people aren't eager to go down into the sewer system."

I have to snort. "I don't think 'eager' is the right word in our situation either. At least it'll get us through the city without having to pass by any scourge sorcerers, as long as we don't need to go to the outer wards."

The underground system of drains and channels was built centuries ago before the city had expanded quite so far. The tunnels only extend beneath the inner wards and partway through the middle wards.

But we need the extra subterfuge where we can get it. The new ally Casimir brought into the fold yesterday, an apparent defector from the Order of the Wild, told us that Lothar has assigned more of his followers to patrol the city streets in search of Petra's allies. A few among them have talents for sensing magic, others for seeking out targets.

If we pass too close to either, even Tinom's concealment charms won't keep us hidden.

Stavros straightens up. "If the sewers are our best option, then into the sewers it is. It's late enough. Let's get to work."

Rheave's eyes flash with a light that actually could be called eager. "I'm ready!"

I give him a teasing nudge as we head for the door. "You won't be so excited once we're down in the stench. I just need to get my cloak."

I expect to simply duck into the bedroom to grab the swath of dark fabric, but Stavros follows behind me. When I tug the cloak over my shoulders, he steps in to fasten it for me.

I hardly need the help, but I release the clasp to his deft grip, his prosthetic managing to hold one side in place while his fingers manipulate the other. His massive frame looms over me, the once intimidating presence now nothing but comforting.

Except I'm not sure why he's here.

A quiver of doubt pricks at the base of my throat. I keep my voice light. "Giving me a closer look to make sure I'm up to the job?"

Stavros sputters a guffaw. "I have no doubt that you are, Lady Thief. I just—I needed a moment away from the others. If you don't mind the intrusion."

His own tone is casual, but not quite enough to disguise a slightly ragged edge that creeps into it. When he lowers his hands, I grasp them between us, both the one of flesh and the one of metal. "Are you all right?"

He gives his head a brief twitch to meet my gaze a little longer before his eyes go distant. A sigh tumbles out of him. "I will be. It's ridiculous. I've felt like a wolf in a cage, cooped up in here, not being able to risk participating in most of the missions we've been carrying out—and now that I have the chance…"

I stroke my thumb over the side of his knuckles. "What?"

His mouth pulls into a grimace. "A lot of the men and women killed or taken captive from that guardhouse will have been people I trained with. People I once gave orders to. People who've counted on me one way or another. I can barely wrap my head around how many lives the Order of the Wild has destroyed in a matter of weeks, and we're stuck picking off pockets of strength bit by bit. It doesn't feel like enough."

I offer him a tight smile, my chest constricting around my heart. "It doesn't to me either. But we've got to build up to bigger things, right? The more the scourge sorcerers falter, the more support for Petra can grow."

Stavros's answering smile slants at a self-deprecating angle. "I know that. It's just harder to accept it when every part of me is screaming to end them all now."

I reach up to pat his cheek. "I'm sure you'll get plenty of chances to end loads of them in the future."

Another choked laugh escapes him, and then he's pulling me to him, claiming a kiss so fierce I wish it didn't have to end.

When he eases back just an inch, his low voice grazes my face with his breath. "The only reason I've made it this far is because I had you with me. Don't you ever let a single one of those fools Tinom pulled together make you feel you haven't earned their loyalty. You know you have all of mine."

I bob up on my toes to hug him, even though his words can't quite penetrate the uneasiness simmering in my gut. "And you have mine. Let's take back some more of what the scourge sorcerers have stolen from us."

We rejoin Rheave in the hall and slip down the stairs, donning our concealment charms as we go. Rheave sets his hand lightly on my back, and I hook my fingers around Stavros's elbow so that we can still see each other fully.

We step out into the night. The windows around us have gone dark, the blackness only broken by the glow of the intermittent lanterns along the street.

Somewhere around a corner, a drunken laugh peals out, but no one's wandering along this road at the moment.

We hurry across the cobblestones, take a turn, and come up on the grate Alek indicated. It's wide enough that even

Stavros should be able to fit without having to squeeze, and only secured by a single, regular padlock.

At the rap of determined footsteps, we pause. A middle-aged man in a thick cloak strides past us down the middle of the street—maybe an Order member on patrol, or maybe an ordinary citizen with some urgent midnight business.

My heart thuds faster with a jolt of my magic coming to attention, but he doesn't glance our way. I don't sense any sorcery emanating from him.

As soon as he's out of view, Rheave kneels by the grate. With a faint crackle, the padlock falls aside.

Stavros hefts up the grate and motions for us to descend.

I find the rungs of a ladder just beyond the opening. Gripping them, I clamber down as quickly as I can manage, wrinkling my nose at the damp grit that sticks to my fingers.

To my relief, the passage below isn't *quite* as awful as I imagined. It rained most of last night, which must have swept the worst of the collected refuse away. Still, the stink of urine and feces turns my stomach.

The men climb down behind me, Stavros shutting the grate in his wake so it's not obvious someone made use of it. More than a few steps beyond the faint glow that seeps through the bars, the blackness is so complete there's no need for our charms.

"Stay close to the walls," I murmur, and start forward in the direction Alek indicated.

The sewage flows turgidly along in the wide channel at our right. I set my feet carefully to ensure there's no chance of slipping into that noxious river.

After a few minutes, Rheave lets out a gagging sound. "Physical bodies do produce some unpleasant substances."

I guess spirit creatures don't shit. I glance back in the direction of his voice with an arch of my eyebrow. "That's the price we pay for getting to eat."

The daimon-man grunts in acknowledgment. "I suppose that is a fair trade-off."

If I had a list of places I'd least like to spend time with any of my lovers, this sewer would be right near the top. But as we venture on through the putrid darkness, my spirits buoy me beyond the stench.

Here I am, in the middle of a scheme that all four of my men have set in motion with me. One that doesn't require any of my unpredictable magic.

Like the old days… except now I'm no longer alone.

In this moment, it doesn't matter what magic fidgets in my chest or what people like Tinom or the Black Talons' bosses think of it. I can make a difference without being seen as any kind of monster.

We mark off the turnings with our hands against the stone wall, noting each passage until it's time to turn. Thankfully the rickety maintenance bridges at the intersections allow us to cross without needing to risk a jump.

Stavros ends up taking the lead, the thud of his boots guiding me onward. Rheave stays close enough to regularly caress my back through my cloak, as if he needs periodic confirmations of my presence to reassure himself.

When we reach our destination, Stavros climbs up to the grate and peers at the street beyond as well as he can from the low vantage point. He swings to the side and motions for Rheave to join him. "I don't see or hear anyone nearby right now. Give that lock a zap."

In less than a minute, we're scrambling out into the fresh if chilly air above. Stavros lowers the grate back into place, and we hustle down the quiet street toward the guardhouse.

It's one of the largest in Florian, just outside the old city walls on the border between the inner wards and the middle. Stavros visited the Crown's Watch here more than once in his capacity as general—and then after while investigating the conspiracy at the college.

He directs us around the squat stone building and down a side alley. There, he points up at a tall window on the second floor.

"That serves as an additional exit if the Crown's Watch needs to move out quickly," he murmurs. "They can pop it open and make the short jump into the alley while others are heading out the front and back doors. Since it's up there, they don't bother guarding it."

So no one should notice if it briefly opens and closes for our invisible figures to enter.

I give myself a shake in preparation. "All right. I should be able to handle the lock."

Stavros bends down and boosts me onto his shoulders. Once he's straightened up, I can easily reach the base of the window.

I pull out the slim metal tool I brought along for this purpose and wiggle it into the narrow gap between the frame and the ledge.

With a little maneuvering, I manage to slide over the deadbolt. I ease the window up an inch, listen, and then push it farther so I can wriggle inside.

My magic jitters with the urge to wrap even more protection around myself, but no figures stir at either end of the hall I lower myself into. Once I've set my feet on the ground, I tug the pane even higher.

Rheave scrambles after me with another boost from Stavros. Then the former general hefts himself after us with the two of us grasping his arms.

We huddle together so we can see each other clearly despite the charms. Stavros points in both directions down the hall, his voice the barest whisper. "The sleeping quarters are all up here—almost every room. They won't be locked. I'll be heading down to the dungeons in the basement."

I give his hand a quick squeeze. "Get through this mission as quickly as we can manage it, and then we'll meet by the grate as planned."

An ache forms around my heart letting him go, but if anyone can look after himself in a potential combat situation, it's Stavros.

As he turns toward the stairs, I nudge open the first of the doors to the police force dormitories.

Some members of the Crown's Watch go back to family homes when they're off for the day, but many choose to live in the guardhouse, especially the younger men and women who aren't married and want to be out of their parents' homes or those who've traveled from outside the city to serve. I guess it must come with a sense of family somewhat like what I've found with my men.

Now, the narrow beds set up along the walls of this room are filled with Order members. Lothar took over all of the Crown's Watch's properties when his people stormed the city, and he's using them as bases of operation.

Which means a significant number of the figures sleeping in these beds aren't people at all but daimon in animated clay bodies.

With one hand on my shoulder so I can see him, Rheave points to three of the beds. Those three are daimon like him.

I set my fingers over his in a quick reassuring touch and move to the first form he indicated.

Casimir picked out the pot of black makeup I retrieve from my pocket. It's a type that stains the skin semi-permanently rather than simply covering it temporarily.

Ever so gingerly, I use a soft brush to dab a few dark streaks on the side of the man's neck, just below the edge of his blanket.

By morning, the dye will have set. A mark will remain through at least a week of washes. But it simply looks like a slightly unusual smudge of dirt or soot, not anything purposefully put there.

Only the Black Talons people prowling the streets will know what those marks signify. They'll kill the captured daimons' bodies in public places so more and more witnesses will see the proof of the Order's unnatural magic—and so those daimon can go free rather than serving their slave masters.

When I reach the third sleeping figure, I have to tug her blanket down a little and brush her hair back from her neck. She lets out a sleepy sigh.

I freeze with a lurch of my heart. Only when she remains still for another several seconds do I lower my brush.

In theory, Rheave could have burned these marks. But the jolt of pain would probably have woken the targets. This way, we can mark them all without alerting anyone.

We move from one room to the next, marking neck after neck. Looking down on all the faces relaxed with sleep, my gut starts to twist with the thought of their future deaths.

They aren't really people, of course. The daimon are trapped inside those bodies, not there through their own will.

But if any of them would have liked to take the bodies as their own like Rheave has, to experience everything mortal life has to offer, they'll never get the chance.

That's the scourge sorcerers' fault, not ours. They set the daimon on this destructive path.

I can't help feeling a little guilty about it all the same.

Neither of us speaks as we work our way through the rooms. By the time we get to the end of the hall, I've marked nearly two dozen sleeping daimon.

I'm not sure whether to be more horrified by how many of the spirits Lothar's people still hold captive or how large a force they've installed in Florian in general. This is only the Order lackeys who didn't take the night shift, and only one of several guardhouses around the city.

The leader of the scourge sorcerers knew how hard he'd need to fight to keep control over Silana's capital. But our current forces might not be enough to tackle even one guardhouse, let alone all of the scourge sorcerers in the city.

I reach the last bed Rheave has indicated and draw back the blanket to reveal the sleeping man. My brush smears the inky makeup across the side of his neck—

And his skin twitches. He startles awake with a grunt.

My power leaps up my throat, but Rheave shoves past me in an instant. As I rein in the frantic call to subdue our target by whatever means necessary, my partner clamps his hands against the man's mouth and chest.

"We want to help you," he rasps in a hushed voice. "I used to be like you, but I'm not anymore. Can you take control? This body could be—"

The man starts to thrash against his blanket. Whether for his own reasons or because of the magic still binding him, he's not interested in a peaceful resolution.

Rheave lets out a pained noise—and a hiss of his daimon magic.

He hits the struggling form with enough power to reduce the clay statue that should have appeared into black dust. A smoky, earthy smell trickles into the air.

I grasp his shoulder, grimacing in sympathy. "You had to do it." Another few seconds, and the guard might have woken up the rest of the room.

We both stare down at the shadowed bed with its heap of charred clay dust, a bizarre murder scene. I gather my resolve. "Come on, we'd better clean up the body so no one realizes what happened."

Rheave nods silently. We gather the remains of the clay

body in a bundle of the blanket and sheets, and Rheave carries it with him on our way back to the window we entered through.

Rheave jumps down first and turns so I can use him as a sort of stepping stool. Several buildings over, we shove the bundle of fabric into a refuse bin where no one is likely to notice it. Then we hurry on to the sewer grate.

Stavros is waiting there, standing right on top of the grate so my gaze can easily find him despite the charm trying to divert my attention. His quest was a lot less time-consuming than ours.

I touch his arm to bring him into focus. From one glance at his grim face, I know he didn't find what he was hoping for.

"One of the captains I'd have counted on has been killed," he tells us as we step back from the grate so he can open it. "I think another may be still alive but held in one of the forts outside the city—Lothar might have hoped she had information that would be useful as the Order establishes itself in Florian."

Which means the advisor will be torturing the woman for her loyalties. I offer Stavros a tight smile. "Maybe we can get her out soon."

He gives a rough chuckle and bends toward the grate. I'm just turning toward Rheave when a sudden blast of magic slams into the side of my head.

The last thing I hear as I topple to my knees is Rheave's frantic shout.

FIFTEEN

Stavros

The shift in the air has me whirling before I'm even sure of what's wrong.

One second, I can't see anything around me except the darkened street. The next, five figures materialize a few paces away.

One of the men is gripping Ivy, her concealment charm snapped off her neck, her head slumped. They must have knocked her unconscious.

But even as my muscles clench to spring to her aid, my gaze lands on the taller man with the pale eyes and uneven frame who's obviously orchestrated this confrontation.

Lothar gestures to the man holding Ivy, who whips a knife to her neck. My stance stiffens, knowing I can't leap in there quickly enough to ensure the blade doesn't sever her throat, even in my currently invisible state.

"I know she's not alone," Lothar says in his thick, haughty voice, his eyes scanning the street. "If any harm comes to me or my people, you'll be sacrificing her too."

At least it seems that Tinom's charm is working well enough that Lothar can't make me or Rheave out when he isn't sure of who he's looking for or where exactly they should be. But somehow he found Ivy.

I adjust my position, my hand balling into a fist. Anger sears through my gut.

How did he know we'd be here at just this moment? It can't be a coincidence. They were lying in wait, concealed by their own magic.

Someone passed on the details of our plan to the Order.

How much else does our greatest enemy know? How much else has he *done* while we were infiltrating the guardhouse?

A jolt of panic spikes through my veins alongside my fury. The royal children—they might already be lost.

Lothar clicks his tongue, his lips curling with a hint of a sneer. "Why don't you show yourself so we can negotiate like proper human beings, hmm?"

He flicks his cool gaze toward Ivy. The man with the knife digs the blade in just enough for a thin line of blood to form along its edge.

My anger and fear congeal in my churning stomach. The former magic advisor would *like* to see Ivy dead. If the only sorcerer he had who could control her is gone, he'll want the threat she poses eliminated.

He's only kept her alive this long to control the rest of us. If he thinks that ploy isn't working, he'll happily murder her and call that its own win.

I can't see Rheave in the darkness. He's kept his charm on so far, though I can only imagine how worked up the daimon is watching the woman he's devoted himself to sagging in the grip of these villains.

It doesn't appear that Lothar knows how many people

exactly would have been with Ivy. Let the daimon realize he should stay concealed. I can be a distraction.

As long as Rheave has enough sense to recognize the advantage we can keep.

With a swift tug, I wrench off my charm. All five of the hostile faces before me twitch in my direction, their attention homing in on me.

I shove the charm in my pocket, my prosthetic raised defensively, and set my hand on the hilt of my sword. Not overtly threatening yet, just where I can draw it the moment I see an opening.

As Lothar's gaze takes me in, a sharper rage cuts through the rest of my inner turmoil.

This prick slaughtered the man I swore to serve, the man I'd have given my life for. He murdered our king and queen with no care for their lives, their children, or what it would do to our country, only thinking of his own brutal, selfish ends.

If I owe King Konram anything, it's seeing the traitor bleeding out here on the cobblestones. He's already destroyed so much, ruined so many lives.

I have to put the cur down.

I just don't know how.

Even if I did the unthinkable and sacrificed Ivy to launch myself at Lothar now, I have no idea what talents he or the lackeys flanking him possess. They might be able to deflect me before I inflicted so much as a scratch.

There's too much on the line to take that gamble.

"Here I am, Lothar," I say, my voice hard, with a flick of my eyes to clear the fog that's rolling over them. "What kind of negotiation are you looking for?"

The one-shouldered man rests his only hand against his belly, a pose that emphasizes what's missing from his uneven body. He tilts his head slightly to the side.

His expression is keenly alert but with no sign of fear. He believes he's fully in control of our stand-off.

As his gaze bores into mine, his face blurring after the first few moments, a sense of rancor prickles over my skin. As if he's radiating fury.

What the fuck does this asshole have to be angry with *me* about?

"There's only one piece of information I'm interested in bartering for," he says. "Where are the false queen and the young Melchioreks hiding?"

I can't restrain a scoffing sound. Does he really think so little of my loyalty as that?

It would tear my heart in two seeing him harm Ivy more than he already has, but I know that she would never forgive me if I traded our future queen's life for hers.

Besides, I'm not naïve enough to believe that Lothar actually would spare Ivy in exchange for the information. No doubt he'd have his man spilling her blood the second I coughed up a location.

Lothar's eyes narrow at my show of skepticism. "You aren't the only vermin we've caught, even if you are the worst." He aims a disgusted look at Ivy before returning his attention to me. "If someone else gives up the royals first, you'll have nothing left to bargain with."

My pulse stutters. Who else has the Order gotten their hands on?

Or is he simply bluffing to try to get his way?

Gods help me, if I could run this man through right now, it'd put an end to this entire mess.

But I don't even know that for sure. How deeply does his followers' fervor run now that he's stirred it up?

My fingers tighten around the hilt of my sword, but I leave it in place, locked in uncertainty. *Could* I offer something in return, a partial acquiescence that wouldn't betray Petra and her siblings but would buy us more time?

Thankfully, getting out of this wretched scenario isn't entirely up to me. As I grapple with my thoughts, a crackle of lightning-like energy blazes through the air.

The bolts slam into all five of the villains in front of me.

Even as my heart leaps, the sparks fizzle out against some kind of magical shield wrapped around Lothar's body, as well as that of his two closest followers. They barely twitch at the impact.

But the other two figures aren't so protected. A woman at Lothar's left and the man holding Ivy jerk and crumple with the surge of daimon magic.

The knife slips from the man's fingers, and Rheave is there, abruptly visible and yanking Ivy to her feet.

Her body trembles, and her eyelids flutter open.

The burst of magic must have jolted her too, back into at least partial consciousness.

My gaze snaps to Lothar—and my gift tickles at the back of my eyes with a sudden flash of imagery that shows me the wretch's next move.

"Pull back," I holler, wrenching out my sword. Rheave has already scrambled backward a few paces with Ivy before Lothar has a chance to snarl and spring at the two of them.

The magic Sabrelle blessed me with might not work as impressively as it once did, but I've never been gladder to have it.

In the tiny window of opportunity I bought him, the daimon spins to the side and thrusts out his arm. He hurls another wallop of sizzling energy at our attackers.

The flare doesn't penetrate their protective magic to char their bodies the way I'd like to see, but it does heave them back several paces. Lothar stumbles into his companions, knocking them all onto their asses.

I raise my sword, but I don't know if the blade could penetrate Lothar's shield any better than Rheave's magic has. And every second we linger is another opportunity for him to bring his own sorcery to bear.

"Run!" I shout to Rheave, and dash over to help him support Ivy.

Our lady thief has gotten her legs into somewhat working order. She only needs a little help balancing as we sprint around the nearest corner and duck into the first alley I spot.

There's no time to find another sewer grate, and I'm not sure we'd be better off down in the enclosed space now that Lothar is on our trail regardless.

Rheave propels out a question between his ragged breaths. "Where do we go now?"

Before I can answer, Ivy lifts her head higher. Her voice comes out slightly slurred but determined. "Can't go back to Petra. Can't risk leading them there."

As little as I like it, I have to agree. "She's right."

We hustle on in a weaving path through the streets. I peer at the buildings around us, my mind whirling. An uncomfortable sense of certainty fills my chest.

I don't want to take this step, but I can't justify the danger I'd be putting our entire cause in if I don't.

I set my jaw against my own misgivings. "We need to leave the city. We're too compromised—we can't guarantee the royal family's safety here. I'll have to signal Alek and Casimir the way we agreed."

We always knew it might come to this—that our situation in Florian might become so precarious we had to make a hasty exit. I just hadn't expected the conflict to reach that point so quickly.

Ivy nods, and I retrieve my locket from my trousers. Still

jogging, I press the pane inside the hinged pendant, pause, press it again, and repeat the sequence once more.

The series of three pulses in quick succession will tell our friends that something's gone wrong—wrong enough that they need to evacuate the future queen, her siblings, and all our other allies who'll join us.

As Ivy said, we can't risk returning to Tinom's tenement building. We'll have to count on our comrades to gather the possessions we left behind.

It isn't as if we've been carrying much with us after all this time on the run.

As a safety measure, we spread out our mounts across several stables at varying distances from the apartment. Taking the lay of the land, I make our next turn to take us to the spot where we lodged Toast and a few of the other horses we can call ours.

Rheave looks over at me, his smooth face unusually tight. Worry turns his voice taut. "What if they know about our escape plan?"

Dread sours my mouth. All I can do is shake my head. "We proceed as if they don't, but we keep our eyes open. If we see any sign that our route out of the city has been compromised, we back up and reconsider."

Ivy swipes her hair back from her face, her skin still wan but her eyes brightening by the second. "There's more than one way. We'll make it out."

I don't like to think about how much that effort might take out of her, though.

Tinom assured us that his hidden passage through the city walls was a closely guarded secret, known about only by the royal family and himself, since he's the one who disguised it. But who knows if King Konram might have trusted his other magic advisors enough to mention it to them?

As we rush into the stable and grab tack for the ride, an

emotion that's more regret than worry twists my stomach. The act of yanking the saddle's girth tight and the hurried snatching of the bridle are far too familiar.

How many times now have we fled from our enemies, running or riding off into the night?

How many times more will we need to before I can stand and fight the man who's inflicted so many horrors on our country?

Every military expert knows there are times when you have to cut your losses and lick your wounds so you can come back stronger. But gods above, each failure pierces me right through the middle.

I *will* destroy Lothar for everything he's obliterated in my world. I'll protect the remnants of the royal family, the woman I love, and the strange family we've made.

I just don't know when.

The uncertainty pulls my gut into a knot. Ignoring it, I lead my horse out of the stable with Ivy and Rheave close behind me, scan the street with a jerk of my head, and heft myself into the saddle.

"Let's ride."

Sixteen

Ivy

Filip's head swivels around as he takes in the landscape on either side of the small country road. Then he squints up at the sky. "We're a little off course for Kevarsi, aren't we?"

A couple of horse-lengths ahead of us, Tinom catches the question and glances back. The magic advisor keeps his voice carefully even. "We've had a slight change in plans. I sent some people ahead to scout out our options, and there's a better place for us to continue building our resistance."

Filip looks as if he's bitten back a protest. From Toast's back, I study his expression as well as I can without being blatant about it.

Has his face paled a little?

In discussions amongst Petra's innermost circle after we first regrouped outside Florian, we all agreed that the supposed Order of the Wild defector was the most likely traitor among us. Casimir said he gave every appearance of wanting our help but acknowledged that he might have been

desperate not to get away from Lothar but to fulfill whatever plan he's been sent to carry out.

So we've created a test. One of Tinom's people mentioned to him as if in passing that we were going to head to Kevarsi to try to gather forces farther from Lothar's current center of power. Since then, we've been watching to see if he's had some way of passing on information back to his former colleagues.

Over the past three days on the less-traveled roads that seem safest, we've also been veering gradually more north on our actual course. This is the first time he's noticed that we can't possibly be heading to the city.

He doesn't say anything else, though, simply keeps trotting along on his mare. After a few moments, his gaze darts briefly toward me with a slight tensing of his shoulders.

That's nothing new. I've caught many similar glances over the days since he joined us. Having me anywhere near him obviously sets his nerves jangling.

He knows about my magic, I assume, since Lothar would have spread the word among his followers to beware of me. The first thing he did when he saw me was jerk his hand through the gesture of the divinities, like the noble heir on the summer estate where Lothar held me prisoner.

I can't hold that against him when Tinom is nearly as wary. I think word might have spread to the soldiers by now, because I've noticed them drawing closer around Petra when I go to speak to her in their company.

This morning, one of them partly unsheathed his knife when I walked by.

The memory leaves a hole in my gut. I understand the reactions; I know how everyone thinks about the riven. But the ongoing paranoia is starting to wear on me.

Gods above, will I ever be able to live my life honestly if most people see me as a villain even when I'm helping them?

I don't let on that I've noticed Filip's anxious glance, just watch him surreptitiously for a few minutes longer. Then I draw Toast to a walk so we fall back to where my men have been bringing up the rear of our procession.

Stavros meets my gaze with a questioning lift of his eyebrows. I offer a noncommittal shrug in return.

When I'm close enough that I'm sure our voices won't carry to the man we're monitoring, I guide Toast into the midst of their group and speak under my breath. "I still can't tell if he's working against us. He hasn't used any magic that I've sensed."

Filip has admitted to having a small talent, one he got in exchange for a few toes, but only for encouraging crops to grow. It seems he's a farmer's son. Of course, there's no way to be sure he's telling the truth about the size of his talent or its purpose.

"He did warn us about the patrols," Rheave murmurs. "If he wanted us to get caught, wouldn't he have kept quiet?"

Stavros grimaces. "It could have been a ploy to earn our trust, knowing he'd find out other ways for Lothar to catch us. But if he passed on information about our plans, he didn't tell them everything. Lothar didn't realize that there'd be three of us, and he didn't arrive soon enough to confront us *before* we broke into the guardhouse."

My lips twist in a wry smile. "It'd certainly have been easier to overwhelm us with dozens of his people right there."

Casimir looks toward the younger man and back at us. "I still think that even if he's acted as an informant to some extent, that doesn't mean he's against our cause. We don't know what pressure Lothar might have put on him, what threats he might have faced if he didn't comply."

"We'll know soon enough if he's continued to inform," Alek puts in. "The men Tinom sent to Kevarsi will catch up with us at the temple within a day or two. If they saw the

Order of the Wild increasing their patrols and watching for our arrival, that's all we'll need to know."

I adjust my grip on the reins, unable to shed the tightness in my stomach. "If they don't see that, we're not in the clear. He simply might not have had the means to pass on the information once we left Florian."

Stavros gives a soft grunt. "Well, he won't have much opportunity at the temple either, if the devouts there are as loyal as Tinom believes. We'll stay alert to any sign of sabotage—from any source."

"It might not have been a purposeful betrayal in the first place," Casimir reminds us in his optimistic way. "If anyone in the know made a stray comment within hearing of the wrong person, Lothar could have put the rest of the pieces together on his own."

I cast my gaze over the two dozen figures traveling with us: three royal guards in their plain clothes at the front, Petra and her siblings behind them flanked by Tinom and one of the clerics, and the rest of our motley assortment of soldiers, devouts, and other miscellaneous allies all the way back to us five.

I can't help feeling a little glad that we left Baroness Sibille and a few other more prominent citizens back in Florian to continue the resistance there alongside the Black Talons. Her attitude always rubbed me the wrong way.

But any of the supporters still with us stand to gain a lot by being instrumental in putting Petra on the throne… or by preventing her and gaining Lothar's favor.

I swallow thickly. "We just have to be careful."

Rheave cranes his neck to the side to look past the riders in front of us. "What's that up ahead?"

A thick wooden post juts out of the terrain along the side of the road. As we come up on it, uneasiness creeps over my skin.

Tattered bits of what could be ruddy fabric or dried flesh cling to the splintered sides. And a rough symbol is carved into the wood near the top of the post—the All-Giver's sigil, but inverted the way the scourge sorcerers like to draw it.

I restrain a shiver and yank my gaze away.

Filip is averting his eyes too. Is that a good sign or an attempt at obscuring his true allegiances?

Our procession continues on past the post with the steady clomping of our horses' hooves. I peer at the open fields around us that stretch to distant patches of forest.

A few figures move around the farms set back from the road, but none of them glance our way. The illusion Tinom cast around us, not having enough charms to conceal us all individually, is still doing its job.

When I asked him how it works, it sounded like he's using a similar technique to one I adopted on the road with my men before. He's conjured a vague impression that there's nothing of interest right where we are and that more compelling sights lie elsewhere.

My magic twitches in my chest, reminding me that I could draw a thicker shield of invisibility around us. I have before with a small group.

Even as my power wriggles against my ribs, a flicker of movement at the edge of my vision makes my head jerk around.

There's nothing there. I haven't called on my magic in days now, but my nerves haven't stopped jumping.

When I return my attention to our group, Casimir is watching me with concern in his dark blue eyes. He's always the most alert to my mental state.

I offer him a quick smile that I hope will reassure him. What's happening to me is what it is. There's nothing he can do to heal the damage my own power has inflicted on my mind.

I'm just stretching in the saddle, wondering if it'll be time to take a brief rest stop soon, when one of the guards at the front of the procession lets out an urgent sound.

A small squad of four riders is trotting toward the crossroad we're just minutes away from, coming from our right. They wear the uniforms of royal soldiers, but one of them is flying a banner with the downward All-Giver sigil.

Order of the Wild devotees. The enemy.

Tinom motions for us all to get off the road. "Gather as closely together as you can. I'll thicken the illusion as much as I have the strength for."

Rheave shifts restlessly, eyeing the approaching soldiers. "We could overpower them."

"If they try to fight us," I say. "More likely, they'd see they're outnumbered and ride off for reinforcements."

Alek nods. "Our main advantage on this journey has been that no one knows where in the country we've gone."

We nudge the horses across the field and bunch together in as tight a cluster as they'll tolerate. Keeping an eye on Filip, I position myself near Petra and her siblings under the dour stares of her guards. Stavros follows suit, helping the guards form an inner ring around our most precious companions.

We can't let enemies beyond our ranks or within them have a chance to strike at what remains of the royal family.

To my dismay, the Order squadron turns left at the crossroads, bringing them on a course straight past us. All of us hold terribly still, our mouths clamped shut.

As they approach, my magic flares sharper, prickling all the way up to my throat. It squirms through my chest and tugs at my heart.

Why am I just sitting here? I could be blasting them to bits or cloaking us so there's no chance they'd ever notice us.

What if Tinom's abilities aren't enough?

Sweat breaks out on my skin beneath my cloak. My fingers clench around the reins, and I summon the imagery that's helped me contain my power in the past: a thick vine winding around my body.

The four riders carry on by without more than a distracted glance in our direction. The pressure in my chest gradually eases, though not without a few final pokes at my innards.

Then a small, sharp jab of retaliation sears between my ribs.

It's little more than a needle prick, there and then gone, easy to ignore. Nothing like the vicious fits that came over me in the past after years of restraining my magic.

All the same, a chill collects in my belly. Is my power already that impatient to be used again?

I can't let myself be distracted by those kinds of worries.

Suppressing a shiver, I scan the faces around me for any concerning signs—and find Petra looking back at me with a pensive expression.

Her lips curl in a brief, muted smile, but her attention doesn't feel entirely friendly. Was she thinking that I should have contributed my vast if chaotic magic to protecting her? Questioning my loyalty for not offering to?

A deeper discomfort seeps through me down to my gut. All the things she must have heard about the riven, all the attempts we've made to convince her family that I'm not a threat… What must she make of my hesitation to trust myself?

The Order's riders dwindle from view and finally vanish down the road. Without a word, Tinom beckons us back onto our course.

I nudge Toast to keep pace with Petra's steed: a black mare that's not quite as elegant as a typical queenly mount.

We'll have to get the royal stables back for our future queen too.

Once we're well on our way again, I pitch my voice low so as not to draw anyone else into this particular conversation. "I hope you know that if you were in immediate danger and the only way I could protect you was with my magic, I would. I just… don't want to risk the consequences unless it's necessary. Since my going mad wouldn't be particularly good for your safety either."

Petra blinks as if startled that I brought up the subject. Maybe I misread her expression earlier.

"Of course you should moderate yourself," she says, matching my tone. "From what you've said, it's understandable both for your well-being and for our security in general. I know my father was hard on you, but I trust you to know your limits."

The thought of King Konram, of how instrumental I was in getting Lothar into a position to murder him—how close I came to murdering him myself—sends a fresh pang of guilt down the middle of me. "Thank you. You should never doubt that if I could save your life, I'll do whatever's in my power to accomplish it."

Petra glances at me again with a similar thoughtfulness in her dark eyes. "But not to save your own life?"

My throat constricts. It takes me a moment to pull together my words. "What good would it do me to save myself only to lose my sanity at the same time? At least if I protect you in the process, I'll have contributed something worthwhile. Balanced out the harm I've done a little."

A furrow forms in Petra's brow. "You know that I honestly don't blame you for what happened in Regica, don't you? That was all Lothar's doing. I've told you I understand that."

I can't keep holding her gaze. My eyes dip so I'm staring

vaguely at Toast's mane. "It was still me there. My power opened the doors for him. My magic murdered loyal guards. But I won't let anything like that happen again. And whatever you need from me, you'll have it."

Petra is silent for long enough that I start to think the conversation is over. Then she speaks even more quietly than before. "It's a difficult balance, isn't it? Knowing how to act and how far to go in any direction… I can't tell you how many times I've thought back to that night when my first instinct was to pull Klaudia and Jacos away from the violence. Maybe if I'd tried, I could have stopped the bleeding…"

Her voice peters out.

I barely manage to stop myself from gaping at her. "Lothar and his sorcerer would have slaughtered *all* of you."

"I tell myself that. That must be why I acted as I did in the moment. But none of us can know for sure what the alternate outcomes could have been, can we?"

The faintest tremor ripples through her words. For the first time, I see a glimpse of the frightened girl behind the queenly façade. The nineteen-year-old who hasn't seen half as much of the world's perils as I have, who never expected to be ruling so soon, let alone in the face of a massive rebellion.

How much of her confidence does she feel, and how much is a front to maintain the authority that could so quickly slip through her fingers?

How much have my past remarks about her father's methods of ruling shaken her confidence?

I had to tell her why the people weren't leaping to support another Melchiorek—that she needed to regain their trust. It wouldn't have helped her to feign ignorance.

But in this moment, the future we're working toward feels unnervingly fragile. Petra's life isn't the only aspect of her existence we need to preserve.

As I grope for the right response, a relieved call carries back from the front of the procession. "I can see the temple! We're almost there."

Peering past the heads in front of me, I make out a pale white spire against the blue-gray sky.

Only a thin flicker of relief passes through me.

It's time to find out what reception we'll receive from this place we mean to make a sanctuary.

Seventeen

Ivy

Cleric Delfis is nothing at all like I expected a devotee of Elox to be.

The godlen of healing and peace casts a calming presence from every painted and carved depiction I've encountered. In fables, he makes himself known in the most subtle and gentle ways.

Delfis moves around his office in the Temple of Tranquil Skies with a jovial energy, never quite standing still. Even when he stops to peer down at the map we've been consulting, the large man cocks his head to one side and then the other while rubbing his hands together.

But strangely, there's something soothing to all that energy regardless. It reminds me of the swift but rhythmic creak of the printing press, back in my early childhood days when my parents' workshop was a comfort.

Delfis sweeps his veiny hands across the unfurled paper. His voice is brisk but reassuringly steady too. "From what you've told me, I think the sacrificial accomplices that the

scourge sorcerers have manipulated could be the key to undermining their stolen authority. And they're the people who most urgently need our help. Their current lives must be a torment."

My lips twist as I think of the few mutilated accomplices I've encountered. "The scourge sorcerers keep them isolated, with only the bare necessities to live. They can barely move on their own. It's horrible."

Delfis nods, his shaggy hair that's as white as his clerical robe swaying with the movement. "We must heal them as well as we can. And when they're ready, they could speak out against the Order of the Wild. Their very existence is proof of wrongdoing."

Casimir smiles at him. "Yes, it'd be hard for Lothar to justify what his followers have done to all those people."

The courtesan's gaze slides to me with a pleased gleam. He, Stavros, and I approached the temple alone yesterday evening to evaluate how safe a haven it would actually be for our future queen. It only took one look at the cleric and one waft of Casimir's gift for him to proclaim his approval.

He told me later that night that the thing he'd seen he could do that would make Delfis happiest was telling him that he could help bring the Order of the Wild down and put a rightful ruler back on the throne. We couldn't ask for a better attitude than that.

Petra peers down at the map from where she's standing across from Delfis. "We need to *find* some of the sacrificial accomplices if we're going to rescue them. Hasn't Lothar been keeping them carefully concealed?"

"We have reason to believe that the factory of sorts where the scourge sorcerers are trapping daimon and animating their clay bodies is up north," I say. "They'd need a lot of power to accomplish that, so they must have quite a few accomplices somewhere in this area."

Delfis hums and taps a spot near the edge of the map. "I have an idea of where we could start our search. My devouts spend most of their time traveling the province, offering their services to any they find in need. Shortly after the Order of the Wild spread their uprising beyond Eppun, one devout reported seeing odd activity at a cluster of farms up here near our border with Eppun. Several carts coming and going, figures in shrouds being ushered inside. When he tried to extend a welcome, he was told off rather aggressively."

Stavros frowns. "The accomplices we've encountered in the past were shrouded—and we haven't seen anyone else working with the Order covering themselves like that. How far away are these farms?"

"Only a few hours' ride. You could be there and back within a day—or over the course of a night."

My spirits lift with a rush of my own energy, for once nothing to do with my magic. "We should go right away, then. It's about time we struck a real blow against the Order."

Delfis steps back with an air of intentness. "All action requires proper forethought, especially in a matter as fraught as this one. I need to consult with my devouts and the records I've kept to confirm the details before we proceed with a plan."

He flashes a smile at me that's almost apologetic, as if he can sense how desperately I want to make progress. "I promise it won't take very long. Your dedication to our royal family is impressive."

As he sweeps out of the room, Petra lets out a soft laugh. "At least we know he's right about one thing."

My cheeks warm with a twinge of embarrassment.

Casimir bumps his shoulder affectionately against mine. "Your enthusiasm does you credit, Kindness. We're on our way now."

I wrinkle my nose at the map. "Isn't there anything we can do *right* away other than wait?"

Every minute Lothar remains in power gnaws at me with the uncertainty of what horrors he might conjure next. What harm he might manage to inflict on the people around me.

Stavros gives my shoulder a quick squeeze. "Why don't you check up on our scholar and make sure the temple library hasn't swallowed him up? He may have found something else that'll be useful."

At Petra's encouraging smile, I peel myself away from the table. It feels like too much time has already passed since we made any real moves against the scourge sorcerers, but I don't want to rush in recklessly either.

The temple's library is located on the lowest level, a series of rooms that manage not to give the same dreary basement ambiance as the archive where my men and I used to meet at the royal college. Thin windows along the outer walls let in sunlight from their position close to the ceiling, amplified by the magic-enhanced crystal fixtures that dangle throughout the space. The white walls and soft, honey-yellow carpeting add to the bright atmosphere.

Books and scrolls pack the pale wooden bookcases built against the walls. It seems this temple has had a scholarly bent for quite some time to amass this kind of collection.

Cozy chairs with tables set next to them scatter the larger fore-room, perfect for curling up with a thrilling story. I tamp down on my own itch to peruse the shelves for folk tales or adventure novels and venture on into one of the side rooms.

I stop in the doorway, taking a moment to enjoy the view before I interrupt.

Alek sits on the smaller room's chaise lounge, the only seating available amid the many looming bookcases. He's bent over a book with tight script and yellowed pages that I can tell must be many decades if not centuries old, with other volumes and a few scrolls lying around it on the low table.

His dark waves have drifted over his forehead, but they can't disguise the passionate gleam in his bright brown eyes. His lips have parted slightly as if in awe. There's a joyful glow to his bronze skin that shines right through the mottling of his scars.

He's dressed in the plain tunic and trousers Delfis provided us all with to change from our travel-worn clothes, which hardly fits his station as a scholar of the royal college and son of a wealthy merchant. But he's never looked more handsome than here, utterly in his element.

I hate to break his reverie, but he glances up and notices me before I have to speak. A brilliant grin curves his lips. "This place is fantastic! I can't believe none of my teachers ever recommended taking a research trip here."

I amble over to the arm of the chaise and consider the assortment of books he's been browsing through. "They have texts you haven't found before—more than just temple records?"

"Oh, they are mostly records," Alek said, his usually even voice as awed as his expression. "That's probably why no one's paid attention. There are all kinds of accounts from past clerics and devouts of people throughout the province they've met—mostly to provide medical assistance, but you can learn so much about how people lived from the details woven in. I've already found several that date back to before the Darium invasion."

His main area of study before he got drawn into investigating the scourge sorcery conspiracy was Silana's history from before the Darium empire's reign.

I perch on the padded chair arm for a closer look at the

book he's currently reading. "Is there anything in there that'll help us knock the scourge sorcerers on their asses?"

Alek lets out a chuckle and gives his head a rueful shake. "Not so far. But I've only just gotten started. Lothar and his followers like to talk about how they're going back to the 'old ways' and how the All-Giver wanted it to be. The more we know about how things really were in the times before the Darium empire, the better armed we'll be to challenge the Order of the Wild. I suppose that's what King Konram was thinking with his own reading."

He has a point. I'm not sure I'd want to argue even if I didn't see it.

The eagerness in his face and voice brings a swell of affection into my chest—and a sudden prickling behind my eyes.

I almost lost moments like this. I almost lost him and everyone else I care about. If my kidnapping by Lothar had ended the way the former advisor wanted it to—if he'd had his man slit my throat the other night by the guardhouse—

I still might lose everything, sooner than I'd like to think about. Because the battle is far from over, and what I said to Petra is true. I'll stretch my magic and my sanity to their limits before I let Lothar hurt her and her siblings.

A lump rises in my throat at the memories. If Lothar had succeeded in his first awful plan, my last words to Alek would have been caustic mockery.

I touch the scholar's cheek and brush my thumb over the ridged skin that's as much a part of this extraordinary man as his beautiful eyes and warm smile. "I can't think of anyone better to do the challenging. I love seeing you like this. Do you have any idea how gorgeous you are right now? You should get to immerse yourself in old books all the time rather than having to run around across the countryside."

A blush adds a ruddy tint to Alek's cheeks. He ducks his

head a little bashfully, but his tone stays light. "So that I can be more pleasing to the eyes?"

I laugh and lean over so I can kiss his temple. "So all that brilliance inside you can shine through in every possible way. I didn't fall in love with you for your looks, as much as I appreciate them too."

A rough note escapes Alek's throat, and then he's tugging me off the chaise's arm, onto his lap.

As my pulse hitches giddily, he cups my face between his hands. He holds my gaze with a hotter light flaring in his eyes. "The books aren't the only thing I want to 'immerse myself' in."

I can't help arching my eyebrows. "Oh, no?"

He teases one hand down to my neck, the other dipping all the way to the hem of my tunic. His fingers splay against the bare skin of my waist beneath, and I lean into his touch instinctively.

"I want to learn everything there is to know about you," he murmurs, his voice gone rough. "Every thought that passes through your head. I want to read every piece of your history that's etched on your body."

His thumb strokes over my collarbone by the neckline of my shirt. "How you got this scar." His other hand finds a mark over my ribs that he must have noticed before. "When you were burned. All the stories in you, even the painful ones."

All at once, I feel naked, even though he hasn't removed a piece of clothing.

How much has he already learned that I haven't told him, just by observing the remnants of my past scrapes and wounds? It can't all be good.

In my awkwardness, my stance tenses, and Alek must feel it. He draws me closer into a full embrace, tipping his face up toward mine. "But most of all, I want to discover everything there is to know about making you happy."

He bobs up to claim a kiss. The press of his lips is sweet enough to erase any momentary insecurities his comments stirred up.

"I love you," he whispers between one kiss and the next. "No matter what happens, I'll always love you."

My heart skips again with a bittersweet pang. He knows me well enough already to have guessed at my insecurities—and answered them with more devotion than I'd ever have dared to ask for.

I shift on his lap to straddle him and kiss him back hard. As our mouths meld together and our tongues tangle, the fondness that filled my chest before flares into a sharper desire.

The same emotion must grip Alek too, because he grasps my hip to center me against his groin and rocks up to meet me to the most delightful effect. As I gasp against his mouth, he fondles one of my breasts with his other hand, making full use of the access granted by my simple temple clothes.

The friction between us leaves me tingling. Every want leaves my head except one.

I nip the corner of his jaw and roll my hips against his. "I need you inside me."

With a groan, Alek yanks at my trousers. As I kick them off, he unfastens his own.

I delve my hand beneath the fabric to stroke his cock up and down. He bucks into my fingers, his gaze burning into mine with an intoxicating mix of adoration and lust.

When he grazes his fingertips over my sex in turn, my breath spills out of me in an eager shudder. My gaze lifts of its own accord toward the doorway to the main library room.

Alek catches my thought before I have to speak it. He lines me up over him, dipping his fingers into the growing slickness of my channel. "I don't care if someone stumbles on us. Loving you isn't shameful any more than loving my studies is."

I laugh, and then he's claiming me again, with both his mouth capturing mine and his cock thrusting up into my body. The confidence he's gained over the past few months is so thrilling I quake with the pleasure that shoots through my nerves.

I sink down on him to take him even deeper, and he kisses me with so much passion my head spins. As we buck together, bliss builds inside me with an unexpected sense of urgency.

Every moment we have together could be shattered. Everything we do hangs in a precarious balance.

But we have each other to hold on to, whatever happens. I never knew how much that fact would matter to me until it became true.

Alek swivels one thumb over my nipple while stroking my clit with the other. At my gasp, he increases the pressure, thrusting faster at the same time.

My head drops beside his, our cheeks pressed together. His breath spills hot down my neck.

"Stay with me," he rasps, as if I'd ever purposefully go anywhere else.

My answer comes out in a mumble. "Always."

I don't know if I can keep that promise, but as I careen into the blaze of my orgasm and feel Alek's chest hitch in tandem, it almost feels possible.

EIGHTEEN

Ivy

I know the woman in charge herself has come to meet us when the cloaked figure approaching through the dusk raises a thumbless hand.

"Ivy," Voleska says in a low voice. "I wasn't sure if I'd ever see you again. I'm glad my doubts were wrong."

She steps into the shadows that drape the front of the shuttered shop where Casimir, one of the loyal soldiers, and I are standing. This small town about halfway between the Temple of Tranquil Skies and Voleska's home city of Pima is quiet enough that it seems to have been mostly ignored by the Order of the Wild. But a few patrons are still coming and going from the pub down the street with bursts of spirited voices.

The corner of my mouth quirks upward with a wry smile. "I'm glad too. And it's good to see you've survived the last several weeks as well."

Voleska dips her head to Casimir in acknowledgment. "I hope the rest of your crew has made it through all right?"

I think of the men I left on the other side of the Eppun border with a mix of fondness and worry. "For now. We're doing our best to stay that way. Is Emor well?"

A note of affection comes into her voice. I've never been sure of her exact relationship with her partner, but it's clearly close. "Oh, yes, and spitting mad that I'm getting to have this adventure without him."

My smile tugs wider. "You can apologize to him for that on my behalf. Thank you for coming all this way to speak with us. We didn't think going right into Nikodi would be wise."

The co-leader of the main resistance group in Julita's former county lets out her breath with a hint of a huff. "A reasonable suspicion. Ever since King Konram's death, the Order members have gotten even bolder. We've shaken them up as well as we can, but it's harder to rally more people against them when there's no clear alternative."

It seems word about Petra's speech in Florian hasn't reached the far edges of the country yet.

I hesitate, glancing at Casimir. His nod reassures me that he hasn't seen any sign that Voleska's goals have shifted.

She's always been just as dedicated to ousting the scourge sorcerers from her country as we have.

I fold my arms loosely over my chest. "What if I told you that we do have an alternative? That it's just a matter of clearing the way so they can safely retake the throne?"

Voleska's pale eyebrows leap up. "What have you got up your sleeve now?"

"The king's heirs didn't die. We have a queen ready to rule, if we can present her without the scourge sorcerers murdering her too."

I don't get into the specifics of exactly who that queen is, since explaining about the former Prince Dunstam's transformation and period in hiding would get a little complicated. We can fill Voleska and her allies in on the details when it's relevant.

Voleska's eyes have widened. She rubs the stump of her thumb along her jaw, beneath the scar on her cheek that speaks of past troubles she's survived.

I don't think her life before the uprising was that much more comfortable than my own on the streets. And I can't imagine what it was like to give up a chunk of her hand and receive no gift in return—to be a child of twelve realizing the gods had judged your intentions as too selfish.

Even without magic, she's proven to be a formidable force. No matter what hardships she's faced before, she's risen to the challenge of protecting her home.

"That's a very good thing," she says in an awed voice. "I should have figured you'd end up in the royal court with all the stubborn heroics you're fond of. What is it that you think our people can do to help?"

The fact that she leaps straight to offering to get involved is one of the reasons I wanted to reach out to her. When we crossed paths with the resistors in Pima weeks ago, *they* approached us rather than the other way around, eager to strengthen their efforts against the Order of the Wild.

Voleska's group is nothing if not dedicated.

My men and I found solid allies during our journeys across the country, even while we were fugitives. And now I can use that luck to Petra's benefit.

We need to gather as large a resistance as we can, stretching across the entire country, if we're going to effectively challenge Lothar's self-appointed authority.

I pull my posture a little straighter. "We're hoping to undermine the scourge sorcerers' power and expose the crimes they've committed at the same time. There's a farm a couple of hours from here where the Order appears to be hiding several of their sacrificial accomplices. We want to steal them away, and it'll be easier with assistance."

Casimir speaks up in his normal, warm tone. "And I'm sure we'll have plenty of future missions we'd appreciate your people joining us for afterward, if they're on board."

Voleska rubs her hands together. "Anything to stick it to the Order and see them finally knocked on their asses. When do we get started?"

I peer through the thickening dusk behind her. We were hoping to act as early as tonight. But as far as I can tell, she came alone, even though the message we passed on mentioned that we'd welcome more of her colleagues to "collaborate" with us.

"I guess that depends on how long it'll take you to get a decent force out here—"

The resistance leader chuckles. "Oh, you don't need to worry about that. I've got a dozen friends waiting on my word right here in town. Didn't want to have them all stick their necks out until I knew what the story was."

Relief sharpened by a tingle of excitement sweeps through me. "Fair enough. We can descend on the farm tonight if you're up for it. The rest of our people are waiting across the border, closer to our target—we already have a plan worked out." With multiple options depending on whether we brought anyone back with us and how many.

Voleska nods and motions to the far end of the road. "We'll meet you on the southern road at the edge of town in ten minutes."

I hold up my hand to stop her. "You know, I realize you and Emor have a lot you're dealing with back in Pima. I didn't expect that you'd pitch in here personally."

"Oh, I'm not missing this. And I'd like to see with my own eyes who all I'm sending my people to work with." Voleska flashes us a grin and darts off down the street.

When I look at Casimir, he's smiling. "I don't think anyone could be more committed than she is." He motions to the soldier who's stayed still and silent during our conversation, only there to intervene in case of a threat. "Come, let's get to the horses."

By the time a distant bell has rung in the second hour after midnight, some twenty of us are clustered in a patch of forest just down the road from the farm Delfis directed us to.

One of the temple's devouts who has a gift for calming nerves has come along to help ease the sacrificial accomplices through what's technically a kidnapping. Four of the soldiers stand among us, along with Stavros and Rheave—and Voleska's dozen resistors. The plan would have been a lot harder to pull off without them in the mix.

Petra almost insisted on joining us, but between Stavros, Tinom, and me, we managed to convince her that ensuring she stays *alive* overrides any concerns about sharing the risks in our mission. She has several guards with her back at the temple.

Tinom's magic will conceal her if there's any significant trouble—and hopefully protect Alek as well. Although he could probably lose himself amid the books in the temple library without any trouble. I wouldn't be surprised if he's still down there reading by lantern-light right now.

Being the one among us most experienced at running military-style operations, Stavros has taken the lead. He's already spoken with Voleska's people to get an idea of their strengths and is now splitting our group into four.

He points at two of the groups. He assigned Filip to one of them, presumably to keep the Order defector and possible traitor away from the most essential parts of the plan. "You and you will go to the left and right of the farmhouse, staying several paces from the walls. Set the fires and keep out of view until our enemies come running to see what the matter is. Disarm and disable them however you see fit."

The former general swivels toward Casimir, one of the soldiers, and a couple of Voleska's leaner followers. "You four will get the wagon into place and come forward to help usher the sacrificial accomplices over there."

He turns to face the rest of us, including me, Rheave, and the devout with the calming gift. "I'll be leading the final group right into the building. We'll deal with any other sorcerers on the premises and retrieve the sacrificial accomplices. They'll be distracted by the fires, but that doesn't mean we should be careless. The faster we can take them down before they realize we're there, the better."

I nod, my heart thudding. My magic wriggles between my ribs and tugs at my gut, but I squash it down.

I've pulled off plenty of schemes like this without relying on it before. If I'm going to risk my sanity, it's not going to be to enhance my stealth skills.

Stavros makes a sweeping motion with his prosthetic hand. "Move out."

Along with a few of Voleska's best fighters and the rest of our soldiers, I follow Stavros through the trees and skirt the edge of the forest until we're directly across from the farmhouse. There's still about a minute's dash across open ground from here to the farm's low stone wall.

Moonlight casts a faint glow over the terrain. A few dark figures prowl around the property's perimeter.

Stavros drops his voice to a murmur. "As soon as the fires flare, we run for the wall, two at a time, on my signal. Stay low and as quiet as possible."

I wet my lips, anticipation thrumming through my veins.

All at once, flames burst through the darkness to the left

of the house. An instant later, another fire roars up on the opposite side.

Shouts ring out as the house's sentries dash to investigate. A few more figures hustle out of the building to join them.

Stavros taps Rheave and me. I fling myself out of the woods.

We dash across the grassy ground and the road that lies between the forest and the farm. More shouts carry through the night along with clangs and thumps of combat, but I don't let myself glance either way.

All that matters right now is the path ahead of us.

We hit the ground on either side of the gate, crouching below the level of the wall. As more figures careen to join us, I pull the knife from the sheath at my waist.

Stavros arrives last and gestures for us to fall in with him as he eases open the gate. We dart along the path through the now-empty yard to the front door.

The hinges squeak at Stavros's push. I wince inwardly.

"What's going on out there?" someone calls from up the stairs. They must assume it's their comrades returning.

My power flares in my chest as abruptly as the flames outside, and I lose a couple of seconds as I tighten my hold around it. My fist clenches, pressing against my chest.

A brief lance of pain shoots through my lungs, and I have to suck in a breath against a gasp.

Most of my companions have already rushed forward. Rheave shoots a crackling arrow up the staircase, and a body crumples against the banister.

Stavros prowls down the lower hallway. As he lunges into a room, two of Voleska's people hurry to follow him while the other creeps up the stairs alongside Rheave.

From the muffled grunts and groans that follow, they're taking down any remaining scourge sorcerers with brisk efficiency. Recovered from the momentary backlash of my magic, I motion the devout over to the narrower staircase I spot leading down through a gloomy doorway.

"This way," I whisper. "The accomplices might be in the cellar."

And so might more scourge sorcerers. I keep my knife in my hand as we slink down the stairs, my ears pricked for any sound in the space beyond.

There's a door at the bottom, keeping whatever's below shut away. My skin crawls.

We've almost reached it when the scuff of footsteps above has me spinning around. A woman who isn't one of our companions is just poking her head through the doorway.

She hisses at the sight of us and jerks her hands as if to direct some kind of magic. But my hand moves faster.

My knife whips through the air and plunges straight into her throat.

As our attacker collapses at the top of the stairs, the devout pales. Obviously I should be the one to deal with the body on our way out.

I test the doorknob and find it turns smoothly. I push it open to reveal a wide, dark room where cots and the figures lying on them form only vague impressions in the darkness.

I've already snatched my other knife from my boot, but no one springs at us. A couple of the figures stir beneath their sheets.

Carefully, the devout lights the small lantern sitting on the floor just inside the doorway. The flickering glow illuminates eight sleeping figures who don't react to the light at all.

Of course not. They've all sacrificed their eyes along with so much else.

"Start waking them and guiding them up the stairs," I murmur to the devout. "You'll probably need to tell them that they're being called on to serve their great purpose or something like that. I'll clear the way and come back to help you."

At his nod, I clamber up the stairs. At least with their blindness, I only have to move the fallen body out of tripping distance, not out of view.

As I wipe my retrieved knife on the woman's tunic, Stavros barges back into the front hall. He takes in the scene with an approving tip of his head.

"The rest of the house is clear," he says.

I point to the cellar stairs. "We found the sacrificial accomplices—I'm going to help bring them up."

"I'll make sure you can get to the wagon safely."

I dash down to the cellar to find that the devout has already roused all of the sacrificial accomplices. They went to sleep wearing their shrouds, but the fall of the fabric reveals the misshapen forms beneath. They're sitting up, a few getting to their feet, mumbling with confusion.

A quiver in the air tells me the devout is employing his calming magic. I try to pitch my voice to be as soothing as possible too. "Come on now, everyone. Let's get up the stairs, and you'll accomplish everything you could have wanted to."

I have to help a couple of the armless forms stand up. They stumble toward the stairs, all of them missing something from their lower extremities, whether merely toes or an entire lower leg.

With my hand on one of the mutilated backs, I support the accomplice's balance going up the steps, then hustle back down to assist another.

A choked sound reaches my ears from above. When I return, I find one of Voleska's people staring at the lurching procession with her fingers pressed to her lips.

I offer her a tight smile. "This is why we're here. Why we're fighting. To make sure this doesn't keep happening."

She draws herself straighter and swipes at the glint of

tears in her eyes before catching an accomplice in mid-lurch. "Let me get you out the door. There's a comfortable wagon waiting."

"Anything to serve," the accomplice mumbles. The devotion in his little-used voice makes my throat constrict.

"You've done so well already," I tell him, not knowing what else to say.

Just beyond the farm's gate, Casimir greets the accomplices with much more grace than I'm capable of. "Thank you for joining us. We're going to ask that you climb up here in the wagon—that's right. I'm sorry for the sudden visit, but what you're going to do is so important for Silana."

I step back, letting him and the devout take over. Gentle reassurance has never been my forte.

The rest of our group gathers around the wagon, returning from their initial posts. One of Voleska's men is wrapping a bandage around a shallow gash on his arm, and a couple of the soldiers are sporting bruises on their jaws, but it looks like we got through the assault without any major injuries.

That thought has just passed through my head when an arc of light flashes through the air toward the edge of our group.

I don't have time to do much more than sense the vicious tang of the magic in that energy and react. No blade can stop that killing bolt.

I thrust out my arm with a surge of my magic.

Training and practice come through—even as I swat at the conjured attack, my mind reaches toward the wood we left and visualizes a branch being pulled toward me in the reverse of how I'm pushing the assault away.

Wood cracks, and the arc of light bursts apart into a shower of sparks.

They dissolve in the air just inches from the faces of the

two men they nearly struck. The soldier takes a step back with a grimace, his eyes flicking to me with an almost accusing look as if I'm somehow to blame for the initial attack.

Filip gapes at the spot where the attack fizzled out before his gaze slides to me too.

"It would have killed me," he says. "I hardly saw it coming."

I inhale slowly, my body tensed for any sign that this one jab of magic has addled my mind. "I want us all leaving this place as unharmed as I can manage."

Was it worth the trade-off? I don't know. But faced with the question, I can't imagine standing back and letting two men simply die to preserve some small shred of my sanity.

Even if the soldier is still eyeing me like I might explode at any second.

A twinge of queasiness passes through me. How long will it take before Petra's followers from Florian pass on what they've heard about me to Voleska's people?

It doesn't matter, I tell myself. What matters is that I'm here, doing what's right for the country, whatever they end up thinking of me.

Rheave has already charged off in the direction the attack was flung from. There's a sizzling noise before he lets out a resolute grunt. "That sorcerer is *definitely* not hurting anyone else now."

Casimir shoots me a concerned glance from where he's guiding the last of the sacrificial accomplices into the wagon, and I smile in return to say I'm okay. Then I clamp down on the rest of the power squirming inside me.

Just a small push. Not that big a deal, and I controlled the consequences. I saved a couple of lives.

But I never want to get back into the habit of using it for anything I don't absolutely have to.

Voleska sets her hands on her hips, watching the devout pull the curtains shut on the back of the wagon. "Well, hopefully this'll put a little dent in the Order's influence. I wonder if it'll affect Lothar's festival plans?"

My head jerks around. "Festival plans?"

She cocks her head with a swing of her sandy blond ponytail. "Hadn't you heard? The Order of the Wild's been announcing it all over the place in the past couple of days. On the next full moon just a few nights from now, he's holding a country-wide party to celebrate King Konram's death."

HISTORIA
TOYTOP

NINETEEN

Alek

The soft rasp of footsteps brings my head up from the book I've been poring over. A twinge of pain shoots down my neck from the cramped posture I've held.

In my research fervor, I've been letting the good scholarly habits I learned in school and under my former mentor slide. I can almost hear one of the professors at Sovereign College chiding me. *A healthy sitting position is essential to keep the body sound for long hours of reading in future years.*

Maybe if my current line of inquiry didn't feel so urgent, I'd find that maxim easier to remember.

The footsteps come to a stop at the doorway of the inner library room. Ivy peers inside with Casimir gazing over her shoulder. Ivy looks a little pensive, but the courtesan offers a smile sunny enough that I don't think there's any reason to worry.

At least, not any more than we already had.

"Can you put the books aside for a little while?" Ivy asks,

a softer smile touching her own lips. "We figured it was about time you got some lunch into you."

"And that you might appreciate some company for that lunch after all the time you've spent tucked away down here," Casimir adds.

Before I can answer in words, my stomach rumbles, which I suppose is answer enough. With a bashful laugh, I get to my feet. "Thank you. My body is reminding me that I shouldn't neglect it while I'm filling my head."

Out of consideration for the many fragile documents in the library, my companions have set up their sort-of picnic on a low folding table in the fore-room at the bottom of the basement stairs. None of the books are kept there, only a small hearth and a few armchairs set along the walls for casual readers.

Stavros and Rheave are waiting for us, Stavros pouring out a ruddy juice into the glasses. He offers me a crooked grin. "I'd have brought wine, but I suspected you'd want to keep your thoughts as unmuddled as possible."

Warmth forms in my chest at his recognition of and respect for my priorities. "That I do. Thank you."

As I sit at one end of the table with Ivy and Casimir sinking down to complete the group, the warmth expands into a sense of total contentment. It's a strange emotion to be feeling when we're up against a country-wide conspiracy of sadistic sorcerers, but I can't bear to dismiss it.

I've never had anything like this before—the kind of connection where you know you can count on each other no matter what you're facing. Where you know you're appreciated for who you are, not some task or favor that's going to be asked of you.

My lover and my friends wanted to have lunch with me and make sure I knew they cared. I don't know what kind of thanks could possibly express how much that means to me.

As is typical in the temple, the meal is simple fare but fresh: a salad of local greens, bread still warm from the oven, butter and cheese from the temple sheep—one of Elox's symbolic animals. Every bite is deliciously tart or creamy.

As Rheave devours his own portion gleefully, he studies me from across the table. He pauses in between bites. "Have you found out anything interesting in all these books?"

I glance toward the stack I left behind with a regretful grimace. "Nothing in much detail so far, but I have a lot more to get through. And I suppose we don't really know that Lothar will draw on actual historic rites with his new festival."

Stavros hums. "It would make sense if he did at least a little, to give his 'celebration' an air of legitimacy. He might be a treacherous prick, but he's a clever one."

Ivy makes a face of disgust. "Yes, why invent a tribute to murder from scratch if you can simply borrow traditions from centuries ago?"

"Not just that." Casimir's voice is gentle but steady. "He may very well believe in his ideals of getting back to the 'old ways' and restoring the All-Giver, as awful as his methods are. In that case, it would make sense for him to incorporate as many of those old ways as he can."

And that's exactly why I've spent the past two days digging through every record from before the Darium invasion that I can find. The more we can anticipate what Lothar might enact with his soon-approaching festival, the more ideas we'll have of how we can disrupt or make use of it to our own ends.

"I've found a few references that might point me in the right direction," I say. "As soon as I find anything I think we should take into account, I'll let you know."

Ivy rests her hand on my arm. "We still have time. And if we can't find anything that could help prepare us, we'll just have to go and see it all with our own eyes. We've come up with pretty good plans in the moment before."

We have, but I'd rather we went in prepared.

Once the meal is done and the remnants gathered, Ivy tugs me close for a quick kiss before following the other men upstairs. I return to my work with both my heart and my stomach full.

One avenue of research that's been somewhat fruitful has been the oldest treatment records I've been able to unearth. I've come across an account of a patient treated by the temple devouts for a chemical burn it was hinted had something to do with a local celebration and another of a broken ankle sustained during a large-scale rumpus.

If any of those long-ago devouts were wordier in their accounts, I might get more details about exactly what those festivities and games entailed.

I finish paging through the book I was in the middle of and pick up another journal with handwriting so faded I find myself squinting even with the lantern near my shoulder. That volume does turn up another account of a similar burn, which the writer notes comes from a dye that's apparently splashed around for reasons he doesn't mention.

As I read, I jot down a few notes that I'm gradually assembling into a somewhat coherent picture.

The next book proves to be both incredibly brief in its notes and half-written in some private notation I can't interpret. The volume I reach for after that I handle especially gingerly, careful of the flaking leather cover that drew me to it where it was buried at the back of a shelf.

It's old enough that even the periodic waves of preservation magic cast through the library couldn't totally protect it from the passage of time.

I'm several pages in when my eyes catch on the word *riven*.

The Temple of Tranquil Skies had dealings with a riven sorcerer? That isn't likely to relate to Lothar's impending festival, but I can't help slowing my skimming to give this section a closer read.

In less than a minute, my heart is pounding as if I've just run up ten flights of stairs. A sickly flush creeps over my skin with each sentence I read.

Patient exhibited a magical gift that wasn't part of his dedication sacrifice... An unearthly voice spoke in his head... Caught up in the destruction that spread out to overwhelm those practicing the most illicit sorcery...

The details collide with my memory of the ancient diary I found at the Haven, written by some long ago riven sorcerer. The one where the writer claimed the gods had torn open their soul not in punishment but to use them as a tool.

I take in all of the account before me and then hurriedly page farther into the book. There are three more cases mentioned involving riven who arrived at the temple for healing.

Each of them only expands my sense of horror.

When I've reached the end of the journal, I double-check the dates and then return to the shelves, yanking out volumes to check them and shoving most back into place. Finally I get my hands on a couple of other books with records of the earliest riven sorcerers, though only one each and not as detailed as the first.

I set those on my stack of reading material and clutch the original journal to my chest. This is the best evidence I have —and all I should really need.

As I stride through the library to the stairs, my pulse keeps racing. My throat has constricted.

It was so long ago—the truth of the situation must have been forgotten, lost with those who lived all those centuries before. I can't blame any of the temple's current staff for being unaware. But now that I've come across the proof...

Exposing it widely will have to wait until we've dealt with the scourge sorcerers, but as soon as that threat is over, all of Silana—all of the abandoned realms—ought to know how wrong they've been.

I head straight to Delfis's office, though I watch for Ivy and my friends along the way. They must be off putting together plans that don't require my academic skills.

That's all right. Delfis should put his authority behind the first announcement. Ivy will believe me, and the other men who've stood with her through so much will, but for the rest of our motley resistance?

I've heard the uneasy whispers, seen the suspicious glances. They need to realize that Ivy's magic isn't any kind of crime.

It was clerics and devouts of Elox who helped the first riven sorcerers. I can't imagine Delfis reading these accounts and seeing Ivy as a monster.

Unfortunately, I find Delfis's office empty. He's got his own work to see to, after all.

Stewing in my discovery, I pace through the temple's halls—and spot Tinom sitting at a table in one of the common rooms, writing a letter.

My spirits lift. Having the magic advisor vouch for this revelation could be even better than the cleric of a single temple. And he's already accepted Ivy as Petra's ally and friend.

As I bustle into the room, Tinom lifts his head. Concern flashes across his face.

He gets up from his chair to meet me. "What is it?"

I hold up my free hand. "Nothing to do with the current scourge sorcerers. But incredibly important all the same. I can't believe—the knowledge has been lost in the library clutter all this time—"

Tinom pats my upper arm, peering at me with his deep-set eyes. He's shorter than I am and even slimmer, but the gravity of his presence makes him feel larger all the same. "Calm yourself and tell me what's bothering you."

"It's not exactly bothering…" I brandish the medical journal. "I found a book with records of patients treated here at the temple all the way back during the Great Retribution. The devout who wrote it witnessed some of the events firsthand and spoke to other witnesses. It proves that we've been completely mistaken about the riven."

Tinom's eyebrows shoot up. "How so?"

I have to fight to keep myself from babbling in my urgency. "They're not a punishment the All-Giver inflicted on humanity for daring to attempt scourge sorcery. They were vessels chosen by the gods themselves to channel divine power! No one's ever really explained how the gods managed to rain down all that hail and fire when standard theology states that the godlen can only encourage people and other creatures to follow their will, not act directly on the mortal world. I always assumed the All-Giver's power allowed it under desperate circumstances."

The magic advisor's expression hasn't shifted, but his stance has stiffened. "Vessels," he repeats. "What exactly do you mean by that?"

I wave the journal. "The first riven felt their souls torn open and heard divine voices telling them their service was needed to punish those who threatened the gods. Then magic rushed through them—calling down the hail, sparking the fires, shattering the buildings… And once the Great Retribution was finished, their souls stayed open like that— like a conduit. The devouts here tried to heal them, but they had no idea what to do."

"Perhaps it was a punishment as well then, that the gods let the effect linger."

I frown. "That wouldn't make sense, unless we believe the All-Giver and the godlen are purposefully cruel. Why would they punish the people who helped them the most? As far as we know, they never imposed their will on any person that strongly before… It could be that there simply was no way to reverse it."

Tinom holds out his hand, and I offer the journal automatically. He flips through a few pages. "This is all really conjecture."

"I don't think you'd see it that way if you read the accounts. The way the patients describe what happened to them, the witnesses confirming that they never displayed gifts like this before—none of them had any significant madness yet despite being adults."

Another memory flashes to the front of my mind. "Ivy's even told us—when Kosmel talked to her last, he said something about making up for the damage the gods have done. We didn't understand what he was referring to. He must have meant her being riven at all!"

Tinom grunts. He drifts through the room, still considering the journal, and stops by the hearth.

I only have an instant for panic to kick in before he's tossed the aged book into the flames.

A yelp bursts from my lips. I throw myself forward, already reaching toward the fire, ready to burn my hands as badly as my face if I can retrieve the precious pages.

Tinom steps in front of me and shoves me backward. I trip over my feet and only catch myself on a side table just in time to avoid landing on my ass.

When I launch myself at him again, this time he eases aside. But we both gaze into the fire to see the book has already disintegrated into embers.

"What in the realms are you doing?" I demand, my voice rasping up my throat. "We needed that book to prove—"

Tinom speaks with an unsettling calm. "There's nothing to prove. All we had was potentially biased reports and speculation."

"Biased reports? Those were eyewitnesses to the catastrophe—at the very least, they confirm that the first riven weren't born that way. They were transformed directly by the gods for a purpose. We could have had clerics appeal to the gods for further signs to support—"

"To what end?" Tinom asks quietly.

I stare at him for a moment before I recover my words through my rage. "How can you even ask that? So we can tell the world that people like Ivy don't deserve to be shunned. There's nothing shameful about how they came to be. They should be helped, not executed."

The magic advisor lets out a soft huff. "It sounds to me as if you're thinking with your groin rather than your brain, young man. If you weren't entwined with one of the riven, would you even care?"

The accusation stings because it comes with a jab of guilt. I can't say the subject would matter quite as much to me if Ivy wasn't in my life. But all the same...

"Perhaps I wouldn't care as urgently, but I would still want the truth to be known. They aren't criminals. They don't deserve what they've faced. If we were prepared to help them adapt to their riven souls rather than executing them on discovery, they might make this world *better* rather than worse."

Tinom shrugs. "There are far fewer of them now than there ever were. The fear runs deep. Telling people a thing can't erase their ingrained emotions. We're dealing with enough troubles without confusing all Silana's people over their beliefs, making them feel guilty for a past they can't change."

I have to pry my gritted teeth apart. "What about the people who'll keep getting hurt? You'd consign Ivy to that fate after everything she's done for the kingdom?"

Tinom fixes me with a look so unwavering it sends a chill coursing under my skin. "I accept your paramour because she's amply proven that, *for now*, she has her magic under control, and because she could make the difference between seeing the Melchioreks retake the throne and letting Lothar win. That doesn't mean I trust her for more than the next few days."

As I grope for an effective retort, he spins on his heel. "If you care about peace in Silana, you won't mention what you just told me to anyone. Not even your lover."

He stalks out of the room, leaving his last statement ringing in my ears like a threat.

Twenty

Ivy

When I come up beside Cleric Delfis by the doorway of one of the treatment rooms, he dips his head in a brief nod and returns to watching the patients inside. An air of sadness hangs over the normally buoyant man.

After I glance into the room, it's not hard to see what's deflated his spirits.

The eight sacrificial accomplices are sitting or lying on the simple but comfortable beds they've been given. A couple of devouts are moving between them, talking to them in soothing tones. One is bringing around glasses of water that she helps each figure drink from. Another rubs a salve into a scar on a man's knee.

The accomplices' mutilations are on full display, the shrouds removed so the temple's people can tend to these poor souls effectively. I have to gird myself against a grimace of revulsion.

It isn't fair to recoil from the marred faces with their blank sockets for eyes and pared off ears and noses. To want to cringe at the sight of their warped bodies, missing both arms to the shoulders, pieces of legs, and more beneath the surface of their uneven chests.

As I watch, one of the figures lurches to her feet. "This isn't where we're supposed to be," she rasps out. "We need to help—we need to give over our power—"

One of the devouts hustles to her side and guides her back down on the bed. His voice trembles a little as he rubs the stump of her shoulder. "Hey there. This is the best place you could possibly be. Once you're completely well, you'll be able to help set Silana back on the right course, just as you wanted."

But not the way the scourge sorcerers claimed was needed.

I swallow the lump that's risen in my throat and glance at Delfis, keeping my own voice low. "How much have they been told?"

The cleric pulls his large frame away from the doorway and rakes a hand through his shaggy hair, which is even messier than usual. "I won't have my devouts lie to them. Elox believes that honesty can heal. But we've avoided getting into many specifics so far. They're still experiencing a lot of distress about their situation. It seems to upset them to be taken care of with kindness. How they must have been treated before…"

My throat tightens further. "I know. It's horrible. Back in Florian, potential accomplices were being recruited from an orphanage—kids who had no family, groomed to be willing sacrifices for what was supposed to be a great and urgent cause."

Delfis winces in horror. I find myself adding, even though I'm not sure it'll make a cleric of Elox feel better,

"The man who orchestrated those particular sacrifices is dead. I made sure of it."

He nods and doesn't ask how. I'd imagine he'd rather not know.

Will there be a time when I admit to this kindly man the truth about my own magic? Would he accept my riven soul as easily as he has these broken bodies, or would he recoil from me like so many others have?

I'm not sure *I* want to know the answer to that question.

Delfis sighs. "They have a long way to come. But this *is* the best possible place for them to find the healing they need. I'll have to meditate on how to make the rest of their existence as comfortable and fulfilling as it can be."

It's hard to imagine how they could have much of a life in their current state. But if anyone can help them, I believe it's Delfis.

I shift my weight, already suspecting what answer I'll get to the main question I came to ask. "The 'Festival of Freedom' is happening in just two days. Do you think any of them would be in a steady enough state to speak on our behalf then?"

The cleric's mouth twists apologetically. "I wish I could give you hope, but I have to say it's highly unlikely. Another disruption when they're having so much trouble settling in here would only set back their recovery. You wouldn't want them speaking in favor of the scourge sorcerers or lashing out at the queen's supporters anyway."

"We wouldn't," I agree, and suppress a sigh of my own. "There were a few other sacrificial accomplices we rescued from a brothel in Pima weeks ago. Voleska is looking into whether any of them are stable enough that they could speak for our cause. If not… we'll find other ways."

Delfis shoots me a smile that makes me feel twice as

guilty about the secrets I'm keeping from him. "Make sure you're getting enough rest yourself. Those who work the hardest need the most time to recover."

"Of course." I manage a strained smile in return.

I head straight toward the room where we've been having our strategy sessions, passing the guest dormitories where we've been sleeping on the way.

Halfway down the hall, Alek emerges from a doorway. He jerks to a halt at the sight of me and holds out his hand to beckon me over.

The scholar's expression looks so haunted that my stomach lurches. I hurry to his side. "What's wrong?"

He takes my arm and guides me into the dormitory. No one else is in there at the moment, though the rumpled covers from this morning have been straightened by the temple staff.

Alek gazes into my eyes for a moment before his head droops. He seems to gather himself, his jaw flexing. Then he raises his chin again. "I found out something. Something I could get in trouble for telling you. But I think you need to know."

Anxiety coils around my gut. "What? Who would you be in trouble with?" It's hard to imagine anything putting us in more personal jeopardy than the scourge sorcerers already have.

Alek exhales in a ragged rush and takes my arm again. He strokes his thumb over my skin as he speaks. "Back at the Haven, I found a journal written by one of the very early riven that said some incredible things. I didn't know whether to believe the story or whether it was only madness, but just a few hours ago, I found records in the temple library that corroborate the account."

My mouth goes dry. This is something about my magic?

Something *bad?*

I force myself to respond. "What exactly did they say?"

"The gist of it is that... being riven isn't a punishment the gods inflicted after the Great Retribution. The first riven souls weren't born in the aftermath. The godlen themselves, and maybe the All-Giver too, broke through the souls of people who were already living so that they could funnel their power through those people and rain down justice on the original scourge sorcerers."

I stare at Alek for a few thuds of my heart before everything he's said sinks in. "The gods *needed* us to be riven? They made people that way to act on their *behalf?*"

Alek dips his head, his expression still fraught. "I know it sounds crazy—but it also makes so much sense when you think about how the gods normally interact with the mortal world, how little they usually can. And there are the things Kosmel said to you about not wanting to make your situation worse than the gods already have... It all adds up."

I press my hand to my forehead as if I can steady my thoughts that way. "But—why haven't the godlen made the truth clear? Delivered some kind of message to the clerics? Stopped people from hunting us down?"

"I don't know," Alek says quietly. "Maybe after the fact, when they realized they couldn't heal the souls they'd fractured, they thought the riven and their descendants *would* provide a useful warning to the rest of humanity. But that doesn't mean any of you deserve to be seen as monsters. I think it matters that the riven started out protecting the continent, not destroying it. The gods didn't create you as a test or warning but as... as accomplices."

A bitter laugh I can't contain spills out of me. "Even if we've destroyed an awful lot since then?"

"It isn't your fault." Alek lifts his hand to cup my cheek. "People like you gave the gods the means to stop the worst kind of brutal magic before it went too far. They used those people and then couldn't fix what they'd broken, so they abandoned you even more than the All-Giver abandoned the rest of us. We should be working with all of the riven to make up for those mistakes, not driving you to desperation and then executing you for it."

He speaks so emphatically that I can't doubt how much he means the words. Tears well up behind my eyes.

What would the world look like if instead of everyone living in fear of the riven, believing that all of them need to be caught as soon as possible and slaughtered, they watched for signs of the power in their children out of caring instead? Gave them training like what Sulla offered me and monitored their progress to ensure they never went mad?

How much more could they contribute to the realms if they were given that chance?

If *we* were?

I'm still in too much shock for my hopes to lift far. I study Alek's face. "You said you thought you might get in trouble for telling me this."

His throat bobs with a thick swallow. "I told Tinom first, when I didn't find you right away. And he—he threw the main proof I had into one of the fireplaces and told me people would be too confused if we made the truth known widely. That it wasn't worth the consequences."

A chill seeps through my innards. I've always known the magic advisor was hesitant to trust my control over my magic, but I didn't realize he'd actively work against me.

Apparently the grace he's given only extends as far as necessary for me to continue protecting the royal family.

"Then we can't do anything about it anyway," I say. "We don't have proof. He'd obviously deny it."

Alek shakes his head. "I might be able to find other accounts. There were a few briefer mentions that at least support the records I found at the Haven… It isn't our most urgent concern right now, but after Silana is set back in order, people should know the real story."

A soft, melodic voice carries from the doorway. "I agree."

Alek and I both jerk around.

Petra steps into the room. Her dark eyes are solemn as our future queen takes in the scholar and then me.

My heart skips a beat and then keeps hammering. "How much did you hear?"

"All the important parts, I think. I'm sorry. I was looking for you to find out the latest news from our allies in Nikodi, and when I caught a little of what you were talking about —" A hint of a blush colors her smooth cheeks. "I should have come in and been part of the discussion properly. I've gotten too much in the habit of hanging back and simply listening."

Before I can decide what to say, she takes another step forward and grasps my hands. "Ivy, you know I trust you. I've seen how dedicated you are and how careful you've been. I want this country to be better to all riven sorcerers going forward. So what I'm about to tell you, please know that I had no part in it. If I'd found out in time, I'd have tried to argue him out of it."

The chill inside me thickens with dread. "What?"

Petra's mouth tightens. "My father—the pardon… Even in the end, he refused to believe that you could be anything other than a danger to the country. He lied in his letter. I think he was going to forgive Stavros and the others, but he'd made arrangements to subdue you and take you into custody when you arrived."

The revelation hits me like a sucker punch. My breath rushes out of me around an ache that fills my lungs. "Oh. Of course."

How could I ever have imagined that the king who's

made it one of his greatest quests to hunt down the riven would welcome me as an ally?

Alek's eyes flash. "That's terrible. He promised her amnesty and—"

"He's dead," I cut in. "Partly because of me. It isn't as if he was entirely—"

"No." Petra squeezes my hands. "He *was* wrong. Absolutely, utterly wrong. And if he'd realized that sooner, Lothar would never have had the opportunity to use you the way he did. I only bring it up now because Tinom was aware of the plan. My father never trusted the riven, and Tinom is holding on to the same opinion out of loyalty. I've been firm with him when he's raised concerns. I'll speak to him again, more forcefully. And when I'm queen, then my word will be the law. He'll have to adapt."

I know she intends to comfort me, but the ache doesn't leave. If anything, I only feel queasier.

She's taking a stand for me against not just public opinion but what remains of her court. Against her father's memory.

Gods help me, how could I repay that?

How can I make sure I don't drag her down in her attempt to save *me*?

After everything I've heard today, it's hard for me to believe that the larger world's view of riven sorcery could ever be shifted. I can't let what's probably a hopeless quest for justice interfere with Petra's true purpose.

A quiver of resolve rises up through the turmoil of my emotions.

I need to justify her faith in me not just to her but to Tinom and everyone else supporting her claim to the throne. Maybe most of them will never see riven magic as anything but an abomination, maybe they'll never open their arms to the others out there, but I can keep showing that *I'm* so much more than that.

I have to make sure we use this upcoming festival to get her closer to that throne, or what good am I to her anyway?

I clasp her hands in return, putting all my will into keeping my voice steady. "Then let's see you hailed as queen as soon as humanly possible."

Twenty-One

Ivy

As we pass through the city gate in the midst of a stream of chattering revelers, the back of my neck prickles with apprehension. Two guards in a new uniform of crimson shirt and dun slacks stand on either side of the arched entryway, their hands resting on the pommels of their sheathed swords.

But the Order of the Wild's version of the Crown's Watch doesn't appear to be monitoring the new arrivals all that closely. Their gazes slide over our humble cart without any more interest than they give the other folk around us.

Of course, Lothar's new Festival of Freedom is being held in every city and town across the country. His people have no reason to think the small group of resistors he wants to stamp out would be here in Tupno.

As far as we know, Filip didn't even pass on word that we were heading somewhere to the north. The men we sent to monitor the Order defector's loyalty returned a couple of

days ago, reporting that they'd seen no sign that Lothar was searching for us at the location we planted as a false lead.

Nothing else has gone wrong since we left Florian. I'm starting to think we weren't betrayed at all, only had a particularly unlucky moment.

All the same, we didn't invite Filip along on this particular mission.

I tap one of the horses' flanks to direct it to the right where the street splits. From the map we studied yesterday, that should lead us to the city's largest square.

It's just a few blocks away from the palace I can already see, silvery spires rising above the nearer rooftops. Tupno is one of Silana's largest cities and also the closest city to the Temple of Tranquil Skies that holds one of the royal residences.

Because of that royal presence, it's a major hub for travel, trade, and all the communication that goes with those endeavours. We're counting on a lot of people seeing our demonstration today—and spreading the word far and wide.

Even this street leading to the square buzzes with activity. Our trickle of visitors mingles with the flow of locals heading toward the main festival areas. Eager voices warble around us in a blur of words.

Crimson banners painted with the inverted All-Giver sigil dangle from lampposts and drape across building fronts. Streamers in the same color wave in the breeze.

Like streaks of fresh blood. After the carnage I've seen the scourge sorcerers carry out, the vivid color makes my stomach churn.

I restrain the urge to glance back at the cart, where our five companions sit in the shade of a canopy. I don't know what Order members might be watching the crowd and whether they'd pick up on my nerves.

Beside me, Casimir takes in our surroundings with a

thoughtful air. When he speaks, he keeps his voice low enough to pass beneath the clamor around us. "We should have a good-sized audience."

I swallow a grimace. "All these people happily going along with a festival to celebrate murder. How can they be okay with it?"

The courtesan shrugs, his shoulder brushing mine. "They aren't necessarily okay. It's been weeks of confusion and uncertainty, especially for people living so close to Eppun where the uprising started. Lothar was smart—he realized they'd be craving a chance to put their fears behind them, to pretend there's nothing to worry about. But the worries will still be lurking underneath."

And I guess a fair number of Silana's citizens have bought into the Order of the Wild's rhetoric. They're not worried at all.

We have to convince them they should be.

My back prickles with my awareness of the figure lying on the bottom of the cart beneath a blanket as if napping. Really, we wanted to conceal the man's mutilated body so no onlookers would notice anything odd before we get into position.

The sacrificial accomplice who agreed to accompany us sounded nervous when we talked him through the plan, even though his loyalties to the scourge sorcerers have faded during his time recovering at a temple near Pima. He thanked Casimir for the courtesan's instrumental role in getting him out of the brothel where he and his few companions were held, but he also tensed up when we talked about speaking to the crowd.

In the end, he agreed. He was the steadiest of the four, according to Voleska—which is why she had her people smuggle him to us for this operation. But that doesn't mean the task will be easy for him.

"Are you sure we should have pushed this role on Poltus?" I can't help asking. "To have to tell a heap of strangers what he's been through—he's risking the Order capturing him again, and gods know what they'd do to him…"

Casimir aims a gentle smile at me. "I wouldn't say we pushed. We told him what we were hoping for, and he embraced the challenge. How many times have you put your neck on the line to protect this country despite the horrors you've already faced? We've got to give the scourge sorcerers' victims the same opportunity."

He's probably right about that too, but it's hard for me to compare Poltus's situation to my own. He was groomed from childhood and left a mangled version of himself. At least I've always had most of the control over my fate.

Possibly I should be more concerned about the other passenger we're concealing. As the street opens up ahead of us to reveal a teeming swarm of festival-goers, Petra scoots to the spot right behind our driver's seats.

The Melchiorek heir has tucked her smooth black hair beneath a mousy brown wig for the ride. A baggy wool dress covers the finer gown that indicates her actual station.

I still would rather our future queen was safe back in the temple while we carried out this mission, but she rightly pointed out how upset people were that she didn't show herself properly when she spoke in Florian. She wants her citizens to see how far she's willing to stick *her* neck out to win them over.

"The river's to the right, isn't it?" she says. "Which building do you think will work best for our… presentation, now that we can actually see the options?"

We pull the cart over to the side of the square, and I take in the sprawling space.

More inverted All-Giver banners hang all around the

square. Not far from us, several long wooden tables have been laid out with glasses of ale and platters of stuffed rolls, dumplings, and cut fruit. The mix of savory and tangy scents wafts through the air.

As far as I can tell, the attendants in crimson shirts behind the table aren't charging for the refreshments. They smile and nod to the people who stop by, many gaping at the spread wide-eyed before plucking up some morsels.

A lot of the revelers look oddly scruffy in their elegant clothes. Most of the men are sporting embroidered tunics or vests, the women in brightly colored silks, but looking a little too loose or too tight. Their hair is rumpled and loose—some look as if they haven't bathed in at least a week.

When my gaze snags on another table across the square, I understand why. This one is heaped with fabric that newcomers are snatching off it.

Casimir has spotted it too. He arches his eyebrows. "It looks as if the Order of the Wild is supplying the costumes too."

And where did they get all those fine clothes? It's not hard to guess.

"Looted from the noble estates they've taken over," I mutter. "And probably the royal residences too."

Or bought with all the gold the scourge sorcerers have looted as well. What is Lothar sacrificing of his own rather than giving away what he's stolen?

"Come play the games of old!" an announcer is calling near the center of the square. "Let's reclaim the heart of our heritage!"

A few older kids are already jostling each other between chalk lines marked on the cobblestones. It looks like one of the games Alek told us he'd found references to.

A game that often ended with broken bones when the revelers of the past got particularly caught up in it. For now, the children are simply giggling, but we'll have to keep an eye on it in case it becomes more intense.

A woman in a deep red dress has gotten up on a platform near the games area. She holds out her hands, her voice projecting over the crowd with magical amplification. "The king can't hold us back any longer! We're free to get back to our roots, what connected us to this world and the gods who made us."

Spirited music blares from a cluster of musicians behind the platform, and the woman whirls into a flailing sort of dance.

We were prepared for dancing too. I was hoping the civilians would be put off by the chaotic cavorting Alek described, that we could point to it as evidence of the Order's ill intents, but I can already see an echo of the woman's movements spreading through the crowd around her.

Oh, well. We can still challenge the Order of the Wild's appeals to history. Something has to snap these people out of their stupor.

I return my gaze to the buildings along the right of the square. We want a position that puts us a safe distance above the crowd but still easily visible to the people below—and within easy reach of the river that'll serve as our escape route.

I point to a two-story stone structure with a flat roof and a narrow alley between it and one of its neighbors. "That place looks promising. Let's go around back and make sure it's got everything we need."

Rheave scrambles out, followed by the soldier and the devout who've accompanied us. They help Poltus off the back of the cart. Thankfully, the winter is chilly enough that the low hood and scarf obscuring most of his head don't look all that unusual. We've padded his clothes beneath the cloak so it's less obvious how much of his body is missing.

Skirting the crowd, we ease through the milling bodies

toward the alley. I scan the revelers around us—and nearly walk right into a little boy who steps in front of me as if unaware of anything except the scene he's staring at.

As I jerk myself backward, the kid—who can't be more than six or seven—stays focused on the mass of festival-goers in the wider square. His gaze is avid, but something about his expression makes me think he's unsettled as well.

Then he turns his head toward me, and I freeze.

His eyes are nothing but whites and pure black, as if the pupils have swallowed his irises. The fathomless gaze takes me back weeks to the strange man we crossed paths with on the road to Nikodi—who warned us of impending doom and then vanished.

But that man had the wizened face and hunched posture of a body that'd passed through many decades, and there's no way the kid in front of me has lived for even one.

The boy peers at me for a moment before his lips curl with a small smile, as if we share a secret. He looks at the revelers again, and the smile falters. "It's all a mirage. They don't know what lies underneath."

"What—" I start, but he's already darting forward to merge with the crowd. In a matter of seconds, I've lost sight of his pale hair.

Petra touches my arm from behind. "Is he someone to worry about?"

I shed the sudden bout of nerves with a shake of my head. It's not as if two people in the country couldn't have the same oddly dark eye color. Just a weird little kid.

"I don't think so," I say. "Let's keep going."

Around the back of the building I suggested, we find there's only a narrow strip of path between the rear door and the walled bank of Tupno's broad river. A rickety fire escape will take us most of the way to the roof.

Petra nods in approval. She motions to the soldier. "Let's

get everyone up to the roof, and then you can scout down the river for a vessel we can… borrow."

Poltus needs both the soldier and the devout supporting him to make it onto the fire escape. As I gird myself to follow them, Casimir touches my shoulder.

"We'll make them see the truth," he says. "No matter what Lothar does, he can't stop us from fighting back."

Then he kisses me, swiftly but tenderly enough to send a tingle down to my toes.

When the courtesan releases me, Rheave pushes in with an intense expression. "I'll be right there with you too," my daimon-man says, and claims a scorching kiss of his own.

By the time I'm scrambling up the fire escape, my cheeks are flushed and some of the tension inside me has loosened.

We aren't going to win over everyone today, but we can make a dent in the image the Order of the Wild has built up. We've come with proof.

I won't let Petra down any more than my men would fail me.

We clamber onto the roof and stay at the back to prepare while the soldier hurries back down. The music, laughter, and excited shouts from the crowd in the square make my gut twist.

What Julita would have thought of this celebration, all this revelry centered around the villains she knew as torturers, I can't imagine. I'm glad she never had to see the scourge sorcerers gain so much ground.

How can the civilians below sound so joyful when this festival is meant to rejoice in their former ruler's *murder*? King Konram might have neglected some of his people and come down hard on the riven, but he never acted like a tyrant.

I've seen more brutality from the scourge sorcerers in the

past few months than in all the years Konram and his father before him reigned.

But then, the Order of the Wild has been hiding many of the horrors of their founding from the rest of the country. That's why we're here—why Poltus is here.

With her wig and plain dress set aside, Petra steps to the edge of the roof. Delfis was able to obtain an amplifying charm for her, which sits on a silver chain at the base of her throat. The devout who came with us stands at her side.

As Petra draws her chin up regally, Rheave and I flank them, ready to protect them if need be. Rheave adjusts his bow against his shoulder.

My magic tingles through my chest, stirred up by all the energies below that have discomforted me.

"Good people of Tupno." Petra's amplified voice rings across the square, and dozens of faces throughout the crowd turn at just the first few words. "I come to you as the heir to the Melchiorek line and the rightful queen of Silana to expose the true enemy in your midst. My family has guided this country for nearly a century without incurring any wrath from the gods, and I intend to take care of all of you as well as I can from here forward. My parents were struck down by the traitors who've wrenched our home from us, not any divine intervention."

The devout tugs his robes straight. His voice carries through the startled silence that's gripped the crowd. "I am swore to serve Elox, and I can vouch that you've been told lies. The godlen haven't given this treachery their blessing. They didn't call for the king's death. That was all human greed, fueled by the same brutal magic that once brought the gods' wrath down on us. Surely none of us wants to return to a history where our cities broke and burned? That's where the Order of the Wild will lead us. The woman beside me is the rightful queen and dedicated to putting Silana on the right path to harmony and happiness."

A muttering is spreading through the civilians below. I tense instinctively, remembering the reaction of the people in Florian.

"If the gods wanted that girl on the throne, she'd be there!" someone hollers loud enough for us to hear, followed by a swell of approving murmurs.

"The gods can't interfere quickly or directly," Petra says. "But the Melchioreks have always served them and you well, no matter what Lothar claims. We pulled the country together after the Darium empire was driven out. My great grandmother started a program of training more medics to be sent all through the country. My grandfather saw new roads built to the most isolated parts of—"

A volley of voices cuts through her speech.

"I don't even remember any of that! What did King Konram do for us lately?"

"Why didn't the rest of them have to fight for the throne like that first king did?"

"Right. King Konram just got the crown handed to him. He didn't care about any of us!"

Petra holds up her hand. She must decide it's time to move from addressing Lothar's lies to stating her own worth as a ruler. "I promise you, I care. That's why I came here to speak to you in person. I realize that my forebearers weren't perfect, and I aim to do better. I want to listen to all your grievances and make—"

The crowd doesn't give her a chance to finish her statement of devotion. More voices interrupt, hollering up at us.

"You care now because you lost your fancy palace!"

"I got to eat more today than I have in years. It's the Order of the Wild who gave us that, not you."

"They're making things better, not just talking at us."

"The royal family never bothered with what anyone except the nobles needed."

"They did one good thing and figured they should get to keep lording it over us forever. We all have to work for anything we want."

The devout spreads his arms pleadingly. "My fellow citizens, if you'd just listen. We can show you—"

"We've seen enough," someone snaps back. "We know who'll look out for us."

"The Order of the Wild set us free!"

Both Petra and the devout glance back at me, with a flick of their gazes toward Poltus, who's sitting awkwardly on the roof's tiles with Casimir. That's my cue to help the courtesan bring the sacrificial accomplice forward.

They must be hoping the sight of him will shock the protests out of the crowd.

I mean to move, but all at once my feet feel heavy as lead. My attention leaps back toward the crowd—the fists waved, the voices raised in frustration. All the shouted words jostle in my brain.

We've been wrong. Both those of us supporting the queen and the Order of the Wild.

The common people of Silana don't give a shit about how people lived hundreds of years ago. They aren't trying to get back to their roots or any of the other metaphors the Order members toss around.

They just want to survive *now*. To have their needs met, to know they have someone to turn to for help.

To be heard.

But Lothar's approach has catered to them so much better than our own, whether by design or inadvertently.

How could it not? He has the manpower to give away a banquet and heaps of fine clothes, to throw a country-wide festival where everything is provided. He has followers in every city and town assuring the locals that they'll set everything right in the most fundamental possible ways.

At this point, is there anything we can show them that will sway their opinion? So many people were fed up under the Melchioreks, tired of seeing those titled or rich favored.

Are they really willing to wait and see if Petra will be better, no matter what we tell them about the Order? Will they believe us even with the proof in front of their eyes?

Poltus sways where he's sitting with a ragged mumbling under his breath. A shudder runs through his body.

He can hear everything the crowd is saying, singing the praises of the people who mutilated him. And now we're going to put him to their judgment when they might hurl the same harsh words at him—when it might not make any difference?

Hasn't he been traumatized enough? How are we better than the scourge sorcerers if we use their victims for our own cause without caring how it harms them?

In that moment, there's nothing I'd rather do than gather my companions and run away from here. Far, far away to some other country where we can escape the Order of the Wild and at least live in some kind of peace.

Maybe that's actually the best thing I can do for Petra and her siblings, before her quest for the throne ends in more tragedy.

Maybe all those people down there deserve to find out exactly who they're supporting when the scourge sorcerers finally stop giving and start taking. What have the people of Silana ever done for *me* except talk about how my kind should be sent to the gallows?

I take a step toward Poltus, on the verge of suggesting we flee, when one more shout reverberates from below.

"The Order is looking out for *all* of us. They want us all to have good lives!"

Poltus flinches and then goes rigid, his jaw clenching. I can see the rejection of those words etched all through his mottled face.

He knows they're a lie just as much as I do. It's like that strange kid said to me—Lothar has created a mirage.

Gods smite me, I can't blame the people for listening to the scourge sorcerers when we haven't given them a chance to see the truth.

I crouch down next to Poltus. It should be his choice.

"Are you ready to give your story?" I ask. "I don't know how they'll respond."

He draws his armless frame taller with an air of resolve. "It doesn't matter. They should know what Lothar's people did."

My chest tightens around my heart, but when I look at Casimir, he nods.

We're in this together, all of us—even the people down there who'd throw Petra's words back in her face.

The scourge sorcerers are the only real villains here.

And maybe Poltus couldn't live with himself any more than I could if we don't expose them in every way we can. This isn't my fight alone.

I help him to his feet, supporting him on one side as Casimir guides him from the other. We unfasten the cloak that's concealed the worst of his deformities and let it fall. He's already discarded the scarf.

Seeing us coming, Petra and the devout step to the side. "Behold what the Order of the Wild has done to your children," the devout calls out. "This is how they fuel their magic—not through their own work, but through the immense sacrifices of others."

"What have you ever—" someone starts to yell, but even that voice cuts out with a gasp of horror.

Cries and startled murmurs pass through the crowd staring up at Poltus. I restrain a flinch.

Even if they believe his story, it mustn't be easy for him to hear their reactions.

Petra sets her amplification charm around the accomplice's neck. He lifts his voice despite the noises of revulsion rising from below.

"Everything Queen Petra has said is true," he says, his voice thick but steady. "The Order of the Wild is run by people who get their magic by borrowing it from other people. When I was little and had just lost my mother, a woman who worked with the Order convinced me that the best way I could protect the rest of my family and the country was by giving the most immense sacrifice I could."

He tilts his head to make it easier for them to see his missing features. "I gave up my eyes, my ears, my nose, my arms. They took even more from inside me. I thought I was helping bring about a better world. But if they want a world that's better for everyone, why did they keep me and all the other people who sacrificed like me shut away like prisoners? Why have they hidden us so that you won't find out?"

A voice breaks through the uneasy tumult below. "They did this to other people too?"

"Lots of other people," Poltus declares, his voice getting even more forceful.

I squeeze his side encouragingly, and he hurtles onward. "There were three others kept in the same room as me. Since then, I've met eight who were kept elsewhere. I've heard of dozens more. How do you think they managed to overwhelm the entire royal army? Where could all that magic have come from? It was stolen from people they lied to, and they'll keep lying to you too until it's too late. Unless we bring this madness to an end!"

An uneven roar of agreement ripples through the crowd. Relief surges through me.

At least some of them believe him. At least some are questioning what they've been told.

Several people have spun toward the Order member who was leading the dances. I see a woman pull a girl away from the dancing area while others jab their fingers as if asking accusing questions.

"Where's the Order?" someone hollers.

"What else are they hiding?"

"We need some answers!"

A flash of crimson at the edge of the crowd brings my head jerking around. A bunch of armed figures in the new Order uniform are shoving along the edge of the crowd toward our building.

My heart lurches. I reach for Petra. "Your Highness, it's time to go. We have to get to the river."

The devout has already dashed to the back of the roof. His face pales. "They're coming from both directions. I don't think we can make it down in time."

We were prepared for that. I sling my arm around Poltus's back and brace myself. "Then we'll have to jump."

Twenty-Two

Rheave

If there weren't angry people waving daggers and swords in our direction, I'd probably enjoy the leap from the rooftop. Soaring through the air like I'm flying just for a moment. Hitting the water with a chilly splash.

The current of liquid consumes me, rushing against my skin and into my clothes and hair. The cold prickles through my nerves in an invigorating way.

Then my limbs push at the water, and my head breaks through the surface. A marshy smell fills my nose, with a slightly rancid note that suggests the river isn't as clean as the streams we drank from during our many travels across the countryside.

Urgent shouts bombard my ears. I grip my bow against my side and blink the moisture from my eyes to see better.

Several figures in red shirts have charged to the edge of the riverbank, which is built up in a stone wall a few feet above our heads. In the water around me, my companions bob.

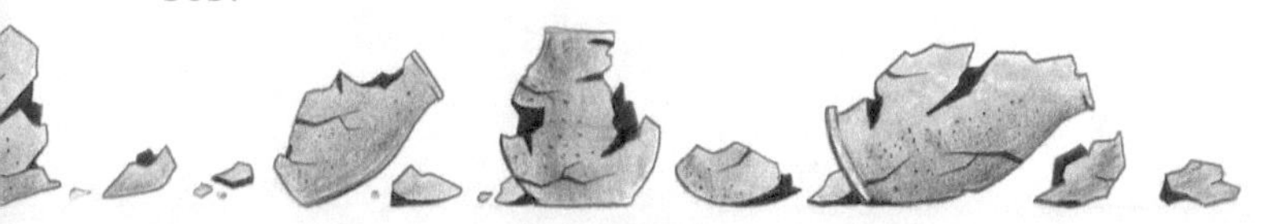

My gaze latches on to Ivy's reddish-blond hair first, turned darker than usual by the wetness. She's swimming with the flow of the water, her slim, pale limbs rising and falling a few arm-lengths ahead of me.

Just beyond her, Casimir and the robed man from the temple sway in the current, clutching the poor victim of the scourge sorcerers between them. Of course—a man with no arms can't swim.

Petra's dark head shows against the rippling gray surface near them. She's rolled onto her side as she kicks at the water, her head tipped to focus on the boat that's just a few paces farther down the river.

Our soldier stands at the side of the curved wooden structure, hunched so he's ready to snatch Petra's hand and haul her into the vessel when she reaches him. He's meant to do the same for all of us, but with a flick of my gaze, I estimate that I can propel myself high enough to grasp the edge of the boat all on my own.

I haul my limbs through the flowing water—and an arrow humming with magical energy soars past me from the bank toward the boat.

The projectile slams into the boat's hull. I know from my own practice that a normal arrow would simply dig its head into the wood and hang there without doing more damage than marring the surface.

But this is clearly not a normal arrow.

With whatever magic the scourge sorcerers have cast on it, the arrow splits right through the boards. A crack opens around the point where it's penetrated, straight down to the surface of the water.

And the river gushes in.

The soldier gives a bark of alarm and turns toward the hole. Even in my limited knowledge of boats, I can see there's no patching it.

Then another arrow whirs through the air and plunges into the soldier's chest.

This time, it's Petra who cries out. The soldier staggers and crumples backward in the already sinking watercraft.

A jolt of urgency races through my veins. Our escape plan has just been destroyed—and the scourge sorcerers are going to keep shooting at us.

I spare one worried glance Ivy's way and then grope for my bow. Maybe I can push myself high enough in the water to launch an arrow of my own. If I can just get into the right position…

As I wrestle with the weapon against the current, I twist to face our attackers. They vanish from view for a moment as I sweep past the capsizing boat. I grope behind my shoulder toward my quiver—

And my other arm slams into the stone wall along the river. My elbow shudders, and my fingers spasm apart.

The bow swirls away from me, caught in the gushing water. I spin around the bend I didn't realize was coming.

The currents shift, whipping me faster along. I surge past Ivy so swiftly that I don't have time to grasp at her.

Heaving myself to the side, I manage not to collide with Casimir's trio. My hands scoop uselessly at the water.

Petra lifts her head all the way above the surface to gasp out an order. "We still have to get to the grate! We can leave the same way. Just swim!"

Just swim. Just swim.

But we can't move through the water as effectively as the boat would have. We don't have the shelter of its wood, as poor a shield as that turned out to be against the scourge sorcerers' weapons.

A fresh volley of shouts rings out on either side of us. More red-shirted figures appear on both banks, having run ahead or caught word from their colleagues.

A woman on the farther bank draws back her bow. Is she aiming at Ivy?

My pulse hitches with panic. The image flashes before my eyes of the arrow smacking into Ivy's skull the way the other did the guard's chest.

No.

I flail at the churning water, but I can't push myself any closer to her. My waterlogged clothes drag at my limbs.

She's too far beyond my reach.

I can't let them hurt her. My Ivy. My little vine.

The arrow arcs through the air—and hits the water just shy of Ivy's shoulder. Instead of relief, more panic surges through my body.

It was so close. So much closer than I am.

They could murder my precious woman right in front of me.

I lift my arm to try to hurl some of my crackly magic at our attackers, even though I'm not sure how much damage I can do from this distance. But the shifting currents throw my aim off-kilter.

The sizzling light I fling out smacks into the riverbank instead, slashing black streaks across the stones.

Another arrow flies at us, and another. We swing around a second curve in the river.

For a second, I find myself spun around, unable to even see Ivy.

As I claw my way through the water to face her again, a thicker fear wraps around my chest, squeezing my lungs.

If we can't make it out of this—if I lose her—all the pain that burned inside me after Lothar took her will wrack me again. Worse than being pierced with a hundred arrows.

I don't know—I can't even wrap my head around the thought— What am I supposed to do?

How can I save either of us?

Watching that man hold a knife to her throat the other night was bad enough. At least I could see right away how to blast him away from her.

Now I'm as caught up as she is. Nothing I can do is making a difference.

Ivy's mouth dips below the level of the water. She sputters and waves her hand toward me. Whatever she says is lost in the swell of desperation that's engulfed my body.

I stiffen and sink. My legs jerk automatically, sending me back to the surface with a sputter of my own.

Petra shouts something too, from off to my left. Casimir glances back at me, his brow knitting.

One of the men on the bank hurls a knife at Ivy's head. She flinches to the side, but a protruding bit of its hilt smacks her temple.

My mouth opens with a wail of protest building in my throat, and her gaze snags on mine, startlingly blue compared to the murky water. Finally, her voice penetrates the haze in my head.

"The grate!" she calls out. "It's time!"

Understanding snaps into place.

I have to carry out my part in the plan—even if we were in the boat, I was meant to fulfill this task.

My fears blotted my duty right out of my mind.

With a ragged breath and a surge of shame, I yank myself around purposefully. Just a few boat-lengths away loom the thick city walls—and the bridge that arches over the river with a steel grate beneath to prevent covert travel by this route.

The opening rises only a few feet above the water—we'd have had to hunch low in the boat to pass through the space beneath the stone arch. That won't matter now that we're in the water, but we still need it to open.

If we hit the bars while they're still closed, we'll be easy targets for our pursuers.

I shove all of my attention toward the metal structure—toward the lock that secures the grate—and thrust my hands forward.

The first smack of my magic warps the metal but doesn't break it.

As I speed ever closer, I will another, sharper blast of the searing energy out of me.

The lock melts away, along with a significant chunk of the deadbolt it held in place. I tip myself backward and slam into the bars feet first, aiming one final surge of magic at the hinges on the other side.

The strips of metal sizzle, and the grate pops off. It rushes beneath the bridge ahead of me, tugged by the river's current.

I right myself in time to see my companions gliding through the opening after me. Yells of frustration carry from the other side, but the scourge sorcerers aren't going to follow us into the water—and they can't jump right over the wall.

They'll have to dash around to the nearest gate on the land. We can be far away from the city by the time they reach the river.

As we bob along in it, the waterway flows past a few farms and into a patch of forest we surveyed ahead of time. The log the now-dead soldier and I heaved most of the way into the current still protrudes from the bank where we left it.

I catch a branch and whirl around to help pull Petra over to safety. Casimir and the devout work their way along the soggy wood to the shore, pulling the sacrificial accomplice with them.

I stay in the water until Ivy reaches me. She extends her arms to stop herself against the log, but I wrap my arm around her first.

The question spills out shakily. "Okay, Little Vine?"

She peers at me, no mark on her except the start of a bruise where the knife hilt knocked her temple. "Just glad to be out of there. Are *you* okay?"

I push my mouth into a smile. "I am if you are."

As true as that is, my heart thumps heavily against my ribs as we slosh to the shore and tramp through the forest to the waiting horses we hid. Toast snorts in greeting as if he's as relieved to see Ivy returning as I am.

She is okay. But not thanks to me.

I almost put her in even more danger when I froze up in the river.

What's wrong with me? Was that paralyzing mix of fear and pain some effect of my human body that no one thought to warn me about?

We set off for the temple as fast as the horses will run, the devout holding his armless companion tight against his chest to ensure his balance. An ache of desire and shame courses from my throat down to my gut—wishing I could hold Ivy like that, wondering if I deserve it after I nearly failed her so badly, hating that I can't say I do.

The journey passes in a blur of tangled emotions. When we reach the temple stable, I slide off my mount's back, planning to gather Ivy to me and hold her until everything inside me settles down again.

But Casimir grasps my arm first.

"Rheave," the courtesan says in a quiet voice, "we should give the ladies a chance to wash off the muck of the river and the road on their own time. Why don't we get ourselves cleaned up too?"

Something about his tone makes me think this diversion is important to him. He might know something I don't.

When I look at Ivy again, one of those unsettling twinges that's both devotion and horror shoots through my stomach. I don't really know what I want right now anyway.

So I follow Casimir through the buildings to one of the temple's bathing rooms, collecting a change of clothes along the way. My river-drenched tunic and trousers have stiffened against my skin.

From what I understand, Elox isn't concerned about sensual satisfaction like Ardone, Casimir's patron godlen. But the godlen of peace and healing does care about comfort. While the bathing room is small and plain, it's filled with warmth, with ample towels stacked on a shelf. A lingering scent of lavender washing oil hangs in the air.

Rather than moving to one of the shower stalls right away, Casimir sits down on the smooth white bench. He motions for me to join him.

"Something's been bothering you for a while now," he says as I sink down at the opposite end. "You haven't been back to your old self even after Ivy returned to us. I'm guessing your disorientation in the river is connected to that problem."

An embarrassed heat prickles up over my face. I suppose if any of my companions were to guess at my feelings, it makes sense it'd be the man who's so in tune with emotions and relationships. At least there's no judgment in Casimir's tone.

Maybe he can help me untangle the muddle I've gotten into.

I look down at my empty hands. "It doesn't make sense to me. The feelings don't fit together."

"Why don't you tell me about it, and I'll see what I can make of them?"

I inhale deeply. "I care so much about Ivy. I don't know… I don't know if I'd still want to keep this body and live a sort-of human life if she wasn't in it. Just being around her makes me so happy. I think that's what you would call love, isn't it? I love her."

The words spark a flare in my chest that's both warm and sharp. I know they're true before Casimir even replies.

"You're the best judge of your own emotions," he says. "But from that description, I'd agree."

I grimace. "But isn't love supposed to be *good*? It's supposed to bring joy and make your life brighter and… It *should* be those things. Why would it hurt me too?"

Casimir rests a gentle hand on my back. "How does it hurt you?"

I grapple with my tangled feelings before I can wrestle a coherent explanation out of them. "When Lothar took Ivy— when we found out what he'd made her do, how she'd had to hurt herself, and we didn't know if we'd be able to rescue her —I've never been in pain like that, not even when I've been injured in this body. And I couldn't get away from it. There was nothing to heal or bandage. It wrapped around me from the inside, like… like I was trapped in the pain."

My voice drops. "It reminded me of when the scourge sorcerers first stuffed me into this body, when it was still clay and I couldn't move it. When I really was trapped."

"Ah." Casimir's voice stays soft. "That must have been very frightening."

"Yes." I swallow thickly. "But it shouldn't matter now. She's here. She's safe. I just—I was worried about her, and then I remembered how it would feel if I lost her, and all of that together was too much for a moment."

"That's understandable," Casimir says. "Especially when you're still getting used to human emotions. The rest of us have had our whole lives to make peace with the interplay between joy and pain."

I glance sideways at him. "What do you mean?"

"Opposites always go together." He takes back his hand

to interlace his fingers in demonstration. "You can't have happiness without sadness, peace without violence, love without heartbreak. They're equal sides of the same coin. One might dwindle to give the other more prominence, but circumstances can always flip it back. And that's how it should be. The joyful parts wouldn't feel as powerful if we could take them for granted."

That's what my old existence was like. Nothing meant particularly more than anything else, all just minor blips in my awareness. It does feel dull, looking back on my past experiences now.

I rub my face. "I don't want to feel anything bad about loving Ivy. I don't want to be afraid of caring about her. I don't want to hold back from loving her more... but the more she matters to me, the more it could hurt. How do you 'make peace' with that?"

Casimir lifts his shoulders in a subtle shrug. "To some extent, we don't. That's why we fight so hard to protect the things we care about—which I think is a virtue, not a flaw. But it's also in how you look at it. Yes, in some ways, love is a cage that chains us to the person we've fallen for. Doesn't it also open up so many possibilities that were once closed to us? How many things have you discovered or experienced that you wouldn't have if you didn't care about Ivy?"

The question sends a flood of images through my mind. The feel of Ivy's cheek against my fingers, the brilliance of her smile. The exhilaration of riding alongside her, the rush of pride when she turns to me for comfort. The heady pleasure of our bodies merging.

There's a whole world inside this love. That's *why* I don't want to lose it.

Will I really, though, no matter what happens? We'll still have been together; I'll still have meant so much to her and her to me.

No one can erase what we've already shared.

The lingering ache melts away with that realization. I smile at Casimir. "Thank you. I hadn't been thinking about it in that way."

The courtesan chuckles. "Very few of us, even those of us practiced at dealing with emotions, react perfectly when someone we love is threatened. I've had my share of conflicted impulses. It's all part of this bizarre but wonderful existence you've found yourself in. Of course, if the rest of us have any say about it, Ivy will make it through any danger that faces her for a long time to come."

I push to my feet, buoyed by my new perspective and a rush of determination. "Yes, she will. And I want to get to feel everything else I can with her, even if there'll be parts that hurt too."

TWENTY-THREE

Ivy

"You aren't even giving me a chance!"

The crisp teenage voice carries from one of the temple doorways up ahead. I expected to find Petra down here, but that sounds like her younger sister.

As I hesitate, Petra's voice follows, not quite as loud but still forceful. "It's not about giving you a chance. This isn't your place. Father and Mother didn't go riding into battle. That's what the army is for."

Princess Klaudia lets out a scoffing sound. "Father and Mother *had* an army. We've barely pulled together a squadron. We'll have a difficult enough time overcoming the damage Lothar's done with all of us contributing. I don't want to keep sitting around here at the temple while the rest of you handle the dangerous parts. I *hate* it."

Spoken like a true sixteen-year-old. But even as my lips twitch with a hint of amusement at the teenage rebelliousness, an ache forms in my gut.

It's her parents' deaths Klaudia wants to avenge, her sister

she wants to see take the throne. Our struggle is far more personal for her than it could ever be for me.

All the same, I can understand Petra's refusal.

There's a rough exhalation, and the future queen says, "You can contribute without putting yourself face to face with the enemy. You could help me clean these—"

"You know that's not what I'm talking about," Klaudia snaps. She barges out of the room with a rustle of skirts.

When the princess sees me, her steps falter for just a moment, the angry flush in her cheeks darkening with embarrassment. At least she doesn't flinch. Then she marches on past me without a word.

She certainly has the Melchiorek pride.

I venture to the doorway and poke my head inside. At the movement, Petra's gaze jerks up where she's standing by one of the tables, wiping down a sword with a cloth.

A flicker of disappointment crosses her face before she schools her expression into her usual stoic calm, although a little tightness lingers at the corners of her mouth. She was probably hoping her sister had reconsidered and come back.

"How much of that argument did you overhear?" she asks in a resigned tone.

I ease into the room, taking in its contents. It's one of the temple's smaller spaces, with only two narrow tables for furniture. But every wall is set with racks holding an assortment of swords, daggers, spears, bows, shields, and helms.

I draw my gaze back to Petra. "Enough to know she wants to fight and you're not letting her. Which I don't blame you for, by the way."

Petra sighs. "Word came in from one of the people from Pima who've been scouting around for us. He thinks he's found the site of the facility where the scourge sorcerers are creating their clay figures to trap the daimon. I made the mistake of mentioning it to Klaudia before we've set a plan in motion."

Her head droops, her hand stilling against the sword. "I don't like that I have to send *anyone* off to fight my battles for me. The facility must have all kinds of protections, guards—that's partly how the scout identified it. Klaudia's never experienced combat outside of self-defence classes."

"She shouldn't be there," I agree. "But it does her credit that she wants to help. Maybe we can find another job for her that isn't quite so dangerous but also a little more thrilling than…" I glance around the room again. "… polishing weaponry. I have to say, even though Delfis told me you'd gone to the armory, I hadn't pictured anything quite like this. Isn't Elox the godlen of peace?"

Petra manages a short laugh. "I said something like that when he showed me to the room. He said that in desperate times, a little warfare can be required to restore peace."

She tips her head toward the weapons around her. "It's clearly been quite a while since this temple needed to put that philosophy into practice. I don't think these arms have been taken off the racks in decades."

I grab a cloth for myself from the bin in the corner and pick out a sword I could see Stavros happily brandishing. The blade is coated with a layer of dust.

As I set the sword on the table across from Petra, I study her stance. Tension shows all through the set of her shoulders and the clench of her hand around the scrap of fabric. But like the droop of her head, something about her posture looks deflated as well.

My stomach knots. "Have you gotten any other news? More challenges ahead of us?"

Petra shakes her head and resumes her cleaning. "What we do have is good news, isn't it? If we can stop the scourge sorcerers from capturing more daimon and turning them into soldiers, we'll have fewer opponents to worry about. Those are the most 'loyal' subjects Lothar has. And there must be at least a few of the sacrificial accomplices there lending power to the process—we'll be freeing them as well."

"It's definitely good news." So why does she seem so unsettled by it?

We work in silence for a few minutes before I speak up again. "You know that the rest of us will be happy to go out there and tackle the scourge sorcerers, right? I want to destroy that facility. I'll go up against Lothar and his asshole followers as many times as it takes."

Petra's mouth twists. Her voice comes out so quiet I could almost miss the words. "But should you have to?"

I pause. "I don't have to. I'm choosing to."

"Because you want to see Silana restored. But what if… what if *I* can't do that after all?"

I stare at the woman I've seen as my future queen for a few thuds of my heart before I can manage to reply. "Why would you think that?"

Petra drops her cloth and swipes the back of her hand across her face. She looks at the table rather than me. "It isn't just Florian… The people in Tupno were frustrated with my family too. I've never ruled anything. I wasn't even acting as a Melchiorek for the last seven years of my life. I couldn't save my own *parents* when the threat was obvious and right in front of us. How can I be sure I'm worthy of the trust we're asking of them?"

My stomach sinks. We won't be conquering any enemies at all if the woman meant to lead us loses her confidence.

She's seemed so unshakeable through all the troubles we've faced so far. I've never caught more than brief hints of vulnerability.

Maybe I should have guessed there had to be more going on beneath the surface.

She did watch her parents murdered in front of her. She's got the weight of the entire country's hopes and security on her shoulders.

How could anyone not start to buckle under the pressure?

But who could take her place if she totally crumbles?

I swallow thickly, searching for the right thing to say. My own doubts swell in my chest.

Scourge sorcerers ravaged this continent once before. Taking them down turned into even more of a calamity. So many people died.

The divinities abandoned those like me, one of whom must be a distant ancestor of mine—cast us aside to be feared and hated by the rest of society.

Who is Petra to set the current catastrophe right? Who am *I* to decide that she should?

For a second, my awareness of all the history looming behind us and the uncertain future spread out ahead suffocates me. My lungs constrict.

I look down at the sword, the gleam of the newly polished blade. My reflection wavers on the metal surface.

Who are any of us to make any of these decisions? We're all just people… but we have to do *something*. If no one steps up, then the whole world falls to pieces.

Or into the hands of psychopaths like Lothar.

"Some people might have their doubts about your family's past reign," I say carefully. "But I don't think they'd see the real Lothar as a better option. They were horrified when they found out how the scourge sorcerers had used Poltus."

Petra lifts her gaze and offers me a tight smile. "I know. And I know I can at least be better than him. I just want to be more for the country than the only not-awful alternative they have."

She still looks uncertain, but my own doubts ease. That statement right there is exactly why I'd want this woman to be our queen.

My mind wanders back to the shouts of the crowd in Tupno yesterday. All the talk about worthy rulers… The Order of the Wild has had a lot to say on that subject too, haven't they?

I tap the tabletop thoughtfully. "You know… Lothar and his followers have been going on about the old kingship trials. Talking about rulers proving their worth—and obviously the common people are starting to buy into their rhetoric now too. What if we could use that idea for ourselves?"

Petra knits her brow, but a glimmer of interest lights in her eyes. "How do you mean?"

"I don't think most people really want us to go back to some distant past, but they like the general idea of their rulers meeting a challenge. There could be some way we can give them what they think they want but designed to fit the world we're in now. Make a new legacy. A version of trials that's our own—not so vicious or deadly, but still showing your strength. Give them a demonstration of your capability as a ruler. Show that you're willing to take risks to earn their favor, that you're more than the name you were born with."

For both them and herself.

Petra cocks her head as she takes that in. "That might actually be—"

She's interrupted by a crash of breaking pottery from the hall outside. With a lurch of my heart, I spring to the doorway.

Filip is standing just a few paces away, holding up his hands and staring down at the fragments of a vase that's shattered on the floor.

The Order defector glances up at me, his face sallow. "I

didn't mean—I bumped into it and tried to catch it, but the glaze was so slippery—"

He just happened to bump into one of the temple's decorations while right outside a room where the future queen was having a strategic conversation? All my past suspicions come rushing back to the front of my mind.

What are the chances he was merely taking a stroll rather than purposefully eavesdropping?

Petra has appeared at my side. She takes in the scene and responds much more gracefully than I'd have managed. "That's a shame. It was a lovely piece."

Filip wrings his hands. "Gods, how old was it? The devouts are probably going to be furious with me." His frantic gaze darts to me. "Unless… you could fix it, couldn't you? With your magic? Good as new?"

He looks so genuinely desperate that some of my hostility fades. My magic quivers in my chest, but I clamp down on it firmly.

"I don't think putting a vase back together is worth trading a little sanity for," I say evenly. "But it shouldn't be a big problem. We'll go tell Delfis so he knows what happened. Petra and I can confirm that it was an accident. I don't think he'll be angry."

Petra nods. "Absolutely not. Accidents do happen. It's only a vase."

"But it was theirs. We're guests here…" Filip rakes his hand through his tawny hair with such a distressed air that I have to wonder who punished him for mistakes in the past.

Considering the company he was keeping, I can make a few decent guesses.

Petra steps out into the hallway. "Here, let's pick up the largest pieces to clean it up some and then we'll go straight to Delfis and sort it out."

For a moment, he just stares at us. "*You* would really

speak for me? You didn't—you weren't even in the hall to know for sure how it happened."

I can't restrain a laugh. "We don't have any reason to think you'd be toppling vases on purpose, do we? It's not that hard to give the benefit of the doubt."

On this particular subject, anyway.

Filip lets out a shaky chuckle of his own and bobs his head to both of us. "I appreciate it."

He crouches to hastily gather the pieces alongside Petra. As I sink down beside him, more thoughts spin in my head.

I don't need Casimir's sensitivity to pick up on this man's fears of being dismissed or outright punished. Even if he isn't perfectly loyal to us yet... couldn't we start the process of earning that loyalty right here, right now?

If we can win over a former scourge sorcerer, the rest of the country shouldn't be a problem.

If Casimir *were* here, he'd be asking what this man really wants. To be treated as a valued colleague? To be trusted?

Well, we have the perfect opportunity right in front of us.

I scoop up a few of the larger shards and glance over at him. "Filip, how would you feel about joining in on a mission to destroy a whole lot more clay vessels?"

TWENTY-FOUR

Ivy

From our vantage point over the top of the low hill, the small stone-block building looks tiny amid the sprawling fields. It's hard to believe that an operation producing hundreds of living clay prisons for daimon could be contained in there, but Rheave quickly provides the explanation.

His eerie eyes widen as he takes in the landscape. "They're under the ground. There has to be—I can't count them all, but I can feel them. Dozens."

Under the ground. I wet my lips as I study the fields, apprehension creeping up my back beneath my scars.

I've spent plenty of time sneaking around in dark, deep passages, some of it fairly recently. The hard part is going to be getting into this underground structure with no cover at all overhead.

The scourge sorcerers couldn't have picked a better position to watch for incoming threats. They placed the outer

building with open land all around, giving anyone watching from there a clear view of at least a mile in every direction.

Stavros must be contemplating the same problem. He makes a disgruntled sound low in his throat. "They'll have people keeping watch up top as well, I'm sure."

Emor shifts on his elbows where he's sprawled next to Stavros, peering over the hilltop. The other leader of the Pima resistors decided to join us for this mission, wanting to meet the prospective queen for himself and see how we're using the people he and Voleska sent to help us.

He rubs his knobby chin. "We've got the magic advisor, don't we? I thought he had ways of concealing people."

Tinom is waiting farther down the hill behind us with Alek, Filip, and the seventeen others we've been able to bring together for this mission. The advisor's presence makes my skin itch, remembering what Alek and Petra have told me about his attitude toward the riven.

"We have a few charms that can keep one person almost completely invisible," I say. "It'd be beyond his power to completely hide our entire force for an extended period of time from people specifically watching for intruders. And I'm not even sure the charms will do much good... The man who defected from the scourge sorcerers warned us that the Order is using magic to guard against us as well."

Emor glances my way with a slight twist of his mouth. I understand why when he speaks. "Couldn't *you* handle all of that?"

My gut twists in turn. I realized I wasn't going to be able to keep my magic a secret from the resistance group as soon as Emor and Voleska's people started working with ours. Someone who knew would gossip about it. But I'd hoped that the subtle signs of discomfort I noticed when Emor first arrived—his gaze getting a bit twitchy when he looked at me, never placing himself right next to me—were just my imagination or for some other reason.

I work to keep my voice even. "In theory, I could. But expending that much magic would have a significant impact on my mental state. I'm not sure how well I could control it even in the moment. We don't need to destroy this facility so urgently that it's worth risking me harming our cause in the process."

Stavros's tone is curter than I allowed mine to be. "Ivy has plenty of other talents that can help us without taking that kind of risk."

He touches his shoulder to mine. "Why don't you take one of the invisibility charms and scout around closer to the facility? You'll be able to sense if they have any magical wards in place. Once we have more information, it'll be easier to strategize."

At least it's a start.

Before I can agree, Rheave jumps in. "I should go with Ivy. When I'm closer, I'll be able to get a better idea of where exactly the underground rooms are. The ones the daimon are in, anyway."

At Stavros's nod of agreement, Rheave scrambles down the hill to retrieve the charms from Tinom. I can't say I'm disappointed that he's spared me from having to speak to the magic advisor myself.

The moment I've fastened the chain around my neck, the daimon-man reaches for me and grips my hand so we stay fully visible to each other. "Should we start by going straight toward the building we can see?"

I square my shoulders. "That sounds like as good a plan as any."

We head over the hill and down the far slope with steady but careful strides. I keep my senses alert to any tingle of magic beyond the faint tickling sensation emanating from the charms.

For the first few minutes, I don't pick up on anything except the rustle of our feet through the yellowed grass. But when we've crossed about half of the distance between our hill and the stone structure, the slightest hum of magic passes over my skin.

I pause and ease forward even more slowly. With just a few steps, the hum thickens enough that I don't dare move any closer.

My magic jitters, eager to shatter the spell in front of us. Always so happy to trade a little more of my sanity in its hurry.

Clamping down on the impulse, I back up a bit so we don't risk triggering the wards. "I think the edge of their magical protection starts just beyond here."

Rheave hums and eyes the ground at his feet. "We haven't come over any daimon yet. The underground rooms don't extend this far, at least not in this direction."

I give his hand a gentle tug. "Let's see if we can chart the entire boundary. Why don't you burn the grass here as a marker—just a little, so no one who's watching from the building will be able to see it?"

Rheave brightens at being given a chance to be of use. He crouches and draws his hand over the ground. His daimon energy sizzles over the grass, leaving a thin black line in front of him.

We walk on, circumnavigating the building, weaving back and forth so I can judge where the magic's effect ends. Every ten paces or so, Rheave leaves another mark.

He's lapsed into silence. There's nothing ominous about it today, but I can't help thinking back to the times recently when he's seemed momentarily awkward in my presence.

My throat tightens, but I force myself to speak. "You

know, you don't always have to stick with me in everything I do. I'd understand if you wanted some time to yourself or to help out in other ways, with other people."

Rheave's head snaps around, his expression so startled that I'm struck by a pang of guilt. "Why would you say that?"

I open my mouth and close it again before I pull my words together. "It's seemed like maybe you've been wanting a little more space, but you felt like you couldn't say so. Like you're not always totally comfortable around me."

A strained sound spills over Rheave's lips. He stops and turns me toward him so he can set his other hand against the side of my face.

As he gazes down at me, his brilliant sea-green eyes shine with emotion. "I'm sorry, Little Vine. It's my fault. I wasn't dealing with everything that comes with being human very well. But I talked to Casimir, and he helped me sort it all out. I'm okay now."

I frown. "What were you having trouble with? You know you can always talk to me if something's upsetting you."

"I don't think in this case that would have worked." He glances down and then meets my eyes again. "I love you, Ivy. It's the most powerful emotion I've ever felt... and it scared me a little. How much it hurt when you were in danger and I couldn't save you. I didn't understand how something so good could also feel so bad. But I want it all the same. I want as much of the good parts as we can have, as much time as I can be here with you. I'm sorry that I made you worry."

I feel even more choked up now, but the sensation is more sweet than bitter. "You don't need to apologize. You've had to adapt to a lot of new things. And... I love you too."

I didn't realize until I said the words how intensely the truth of that confession had been building in my chest. The words tumble out of me like a creature I've set free. Joy blooms in their place.

Rheave beams at me and leans in to claim a kiss. As his mouth melds with mine, I pull him into a tighter embrace.

How could I explain to him that for me accepting love has been the exact opposite? Everything I've loved before the past few months has brought me far more pain than happiness.

It's this joyful part that's new to me—that I could hardly bring myself to trust when I first started falling for the men who've won my heart.

I guess you could say Rheave and I have met each other halfway.

There isn't time to do much celebrating of that fact. We do have a military mission to carry out. But as we walk on around the scourge sorcerers' facility, Rheave twines his fingers with mine and swings my arm lightly back and forth, as if we're engaged in a dance as well.

"Have you been all right?" he asks. "What Alek found out about the origins of riven sorcerers is good, isn't it? But sometimes you've seemed more… sad, or tired maybe."

I'd hoped I was hiding my emotions better than that. A sigh slips out of me. "It's nothing new. I just keep getting reminded that no matter what the truth is, most people are going to be scared of me. Maybe even think I shouldn't exist. Even once Petra's on the throne, I'll probably have to keep hiding what I am."

Rheave growls defiantly. "Not with me. Not with Stavros or Alek or Casimir either."

The glow of affection he stirred up earlier lightens my melancholy thoughts. "I know. You have no idea how grateful I am to at least have the four of you."

It'll be enough. I can hardly complain when I've gotten so lucky already.

By the time we complete the full circuit, it's clear that the scourge sorcerers have wards monitoring about half a mile all around the outer building.

I stop to squint across that distance. Maybe a hundred paces away, a small metal grate shows through the grass.

It must be providing ventilation for the underground chambers. I suppose they probably need several of them. But we can't reach those access points, small as they are, while the wards are in place.

The sight of the barred metal circle reminds me of a different hatch many weeks ago—the entrance to one of the royal army's underground equipment stashes. It was guarded by a different sort of magic.

But that doesn't mean the same solution wouldn't work.

I look over at Rheave. "Do you remember how you've used your power to shatter other magic in the past? Do you think you could do the same thing to the wards around this place? Just… knock them out and dissipate the magic so the scourge sorcerers don't get any warning?"

Rheave studies the landscape intently. He lifts his hand, and a few sparks shoot from his palm. They fade into the air ahead of us.

"I can feel it there," he says. "It's coming from different places… Let me try doing one."

His stance tenses with his focus. He curls his fingers toward his palm and then splays them again in a sudden movement.

I don't even see the power he's sent out this time, only hear the soft crackle of it. But all at once, the tingle of nearby magic snuffs out completely.

"That did it!" I said. "At least near here. Let's see if anyone seems to notice…"

We hold perfectly still for the space of a minute. The cool

breeze tugs at my hair, but no one emerges from the building.

A smile stretches across my face. "All right. Let's knock the rest of them out."

While Rheave prowls around the facility in a second circle, I dash back to our companions to fill them in on the progress we've made. As soon as I mention the grate, Alek perks up. "I should take a look at that."

The main reason the scholar joined us on this mission was to share his ideas for the best places to hit the facility to destroy it as quickly as possible. He's studied plenty of architecture in his years of research into Silanian history. The fact that this architecture is mostly under the ground apparently isn't too much of a setback.

With the third of Tinom's concealment charms, he follows me back to the field. My breath comes easier when we walk past the marks Rheave made without any hint of magic touching my senses.

Alek kneels down by the grate, dangles his fingers between the bars, and then holds his hand flat over them to test the air flow. "I'd definitely expect there to be more than one if the underground structure extends this far from the center point," he says.

With a quick search, we discover three more just on the hill-ward side of the facility. A light of inspiration gleams in Alek's eyes that would make me nervous if he wasn't on my side.

By that point, Rheave has finished disabling the wards. We all hustle to the hillside to confer with the full group.

"Exactly how many concealment charms do you have?" Alek asks Tinom first. "And how many other people do you think you could effectively divert attention from for several minutes?"

The magic advisor digs into his pouch. "I've managed to

have two more blessed, which brings us to five. To be sure that no guards spot you, I wouldn't want to risk extending my gift to more than three others. Eight won't make for much of an offensive force."

"The people won't be doing most of the work. It's about what they can carry." Alek swivels toward Stavros, who's acting general for this mission. "We brought those explosive materials. We can still use them even if we can't see the building—through the grates."

Stavros catches his enthusiasm. "Yes. We'll have to set them off simultaneously for the best effect, because as soon as one goes off, the scourge sorcerers will go on the defensive. But that shouldn't be difficult to manage. I'll give a signal."

The massive man turns toward our varied group of royal soldiers and local resistors. "We'll need volunteers to launch the explosives. The rest of us will wait until the blasts have gone off, and then we'll charge the building. Anyone who emerges from below on the attack, we end them as quickly as possible before they can make much use of their magic. In the chaos, we should be able to get the upper hand and make our way below to finish the job."

I lift my hand before anyone else needs to. "I'm obviously going with the first group." If someone needs to jump in to prevent an unexpected disaster, I'll have the best chance of averting it, as much as it might cost me.

Unsurprisingly, Rheave volunteers too. Alek raises his chin with an air of defiance. "It's partly my plan. I should bear some of the risk."

I want to protest that my brilliant but not particularly soldierly scholar should stay back here where it's safer, but I can see how much it means to him to contribute in every possible way. My heart swells with more affection.

Tinom hesitates but offers to join us since it'll be easier for him to conceal himself than anyone else—and easier to cast his gift for illusions over others if they're nearby. Emor calls on a couple of his people to join him on the front lines, and one of the royal soldiers steps up as our eighth.

With an air of urgent anticipation hanging over us, we distribute the explosive supplies and the flints to set them off between us. Our other companions gather weapons and shields, Filip among them with a grim expression.

Stavros demonstrates a whistle that sounds like a hawk's cry to set us in motion. "I'll use my gift as well as I can to scan the grounds before I signal you. I don't want any unexpected surprises if we can avoid them."

As we nod, he reaches to give my shoulder a quick squeeze, as if willing me to return safely. I shoot him the most reassuring smile I can manage before we set off to do our duty.

The bundle of volatile substances in my hands makes my heart thump hard. I cradle the waxed tubes carefully as I lope across the grass, making for the far side of the facility.

So far there's still no sign of the scourge sorcerers from the upper building, so our initial efforts must have gone undetected.

When I reach my chosen grate, I brace myself above it and loop the far end of the oiled cord around a bar to ensure I don't lose hold of it. Then I sit back on my heels and wait.

My pulse thuds in my ears for what feels like an eternity before Stavros's whistled signal carries across the fields.

I drop the explosives between the bars and strike my flint. As the tubes tumble down the tunnel beneath the grate, a hissing flame darts along the cord after them.

I snatch one of my knives from my boot and scramble backward to avoid the worst of the explosion.

A stuttered booming shatters the quiet of the afternoon. One set of explosives and another and another blast apart in quick succession. The ground shakes, a puff of dark smoke rising from my grate.

And four figures burst from the inner building.

Flares of magic send a tingling rush over my body, but the scourge sorcerers don't know where to aim. I dodge the searing bolts of energy and charge right into one of the men, slamming my knife into his throat in the same motion.

The woman next to me staggers and collapses into a blackened corpse, telling me Rheave has made it to my side. Shouts ring out from the other side of the building, along with the thunder of more than a dozen racing feet.

I dash around the building in time to see Emor wrenching his dagger from a body that's turned to clay. Two more forms hurtle out to attack us, but Stavros is there, cutting through one with his sword. One of the soldiers slays the other attacker.

Another tremor ripples through the earth, followed by an unearthly creaking. I spin around to see the ground collapsing around one of the grates, opening a sinkhole as big as the building we're standing by.

As my jaw drops, someone yelps behind me. I whirl back around.

Filip is stabbing his spear into the side of a man who was ramming a sword toward me. He jerks backward as my would-be murderer transforms into a statue of clay.

I stare at the Order defector for a second, the hairs on the back of my neck on end. I shouldn't have gotten distracted.

I never would have thought the man who once associated with the scourge sorcerers would save me from one of their creations.

"Thank you," I manage to say.

Filip blinks at the spear he's holding as if startled by his own act and then flashes a sudden grin my way. "I owed you, didn't I? We'll take them down together!"

I can't help smiling back. "Yes, we will."

Our group storms into the building and catches another wave of fleeing sorcerers and captured daimon just emerging from a deep stairwell. They don't have even a chance to lash out with their magic before Emor's followers leap in to cut them down.

It all goes quiet except for a few gasps and groans from below. Tentatively, we descend the stairs.

A short hall leads to a huge room. At the far end, chunks of the ceiling have collapsed by the doorways to other parts of the facility. The idea of rocks bashing down on the heads of the scourge sorcerers gives me a grim satisfaction.

The rest of the room is laid out with cots. More than half of those cots hold a body, some still clay, some looking like flesh, their chests rising and falling with shallow breaths.

A shiver travels down my spine.

Rheave rushes to the nearest beds holding bodies of flesh. He grips one figure by the shoulders. "Can you get up? Can you talk to me?"

The form doesn't so much as twitch. I wince in understanding. "They mustn't be fully animated yet."

The daimon-man's face falls. "We can't do that awful magic ourselves."

Alek speaks up quietly. "We'll have to break the bodies so the daimon can go free. At least there won't be a struggle."

Rheave nods, but he still looks unsettled.

Stavros waves to us. "Come on, let's do what we can for them and then blast the rest of this place to bits before the Order realizes we're here."

Tinom calls out from another doorway. "I've found at least a few of the sacrificial accomplices!"

As I hustle over to join him in helping the mutilated figures, the images of the vast room with its rows of bodies stick in my head. My skin turns clammy, and not just because of the dank atmosphere of the underground facility.

I'm surrounded by the beings the scourge sorcerers have used for their purposes—to expand their power and their reach.

It isn't so different from how the gods apparently used the first riven, is it?

And the scourge sorcerers have called on their captured daimon again and again. They even managed to alter Rheave's behavior briefly a few times in the past after he'd shaken off most of their influence.

How can I be sure no godlen will ever tap me again to use me for their own agenda?

Twenty-Five

Ivy

My uncertainties gnaw at me until a queasy sense of resolve forms in my gut. As we ride back toward the Temple of Tranquil Skies, my gaze shifts along the horizon, searching for a landmark I spotted on our journey to the clay factory.

We have to keep a slow pace with most of our number—which now includes the seven sacrificial accomplices we were able to rescue—piled into two wagons rather than on horseback. The sun has dipped to the horizon by the time I spot the crooked spire in the distance.

I nudge my horse forward to ride next to Stavros, knowing Rheave will keep pace. "That's a temple of Kosmel. Alek mentioned it when we passed the first time."

Stavros considers the distant building with its irregular architecture, presumably designed to echo the godlen of luck and trickery's interest in aiding those who aren't following the straightest paths in life.

His gaze slides back to me. "What are you thinking, Lady Thief?"

I adjust my grip on Toast's reins, abruptly nervous even though I have no real reason to be. "I'd like to make a detour over there. On my own," I add quickly when Rheave draws in a breath to speak. "There's a matter I'd like to take up with the godlen who's called on me."

Both of my men pause in pensive silence. We haven't broadcast Alek's discovery about the riven to all of our allies for fear of how Tinom will respond, but the scholar informed the rest of my men not long after he revealed his findings to me.

Rheave makes a disgruntled sound. "I could come with you and stay out of the way once we get to the temple. It might not be safe for you to go off on your own."

I shake my head. "I'll be less noticeable than the bunch of you. No one will be looking for a single rider. You should stay together in case the scourge sorcerers come looking for us for revenge. I'll meet you back at the Temple of Tranquil Skies—I might even make it there before you do."

Stavros lets out a sigh but reaches across the space to bump his elbow against Rheave's arm. "You're going to have to learn that there's no subduing our woman's independent streak. And she has a point. You're the most powerful protection we have other than her magic."

The former general tips his head toward me with a fond smile and compassion smoldering in his gaze. "Go on and see what the trickster can tell you. I'd like to hear it too."

I meet his eyes with a wave of affection. "Thank you."

Tapping Toast's sides, I send him cantering across the open plains toward the temple. It's far enough away that after a time I have to draw him back to a brisk trot to avoid exhausting him.

By the time I reach the cluster of ramshackle homes

around the temple, where I guess the devouts and maybe eager dedicats take their rest, evening has fully set in. Lanterns gleam against the darkness in the temple's mismatched windows.

I tie Toast to one of the posts outside the temple. Kosmel is a patron of thieves, but I'm not especially worried about losing my mount.

Anyone who tries to make off with this cantankerous creature against his will is going to regret it.

Several crows perch on the crooked points of the roof. They let out a few hoarse caws at my arrival.

I step through the doorway of dark gray stone into a high-ceilinged chamber. The floor tiles are both cracked and polished.

Off to the side of the room, a devout in gray robes nods to me in welcome before resuming his current task—tossing scraps of bread and cheese onto the floor. At least a dozen small, furry bodies wriggle around him, snatching tidbits with the scrabble of tiny claws against the floor.

The rat is Kosmel's other holy animal. Apparently this temple hosts a colony of them.

I restrain a grimace and walk to the silver statue of the godlen looming at the far end of the worship room.

This depiction of Kosmel stands only twice as tall as me, less impressive than the massive statue in the one other temple in his honor I've visited back in Florian. Beneath his hood, his lips are curled in a typical sly smirk.

One hand extends to beckon me closer—the other is tucked behind his back as if concealing a gambit. A silver crow perches on his left shoulder, and two rats sprawl across his feet.

One of them is a living rat rather than part of the statue, I discover when I get closer and it darts away with a squeak. I raise my eyebrows at the image of the godlen, but I can't really complain about the company he keeps when it includes me.

Kosmel stood up for me when everyone else in my life would have had me hung for my magic. He helped me guide my power away from doing harm.

As frustrating as he can be, I have to give him credit for that.

As usual, a few dice lie scattered on the platform around the statue's booted feet. I pick up one, so many questions whirling in my head that it's hard to know where to start.

Let's cut right to the core of the matter. I squeeze my fingers around the hard cube and close my eyes, thinking as loudly as I can at the godlen.

Did the gods channel their power through human beings to bring about the Great Retribution?

I open my eyes to toss the die. It rattles across the platform and lands on three.

A moderate yes. My stomach clenches.

I grasp the die again. *Did channeling the power turn those people into the first riven sorcerers?*

Another roll, another three. I stare at it for a moment, letting the answer sink in.

There's my confirmation. Kosmel isn't trying to deny it. But then, in the past he's hinted at the damage the gods have done to people like me.

Maybe he wants me to know.

There are all sorts of other questions clamoring to be voiced, but one rises up so swiftly it overwhelms them all. I clutch the die against my palm.

Did you leave us broken like this on purpose, as punishment?

The die bounces across the platform with more force than I intended. It seems to take forever to come to a stop.

When it does, six dots gleam up at me.

The most emphatic no.

I glance up at the statue poised over me. A streak of shadow falls across the godlen's face just for an instant, like a tear trickling down his cheek.

I blink and it's gone, but a lump fills my throat. A prick of my own tears burns at the back of my eyes.

All this time, the recriminations, the pain, the executions —it's all been a terrible mistake?

I snatch up the die and roll it with a thought that races through my head. *Can you fix us?*

I'm left gazing at another six. Fuck.

A brief pressure grazes my shoulder, as if some invisible presence is offering me a reassuring—or perhaps apologetic —pat.

The gods have so much power, but there are things beyond their reach. Cracks that can't be sealed.

I don't think I even really hoped there was a way, but I find myself swiping at my eyes all the same.

This is how I am. This is how I'm going to stay.

As I reach the stable next to the Temple of Tranquil Skies, I can tell I did arrive ahead of the rest of our makeshift squadron. My pulse hiccups at the thought that they might have been waylaid after all, but one of the devouts emerges from the main temple building just as I'm dismounting.

"You separated from the others," she says without any significant sign of concern.

I nod. "I had an extra errand to take care of. I don't think they should be too far behind…"

She grins. "Not at all. Zevim's been watching from one of the towers—he says he can see their lanterns about a half hour's trek out."

I exhale with a rush of relief. "Good."

When I've left Toast comfortable in the stable, I emerge to find Casimir just crossing the yard. He hurries the last short distance to join me, his smile fond but his tone urgent. "How did the mission go? Is everyone all right?"

I lean toward him, grasping the front of his shirt, and he tucks his arms around me automatically. Even more tension unwinds as I rest my head against his shoulder, although nothing can budge the tightest knot that's formed in my gut since my talk with Kosmel.

I force out my voice. "No significant injuries, seven accomplices rescued, and no one will be using that facility to make more clay bodies any time soon."

Casimir hugs me a little closer. "Perfect. What was your extra errand, then?"

The devout must have passed on what I told her.

I swallow thickly. "I went to a temple of Kosmel to have a little chat."

The courtesan hums. "And was it enlightening?"

"Kind of."

I inhale, taking in his sweet sandalwood scent, and so much more I want to say fills my chest. Casimir has always seemed to have the closest relationship to his chosen godlen out of all of my men.

But what I want to discuss now, I don't think I want to bring up within hearing of the devouts serving their godlen so avidly.

"I'm tired," I say. "And I could use a bath. How about you practice some of that pampering skill on me?"

Casimir chuckles. "I'd be delighted to."

He guides me into the temple to one of the smaller bathing rooms and starts the water running.

As he considers the limited selection of oils and soaps, I twist my hands together in front of me rather than starting to undress. "Casimir... do you ever get frustrated with Ardone?

Have there been times when you felt like there was more she could do for you that you deserve, and for some reason she hasn't come through?"

The courtesan turns to look at me. "I think it's totally normal for any human being to have moments of frustration. But I don't dwell on them. I know every godlen has a lot of dedicats to watch over—and what they want most is for us to thrive by our own abilities rather than relying on them."

He pauses. "What did Kosmel tell you about the riven?"

The lump returns to my throat. I have to gather myself before I can go on. "If I believe the die's answers came from him, he confirmed what Alek discovered. We were created to destroy the first scourge sorcerers. And they—they didn't leave us this way on purpose. The gods can't heal us."

"Oh, Kindness." Casimir walks straight to me and pulls me into another embrace. "At least you know that none of *them* see you as a monster, then. But it isn't fair that you and others like you have to continue suffering the consequences of their misstep."

"I don't understand," I mumble against his shirt. "Surely there was *some* way the godlen could have let people know that it wasn't our fault, that we could use help."

"Maybe they did, as well as they could. You've seen how stubborn people can be even when presented with facts. Once the idea became ingrained... Humans do like picking scapegoats so they have something concrete to aim their fears and angers at."

They do. And maybe I'm doing the same thing with the anger simmering in me—aiming it at the gods when it's really a huge mess of blame that I doubt anyone could pick apart.

I manage a rough bark of a laugh. "So you don't think any divine beings are going to smite me for thinking some not particularly kind thoughts their way?"

Casimir strokes his hand up and down my back. "I think they'd see that anger as your right. We all need to be allowed some grace."

He says it with so much calm certainty that I believe the words. As I tuck my head against his chin, I can't help thinking that this man deserves that grace at least as much as I do.

How much has he endured over the years, trying to live up to his mother's expectations to honor Ardone? How many sacrifices has he made that aren't visible like his jeweled teeth?

He's been here for me every time I've doubted or stumbled... Does he even understand just how much he means to me?

Love beams through my chest, softening the last of my frustration. I pull back just far enough to reach for the ties at the neck of Casimir's tunic.

The corner of his mouth quirks upward. "Looking for company in your bath?"

"It's always better when you join me." I tug the ties loose. "But I've changed my mind. This time, I'm going to pamper *you*."

Twenty-Six

Casimir

As Ivy tugs my shirt up over my head, my first instinct is to protest. Pampering is my job—it's sometimes been the only significant contribution I can offer.

I'm the one who stayed back here at the temple while she risked her life today.

But when I see the bright smile that's crossed her lips as she gazes at me, my resistance melts.

The idea of offering her love this way makes her happy. How can I deny her that joy?

That doesn't mean I'm going to be totally passive in this encounter, though.

I reach for her shirt in turn, the fitted tunic she wore rather than her usual dresses for the mission we knew might require a lot of physical maneuvering. "I still want you in that bath with me."

Ivy's laugh is as bright as her smile. "I'm not going to deprive myself just because I'm taking care of you."

With rustles of cloth, fleeting caresses, and a few stolen

kisses, we shed all our clothes. My cock stirs just at the sight of Ivy's slim but wiry body, that beautiful combination of delicacy and strength.

Before I can do more than stroke my fingers along the side of one of her pert breasts, she pulls me over to the bathtub. "I do want to get washed first. And I'm going to wash you too."

I force myself to remain where she positions me at the side of the large tub rather than aligning myself with her in the water. Ivy lathers a bar of soap between her hands and rubs her fingers over my shoulders, then down my arms and chest in a gentle massage.

I'm getting harder by the second, but her touch generates more than lustful heat. A soothing warmth spreads from beneath her hands as well, releasing tensions I hadn't known I held in my muscles.

Her expression has become intent, but her eyes still shine with affection every time our gazes meet. There's a warmth in that too—in the devotion she's offering with every swivel of her fingers.

I could be molded like clay in this woman's hands.

It's not a feeling I've truly gotten to experience before, somehow. In our training for the companionship division, we sometimes worked our arts on each other for practice, but I never completely gave myself over to any of those experiences. I was always thinking like a courtesan still, noting the techniques used and the reactions they provoked in me for any aspects I might want to incorporate with my future clients.

And I didn't care about any of those partners beyond friendly acquaintances or casual friends, nor they about me. The pampering that Ivy's offering me right now really is an act of love.

She's not afraid to bring a little more heat into the mix.

As her hands drift down to my hips, she slides her fingers around my rigid cock for a few quick pumps.

The rush of more intense pleasure propels a groan out of me.

I'm rewarded with a sly smile that only makes Ivy more gorgeous. She works her way down my legs with the same care she brought to my upper body and then motions for me to dunk my head. "Let's wash that lovely hair of yours too."

I drop my head back into the water obligingly and then lean forward so Ivy can reach the drenched waves more easily. She drizzles the liquid soap over my hair and then works it in with teasing circles of her fingertips.

An appreciative hum resonates from my chest. "You're very good at this. Maybe we should add courtesan to your list of titles."

Ivy lets out another laugh and deepens her massage of my scalp. "Only when I'm properly inspired, and I'm very happy limiting myself to four lovers who spark that inspiration."

She has me sink down so she can rinse the suds from my hair. Fully refreshed, I reach for her. "I think it's my turn."

Ivy's sly smile grows. She looks at me through her eyelashes with a coquettishness I'm not used to from her. "I think it could be more fun if you simply relax and watch."

Before I have to wonder what she means, she rises up on her knees so her breasts are on full display. She strokes her lathered hands over her own body with the same sensuality she brought to mine.

I can't help imagining my hands following those same paths. My cock is outright throbbing now, but it's a delicious sort of teasing.

And my heart swells at the same time, full of my love for her.

Ivy's gained so much confidence since the first bath I arranged for her, when she was nervous to even take off her dress. The trials we've faced have wounded and shaken her, but she's also come out of them even stronger than before.

Once she's finished washing her torso, she stands right up so I get a clear view of her sex and ass as she tends to them too. Desire thrums through my veins.

I manage to hold myself back until she lowers herself back into the water for a rinse, and then I surge forward.

I pull her to me and bury my face against her damp hair by her ear. My voice comes out in a ragged murmur. "I don't think I can stand one more second without being inside you."

Ivy shivers eagerly against me and adjusts her position to straddle my thighs. "I certainly didn't start this interlude to leave you wanting."

As she takes me into her slick heat, our mouths collide. A blissful flush spreads across every inch of my body.

I cup her cheek with one hand and grip her hip with the other, thrusting into her at the angle I know will spark just as much pleasure in her.

Even through her gasps, Ivy doesn't give herself completely over to me. She tangles her fingers in my hair with the most delightful tug and strokes her other hand over my chest, pausing to pinch one of my nipples.

Still determined to offer me every bit as much attention as I'm giving her.

There's a deeper sort of joy to this exchange, isn't there? To be receiving adoration as well as offering it?

It's not something we learned at the royal college, but as courtesans, we weren't meant to seek out partners who wanted more than a temporary liaison. I have to think Ardone must value this balanced love just as much as that offered totally selflessly.

It feels like a kind of magic.

It's my honor to be a part of it.

Our mouths crash together again and again. The water sloshes around us just as wildly.

My release builds at the base of my cock, but I need Ivy to come with me. Plunging into her at a faster rhythm, I slip my hand between us to strum that sensitive spot just above her opening.

Ivy moans and bucks faster with me. Her fingernails dig into my back with a sting I find more thrilling than painful.

I will back my climax, but in the same moment a tremor ripples through Ivy's frame. She clamps around me with a stuttered sigh, and I give myself over to the blaze of pleasure now that I know she's satisfied too.

Ivy relaxes into my arms and snuggles against me for a minute, not making any move to untangle herself from me. I nuzzle the side of her head and allow myself to revel in every bit of the pampering she's offered.

It's not long before her practical side kicks in, though. She peeks over the edge of the tub and winces at the puddles left behind by our fun. "We're going to need more towels."

I chuckle and give her one more kiss before getting out of the tub with her. We dry ourselves off and mop up the watery mess until there's no evidence of our intimate adventures except the sodden towels.

I help Ivy back into her clothes and don my own. "How would you feel about a little stargazing?"

She beams back at me. "That sounds wonderful. The rest of our expedition should be back by now, but there won't be much planning to do until the sentries report on how Lothar's responded to our attack. I think we've all earned a night off."

We're just coming around the bend into the temple's main hall when Filip bursts out of one of the other hallways. The Order defector halts in his tracks at the sight of us, his expression twitching with a flurry of emotions that makes me uneasy.

I step toward him, gentling my tone to avoid putting him on the defensive. "Are you all right, Filip?"

He stares at me for a second and then glances at Ivy. Her brow has knit with worry. He seems to waver before dragging in a sharp breath and hurrying closer.

"Ivy," he says with a respectful dip of his head. "If anyone will be able to stop them, it's you. I'm so sorry. I should have said something earlier. I never should have gone along with it at all."

As my heart lurches, Ivy's posture stiffens. "Gone along with what? Stop who?"

The Order of the Wild defector shoves his hand back through his tawny hair. "When I joined you—it was supposed to be a trick. I didn't *want* to lie to anyone. I haven't felt right about what's being done under the banner of the Order of the Wild for months. But I was afraid of what they'd do to me if I didn't go along with the plan…"

With every word that falls from his mouth, it's obvious how anguished he feels about his decision. Anger flares in my chest at the thought of the danger he's put us in, but my fury is tempered by a corresponding rush of compassion.

I don't know what this man has been through—what the scourge sorcerers put him through before he got to this point.

He's confessing to us now. That counts for something.

Ivy's hands have clenched at her sides. I jump in before she can speak. "It's understandable that you'd have been afraid, and it does you credit that you're owning up to your missteps. We can deal with the past later, on our own time. What is it you're worried about now?"

His expression turns even more miserable. "The last thing I did for them—I managed to pass on a message a few days ago, not long after we got to the temple, to let them know where Princess Petra had gone. They signaled me just now, through a charm they gave me—they're on their way. I'm supposed to distract you so you don't realize they're coming, but I don't want to. I want you to get out of here before they can do whatever they're planning. I—I want to come *with* you."

He drops to his knees in appeal, his hands clasped in front of him, his gaze fixing completely on Ivy. "You know what it's like to hurt people and regret it. To want them to see you as something better. I know I can do so much better too. Please, give me the chance."

As she stares at him, I reach for my gift with a tingling through my teeth and focus on the man in front of me. In the rush of sensations that flow through my mind, my certainty locks into place.

It's a much more specific impression than what I first got from him, when he needed us to welcome him to carry out his trick. What I could do that would make this man happiest is to help him escape the horrors he's already seen from his former colleagues.

"He means it," I say.

Ivy's gaze turns fierce. She motions Filip back to his feet. "How far out are they?"

He splays his hands helplessly as he scrambles up. "I don't know. I assume they'd give me a decent amount of warning, but it could be less than an hour."

Ivy's stance is still rigid, but my calm approach appears to have tempered her anger as well. She turns to me. "Come on. We need to get everyone out of the temple."

Her head jerks back toward the defector. "And you'd better stick with us. You're going to need to prove that we *can* trust you now when we shouldn't have before."

He hangs his head. "I know. I thought… I thought I'd

already been dragged into so many messed up things that there wasn't any hope for me. I haven't really felt like myself in years… until the past week with all of you. This is where I want to be, and I'll do whatever it takes to prove it."

Ivy gives him a sharp nod and jogs down the hall. She raises her voice so it carries through the building. "Delfis? Tinom? Petra? We have a problem!"

In a matter of minutes, the temple is consumed with activity. Delfis directs most of his devouts to help us in our frantic packing of supplies while several others usher the rescued sacrificial accomplices into a hidden entrance that leads to a secret basement chamber.

"A security measure I wish we could offer all of you," he says. "But if the Order is suspicious of us, they'll watch the temple closely for weeks. I don't think you'd be able to leave to carry out the rest of your mission unless you do it now."

Petra bobs her head to him with a tap of her fingers down her chest, acknowledging both him and the godlen he serves. "I understand. We're grateful for the hospitality you've already offered."

I hurry out to the stable to gather all the horses we brought and a few extra steeds the cleric says he can spare. When I lead the last couple out to meet the emerging crowd, Petra is deep in debate with our allies from Pima.

"I don't know how far we're going to have to flee to be safe," she's saying to Emor. "And Nikodi was right at the heart of the uprising. We can't go there. But I can't ask your people to travel so much farther from home either."

He waves off her concern. "I'll return to pass on word of what went on here. But what matters the most to us has always been seeing the scourge sorcerers taken down."

He glances around at his followers. "Is there anyone who'd rather go back to Pima with me than continue helping our future queen secure her throne?"

At the chorus of refusals that rises up in response, Petra looks both awed and nervous. Her mouth sets in a firm line. "I'll do my best to keep you all safe."

Ivy secures a bag to Toast's saddle and swings onto his back. She scans the yard as if seeing beyond the temple walls. "I can't sense any magic extending this far yet… but that doesn't mean they aren't close."

Petra hefts her younger brother onto her horse in front of her and checks on her sister, who's sharing a horse with Rheave. Once we're all mounted, Tinom extends his arm, sweeping his hand through the air.

"I'll do my best to deflect their attention from us in the darkness. Let us go quickly and quietly. If anyone gets separated, make for Tupno, and we'll regroup outside the city. I think we're best off heading south. There are a few noble families on the far side of Florian I'd expect to take the Melchiorek side. It's about time we called on them."

We set off through the gate at a brisk trot.

The night drapes around us, the temple's lanterns quickly dwindling behind us. All my companions are reduced to faint shades of gray in the dim starlight.

Stavros, Ivy, and the soldiers form a circle around the royal children. I hang a little farther back in the procession to watch both my companions and our surroundings.

Filip sticks near me, his shoulders hunched and his expression pained.

I don't see any sign that my gift's judgment was wrong. He didn't see a way out before—now he believes there is one. And that's made all the difference.

Ahead of me, Ivy's head snaps around. She nudges Toast faster to pull ahead, as if tracking something. "I felt a twinge… some magic I don't think is ours—"

The last word has barely left her lips when a flash of searing energy shoots through the night toward Petra. Ivy yanks her stallion around; one of the soldiers jostles the future queen's horse to the side.

And Prince Jacos yelps in pain.

"Ride!" Petra shouts. "Ride, as fast as you can, before they can keep attacking."

She hugs her brother to her. I catch a glimpse of a slash cut through his cloak, blood welling on his arm, before she bundles the fabric to stop the bleeding and kicks their horse to a canter.

"They aren't close," Ivy calls out in a low voice as she follows suit. "They might not even know the blow hit. We can still outrun them."

As our procession surges forward, Tinom aims a glower at her that raises my hackles.

He's looking at Ivy as if he thinks it's her fault the prince was hurt. As if she should have sounded a better warning when it's his concealing magic that failed us most.

Is he always going to see her as a villain?

Gritting my teeth, I tap my horse's sides and race after the others.

TWENTY-SEVEN

Ivy

I stride into the dining room turned resistance headquarters, waving a pamphlet fresh from the press. "We've got a new batch!"

The many figures crowded around the table look up. Petra smiles from her spot at the head, but I catch plenty of skeptical or even anxious expressions too.

I'm not sure yet how to feel about the way our resistance group has grown. Since we arrived at the summer estate of one of the court barons a few days ago, our numbers have more than doubled.

Tinom chose well, I can admit. Baron Cyris and his wife showed nothing but pure relief when the remaining Melchioreks arrived and immediately started venting about how awful Lothar and his Order of the Wild are. And this particular baron has a gift for illusions similar to Tinom's, which means he can join the magic advisor in concealing signs of our comings and goings from the estate.

But he is a noble, and the others who've joined us are also

nobles or the close comrades of nobles. Every time I see a lip curled in disgust aimed Alek's way, my well-practiced will-power is strained resisting the urge to punch that face. I'm sure our allies who came all this way from Pima with us have noticed the upturned noses and uneasy mutterings just as I have.

Gods forbid anyone be in their presence wearing peasant clothes rather than embroidered silks.

Petra beckons me over, and I skirt the various nobles and staff to reach her. Most press closer to the table even though there's plenty of space at the edge of the room for me to get by.

It's obvious word has worked its way through our growing numbers about my powers as well. No one's dared to speak against me, since I'm sure they've also heard that their future queen has defended my presence, but there's no denying the tensed postures and lowered voices whenever I pass by them.

I can't really complain. We need all the help we can get. The nobles have sway over their domains and plenty of staff they can call on.

They have access to resources we might need… including the printing press I heard the baroness mention she fiddles around with as a "hobby," which gave me an idea for a new strategy.

A sense of satisfaction takes the edges off my nerves as I set the pamphlet I'm holding in Petra's waiting hand.

My father always talked about how the press was the best tool for reaching people's minds. *You can put any message on pieces of paper and send it all over the realms in a matter of days.*

We haven't needed to win over anyone outside our kingdom, but we have to build all the support we can manage within it. I've spent a large part of the last couple of days working with Alek and Casimir, putting together simple messages and pictures to convey the threat the scourge sorcerers pose and the good Petra can offer the country instead.

The images will give the gist of the idea to those who haven't learned to read. Those who can will explain the rest in the undercurrent of nervous chatter we hope to encourage throughout the country.

This afternoon's set of pamphlets warn Silana's civilians that a group that would murder the king won't hesitate to kill others as well, prompting them to think about the acts of violence they've witnessed carried out by the Order. The stark letters at the bottom ask, *What if they come for your sons and daughters next?*

It's pointed propaganda, but the scourge sorcerers deserve it.

As Petra scans the one I gave her, several of the more luxuriously dressed figures nearby stir restlessly.

The local countess who's thrown in her lot with us clears her throat. "Are we really sure that tossing those papers around is the best use for our limited manpower?"

One of Voleska and Emor's people speaks up before I have to. "It's not like we've had that many other jobs to take care of. And you should have seen 'em in the square this morning when we launched the latest batch!"

The colleague next to her lifts his head eagerly. "Yeah, they were snatching at them and chattering away about it. Word is spreading fast. The tide's turning in Queen Petra's favor."

We've had to come up with creative ways of distributing the pamphlets, since the Order members who've spread across the country aren't going to stand by while someone shouts about their misdeeds in the city squares. With a combination of stealth and a few handy magical gifts our allies can bring to bear, we've been showering them over the crowds from the highest vantage points we can find.

If all's gone well, some of the riders who headed out yesterday will have sent papers blustering down as far as Florian with the help of the Black Talons, as well as other royal cities like Zulina and Mipone.

It won't be long before the scourge sorcerers can guess that we've relocated in the south end of the country, but we want to spread out our activities enough that it isn't easy to guess what province, let alone county, we're in.

If they find us again, I'm not sure where we'd be able to take shelter next.

A merchant friend of the barons raps an impatient hand on the table. "We need to 'turn the tide' with more than just words."

Petra lifts her gaze to consider her supporters. She keeps her tone mild. "I think words are a very good start while we gather ourselves for a more intensive effort. This is perfect, Ivy. Do we have people ready to carry them out?"

I nod. "I just have to give them the word."

As I duck out of the room, I catch a not-especially-hushed voice mutter, "Where did that one come from?"

Stavros's voice follows an instant later with a hard edge of warning. "Ivy's been protecting Silana from the scourge sorcerers from the beginning."

I hurry to the out-building that holds the press, discomfort itching at my skin. I don't like leaving my men or the future queen who's accepted me to defend my role in the resistance, but I'm not sure how to speak up myself without making our new allies even more nervous.

I find my self-appointed assistants just finishing stuffing the latest batch of pamphlets into saddle bags.

"Queen Petra approves," I tell them, and they flash grins at me before hustling off to the waiting horses.

I raise my voice to call after them. "Safe travels!"

Some part of me wishes I was riding off to carry out more capers rather than debating with the stuffy jerks around here.

Of course, the current caper might not be possible without those stuffy jerks and all their possessions. So I bite my tongue and march back to the meeting room.

I return to find the table debating the need for weapons. Princess Klaudia is just looking around at her companions with a worried expression. "I thought we were going to win over the people as peacefully as possible. We're not like the scourge sorcerers. We can't just *kill* citizens who've been deceived."

Tinom shoots her a condescending glance. "We can't be unprepared. It's unlikely Lothar will back down without any fight at all."

Stavros dips his head. "I'm sorry to say that I agree. I'd rather not have to draw any more blood, but it's better that we have blades we don't need to use than need them and find ourselves empty-handed. The scourge sorcerers and the most avid members of the Order of the Wild know what they've gotten themselves into by now."

Petra sighs, her gaze sliding to Prince Jacos. Her brother is sitting next to Klaudia, his sleeve lumpy around the bandage he's still wearing from the magical attack while we were fleeing the Temple of Tranquil Skies.

"We do need to be ready to defend ourselves," she says. "And to strike at our actual enemies when we have the opportunity. The Order has hurt too many people to deserve our mercy. We'll do our best to avoid any collateral damage."

Alek pushes to the table from where he's been hanging back from the discussion. His jaw looks tight, his posture a little awkward under the stares, but he hasn't been so bothered that he's returned to wearing a mask over his scars.

His voice comes out perfectly steady. "I may be able to arrange a large supply of new weapons. I can reach out to my family. They've handled a steady production and acquisition of quality arms for decades, and I've never heard my parents be anything other than supportive of the Melchiorek reign."

My stomach knots at his proposition. His family might be loyal to the Crown, but they never supported *him*. I don't think he's been back to see them since he first enrolled at the temple school where he got those scars.

Petra aims a smile at him. "If you trust that it's safe to reach out to them, I know you'll handle the discussion well. The sooner we find out our options, the better."

The scholar draws himself up straighter. "I'll prepare for the trip right away."

I watch him head for the doorway, my gut tugging at me to follow him.

Before I've quite made the decision to leave, Petra taps her hands against the tabletop. "Now I think we should discuss the possibility of the kingship trials."

My gaze jerks back to her in the same moment as a few grunts and other disgruntled noises sound from around the table.

"Trials?" Baron Cyris says. "Isn't that one of the bizarre ideas Lothar's people have been babbling about?"

Petra inclines her head in acknowledgment. "It is. But I believe we can adjust the concept to work in our favor."

One of the other nobles lets out a sputter of a laugh. "How could they possibly be a benefit to us?"

Petra's eyes seek me out by the other end of the table. I'm the one who suggested this idea to her—but she isn't singling me out or demanding that I justify the strategy.

Somehow that makes me feel even more compelled to step in.

I raise my voice to carry over the uneasy murmurings. "A

lot of Silana's citizens have shown that they don't trust the Melchioreks to have their best interests at heart. We heard demands that the next ruler prove themselves worthy in both Florian and Tupno. And they don't really know Petra. Even if they're starting to doubt the Order of the Wild, that doesn't mean they believe in *her* enough to risk their livelihoods and their lives on her behalf."

Most of the heads around the table swivel toward me. The baroness's lips curl with a hint of a sneer. "So you think our queen should put her life on the line to convince them?"

"Not her life," I say quickly. "That's why we'd adapt the idea. Nothing brutal or as dangerous as I'm sure Lothar is imagining—or as skewed in the Order's favor. We'll come up with tasks for Petra to complete that would make people feel more confident and prove her strength without taking too immense a gamble."

"Exactly." Petra folds her arms over her chest. "And there's another very good reason to put on such a demonstration. We can call for Lothar to submit his own candidates. It won't be much of a trial if I have no competition. If he wants to prove *himself* a fair player, he'll need to show up. We'll have our first real opportunity to expose his and his top followers' treachery directly—and to address it as we see fit."

With a sword through Lothar's skull, preferably. But even as my spirits stir at the thought of confronting the villain on equal ground, my stomach flips over.

Petra never mentioned that element before. It wasn't part of my initial idea. And it sounds as if…

Klaudia puts my concern into words before I can. "You're talking about using yourself as bait."

Horror tinges her tone, but Petra responds calmly. "I'm the only bait that would work. I trust that you all will ensure

I'm never under more threat than is worth it to see our purpose through."

No one quite seems to know how to argue against that statement. Our future queen gazes around the table. "Let's get on with it, then. We need to brainstorm what our trials might look like, how we would spread the word, where we should hold them."

Her call to action finally spurs the uncertain to speak.

Tinom frowns. "I'm not certain this is a wise tactic, Your Highness. Regardless of what precautions we try to implement, the risks you'd need to take—"

"It's absolutely inappropriate," Countess Mirina breaks in. "Our queen, dueling against whoever the riffraff throws up against her?"

Petra gives a cough that might cover a laugh. "I don't think we'd include any actual dueling, Mirina."

Baron Cyris waves his hand dismissively. "A queen shouldn't lower herself to that level. You have to think of how it would appear to your most devoted supporters, Your Highness."

My hackles rise. Supporters like him, he means.

The words burst out before I can catch them. "Unless you can win the throne back for her—and keep it—all on your own, we *need* the support of the common people too."

He turns to me with a huff. "What do you know about the ways of the court? I never saw you before three days ago." He shifts his attention back to Petra. "You must heed our advice, Your Highness. Nothing good ever comes of giving way too much to the masses."

A flurry of other voices follow his, most of them echoing his protest.

My magic shudders, prodding me to shut them all up, preferably by knocking them on their pompous asses. I clamp down on it instead and gather myself to jump back into the argument.

Then my gaze catches on Petra's face.

Her mouth has tightened, her expression momentarily uneasy.

She isn't totally committed to this course. They've shaken her resolve.

If she isn't sure it's the right plan, who *am* I to insist that it is? The baron isn't entirely wrong.

All at once, I feel like I'm back in the bow of the oak tree in Slaughterwell, watching life happen beneath me from a distance. I've witnessed plenty, sure, but how much have I truly lived before the past few months?

Do I even really know what I'm asking of Petra?

The doubt rises up in me so fast it steals my breath. I step back from the clash of voices and then stride out of the room.

On a matter this immense that involves her so personally, Petra should make up her own mind. She has plenty of other people in there who can advise her from various levels of society, all of whom probably have a better idea what's really at stake than I do.

I walk almost blindly until I find myself stepping out the front door. The cool air washes over me, settling my thoughts and leaving my mind clearer.

I take a few more steps into the yard, breathing deeply and getting a grip on myself.

I'm not used to being an active participant in Silana's politics. I'll get more comfortable with it in time. Just a few minutes to sort myself out, and I can go back in there and say my piece if I feel I need to.

The door squeaks behind me. I barely have time to turn before Stavros's well-muscled arm has wrapped around me.

I turn to meet his embrace instinctively, soaking up his

warmth and his smoky, peppery scent, even as the question I know I have to ask creeps up my throat. "Shouldn't you still be in there with the rest of them, figuring out the best approach? You're the only general we've got."

"Former general," Stavros mutters, and teases his prosthetic down my back in a gentle caress. "I needed a break from them too. It was either that or there'd have been several broken noses and a not particularly happy queen-to-be."

The corners of my mouth twitch with the start of a smile. "I think she might have understood a little."

Stavros hums to himself and eases back just far enough to peer down at me. "You're not letting them shake your confidence, are you, Lady Thief? The Hand of Kosmel knows more about schemes and treachery than those nobles could even conceive of."

My momentary good humor fades. "They know a lot about plenty of other things I've never experienced."

"Which is why we're all at the table together, weighing in." He cocks an eyebrow. "You didn't let the horde of highborns at the college intimidate you."

I open my mouth and hesitate as I form a full answer. "I had Julita giving me an inside edge. And… I wasn't there as myself. I was playing a role. It was easier."

Easier not to care what they thought of me. Easier to drape myself in noble-style self-assurance like yet another fancy gown.

Of course, even if I'm not outright pretending to be someone else these days, I'm still not really being myself. I'm downplaying one of the most significant parts of me as much as I can, willing everyone around me to forget that I'm one of the riven.

Somehow that's more uncomfortable than simply hiding my whole self away like I once did. But I'm going to have to get used to it.

Stavros dips his head closer, his voice dropping low with it. "I just don't want to see you backing down. The woman I love has never shied away simply because a situation gets hard."

A flush spreads over my body with his nearness, and I leap at the opportunity to focus on that heat rather than my worries.

I trail my fingers down his brawny chest, appreciating every ridge of sculpted muscle I can trace through his tunic. "I suppose that's true. Certain things I particularly appreciate when they're hard."

The suggestive note in my voice clearly isn't lost on the former general. He chuckles and catches my mouth with his.

As Stavros worships me with his kiss, our bodies press closer together. Desire pools low in my belly with the image of him pushing me right up against the side of the house, plunging into me without regard for noble sensibilities.

I'm not sure either of us would actually go quite that far. But before I get the chance to find out, a current of magic tickles across my skin from across the yard.

My back goes rigid, and Stavros yanks back. "What's wrong?"

I pull back from him, scanning the landscape around the estate. "I felt… Someone extended magic this way…"

As I move forward, his hold on me loosens. We stalk over to the gate together.

The whiff of magic keeps drifting around me. I don't sense anything aggressive about it, but that doesn't mean the caster has good intentions.

Stavros tilts his head as if pricking his ear. "Someone's coming."

I hear the distant hoofbeats a moment later. Only one set, from the sounds of it. Not anything like an army.

Still, we stay braced and waiting as they approach the

estate. If it isn't an ally, we don't want them seeing me or Stavros here under Baron Cyris's roof.

My own magic unfurls through my chest, reminding me of how easily it could spring to our defense if need be.

The hoofbeats slow. The guard posted on the other side of the gate calls out. "Who are you, and what business do you have here?"

A dryly feminine voice replies. "I'm looking for a woman named Ivy."

The tone is so familiar and yet so unexpected that for the first second I remain frozen. Then I reach to open the gate.

It swings open to reveal the last person I'd ever have expected to see outside her home. The woman who taught me what I know about controlling my riven power—and who insisted it would never be safe for people like us to return to society.

Sulla meets my gaze with a tentative smile, her hands tight around her horse's reins. "There you are. I thought... I thought it was time I came down from my mountain."

HISTORIA
TOTOP

Twenty-Eight

Alek

The smell of the forges taints the air even half a mile away. Memories come flooding over me with it: the nights when I tucked myself away in the attic so my parents wouldn't notice how late I stayed up reading, the ache in my muscles on the days when Dad insisted I take a turn with the hammer and anvil as if that might wake up some love of weaponry in me.

The disapproving glowers when not even a flicker of interest ever lit.

As I ride on toward our family's sprawling shop at the edge of the small city, the breeze washes over my face. The air is starting to warm with the first hints of spring, but I'm starkly aware of the currents catching on the ridges of scar on my face.

I've thought about my deformity less and less over the past few months since I first started removing my mask. Even the stares of the nobles we're allying ourselves with barely

matter anymore when I can simply look at Ivy and have her beam adoration at me.

But my family already has a picture of me in their heads, and I don't fit it anymore. I haven't been home since I was expelled from the temple school.

They may have heard some of the details of my teenage disgrace, but that's different from seeing it in front of them.

I can already picture my mother wincing in horror, my father's lip curling with disgust. They'll probably blame my ruined face on my strange inclinations toward books and scholarship, as if my studies warped my morals.

I glance down at the small bag attached to my saddle. I brought a mask with me in case I decided it was best to cover the consequences of my long-ago crime.

My fingers itch to reach for it, to shield my face from judgment like I did for so long.

But what difference will it make, really? They'll imagine something terrible lies behind it regardless.

It isn't as if my family is unfamiliar with how ravaged a human body can become. I remember plenty of scarred figures crossing the shop's doorstep.

The difference is those figures earned their scars in battle as badges of honor.

I suppose I received mine in a battle of a different sort—one with my personal flaws. As much as the shame of my actions might have marked me, I did win in the end.

I've come a long way from the boy I was.

So when I reach the hitching post down the street from the shop, I leave the mask in my saddlebag. I walk over to the shop through the thickening smells of smoldering coals and hot metal with all the confidence I can bring to my stride.

The clang of a hammer striking steel rings through the doorway. I know before I reach the threshold where to look for my father.

He still has his personal forge and anvil in the same corner of the workshop. He hefts the hammer and brings it down on the blade he's working, presumably a private commission for a particularly moneyed client.

The rest of the front room is dedicated to displaying the results of his craft and other pieces of weapons and armor he's carrying in his inventory. Most of the arms he and my mother deal in he doesn't make himself. He oversees multiple apprentices in one of the back rooms and sources more from other blacksmiths who don't have quite the same business sense.

He has his back to me, his broad shoulders flexing as he lowers the hammer to examine the sword. It seems like as good a time as any to make my presence known.

I clear my throat. "Dad."

My voice peels out louder than I expected over the warble of the forge's fire. Dad startles and whirls around, my name already on his lips. "Aleks—"

The last syllable dies as his gaze jars on my face. He doesn't quite flinch, but his jaw tics as if he's restrained one.

And there's that curl of the lip.

I step farther into the shop and continue before he can say anything else. "I won't be staying long. There's something important I need to talk to you about."

Mom's surprised voice carries from the large warehouse room at the back of the shop. "Is that Aleksi?"

She comes hustling out with wide eyes and a hesitant smile. When her gaze finds me, her eyes widen even more— and the smile vanishes.

"Hello, Mom," I say through the constricting of my throat. Imagining their reactions wasn't a tenth as painful as experiencing them firsthand.

She doesn't even bother to return my greeting. "What happened to you?"

I'm not going to lie. "I made some bad decisions—but I learned from them. It was years ago. I've put it behind me."

My father finally manages to sputter a response. "It's right here in front of us. This is what you let happen to you at that useless school? This is the face you show the world now?"

My hackles come up in an instant. Just like old times.

"It's the face I have," I grit out. "And the school wasn't useless."

Mom moves tentatively toward me, her arms crossing in front of her. She shakes her head. "I knew there wasn't anything good to come of surrounding yourself with people who'd rather think about words than what's real. But you were so stubborn."

"It was still the right choice. Everything I studied was real. What I look like doesn't matter in—"

Dad cuts me off with a dismissive snort. "Tell that to anyone you need to barter with while you're showing them that mug. What are you doing here? Did you finally get tired of those stuck-up scholars?"

Another sharp retort prickles up my throat. In the same moment, my hand clenches by my hip—and my fingers brush the lump in my pocket that's my most vital cargo.

That object is the reason I'm here at all. It has nothing to do with my career choices or my parents' opinion of them.

The mission I'm on is so much bigger than all the bitter past behind us that I've nearly stumbled right back into.

I'm *not* the boy they knew. I have the ear of the future queen. The love of a riven sorcerer.

I'm not someone for a couple of weapons merchants to sneer at—I deserve their respect.

Gods above, would I ever have stooped so low in the first place if I hadn't been so desperate for respect back then? If I'd gotten even a smidgeon of support from the people who raised me?

My scars are marks of my shame, but I had a childhood of rejection and disdain to bring me to that point. Everything I've earned since then, all the things I've accomplished are completely thanks to my own strength, rising above the foundation these two people built for me.

I draw my stance up straighter and swallow down my rancor.

I won't speak to them like their disappointing son. I'm here as Queen Petra's representative.

My tone evens out, both harder and steadier than before. "I didn't come to discuss my schooling or what happened to my face. There are more pressing matters to address. Have you been doing business with the Order of the Wild?"

Dad's momentary shock at my change in tone shifts into a disgruntled expression at my last words. "Crazed rabblerousers, throwing the whole country into chaos," he grumbles, setting his hammer down on the forge. "What business is there anyone can do with them? They don't think they should have to pay for anything. Marched in here not long after King Konram's death was announced and took half our inventory."

As he says King Konram's name, he taps his fingers down his front in the gesture of the divinities, honoring our former ruler. The hope that brought me here expands in my chest.

Mom lets out a huff and then lowers her voice as if afraid she might be overheard. "They're meddlers, is what they are. Want to take over *everything*. Seems like every other day they send someone in here wanting to know what orders we've gotten and from who."

"Trying to dress themselves up as some sort of salvation when they're nothing but murdering traitors." Dad grimaces.

Then he gives me an abruptly wary look. "You haven't fallen in with *that* lot now, have you?"

I have to swallow a slightly hysterical laugh. I'm not sure what's more insulting—that they think so little of me it didn't occur to them that I could be a threat when I first asked the question or that they don't realize I'd reject everything the Order stands for even more vehemently than they do.

But the fact that he stopped to ask—and looks nervous about it—only confirms his loyalties. He wasn't spouting off insults because he thought I'd want to hear them but because he wasn't filtering his true opinions at all.

"Absolutely not," I say. "They're a menace to this country. And that's why I'm here. What would you say if I offered you the opportunity to oust those traitors—and win the esteem of the royal family?"

Dad knits his brow. "I'd say all those books have finally addled your brain beyond repair."

I do let myself chuckle then and take another step toward my parents. "Not at all. It turns out all my book-learning has actually been useful to your future queen. You must have heard that the Melchiorek heirs escaped the murder plot and have been speaking out against the Order of the Wild as much as they can. I've come on behalf of the legitimate Queen Petra to make you an offer."

The skepticism hasn't left my parents' expressions, but Mom's eyes have lit up a little all the same. "What kind of offer?"

"If you supply our resistance efforts against the Order of the Wild with weapons and armor—as much as you can manage—you'll become the official arms supplier for the royal family."

Dad goes rigid, his lips parting with an eagerness he can't suppress even as he grapples with his doubts. He's probably picturing the new sign he'd get to add to the front of the shop once he earned that honor.

"You," he says uncertainly. "The queen— How—"

"It doesn't matter," I interrupt. "Our paths crossed, and I earned her trust. Enough that she believed me when I said there was a good chance you'd support her. She's laid out her terms in this letter."

I draw the folded paper from my pocket, holding it out with the Melchiorek family seal showing in the wax that seals the missive.

Dad takes the letter gingerly, as if he's afraid he might damage it. As he unsticks the seal, my mother hustles over to join him so she can read too.

It isn't a long letter. Their eyes skim over the words a few times in the space of a minute.

Then Dad looks up at me again. "She says the condition of being named the royal arms supplier is dependent on…"

He can't quite bring himself to say it?

I allow myself a thin smile. "On my judging that you've served her well. I know what our family is capable of. She knows I can confirm that you've contributed all you can."

"Oh." Mom lowers her hands to clasp them in front of her before combing one back through her hair as if she's afraid I'll be judging *her* looks. "Oh, that's— You really have found a place for yourself, haven't you?"

I've heard that fawning note in her voice before—when chatting up potential customers of high status. Somehow it isn't remotely gratifying.

Because it has nothing to do with who I am, only what she thinks I can do for them.

Dad claps me on the shoulder, a smile springing to his lips but a slightly panicked gleam in his eyes. "Of course we'll do whatever we can to see the rightful queen on the throne where she belongs. You know what I said before—it builds character to have to defend your passions—you've always had impressive dedication."

What they moments ago referred to as stubbornness instead.

He nudges me toward the doorway into the adjoining home. "We should have taken this into the house in the first place. I'll pour you a drink, and we can discuss specifics man to man."

"Thanks, Dad," I say, with only a trace of irony creeping into my tone. The last of the unsettled nerves that gripped me melt away.

I craved these people's approval for so long... but it's absolutely hollow, isn't it? Focused only on their narrow and frequently superficial priorities.

I don't require their pride or their blessing. I only need their cooperation so that *I* can serve Petra the way she deserves, and I've got that. I've earned my own pride.

Now it's time to get down to the business of overthrowing an uprising.

TWENTY-NINE

Ivy

At the head of our procession, Sulla draws her horse to a stop amid the trees. She turns her head, the fragmented sunlight glowing off her lined face. "You can feel that, can't you?"

I hadn't until she halted us. Now, as I concentrate on the sensations around me, a faint tingle of magic brushes over my skin.

I tense, swiveling my head to try to track its source.

I don't get the impression of any specific direction or purpose. It's more like the energy is simply drifting in the air.

Just behind us, my men shift in their saddles. None of them can pick up on supernatural eddies the way I can.

"There's magic being worked somewhere nearby," I say for their benefit as well as to answer Sulla's question. "Are you sure it's from the scourge sorcerers?"

The older sorcerer purses her lips. "I can't tell for certain. But it gives me the feeling of a large cistern dribbling water as

it overflows. That much power in one place… I would expect a temple, but there are none nearby."

Alek speaks quietly. "But a group of sacrificial accomplices could also wield that kind of power."

"Exactly."

He and the rest of our procession—royal soldiers, noble staff, Pimanian rebels, even my former general—look to me for confirmation. Whatever some of our allies might think of my magic, they see me as the expert on that subject. They barely know Sulla.

I wet my lips and turn my head again. Another whiff of energy quivers over me.

What are they working on out here for traces of their magical practice to be seeping through the woods? What new threat are they conjuring?

We're only a couple of hours' ride from our current stronghold. If there are scourge sorcerers performing their darkest magic nearby, it's better for us to root them out and determine what new schemes they're setting in motion before they have a chance to discover our presence.

If we can free more of their accomplices and weaken Lothar's power that way, all the better. The more we can diminish the threat of retribution from the Order of the Wild, the easier it'll be for our allies to take a stand with us, however Petra decides to make it.

On the other hand, I don't want to lead two dozen followers into a battle on totally uncertain ground. My comrades came prepared to fight but expecting me to guide them.

I consider for a moment, uneasiness twisting in my belly. "Let's move closer to get a better idea of what we're dealing with. We should go ahead on foot—just a few of us to start."

Stavros nods and makes a couple of gestures to the rest of our company that those with military training must understand. As I slide down from Toast's back, he, Sulla, Rheave, and one of the soldiers follow suit.

We set off through the forest, Sulla and I remaining in the lead. I tread forward carefully so I can adjust my route with the minute shifts of the magic lacing the air.

For a few moments, it seems to grow stronger to the east. Then the impression dwindles, and I find myself backtracking onto a more northerly route. I can see what Sulla means about the magic feeling like stray dribbles rather than a focused effect.

But after maybe half an hour of rambling, a more solid sensation brushes my face. I ease toward it even more tentatively than before and stop in my tracks at its swift thickening.

I motion toward the terrain ahead of us. "This part of the forest is warded. If we go much farther, whoever set those wards will probably set off an alert."

More proof that whatever the sorcerers are working on, it's important. Or maybe they've simply become increasingly cautious after the raids we've already pulled off in the north.

Rheave steps up beside me without hesitation. "Let me see if I can break the magic so we can get closer."

He glances over at me with a brief flick of his gaze toward Sulla as well. "There isn't much chance anyone other than the scourge sorcerers would be protecting themselves like that, is there?"

Sulla shakes her head before I can answer. "The enchantment they've laid down is stronger than any I've felt from even a devout. No ordinary homesteader would have the means to place that kind of magic." She shivers. "Our foes are formidable."

As Rheave reaches his hands toward the wards, I study my former mentor. Sulla told me that was why she'd come— because even on her mountain, she became aware of the tragedies and violence spreading across the country. The Haven no longer felt secure.

She remembered what I'd said to her about us standing up to the blight of scourge sorcery together and decided to seek me out. Her magic led her to me.

I'm glad for her help, but *I* remember how she stole our equipment and tried to bar us from leaving the Haven. How she insisted that it was too dangerous for me to leave—not for my safety but everyone I'd encounter in the outside world.

She's declared her loyalty to Petra and her siblings. She warned us of the magic she'd sensed on her journey so we could investigate it. But I have trouble completely trusting her just yet.

Rheave's face hardens into a mask of concentration. His fingers twitch, sparks leaping between them.

The aura of magic in this part of the forest ripples and then fades away.

Stavros scans our surroundings. There's still nothing visible but trees and underbrush.

"We should proceed cautiously but quickly from here," he says. "We don't know how long it'll take before the sorcerers notice that their wards have been disabled."

He motions to the soldier. "Hovi, return to the others and have them follow. The sooner they can catch up with us, the better."

The guard bobs his head and lopes off in the direction we came from. We continue onward at a faster pace, but all my senses stay vigilant for further magical protections.

Only the vague, drifting impression of magic remains. It intensifies as we continue, until the trees start to thin up ahead and I make out a couple of squat wooden buildings in a clearing some fifty paces away.

We all go still, peering between the trunks. We have a

little illusionary magic wrapped around us to deflect attention, but that won't hide us from magical surveillance or particularly attentive guards. We don't have enough of the more potent charms to conceal much of a fighting force.

And whoever strikes the first blows will automatically become a target.

As we study the buildings, the rest of our force catches up with us. Most of the group hangs back several paces, but Casimir and Alek tread carefully over to where the four of us are standing.

A couple of men emerge from one of the buildings and amble around it with only brief glances toward the trees. They look as if they're pretty confident that their magical protections are all they need to fend off intruders.

Rheave sucks in a breath and speaks under his breath. "One of those is a captured daimon. This is definitely a place of scourge sorcery."

"Then we need to find out what they're up to," I mutter. "But we don't know how many of them are here right now or what kind of magic they can wield."

A few deep gouges mark the ground farther out from the buildings. Their edges gleam with a sheen that doesn't look like soil or grass. When I squint, I make out a mottling of ruddy gashes on some of the nearby tree trunks around the edge of the clearing.

Whatever magic they've been experimenting with, it doesn't look like the peaceful type.

Sulla offers a small smile. "It shouldn't be difficult to create a distraction with our own magic."

I stifle a laugh. "I don't think we want Rheave setting the forest on fire. That would be bad for us too."

A crease forms in her brow. "I was thinking the two of us could manage enough of an effect."

Oh. With a lurch of my pulse, my body stiffens even more than it had already.

Since she arrived, I've avoided talking with Sulla about the exact results of my magic usage, but I can hardly hide it now.

I force my hands to unclench, willing my voice to remain steady. "I'm only releasing my power when it's absolutely necessary. I—I've already felt the madness coming on. I don't want to push myself farther toward it unless there's no other option."

The older woman stares at me for a few heavy thuds of my heart, the color leaching from her weathered skin. "You only left the Haven a matter of weeks ago. You've already let yourself go so far— You threw aside everything I taught you—"

I wince. "I didn't throw it aside. I followed your teachings as well as I could. But there was so much we needed to do, and I didn't know it would affect me so quickly."

"I warned you!" Sulla's whispered voice sharpens into a hiss. "After all that insistence that you knew what you were doing—"

Stavros cuts her off with a sharp sound. His voice comes out low but fierce. "Ivy risked her life and her mind to protect this country from the scourge sorcerers. If it wasn't for her, the entire Melchiorek family would be dead right now."

As Sulla jerks around to stare at him, Casimir dips his head where he's standing by my shoulder. "And as soon as she realized she was in trouble, she restricted her magic to ensure she wouldn't lose control. As she's shown just now. You should be pleased that she recognizes her limits."

The courtesan's normally gentle voice takes on a chiding edge with that last sentence. Alek rests his hand on the small of my back in reassurance, and Rheave has bristled as if he thinks he might need to leap to my defense with more than words.

Their automatic support brings a flood of warmth into my chest, but a pang of guilt resonates alongside it.

What they've said is true… but it's also true that I pushed myself past what I should have known I was ready for. What any riven sorcerer would ever be ready for.

Sulla takes in their expressions and mine, and her stance gradually relaxes. The smile she gives me next looks tight but also sad.

"All right. Maybe I shouldn't judge. I wasn't there, because I was hiding away on my mountaintop. I still think…" She shakes her head with a sigh. "Let me handle this. For when you do extend yourself in the future… It's important to remember that even very small acts can have a large impact."

She scans the trees around the clearing and points to a broad oak with mottled greenish bark. "That tree's sick—the branches will be weakening. With just a small nudge…"

Her eyes narrow in focus. Her fingers twitch at her sides —and one of the thickest branches on the tree cracks off the trunk.

It plummets with a thunderous crash. With another magical nudge, Sulla sends a second branch tumbling after it.

Shouts reverberate through the buildings' walls. Several more figures slip from the doorways while the two guards we already spotted jog over to the tree to investigate.

A few of their colleagues join them while the rest of the group hangs back near the buildings. But now we can see them—and they haven't noticed us yet.

Stavros raises his hand. "Those with the concealment charms first. The rest follow behind. Take them down as quickly as you can… *Now.*"

Rheave, Hovi, one of the women from Pima, and I have

already yanked the charms on their thin chains over our heads. As my companions disappear around me, I hurtle forward and snatch my knives from their sheaths.

We burst from the trees, invisible to the confused guards, amid arrows flying from unseen sources. More than half of them sizzle with Rheave's daimon energy, launched from the new bow Alek brought back for him.

The arrows streak through the air, felling foe after foe. A few of the figures topple into clay statues. Others crumple limply like the mortal men and women they are.

Blood splatters the grass before the remaining few have finished whirling around.

I race straight toward them, swinging one knife in a deadly arc and plunging the other into the nearest chest. Hollers from behind tell me that the rest of my comrades have flooded the clearing.

A blast of magic slams into me from the direction of one of the buildings—and the charm lying against my chest cracks. Suddenly the scourge sorcerer to my left is staring at me.

I'm visible again.

My magic blares through my body so forcefully I bite my tongue clamping down on its call. The battle around me blurs in my struggle for control.

Another body barrels into me from the side. Rheave heaves me out of the way of a sharper bolt of magic, shielding me with his well-muscled frame.

He spins us around and manages to send his final arrow soaring into the air, through an open window on the nearest building. A thump on the other side confirms that it hit its mark.

My power lashes out at me again, this time in pure frustration. A stabbing pain spikes through my gut.

As the momentary agony fades with my restrained gasp,

the daimon-man remains poised next to me. Other magic flares around us in a muddled barrage of light.

"I freed more of my kind," Rheave says. "And killed many of yours."

His gaze slides to me with a hint of concern and longing. As if he needs my approval, even after everything we've already been through.

I give his arm a quick squeeze. "You were amazing. We just have to topple the last few of them and—"

Another supernatural attack rains down on us with a roar of flames. This time, I shove Rheave to the side.

As the two of us roll across the grass away from the now smoldering patches, a cry breaks through the air. One of Voleska's men kneels by a woman who's slumped on the ground, her body charred from head to waist.

My stomach flips over. His friend won't be getting up again.

A man who joined us from Baron Cyris's staff jerks his hand toward a second-floor dormer. "Up there. Someone's—"

A glinting bolt slices through the air before he can finish his warning. It gouges straight through his neck. He crumples backward.

I inhale in a hiss through my teeth and launch myself forward. The first-floor window frame gives me enough of a foothold. I wrench myself up the side of the building and plunge through the upper window feet-first.

My heels slam into a body that didn't dodge fast enough. Ignoring the renewed clamoring of my magic, I jab out with my elbow, smack a cheekbone, and whip around the knife that's leapt back into my palm.

The sorcerer slumps beneath me into a pool of blood from her slit throat.

I crouch there, panting silently, listening for any other

signs of attack. My magic's call reverberates through me, but it's more a simmer than a boil when there's no direct threat.

A clatter rings out below me, followed by Stavros's voice shouting, "All clear!"

Cautiously, I move back to the window. My comrades are still scanning the clearing warily, but no further attacks batter us.

Blood streaks several sleeves and pantlegs. To my relief, no one appears to have taken fatal wounds except for the woman from Pima and the baron's man.

My throat tightens. That's still more losses than I'd prefer.

How are we ever going to confront Lothar's full force? Eventually we're going to have to go head to head with him… and we've just witnessed how much damage even a few scourge sorcerers can do.

Sulla looks up and catches my eye. "I see you get plenty done even without turning to your magic."

Her tone is dry, but I can't summon enough amusement to form a smile.

I lift my voice to carry to our companions who remained in the forest. It comes out ragged. "Come on. Let's give this place a thorough search."

I decide to take the stairs down rather than flinging myself back out the window. Along the way, I peer into the other rooms along the hall.

The door right by the top of the stairs is locked. I break the deadbolt and peek inside to find myself gazing at three mutilated forms draped in gray shrouds.

"Mistress?" one of them mumbles.

My heart sinks. We were hoping to find more of the sacrificial accomplices, but it still horrifies me to see the results of the scourge sorcerers' greed.

"We'll be taking you somewhere else," I say. "Somewhere safer." Then I hustle down the stairs in search of Casimir, who'll know how to reassure the Order's victims leagues better than I can.

"Cas—" I'm calling out as I reach the bottom of the stairs, and jar to a halt at the sight of Stavros, Alek, and a couple of the royal soldiers leaning over a table on the other side of a nearby doorway.

Alek's face looks grimmer than I've ever seen it. Stavros's jaw is clenched tight.

I march over to join them. "What did you find?"

Alek taps the papers scattered across the table. "I think these are some of the Order of the Wild's plans for their kingship trials. They've been testing out different strategies… If they go through with something like this, Petra won't stand a chance. They're setting everything up as a trap."

A chill races through me. "Then she'll refuse to compete."

"And Lothar will say that proves she isn't worthy." Stavros lifts his head. "He must intend to move forward with them soon if they've gotten this far with their plans. We're going to need far more allies than we've already pulled together—and quickly. If we don't present our own version of the trials soon, the scourge sorcerers will steal the chance right out from under us."

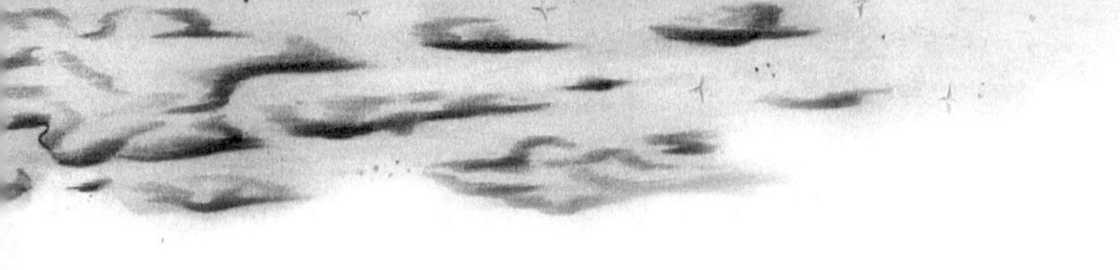

THIRTY

Stavros

Every hoofbeat of the horse next to mine sends more tension coiling around my innards. I glance over at my foremost companion on our journey. "You didn't need to join me for this expedition, Your Highness."

Petra lifts her chin with the stoic determination I'm becoming used to in our future queen. "I know you and Ivy want to keep me out of danger, but I can't hang so far back that I'm shying from my duties. We're going to be asking a lot of Provinca Yessaine and her household. She should know I'm taking my fair share of risks as well. The request will mean more coming directly from me."

I'm sure that's true, but every instinct of my military training tells me that the meeting we hope to initiate could easily turn into an ambush. I trust Provinca Yessaine's loyalties enough to be riding out to one of her homes with a small entourage of associates, but not so much I want to stake the security of the royal family on it.

As if she's read my mind, Petra shoots me a pointed look.

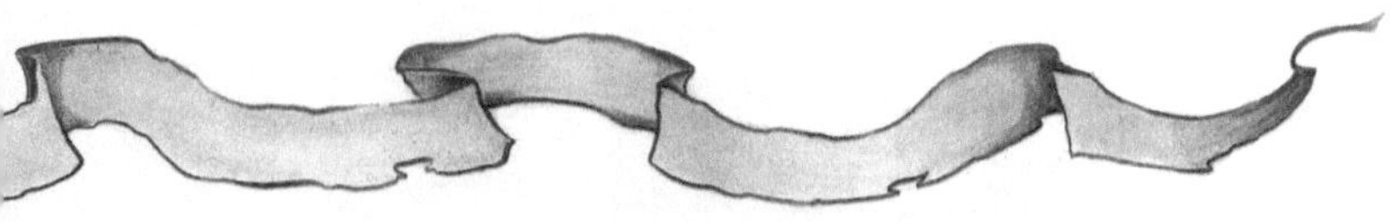

Her tone is dry with amusement. "If something happens to me, you still have two other Melchioreks currently safe under Baron Cyris's roof to take the throne."

I grimace at her. It's obvious why she and Ivy get along so well. They're both damned stubborn and far too good at arguing their case even when I want to refuse them.

"I'll endeavor to ensure that's not a concern," I say, smoothing my frustration from my voice. "But please don't stray from your guards."

If I were coming on my own, I'd have brought only one or two comrades with me to assist the provinca and her staff if they agree to set our plan in motion. Because we have a Melchiorek among us, I insisted on four soldiers on top of that, and even that number feels insufficient.

Petra's mouth slants as if she's going to reject that suggestion as well. "I suppose I should be grateful for the freedoms I had in those years when no one knew I was anything other than a distant relative of the queen's."

I study her as I formulate my answer. How can I know what goes on in the head of a woman who's lost her parents and found herself thrust into the highest leadership role so suddenly and violently?

Especially when she's talking to a man who should have been there to protect her father but wasn't.

But I did know her father. I might not have agreed with every decision King Konram made, but I can imagine the lessons he passed on to all his children while he could.

I adjust my grip on the reins. "There are different freedoms that will replace those you lost, once we see you back where you belong. You can't protect your people as you're meant to unless we protect *you* in turn. But you'll wield more power than most of your subjects could conceive of."

A faint smile flickers across her face. "Of course you're

right. I apologize. I didn't mean to complain when I've had so much handed to me by virtue of my birth."

"Both boons and responsibilities. The latter can be heavy to carry. We all have our own burdens to shoulder if we strive to serve well—and I know you mean to."

"Yes." The word comes out of her like a sigh. "I hope Provinca Yessaine can recognize that too. And if we can prepare these trials in time, I can prove to all my people that I deserve the trust I'm asking them to put in me."

"It isn't only birth regardless, you know," I remark. "It's experience and training. You've seen the inner workings of a kingdom as no one except your siblings has. You understand what it takes to rule. I can't say even I would feel prepared to take on a role that immense."

A teasing lilt returns to her voice. "Not even the great General Stavros? I don't imagine you'd do a terrible job as monarch."

I glance away, taking in the landscape and the buildings of the city we're approaching for the fleeting moment before they blur in front of me. "I wasn't hale enough to continue as a general. King is another order altogether. I failed to protect the king I'd sworn to defend from the worst threats he faced. I'll be happy if I can simply ensure that you're restored to the throne."

Petra lapses into a momentary silence. She glances at me sideways, her expression gone solemn. "You didn't fail my father, Stavros. Surely you don't think that."

I lift my shoulders in a slight shrug, tamping down the swell of guilt inside me. "I did everything I could to save him, but it wasn't enough."

"Because he didn't let you. He pushed you away. If there were any failures in that equation, *he* failed *you*. Even this conversation proves why he should have trusted your judgment more." She shakes her head. "I think you see perfectly well in the ways that matter most. I appreciate your guidance, even if I don't follow every caution."

I don't know if I can fully agree with her, but the words spoken in her steady voice take the sharpest edge off my regrets.

We veer onto the lane that leads to the sprawling estate just beyond the city walls, where Provinca Yessaine enforces her authority over Aberni province.

I'm reasonably sure of the provinca's loyalty because I collaborated with her local military efforts more than once, whenever they needed to push back incursions from the Darium empire across the Seafell Channel. Our association also means I know about the hidden back entrance in the estate wall where her family accepts visitors they don't want to draw attention to.

After a short trot longer, we turn off the road, give the main entrance a wide berth, and circle around the back. When we've drawn close to the section of mortared stone I was aiming for, I motion for the rest of our company to stand their ground, dismount, and walk the last several paces on foot.

I press my hand to the keystone and then rap out a pattern only a few recent generals will have been given. I suspect Provinca Yessaine will be able to guess which one is calling on her.

Luck willing, she's heard enough about the Order of the Wild to realize that I'm fighting for our country as always, not against it as Lothar would claim.

I have no way of telling exactly how much time passes while we wait. The city bells ring in the late afternoon hour. Finally, footsteps crunch through the brush on the other side of the wall, where the estate's hunting woods lie.

Several sets of footsteps. If the provinca intends to meet us herself, she hasn't come alone.

Then again, I wouldn't have expected her to.

There's nothing wrong with my ears. I listen closely and then raise my hand toward my companions, splaying my fingers twice to indicate that we should expect ten figures in this confrontation.

Just as I'm lowering my arm, the hidden doorway grates open.

Provinca Yessaine peers out at me, her face framed by the raised swords of the guards standing half a step ahead of her on either side. She folds her arms over her lean chest and raises a thin eyebrow at me without a word.

I dip my head to her respectfully and catch a familiar face behind her that I hadn't expected to see here. It appears the provinca has called her daughter back from the royal college.

Further evidence that she's unsettled by the current state of affairs in Silana.

"Provinca Yessaine," I say in acknowledgment. "And Romild—it's good to see you're well."

My former student fixes me with a stare as steely as her mother's. Does she still resent that I chose Ivy as my supposed assistant rather than opening the position more widely? I know she coveted that spot—and made no secret of it with the woman I love.

I would hope we can put any sour feelings from before behind us. But there is a reason Ivy didn't join us on this particular expedition, just in case.

Romild nudges her mother with a brief murmur, and the provinca's gaze slides past me to the riders in the shade of the trees. Her normal unflappable expression twitches.

Romild must have pointed out the face she can recognize from their time as classmates.

Provinca Yessaine drops into a deeper bow than mine. "Your Highness. I didn't realize—if I'd known—"

Petra offers a small smile. "It's perfectly all right."

Relief trickles through my knotted stomach, but not enough for me to let down my guard. "The rightful queen wishes to speak with you. I'm not sure it would be wise for many to see her entering your home. Are you willing to conduct the conversation in a less conventional setting?"

Yessaine lets out a soft chuckle. "That sounds fair enough. We will come out—but I hope you won't take insult if my guards accompany me."

"Absolutely not," Petra says. "We all have reason to be wary in the current climate."

I draw back to stand near Petra while the provinca, Romild, and their eight protectors ease out through the doorway. As we face each other in the lengthening shadows, Petra and our own small squadron of guards descend from their horses.

I'd like to shield my future queen, but I know she won't accept being hidden behind me. So instead I flank her alongside one of the royal soldiers who's been with us since Florian, with the rest of our company in a semicircle around us.

A lightly sweet scent laces the air from the first early spring blooms. Petra draws her posture up commandingly straight and holds Yessaine's gaze.

"You must have heard about the horrors Lothar and his followers are carrying out. I need help to put down this uprising once and for all and end the slaughter that's come with it."

The provinca's mouth tightens. "I don't care for the stories that've been passed on to me or the scenes I've witnessed myself. But this Order of the Wild has spread through every city and town in the country, it seems. Two of my counts tried to stand against them when they first swept through the province, and their entire families were slaughtered." She touches Romild's shoulder. "I'm not throwing away our lives on a principle."

I clear my throat. "That's why we came to you discreetly, Provinca. We have no interest in putting you in danger."

"I assume you want me to offer my military forces to fight these scourge sorcerers. I'm afraid many of the soldiers stationed here have deserted."

Petra speaks up again, clear and calm. "Your strength would be valued if it comes to a battle of force, but I came here today seeking a subtler sort of assistance. I don't believe we can defeat the chaos Lothar has stirred up unless the people are convinced that I truly am a better choice to offer peace and security."

Up goes the eyebrow again. "And how do you expect to do that?"

"The Order of the Wild has spoken of the old kingship trials," Petra says smoothly. "We will hold our own trials to show I'm prepared to prove myself. But we need to move swiftly so we can ensure they happen fairly and not through the scourge sorcerers' twisted means. Aberni is renowned not just for defending our country from invasion but also the speed with which you've alerted the rest of the country about impending threats."

One of our other companions steps forward, holding a thick bundle of paper. "We've printed pamphlets to be passed around in every town and city your best messengers and their connections can reach."

I nod. "Your people know the fastest and most surreptitious routes, as well as who will pass on the word farther. They won't need to linger anywhere long enough for the Order to confront them."

Yessaine shifts on her feet, still looking uncertain. "If even one of them is caught and Lothar traces them back to my family…"

"I will protect you in every way I can," Petra says. "But I expect by then he'll be too concerned with addressing the impending trials to waste manpower trying to destroy a province with such a formidable reputation."

"Are you sure these trials are even worth the risk to *you*?" the provinca asks. "With the rumors flying around, public opinion has been turning against the Order. The unrest might reach the point of an opposing rebellion in time."

Petra grimaces. "We don't have time. Lothar is already preparing for his next move against me, and if we don't beat him to the punch, he could shatter any trust I've gained. I need the people to see how far I'm willing to go to earn their loyalty."

Yessaine drops her gaze. Like the baron and his friends, I'd imagine she finds the idea of a Melchiorek agreeing to compete in some sort of trial distasteful, which can't help our appeal.

With a twitch of my eyes, I focus on her and prod my gift. A prickle quivers through my nerves. If I can get some glimpse of how she'll react, prove that *I* can still anticipate the country's needs as I once did—

The vision that flashes before my eyes isn't of the provinca's response. I catch a movement from the corner of my eye—the man two over from her left springing forward with an abruptly drawn blade he stabs into Petra's heart.

My body stiffens. With another tick of my gaze, my vision reforms into the actual tableau in front of me.

Our groups are still facing each other in our discussion. No one has made a hostile move.

But that guard is planning to. His jaw has tensed, his hand resting on the hilt of his dagger in its sheath.

My first instinct is to leap forward and slam him to the ground before he can think for another second about hurting the future queen. Only my two dozen years of training back to when I could first hold a sword hold me in place.

I didn't become the lauded General Stavros through brute force. I was known for strategy above all else.

The common people aren't the only ones who'll be swayed by visible proof. If Provinca Yessaine is going to believe that the current danger is urgent enough to warrant the favor we're asking of her, she needs to see the severity of the threat play out with her own eyes, not simply hear a claim I make.

I have to protect Petra not just against the most immediate threat, but against everything that could go wrong spiraling out from this meeting.

My fingers itch for my sword. If I draw it, I might frighten the traitor into thinking better of his scheme—for now. He could simply bide his time for later, when I'm not close enough to act.

My glimpses of the future are never more than a minute or two ahead of the event. All I have to do is hold myself braced and ready—

I've missed a couple of exchanges between Petra and the provinca, but my attention doesn't fail me. My eyes catch the instant the guard adjusts his stance to lunge forward.

He springs at Petra with a hoarse cry and a hiss of his blade from its sheath—and I hurtle between them at the same moment.

The dagger clangs off my metal prosthetic. I slam my knee into the man's belly and wrench his wrist behind his back as I shove him to the ground.

Sweat cools the back of my neck. My heart hammers as the iron flavor of panic laces my mouth.

There's no need for fear. I intervened in time.

My monarch trusted me, and I didn't fail her. I played this game of swords as well as I ever have.

But even with the relief of that knowledge sweeping through me, I need to play politics too.

Yessaine cried out in the moment. When I lift my head to meet her eyes, she's staring at her guard, white-faced with horror.

"Baldric," she mumbles. "He's been in our service for nearly a decade. He's never spoken—never acted—"

I firm my voice to its most authoritative tone. The voice that commanded armies of thousands against our greatest foes. "Scourge sorcery is like a sickness. They've infected more people than we can guess with their toxic claims and ideals. Lothar and his followers must be stamped out *now*, before they spread their poison even farther."

Petra speaks up after my last words. "And we will conquer them as Stavros did this traitor in your midst—if those who have the means to stand with us will do so."

Yessaine shakes herself. "I…"

Romild touches her arm. For a brief moment, I'm worried she'll pull her mother back into hesitation.

But there's a reason I would have seriously considered the provinca-to-be as a potential assistant if Ivy hadn't claimed that position by necessity.

My former pupil squares her shoulders. "Mother, we *have* to. They're barely asking anything at all. We should do more. You didn't raise me to cower when there's work to be done."

The provinca exhales sharply and matches her daughter's stance. "Indeed, I didn't. Queen Petra, you'll have your messengers—and all the soldiers I can offer, when you need them too. Let's take back our country."

THIRTY-ONE

Ivy

I lean my hands against the tabletop as if I can push more information out of the polished wood. "What about the other scourge sorcerers you met in Florian? What talents did you hear of that they could wield?"

Filip rubs his hand across his mouth, knitting his brow as he thinks. His shoulders have slumped during our conversation as he's admitted how little the higher-ups in the Order of the Wild let him in on their larger plans.

"I know there was one who had some kind of gift for heat," he says. "She could use it to burn people to encourage them into compliance or destroy things the others didn't want seen. At least a few had gifts for stirring emotions—trust or fear... There was a man recruited at the same time I was who could run twice as fast as anyone should be able to for short distances."

At the other end of the table, Alek nods. His quill scrawls across the notebook where he's recording everything the defector can tell us about the Order's plans and abilities.

He writes the last word and glances up. "I suppose just about any gift could be useful to the Order's aims in one way or another."

Filip offers a miserable grimace. "They wanted to bring in as many people as they could. People with gifts who could expand them with the scourge sorcery, people who didn't have gifts just to spread the word and silence anyone who argued…"

He looks down at his hands. "I was so stupid to get caught up in their talk to begin with. I wasn't brave enough to give more than a few toes for the small gift I got, and somehow I thought I deserved to make it more?"

I don't know how to answer his self-recrimination when the fact that so many people have gotten swept up in Lothar's treacherous conspiracy frustrates me beyond end. The best I can offer is a brief shrug. "Maybe that small gift will make some difference against them now."

It seems unlikely. Growing crops a little faster isn't going to win over those who are already caught up in the Order's propaganda.

Even his former colleagues couldn't find much use for him if they sent him off on this potentially suicidal spy mission.

It'll be a perfectly good talent when we have peace, though.

I lean back in my chair, sorting through the questions I meant to ask. "Their precautions beyond the city walls—how much are they monitoring the area around Florian? How far out?"

Filip wets his lips. "It may be more now that you've disrupted their influence. But when I was there, the Order was focusing most of their efforts on keeping control over people *in* the city and securing the walls themselves. They didn't care much about the farmlands nearby."

Alek lets out a rough chuckle. "Very efficient of them. Reserve their efforts for where the population is most concentrated."

I exhale in a sigh. "Well, if they've kept up that approach, it'll at least be a little easier for—"

A voice cuts through my statement, bellowing through the halls of the country residence. "Baron Cyris! General Stavros!"

The urgency in the yell has me shoving back the chair with a rasp and springing to my feet. Alek and I exchange a fleeting glance before we both hustle to the front hall to find out what the ruckus is about.

I jerk to a halt on the threshold of the foyer. Three of the baron's guards stand in a tense ring around a slumped man who's bound tight with rope and dripping blood from his forehead. The slackness of his pose against the floor suggests he's unconscious if not dead, possibly from the blow to the head.

Alek and I aren't the only ones who've been drawn by the clamor. Casimir and Rheave both appear within moments of our arrival, along with a few of the rebels from Pima, a couple of the estate's staff, and all three of the royal heirs.

At the sight of the future queen, the guard who appears to be in charge holds up his hand to ward Petra back. "Don't come closer, Your Highness! We don't know what he might be capable of."

Petra reaches out to hold Princess Klaudia and Prince Jacos with her, but even as her jaw tightens, she arches an eyebrow. "He doesn't look as if he's capable of doing much harm at the moment. Who is he?"

Before they can answer, Stavros strides into the hall. The title may no longer be fully accurate, but the massive man still looks every inch a general.

Baron Cyris hurries in close behind him. "What's the meaning of this commotion?"

The lead guard dips his head to his employer. "Sir, we found this man sneaking around near the estate. He attempted to run when he realized he'd been spotted, but we were able to subdue him. I think he's a spy for the Order of the Wild. I expected you'd want to—"

Rheave breaks in with a sudden step forward. "He's a daimon."

Everyone in the room goes still and silent as they absorb that declaration. Then my daimon-man takes another step toward the bound captive, and two of the guards jerk up their swords.

Rheave blinks at them with obvious confusion. "*I* wouldn't harm you."

The lead guard seems to prefer to ignore him when he isn't approaching, looking instead at the baron. "The spy isn't even human, then. One of their animated slaves. He won't tell us anything. We should end him now before he comes to and has a chance to blast us with that magic of theirs."

I'm not sure which part of the scene jolts the hasty words from my throat. Maybe it's the sorrow that flashes across Rheave's sweet face or the helpless sprawl of the captured daimon, or maybe the hint of a sneer in the guard's dismissive words.

Whatever the case, I find myself pushing forward to stand by my inhuman lover. "No! Not like that."

The guard's expression turns incredulous—with a flicker of fear he manages to master quickly. "You're not the one who gives my orders."

"Her judgment is worth listening to all the same," Stavros says firmly. He folds his arms over his chest. "What are you thinking, Ivy?"

I glance at Rheave and then at the rest of the spectators.

My gaze catches on the faces of the royal children: Klaudia's, pale but determined; Jacos's, wide-eyed with obvious anxiety.

They've accepted the one daimon among us as an ally because it's hard to speak to Rheave and not see him as a sort of person. But all the other daimon the scourge sorcerers have captured have blended into a nameless mass simply labeled "the enemy."

None of the spirit creatures ever wanted to hurt us. Don't we owe each of them a chance to be something else when we can offer it?

Isn't that the kind of compassion I want our future rulers to see is possible?

I don't know if that explanation will win me any ground with the baron, so I consider the practicalities. "Even if the sorcery compelling this daimon means he can't tell us anything on purpose, we might be able to get him to reveal a little bit involuntarily. It'd be incredibly useful to know why he was lurking in this area—how much the Order already suspects. Whether there are others roaming around here."

The baron's mouth sets in a hard line. "Is it worth the risk of the damage he could do when he wakes up? I wouldn't want you to need to strain yourself defending us."

The edge in his voice makes my hackles rise. Before I can respond, Rheave interjects.

"I can stop him," he says quietly. "Our powers will deflect each other. And as long as he's tied up like that, it'll be easy to keep him under control."

Petra lifts her chin imperiously. "Then please do that, and we should hear if the daimon will say anything to us. He's as much a victim of the scourge sorcerers as those they've maimed and murdered."

She flicks her fingers down her front in a gesture of the divinities, as if asking for the godlen to bless the upcoming conversation. My eyes meet hers, and she dips her head slightly in acknowledgment.

She understands my concerns without my needing to say the rest.

Gods help us, we do need a ruler like her on the throne. Someone who'll listen before taking action.

Someone who cares for all her country's inhabitants, no matter how unusual.

The baron isn't about to argue with his future queen. He clears his throat. "Take him to one of the holding rooms, and let us know when—"

Before he finishes his order, the captured daimon twitches. A faint groan spills from the man's lips.

Rheave rushes closer and kneels a couple of paces away from the captive, braced in case the sculpted man attempts to use his magic. The guards each take a wary step backward but keep their swords pointed at the bound form.

The captive's eyelids flutter. He rolls onto his side and stares blearily at the assembled crowd.

Petra nudges her siblings a little farther behind her, but to my relief, she doesn't insist they leave. She must know she can't protect them from every danger of ruling—she wants them to see the hard decisions that might need to be made.

Rheave speaks first, in a low but steady voice. "Friend, I'm sorry for how you've been treated. We know you're being pushed by magic, but your masters have used other daimon to hurt us before. Will you speak with us?"

The captured daimon only manages a grunt.

Rheave leans closer. "I was once caged by the sorcerers too. I shook off their hold. If you try, you might be able to as well."

The man's face tips toward the floor. For a moment, there's only his ragged breath. Then he mumbles, "So long… So much power."

The lead guard huffs. "Like the rest of them. They've got this one completely under their thrall too."

He raises his sword, but the daimon's words have snagged inside me with a tug of my gut.

I shake my head. "I don't know... The others we've talked to wouldn't say anything at all—or couldn't. He's trying."

Petra's tone gentles. "Ivy, freeing the daimon from that body may be the greatest kindness we can offer."

I know she's right, but something about this one's behavior doesn't feel quite like the captured spirits we've encountered in the past.

I walk closer so the slumped man can see me beyond Rheave. "The scourge sorcerers who made your body do have a lot of power—but we've been breaking it down. They have less than they did before. It's worth fighting their control again, even if you couldn't in the past."

"Yes," Rheave says. "We'll help you. We *want* to be your friends, if you can pull away from the sorcerers."

He sounds so hopeful that an ache forms around my heart. Should I have pushed this hard if the moment is probably only going to end in more disappointment for him? I know how much it's bothered him that none of his fellow daimon have been able to make their new physical lives their own.

The captive's jaw looks as if it's clamped tight. He shivers in his bonds—testing them or simply showing his discomfort?

Rheave tries again, the usual brightness in his voice dwindling. "If there's anything at all you can manage to tell us about why you came here, what your masters know and want to find out..."

"I can't," the man mutters. "I can't. I—"

All at once, he twists at the torso, straining against the

ropes. The guards cry out in warning. But as the man's head yanks backward, an unearthly glow flares in his eyes that looks more desperate than fierce.

His voice spills out of him. "They told me to wander this county searching for signs of other daimon. And to find where those were, who they were. They know there's one they can't control staying with the queen."

His gaze settles on Rheave, and a sudden smile curves his lips. "I found you. I found you, but they won't, because I won't tell them. We won't let them bring me back. Right?"

Rheave beams at him so brilliantly he takes my breath away. "We won't. We can stand up to the vicious ones together, all of us."

A rush of my own hope smacks me in the chest.

I whirl toward Petra. "This is the first daimon who's snapped out of their control. It's been weeks since I killed the sorcerer who was doing some of the compelling—we've taken more than a dozen of their sacrificial accomplices away since then. The compulsion the Order imposed on the daimon *must* be weakening."

Petra studies me with more reserve. "Where are you going with this, Ivy?"

I fling my hand vaguely toward the world beyond the estate's walls. "If we can bring the rest of the captured daimon over to our side, we'll have stolen one of the Order's biggest advantages. All we have to do is get to them."

THIRTY-TWO

As the wagon jostles over the pits in the road, I keep my shoulder leaned against Ivy's. While the charms we wear mostly conceal us from sight when we're not touching, I can still sense her beside me, but I prefer to be able to see her clearly too.

Maybe it's the same for her. She tucks her hand around mine and tips her head closer when we sway with the movement of the wagon. From the blurred form I can make out at her other side, I think she must be holding on to Casimir as well.

It's good that she has both of us. We won't let any harm befall her on this precarious mission we've set out on.

The memory of how we ended up here brings a swell of deeper affection into my chest. I twine my fingers more tightly with hers.

If the baron's people had their way, my fellow daimon would have been severed from the body the sorcerers forced

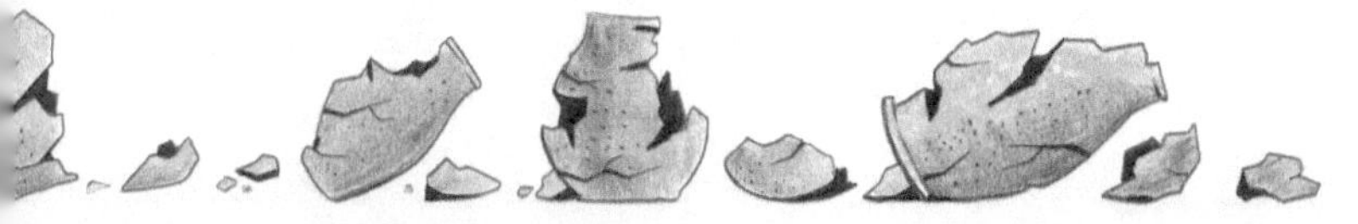

him into. He may still choose to leave it—but now it will be his choice and not anyone else's.

I spent much of this morning informing him of many of the delights I've discovered that our more physical forms allow. He was especially fond of the sounds he could form with the lute in the baron's music room.

Now, if our mission is successful, dozens more captured daimon might find their freedom without needing to give up all those new opportunities. They can make the bodies that started as our prisons their own like I have.

They can help us stand up to the scourge sorcerers and create these trials in time to stop Lothar's plans.

As long as we're not caught before we can even get started.

The wagon slows, I assume because we're approaching the city gate. Wheels rattle and hooves stomp ahead of us and behind. We hold perfectly still in the cramped covered space where we're huddled among sacks of grain and crates of nuts supposedly for sale at the markets.

The woman driving the cart is a stablewoman who normally works under one of the noble allies we've gained. There's no reason for any scourge sorcerers to see her as a threat. But we'll still be in trouble if they realize what she's concealing.

Somewhere off around the far side of the city, a few other allies will be setting off a magical disturbance. If all goes well, that should draw the attention of any sorcerers who are monitoring supernatural activity in the city—draw it away from checking the new arrivals all that closely.

The wagon rolls forward and stops, forward and stops. We chose a time of day that Ivy said isn't often busy, but there must still be a bit of a line.

Finally, footsteps thump around the side of the wagon. A

couple of bulky men lift the canvas flaps at the back and peer into the dim space.

They can't see us thanks to our charms, and the sacks and crates are small enough that they couldn't suspect any human is hiding inside them. Their eyes sweep over the interior for several long seconds during which Ivy's grip tightens on my hand.

Then they step away with a satisfied nod. "Continue."

The wagon jerks forward and continues rattling along for many minutes with slight hitches to one side or another as we take a turn. Ivy gives my hand one more squeeze and lets go.

Her form turns wavery, but I know what she's doing because a moment later, the lid lifts off one of the crates she's moved to. She's retrieving the other cargo we hid.

Carefully, she pulls out the cube of fine netting. A few dozen small butterflies cling to the sides with faint flutters of their wings.

I smile at them, though the insects can't see me. I called them into this temporary home, making an appeal to Inganne and pleading for her help. The steady current of the winged insects that trickled to us through the air made my heart leap—almost as much as the startled joy it sparked in Ivy's eyes.

The wagon's wheels grind to a halt. We must have reached our chosen stopping point.

Casimir touches my shoulder lightly so I can see him properly for a moment. "Safe travels," he murmurs, and then stoops to tug one of the lower sacks out of the pile.

That one is full of printed pamphlets that he's going to bring to the Black Talons. We're hoping that the gang members will stick to their promise to help by both distributing information about the upcoming kingship trials and taking in any daimon we can snap out of the scourge sorcerers' spell.

The canvas flap sways with his departure. The mesh cage of butterflies has disappeared into the circle of Ivy's arms, but it comes back into view along with her form when she bumps her shoulder against mine. "We'd better get going."

I follow Casimir's example, nudging the flap aside, confirming no one is in view of the small space next to a wall where our driver backed up the wagon, and slipping out as quickly as possible. I know from our planning conversations that we're in the middle wards, not too close to the prominent center of the city but near enough that there should be a fair number of Order members watching over the inhabitants.

When I emerge, the many voices carrying from around the square reach my ears more distinctly. I make out sellers hawking food, clothes, and other goods for sale and passers-by chatting about their shopping or how their day is going.

Amid it all, my mind prickles with the vague awareness of other beings who share my unique energy. I get the impression there are a few close by and several farther out but still within decently easy reach.

The scourge sorcerers like to use their captured daimon to enforce their rule over the city. Expendable lives. They can make them handle any outbursts of violence rather than subjecting themselves or their less easily controlled human allies to it.

The knowledge gnaws at me as I survey the square. A medley of smells both intriguing and unsettling trickles into my lungs. Music wafts from an eatery farther down the square with an upbeat melody that would have made me bob with it if we didn't have such a serious task ahead of us.

Ivy curls her fingers into the back of my tunic so she can

keep track of me. I ease away from the wagon and meld with the crowd, sticking to the small open spaces between the other pedestrians as well as I can.

No one can see me, but they can still bump into me.

It only takes a few steps before my sense of a nearby kindred spirit heightens. I turn my head and spot the figure it's coming from some ten paces away.

A broad-shouldered woman in the Order's now-standard red uniform surveys the crowd as she prowls through it.

I stop and reach toward the mesh cage. Ivy loosens the panel on the top for me.

When I dip my hand in, making the gesture of the divinities at the same time with a hasty prayer to Inganne, one of the fragile insects settles on my forefinger.

I draw the butterfly out and point it toward the daimon I've spotted. Lowering my head, I speak in a murmur. "Go to the other one with a spirit like ours. Remind her that there's more to this world than what the sorcerers say."

Does the butterfly understand any of that? I have no idea. But we believe that the godlen of play and creativity has a particular affinity for mischievous spirits like mine, and butterflies are one of her symbolic animals. An injured one that was drawn to me helped bring Ivy into my life.

It's our test to judge whether my counterparts might be ready to shake off their magical bonds as well.

As the insect swoops through the air, Ivy and I trail along behind it. We need to be close enough to judge our target's reaction.

The butterfly flits back and forth before plummeting to perch on the woman's shoulder. She twitches and glances over at it. Her expression shifts from startled to puzzled.

I pause, braced for my cue to move. How will she respond?

After a few seconds marked by the thudding of my heart,

she reaches toward the butterfly with her other hand and offers her fingers for it to hop onto. As she takes in the delicate bobbing of its wings, her eyes widen with a hint of awe.

I exchange a glance with Ivy, and she nods with a hopeful smile.

Ducking down beneath the eye level of the crowd, I hastily remove my charm. I straighten up, abruptly visible, and amble the last short distance to my target.

The woman's gaze jerks from the insect to me. I can tell she recognizes me as our kind just as well as I can her. A crease forms in her brow.

Before she says anything, I offer the friendliest smile I can and nod toward the butterfly. "They're wonderful, aren't they? Inganne is sharing a blessing of delight with us."

The woman seems to struggle to catch her breath. "I—I have a job to do—"

I touch her arm, lightly but steadily. "A job they forced you into. But their control is fading. You can shake it off. Make this life your own. I have. There are so many other wonderful parts of the world you can embrace now."

I wish I could shatter the magic that's acted on her the way I have the scourge sorcerers' wards. Their spell of compulsion is so much more delicate, woven into the spirits themselves, I'm not sure how I could pick it.

The woman's body goes rigid, a shaky exhalation spilling out of her. A tremor runs through her sturdy frame.

The corners of her lips twitch with a smile of her own. "Yes. *Yes*, I can."

"Hold on to that freedom," I urge her. "We have more friends who can help. Wait outside the Newt's Goblets Pub in Tangleside at sunset, and the ones who made these bodies will never use you like a puppet again."

She shivers again, but her smile grows.

"Thank you," she mumbles eagerly, and steps away toward the edge of her square. There's a new bounce of joy to her step.

With a pleased thrill ticking through my chest, I turn to scan the square for another of my kin.

Ivy sticks close to me without removing her charm, keeping both herself and our insect cargo hidden. We send butterflies frolicking toward four more daimon-in-human-form who have similar reactions to the first—confusion, interest, and a brief struggle to test the magical influence they hadn't realized was fraying.

I haven't felt the scourge sorcerers calling for me since Ivy's kidnapping. It seems likely that the one she killed to save herself was the same one who tried to steal me back more than once.

With each of my counterparts we send to what should be a meeting with our Black Talons associates, my own sense of freedom expands. The ground might as well be softening beneath my feet, leaving me floating as much as walking.

It still amazes me how many physical sensations have nothing to do with the concrete world at all. The way emotions shape these bodies of matter into something more than flesh.

A man marches into the square out of a side-street. He doesn't have an official uniform on, but my senses give another twinge.

I hold out my hand to Ivy, and she passes me another butterfly.

After my murmured instructions, it weaves through the air toward the man. It circles over his head once and descends to cling to the cuff of his sleeve.

The man stares down at it with a tighter expression than any of the other daimon we've approached. Before my pulse can do more than stutter once, he gives a sharp yell of alarm. His head jerks around, searching the crowd for the source of the intrusion.

My heart outright lurches—and then Ivy is shoving the mesh cage into my hands while yanking off her own charm.

She grips my forearm. "I'll divert him like we planned. Get back to the wagon and go to the next square."

With that, she's off and running, pushing through the crowd much more clumsily than I know she's capable of.

Because she wants the guard to notice her. She wants him to notice her *before* he notices me.

In that first instant as I see him spin toward the disturbance, a flood of panic rushes through me. A cry of my own jolts to the back of my throat.

We did talk about this strategy. Ivy's better at sneaking away from people—I'm the one the willing daimon are most likely to trust. It makes sense.

But if that guard or the other Order members catch her —if Lothar gets his hands on her again—

I could yell. I could bring the guard's attention back to me, and she wouldn't have to put herself in that danger.

I wouldn't have to risk losing her. Only myself.

My pulse is pounding frantically, but somehow that hasty rhythm is what grounds me. It reminds me of the way my heart skipped the first time Ivy kissed me, the first time our bodies melded together. The first time she told me she loved me, not that long ago.

I love her too. I love her. I love her.

That's all the frenetic beat is telling me. Not that I'm doing something wrong or that she won't escape this danger.

I want her to come back. I want her to be okay.

It will hurt so much if she doesn't.

But she'll be hurt if I break from the plan. If I act as if

she can't look after herself and ruin everything we've been fighting for out of my fear of pain.

And how good will it feel when she comes back to me, grinning at her success and wanting to hear of mine?

A girl near me is gaping at the mesh cube I'm clutching. I shake myself out of my frozen daze and hustle back to the wagon.

As I go, I grab my charm from my pocket. I duck behind the vehicle, slip the chain back over my neck to vanish, and dive inside.

"It's time to go to Finnacle Square," I call to the driver. "Ivy will meet us there."

She will. I know she will. She always makes it back.

That fact doesn't stop me from fidgeting as the wagon rocks its way to the second square we picked out about a half a mile across the sprawling city from the first. When the wheels halt, I hesitate and force myself to inhale deeply, settling my nerves.

I have my own work to do here. A real partner would focus on that, not on worrying about the part that's not his.

Easing out of the wagon, I spot the first daimon right away. There's a slim, sinewy man in an Order uniform patrolling around the edge of the square.

Since I'm on my own, I have to leave the butterfly cage in the wagon. I bring just one of its residents with me and send the insect flying off toward my counterpart.

It lands near the man's elbow. I brace myself for him to flinch like the last daimon did, but instead he simply peers at it. The glimmer of intrigue I've seen before lights in his eyes.

With a smile crossing my lips, I move across the square to reach out to him with my words as well.

I've just told a third compatriot in the square about the meeting place and watched her lope off with a breathless giggle when a soft pressure brushes my arm. I turn toward it, and Ivy's scent wisps over me, sharp but sweet.

"You've been keeping busy," she says in a low voice, her form swimming into sight in front of me. "We're really doing this."

Then she bobs up to kiss me, quick but so tender a flush warms my cheeks.

We are succeeding. We worked together and did what we're both best at, and Ivy ensured we could keep going.

We're bringing my people home.

I close my hand around her invisible one as I head back to the wagon to collect another butterfly. In the shadows behind the vehicle, I slip my own charm back on just for a few moments so we can embrace in our pocket of invisibility together—so I can revel in having her back despite my panic.

Ivy tucks her head against my neck. "Were you all right on your own?"

Her hand rests on my chest over my heart, and I feel the truth of the words before I say them. "I wasn't really alone. You're always with me, in here."

I set my hand over hers, and she beams at me before rising to claim another kiss.

We finish our rounds in the second square and move on to another and then another. By the time the shadows start stretching long, I've helped more than thirty daimon shed the last lingering influence of scourge sorcery.

A few others have balked—swatting at the butterflies or pushing forward to search for the source with obvious hostility—but none quite as aggressively as our first failure. When it happens, we simply vanish and move on to another part of the city.

I'm starting to get a sense of who is under more tenuous hold and who is caught in a firmer grasp before we even test them, just from the vibration in the energy I pick up on. I'm studying yet another possibility, debating whether she's worth risking a butterfly on, when an amplified voice rings through our current square.

"The regent Lothar calls Florian's citizens to the Temple of the Crown! He has news that could mean life or death for all of you."

THIRTY-THREE

Ivy

Rheave tucks his arm around my waist in the wagon, pulling me even closer than he did earlier on this journey. "Do you think Lothar knows what we've been doing?"

I can't help pricking my ears to the warble of city noise beyond the vehicle, as if I might hear something to inform my answer. I get nothing but a blur of rattling wheels and jumbled voices.

I swallow thickly. "I don't know. We have been at it for a few hours now. His people could have already noticed that a bunch of their captured daimon have left rather than following orders. But with the sorcery on them waning, that could have happened eventually without us interfering."

The daimon-man makes a rough sound. Everywhere our bodies touch, his muscles are tensed. "Should we leave instead? While so many people are distracted by the announcement?"

I've already thought that question through more than

once since we made our first hasty decision to have our driver direct the wagon toward the inner wards. The answer comes automatically now. "No. If it's a matter of life or death… we need to know what's going on. *Especially* if it has anything to do with Petra or our efforts to see her on the throne."

Rheave nods, accepting my statement without argument. For just a second, I wish he would push back, insist that we get out of here, even though I'd have to stand firm.

I'm not sure I really *want* to. Something about the messenger's call in the square has left a clammy sensation seeping into my skin.

But what I said is true. If Lothar is about to unleash some new horror, we have to know as soon as possible so we can protect ourselves. Even if the Black Talons have people listening in, we don't know how long it'd take them to get a message to us.

The Order's leader could be counting on us thinking that way, though. He *could* suspect that members of the resistance have infiltrated the city and want them to find out just how awful things could get for them next.

With that possibility in mind, I have the driver stop a couple of streets shy of the old city walls that border the inner wards. Rheave and I remove our charms, keeping them in our pockets where they'll stay inactive.

We don't want there to be any chance of the scourge sorcerers seeking out their magic.

I smear some grit from the side of the wagon across my face as if I've been doing grunt work in the outer wards all day without a bath. Rheave follows suit. Then we pull on our cloaks, tugging the hoods low over our heads.

Spring is creeping closer, but enough winter crispness lingers in the air that plenty of other civilians are wearing their own cloaks. Once we emerge from the wagon and merge with the current of figures flowing through the streets to the Temple of the Crown, we blend in perfectly.

I spent twenty years of my life in this city and seven of those making the streets my home, but somehow the territory I've roamed through more than a hundred times feels like foreign territory today. I know the twists and turns of the roads, the steep slope that takes us the last short distance to the huge courtyard outside the grand temple, and yet nothing looks quite as familiar as it should.

Maybe it's the murmurs passing through the growing crowd around us—not eager with anticipation the way they might have been for past events at the city center, but hushed and uncertain. My fellow citizens can't have any more idea what their self-proclaimed ruler has in store for them than I do.

We've been sowing doubt and fear throughout the country as well as we can. I'm sure plenty of Florians have heard the claims against the Order. Some who first supported them will now wish them gone along with their horrific sorcery.

But how many have the means to stand up to the scourge sorcerers? How many would be prepared to risk their lives speaking out when even the queen has only done so through stealth?

They're waiting for us—waiting for someone with real power to stand with.

My lungs tighten with the thought.

We're working on it, I want to tell them. *We're coming to rescue you from these villains. We just have to make sure we do it right, or we'll be lost too.*

The stream of pedestrians we're caught up in spreads out at the mouth of the courtyard. The vast space is already teeming with bodies pressing close together to make room for more. Other figures peer from the windows and balconies of the stately buildings around the courtyard.

I suspect by the time Lothar begins his announcement, even the side-streets will be packed with spectators. All of them poised to spread the word back to their neighbors who didn't make it in time.

I grasp Rheave's hand and lead him through the jostling bodies to one spot that is still familiar. Nothing's changed about my favorite alcove where months ago I watched the execution of the last apprehended riven sorcerer.

The daimon-man's height means he doesn't need much of a vantage point to look over the milling crowd. I clamber up to my usual perch so I can peer over his head.

The sun has nearly completely set. The daimon we shook out of their sorcerous bindings will be gathering near Crow's Close for the Black Talons to collect. Casimir hasn't sent any signal through my locket, which should mean his end of the plan has gone smoothly.

He'll be waiting for our wagon to pick him up. I hope he's heard about this announcement and realizes we'll have delayed to learn the news.

To my relief, no corpses dangle from the walls of the temple like they did the last time we visited this place. Dark stains still mar the pale marble where the murdered clerics and devouts once hung, a stark reminder of the penalties for drawing the Order's ire.

As lights start to glow on the balcony where King Konram used to speak to the masses, my magic wriggles in my chest. If Lothar appears directly—if I can set my eyes on him and know exactly where he is—I have a chance to end this now, before he says anything at all.

But when the head scourge sorcerer's looming, lopsided form appears by the stone railing, I'm not surprised to catch a faint flicker at the edges of his body. The former advisor isn't taking any chances. He's projecting himself as an illusion again.

Before he even speaks, the crowd below falls into an ominous silence. Clothing rustles as the spectators shift uneasily on their feet.

"People of Florian," Lothar says, his voice resonating through the courtyard as if it's coming from all sides at once, "I've gathered you tonight to make two important announcements. The first is one we can rejoice. You may have heard rumors that a series of kingship trials will be happening soon. That's true—the ones the Order of the Wild will enact. We'll determine the best ruler of Silana and discover whether the supposed princess will participate in a fair competition or forfeit the crown."

I can almost hear Julita scoffing. *Fair? Fairly rigged, I'd imagine.*

No doubt. But any dark amusement I can take from that thought vanishes with the former advisor's next words.

"You can look forward to witnessing the spectacle of royal worthiness in just four days, when Creadenala is upon us!"

My entire body goes cold. He expects to pull together his trials in just four days? I'd forgotten to even think of the standard festivals, let alone the one for Creaden soon approaching.

Will we be able to pull our own spectacle together in the fleeting time before then? If we can't—

Lothar's voice breaks through my thoughts again, taking on a dire tone. "To my dismay, I must also warn you of a grave threat that's come to my attention. Many other stories have been circulating through rumors and hearsay, but they've been spread by a source far more terrible than any of the supposed villains they point to."

I frown, peering at him as intently as I can. What's he

talking about now? Is he going to say that Petra is some kind of brutal fiend?

I find it hard to believe this will simply be more bluster about how exploitive the royal family was. He must have something specific to say that he thinks will sway public opinion.

What could that be? Petra didn't act in her royal capacity at all until after her father was murdered. I know she hasn't done anything remotely criminal since then.

Lothar continues with a thump as if he's stomped his foot for emphasis. "You've been deceived, but it's understandable in the face of a vicious power like this. All of us in the Order of the Wild put our own lives on the line to bring you the truth."

A deeper prickling of discomfort digs into my chest. Something about the way he's phrasing his remarks—

He waves his hand, and another figure steps forward, her face shadowed by the hood of her cloak. I think she might actually be standing on the platform rather than an illusion herself.

Lothar's mouth forms a tight smile that I suspect is holding back a smirk. "You can hear just how long this poison has been tainting our city from the woman who witnessed it emerge into being. Who has come to us now to warn us."

The woman pulls back her hood, and my heart stops.

It's my mother. Even across that distance, with the stark shadows of the magical glow sharpening the angles of her face, I recognize her in an instant.

My legs wobble under me. I have to press my hands hard against the walls I'm braced between to catch myself before I fall.

My head spins. What— How—?

The woman I once called "Ma" steps forward to rest her

hands on the stone railing. Her face looks pale and taut as she gazes down over the gathered crowd—the expression I can remember from when she'd take the whip to me all those years ago.

The scars on my back itch.

"I had to come forward," she says, her familiar if roughened voice flooding the courtyard through the same magical amplification as Lothar's. "The more I heard about the vigilantes who are attacking the Order of the Wild, the ones the supposed queen is working with, the more I realized what must really be going on. If only I'd seen it sooner…"

Her voice fades with a rasp. I can barely breathe. Then she squares her shoulders and goes on.

"Thirteen years ago, my beloved younger daughter died suddenly under unexplained circumstances. My husband and I never had any proof, but I couldn't shake the feeling that something was strange about our older daughter. That she might be hiding dark intentions of the kind a mother would never want to imagine."

My fingers curl against the walls holding me up as anguish twists my gut.

She didn't want to imagine it? But she did, over and over, no matter how much I pleaded.

She beat me and shunned me and left me hungry and loveless, all because of what she suspected but never brought herself to say outright.

Ma raises her voice even louder. "When she turned twelve, right before her dedication ceremony, she ran away rather than accept the gods. I had no idea what happened to her—until I started hearing the stories. A young woman with pale orange hair and blue eyes who seemed practiced at criminal acts. Who could call down unspeakable magic of all sorts with her will alone. It's her, and it's undeniable. My daughter is one of the riven, mad with her power, and she's out to destroy all the rest of us!"

Gasps and mutterings of concern ripple through the crowd. My gut clenches tighter.

Rheave glances up at me with a matching anguish etched on his gorgeous face, his body tensed as if he could literally leap to my defense.

"If I had an arrow, I could quiet her," he says in a low voice. "Strike her down like lightning…"

I could do the same right now with the magic she's condemning, the power writhing between my ribs. A sour taste laces my tongue.

My magic sears all the way from my jaw to my gut, burning to be let out. To strike her down for the awful picture she's painting, the blame she's shirking.

But it's not even a question.

I shake my head. The words scrape their way up my throat. "Nothing she's said is exactly a lie. And we'd only be proving her right."

How much does she really believe that I'm the brutal monster she's claiming, and how much has Lothar coached her on what to say?

I'm not sure it makes any difference.

My mother is still speaking, with a quaver in her voice that makes my teeth grit. "I don't know how anyone who claims to want the best for us could ally with a riven sorcerer. Maybe she has whatever's left of the Melchiorek family under her control. Maybe she's the one who murdered King Konram! But we can't let her or the people she's swayed to join her tear down all the good the Order has done for us."

The murmurs of the crowd are becoming more urgent. Some are waving their fists in the air in apparent anger.

My power roars louder, and I squeeze my eyes shut as I

pull my imagined vine tight around me. At my continued refusal, a slash of magic cuts across my lungs.

I flinch and clamp my mouth shut against a sob. The pain radiates through me for a few thuds of my heart before finally dissipating.

And Lothar isn't even done yet.

He takes over the speech with a coolly forceful tone. "You've heard it from the mouth of the woman who endured the tragedy of having birthed this monster. Our entire country teeters on the edge of disaster as long as this ruthless riven sorcerer runs free. We must find her and execute her before she can do any more harm!"

At the sharp cheer that rings out, I wince. Another tremor runs through my body.

Rheave touches my leg as if to steady me, but I barely feel the warmth of his hand.

Then more light flares beside the temple platform, and an image of a figure that's closer to my looks than I want to admit shimmers into being. An illusion drawn from Lothar's memories and those of his followers who've seen me?

My pulse hiccups, and I drop down from my perch.

Lothar's voice booms through the courtyard again. "This is the woman you must beware. This is the riven who intends to destroy us all. The Order will be showing this image all across the country so you can protect yourselves—and inform us if you've spotted her. Don't approach her yourself. We'll bring our own magic to bear and ensure Silana's people are safe. But any information will be hugely rewarded."

Gods smite me. I fumble for the invisibility charm and yank it over my head. Rheave does the same and snatches my hand.

Without another word, we bolt along the edges of the crowd and out of the courtyard, fleeing the mass of my fellow citizens now baying for my blood.

Thirty-Four

Ivy

The wagon jolts to a halt when we're still half a mile distant from Baron Cyris's summer residence. The driver calls back to us in a wary voice. "There's someone coming to meet us. They're signaling for us to stop. I'd better wait and see what she's about."

I rub my eyes, bleary after the fragmented sleep I forced myself to attempt on the trip back, and peek through a gap in the canvas covering. A figure on horseback is riding toward us at a gallop through the thin dawn light, braided hair streaming behind her.

It's hard to read her expression at this distance and with her moving so swiftly, but her rigid stance makes me tense up in turn.

Rheave adjusts his position beside me, setting his hand on my shoulder. I'm aware of Casimir sitting across from us, though I can only see a hazy impression of him if I squint.

Even though we've almost reached our current "home," it doesn't feel safe to remove the charms concealing us just yet.

The rider arrives with a thunder of hoofbeats and a disgruntled-sounding huff from her horse. She cranes her neck to eye the wagon before focusing on the driver. "You've brought the three of them back from Florian?"

"Of course. Is something the matter?"

"Word's been spreading." Her voice drops to a hush as if she's hoping I won't hear. "About *her.* The baron doesn't want her on his property anymore. I'll let the others know you've returned. Wait here."

She whirls the horse and races back toward the residence without waiting for a response. My stomach has plummeted to somewhere in the vicinity of the floor.

Word's been spreading… about my riven magic. About the sister I killed with it.

About how my own mother is condemning me and calling for me to be struck down.

Some of our allies already knew, but my men and I never emphasized it. I've rarely used any magic in front of any of them.

I made it as easy as possible for them to dismiss or ignore the nature of my power. Now Lothar has shoved it in all their faces.

My throat constricts, and a hand wraps around mine. Casimir has pushed forward and found me in the dimness of the wagon.

"Petra will sort this out if no one else does," he says. "*She* knows you're not a threat—she knows how much you've done for her and her family."

She does. And one of the things I did, no matter how many times she says she doesn't blame me for it, is get Lothar access to the room where he slaughtered her parents.

My stomach settles into a simmer of nausea while we wait for the rider to bring additional orders. We have our own urgent news to pass on, but the messenger didn't give us a chance to say anything. Every minute could make a difference.

Doesn't the baron care about that?

Finally, I peek outside and spot a small procession on their way.

Whoever that woman was, she isn't with them. It's just Stavros, Alek, and Sulla, on their usual horses and leading three other steeds including Toast, with Petra and a couple of her guards riding behind them. Our horses are loaded with bulging saddle bags.

My queasiness bubbles right up to the base of my throat. It doesn't look as if they're coming to say all is well and we should return to Baron Cyris's residence after all.

The concealment charm seems pointless now. I don't need to hide from my lovers and the one consistent friend I've got in this mess.

As I tug off mine, Casimir and Rheave follow suit. We clamber out the back of the wagon and come around to meet our ominous welcome party.

Stavros's face is as grim as I've ever seen it, his eyes dark with restrained fury. He hops off his horse the moment he's near enough and strides over to meet me.

His voice comes out taut. "I'm sorry, Ivy. I tried to reason with Cyris—he *has* to see—I don't know how he could think it's worth jeopardizing everything we've worked for—"

I lift my hand to cut him off, forcing a sickly smile. "Unfortunately, we've got bad news that's even more urgent. I don't suppose anyone passed on word about Lothar's trials as well."

Alek's eyes widen. "What? No." His tone turns bitter. "They were too busy smearing your name."

I can't let that fact distract me from my most important purpose. "Lothar also announced that the Order of the Wild will be holding their kingship trials in four days, when we'd normally be celebrating Creadenala. He made a challenge to Petra to show herself there or forfeit the crown."

For all his fury on my behalf, even Stavros draws up short. "Four days?"

Petra sucks in a breath with a hiss, her tan skin graying.

"So we have to pull the rest of whatever we're doing together even faster," I say, supressing the ache in my gut. "However we can. What exactly has the baron decided about me? I'm guessing he hasn't called for my arrest."

Stavros's lips draw back from his teeth with a restrained growl. "I'd stuff him in one of his holding cells before I let his guards set a finger on you."

Alek speaks up again, his voice quieter now but still strained. "Hunting parties have already gone out from the nearby towns—people hoping they can spot you and get some kind of reward for reporting you to the Order and allowing 'justice' to be done. Baron Cyris doesn't feel secure having you on the premises in the current atmosphere. And obviously we weren't going to stay if you couldn't."

Sulla bows her head. "No one's hunting for me, but *I* wouldn't have felt safe staying among such fickle allies."

Petra brings her horse around the others, shooting a brief glance of stifled irritation toward the guards who insist on flanking her. "I still want your help—now more than ever if we only have three days left to finish our plans. Our scouts previously identified a reasonably secure location nearby where you can stay and avoid notice. There's an abandoned cabin about a half hour's ride from here in a patch of woods. And I'll keep working on the baron to have you back in comfort."

It's not my comfort I'm worried about. Despite my best efforts and maintaining my composure, my stomach has not just sunk but had a hole punched through it.

My voice comes out with a rasp. "Don't bother with that.

You need to put every bit of your energy and concentration into overseeing our final preparations."

My daimon lover clearly disagrees with my priorities. "How can the baron cast Ivy away?" he demands. "She's helped so many people—she hasn't hurt anyone."

I give Rheave's arm a quick squeeze. "You know that isn't entirely true. I'm lucky my presence was tolerated for as long as it was. Let's find this cabin and let Petra get back to her work."

Willing my posture to remain steady, I walk over to claim Toast and swing onto his back. Rheave and Casimir take their own mounts, Rheave's expression still fierce and Casimir's downcast in a way I've rarely seen on the courtesan.

No one wants to say it, but this is the end. The end for us, at least.

I think I've known it since I first saw my mother standing on the platform next to Lothar's projection, but I didn't want to admit it to myself.

The wrenching sensation inside me pulls my gaze to Stavros. "You should stay with Petra and the others at the estate. You're by far the best strategist they—"

Stavros cuts off my suggestion with a sharp shake of his head. "Our future queen knows she has all our support, but I'm not going to act as if I condone the way the baron is treating you. I'll only be a half hour away, and I can think just as well outside those walls."

Petra lifts her chin. "And for the actual construction, we'll probably end up closer to you than the residence regardless."

She turns to one of the soldiers. "Ride back to the estate and let the others know our new timeframe. If there are any clerics we haven't heard from to supervise the trials, we need to approach our second choices now. And all the blueprints need to be finalized so we can start construction today. I'll be back as soon as *these* allies of mine are settled."

The man bobs his head and gallops off.

With a tap of her heels against her horse's flanks, Petra leads us around the estate. As I follow her, I tell myself it's all right.

I've pitched in plenty already. I've played a key role in building our cause from our first tiny group to a network of hundreds of allies across the country.

I should be satisfied with the fact that I accomplished as much as I did. Who knows whether I could have really done much more anyway?

I still can't shake the sensation of a jumble of rocks piling up in my belly.

Sulla prods her mare to walk beside Toast. We ride in silence for a few minutes before she clears her throat.

"There's too much history. Too much fear. Those who don't have the power don't know how to see us as human."

That's part of the reason she didn't want me inserting myself into the affairs of the country in the first place. I wince inwardly. "I know it's hard. But a few of them have accepted me as I am. If Lothar hadn't sent the whole country into a fury to hunt me down…"

She sighs. "They're only acting on what they think is right. What they think even the gods would want."

But it isn't. The gods wanted us to wield this magic, at least while it was useful to them. If anything, we're blessed more than anyone else, not less.

Even that revelation sits heavily in my chest right now. No matter what we say to most of Silana's citizens, how will they ever accept the idea that the riven are more than monsters?

It certainly didn't look possible in the temple courtyard last night.

Even the men and women who've worked alongside me

have remained wary through the weeks. There are still more of our allies who'll dodge my path than smile at me.

Casimir seems to have picked up on my train of thought. He speaks in the steady, soothing tone that comes to him so naturally. "Once we've fully exposed Lothar for the villain he is, it'll be easier to convince the rest of the country that the things he said were wrong as well."

It isn't just Lothar saying riven sorcerers deserve nothing but execution, though. Gods smite me, *I* had trouble believing anything else for most of my life.

Those uneasy thoughts stew inside me through the rest of the ride. We pick our way along narrow paths trampled by wildlife through a stretch of forest, Petra studying our surroundings and adjusting our course a few times. She makes a wordless sound of relief when a low, log building comes into view up ahead.

Once we've dismounted and examined the cabin, I can't summon much of a mood for gratitude. The building contains only a single room, scattered with dirt and twigs that have blown through the broken window. It smells dank, and the door doesn't close all the way.

It must be years if not decades since anyone last stayed here.

Oh, well. If we're still here after three more days, then we've lost to the scourge sorcerers, and it'll be a far cry better than a dungeon.

Alek pats the wall with forced cheer. "At least the roof looks solid enough. We'll have shelter if it rains."

Stavros grunts. "It beats a tent of branches. We've made do with worse."

Petra steps toward me and my men. "You can keep the one concealment charm, Ivy. If anyone does stumble on you, you'll want to be able to disappear."

She glances apologetically at Rheave and Casimir. "I'll

need to bring back the others. We don't know how quickly we might need them."

Rheave opens his mouth with a look as if he's about to protest, but I jump in first. "Of course. The first priority is keeping you and your brother and sister safe. There aren't many to go around."

The daimon-man frowns, but he doesn't want to argue with me. And he'd probably rather blast anyone who comes hunting around here than stay hidden anyway.

"Thank you for understanding," Petra says softly as the two men hand over the charms on their chains. "I haven't asked you yet—did you accomplish everything you hoped to in Florian?"

Casimir pipes up first. He already filled me and Rheave in on his success when we reconvened at the wagon. "The Black Talons came through admirably. Their people should already be distributing the pamphlets so that most of Florian will be ready for our trials when we give the signal. We decided it was best if most of the recovered daimon remain in the city so they'll be close at hand when we arrive, but they might send a few to Baron Cyris's estate."

"How many *did* you recover?" Her gaze slides to me and Rheave.

"A little more than thirty, in the end," I say, the memory of the freed daimon, the delight that crossed their faces at realizing they could make their own decisions, softening a little of the turmoil inside me.

Rheave sighs. "There were a few who were still too deeply under the scourge sorcerers' spell for us to break them out of it. But their hold has weakened a lot."

Petra smiles at him. "That's wonderful. I suppose we can hope that within the coming days and weeks, some of them will start to emerge from the Order's influence on their own."

She pauses and seems to gird herself. "Not that we can wait on that possibility."

She's going to put herself on display in front of many of the same people who cheered at the thought of my death just last night. A shiver travels down my spine.

Our fellow citizens *have* to see that she's meant to rule. It's in her blood, her training—and every honorable, determined word she says.

If we can pull together our trials in no time flat.

I attempt to offer a reassuring smile. "We've laid the groundwork."

"Yes." She brushes her hands over the skirt of her riding dress and glances back at her guards. "We haven't yet determined the best approach for a few of the godlen's domains, have we? I'd appreciate you giving that matter as much thought as you can—what you think would prove my strengths as a ruler. We also need to solidify our strategies for preventing the Order from doing any harm during the tests —how you'll all factor in. I'll return this afternoon with Tinom so you can fill each of us in on the parts we're meant to hear."

My gut lurches. She still wants *me* contributing to the trials somehow—even helping orchestrate them on the actual day?

The words tumble out before I can think better of them. "Are you sure that's a good idea?"

Petra shoots me a puzzled look. "What do you mean?"

I motion helplessly with my hands, the weight of all my failures pressing on my lungs. "Should I be involved in the trials—or anything else you're doing—in any direct way at this point? Just the fact that people know you've had a riven sorcerer on your side, that I've supported you, is hurting your cause."

My voice falters, but I force myself onward to the inevitable conclusion. "You should probably remove yourself completely from any hint of an alliance with me. Forsake any past connections."

My chest clenches even tighter with those statements, as true as they are. If Petra sets herself apart from the riven—if she claims she didn't realize what I am and that she's now set herself apart from *me*—maybe there won't be too much fallout in the public's opinion of her.

But if she does that, it'll be even harder for her to turn around and speak up on the behalf of riven sorcerers later. I don't know how long it'd be before she could broach the subject of our origins.

Possibly never.

The future queen considers me for long enough that my skin itches with uncertainty. "I never took you for someone who'd give up and abandon a cause that easily."

The accusation stings. I can't hold back my instinctive response. "I'm not giving up—I'm not abandoning you. I'm trying to *help* you."

"By refusing to help me any further."

"By—by refusing to harm you any further."

My arms come up to hug myself. Casimir rests a gentle hand on my shoulder, and Rheave stirs behind me with a noise of concern, but I have to say this. The thoughts have been rattling around in my head since my mother first raised her voice to the crowd in Florian.

"I've tainted your legacy. I might have done more damage to the cause than good." A raw chuckle escapes me. "That's how it always seems to go."

Trying to save someone only to cause a worse catastrophe isn't exactly new to me.

Alek's lips part where he's standing by the doorway

behind Petra, but she speaks before he can. "I should be the judge of that. I still want you standing with me. Most of what Lothar is spreading is lies."

"Lies the people believe. You didn't see them last night while my mother told them what a monster I am."

"I wouldn't ask you to make a public exhibition of yourself."

"I don't need to appear before them to be a problem." I spread my hands. "I've just divided your allies, simply by existing. I've created discord right when we need to be as united as possible."

Petra grimaces. "You didn't cause that—Lothar did."

"And he only could because of what I am."

"Ivy—"

Before she can go on, Sulla steps in with a gesture for attention.

Petra falls silent. We both stare at the older woman, me with my hands clenching where they're tucked against my sides.

She's going to tell Petra she agrees with me. Maybe even suggest that she whisk me all the way back to the Haven where I'll be completely out of the—

Instead, my former mentor faces me. Her voice comes out unexpectedly soft. "I might have only arrived a few days ago. I might not have witnessed most of what you've accomplished directly. But I've seen and heard enough to feel sure when I say that I was wrong, Ivy. You've set things right much more than you've created new troubles. I—I'm sorry if any of the doubts I expressed before are making you doubt yourself now."

I gape at her for a second before I manage to reel my jaw in.

Petra jumps into my silence. "She should know, shouldn't she? You have to listen to us."

I step back to slump against the wall, a sense of defeat sweeping over me that I can't totally explain. "I don't want to make another mistake. Not when the consequences could ruin the entire country."

"You wouldn't," Rheave insists, but of course he'd say that.

Petra hesitates. Then she moves so she's directly in front of me and waits until I lift my gaze to meet hers.

"Ivy, I won't force you to stay involved. I won't give you any royal commands or demand your obedience against your better judgment. That's not how I want to rule. But you have to know how much everything you've done for this country and for my family means to me. And it's more than that. What kind of reign will I have if it's founded on old, unfair prejudices? I'm making my stand now—in every way I need to."

I choke up abruptly. It takes me a moment to recover my tongue. "That means a lot to me too. I want to be ruled by a queen who follows those principles. I just… I don't know."

The conflicting desires twined inside me send a lance of pain through me from throat to belly. My arms shift, my hand coming to rest on the spot on my sternum where most people have a godlen mark.

Where the godlen who went out of his way to claim me once marked me temporarily to save my life.

I don't fully know how I feel about the gods' role in creating riven magic. I don't expect Kosmel to step out of the clouds and point the way. He's never been so blatant with his advice.

But he has offered guidance when I've needed it. I can't say he's ever led me astray.

If I'm willing to bow down to a mortal queen, maybe I should welcome the gods all the way into my life, into whatever roles they're meant to fill.

I push myself off the wall and slip over to the cabin doorway. No one moves to stop me, probably waiting to see what I'm up to.

On the threshold, I scan the forest and pick a dense grove of trees several paces from the building, where the shadows lie most thickly.

Kosmel is the master of the shadows, just as I once liked to think I was. If I can find him anywhere, it'll be there.

I walk to the grove and kneel at the base of the tree trunks. The roots jutting from the soil dig into my shins.

I tip my head up to the patch of gloom cast by the overlapping leaves above me.

Kosmel, I think, sending my mental voice out into the world, *you helped me get this far. I don't know what I'm meant to do now. Have I accomplished everything you hoped for? How should I go forward if I want to see this woman reclaim her throne?*

I'm not surprised that my head stays silent. The leaves rustle overhead, and a faint caw reaches my ears, as if a crow has flown nearby.

Then all at once a breeze gusts up and blows through the high branches.

Even as my hair whips around my face with the blast of wind, I take in a sudden burst of light. The leaves sway to the sides, and sunlight pours down where once there was only shadows.

A quiver of understanding runs down the center of me. I keep staring up at the branches as they settle back into place.

Thank you, I say silently.

The sign he sent has left a renewed light in my chest as well. As I get to my feet, an almost giddy sensation tickles through my limbs.

I never really wanted to back away. I've fought so long to protect my country.

I want to see that mission through to the end.

I choose my words carefully through the growing thrum of my pulse. "I think… I think I'm meant to show the truth. To help you come out of the shadows so people can see you as you truly are. Which means we need these trials to happen fast, so I'd better start brainstorming."

THIRTY-FIVE

Casimir

The rasp of saws and hiss of sandpaper travels through the wide forest clearing. I could barely make out the sounds of human work when I was approaching this spot, thanks to a combination of magical effects created by a few different gifts working together, but now it drifts around me in an almost comforting rhythm.

Almost, because despite the care the workers are obviously taking, a sense of urgency permeates the air. Everything needs to be finished within the next day if we're going to have any hope of superseding Lothar's trials.

This is our last chance. No matter what doubts about the Order of the Wild we've sown, no matter what promises Petra has made, if the scourge sorcerers can set her up to look like a failure of a ruler in a public spectacle, I don't know how she'd ever win over the country.

If she'd even survive the day.

My heart thuds along at a faster rhythm than the work

around me. I can't quite settle it even with all my calming techniques brought to bear.

I pause here and there to consider the blueprints laid out on the forest floor and the corresponding slabs of wood the workers Baron Cyris assembled are cutting, but physical building isn't exactly my area of expertise. I'm here mainly to evaluate the emotional impact of the finished apparatus.

The pieces already shaped and smoothed lie in careful rows across the ground at the other end of the clearing. The pale wood gleams in the late afternoon sun.

We'd have some trouble explaining what we're up to if any members of the Order stumbled on this work site. The large, irregular pieces with their knobs and indents to allow them to fit together securely don't look like any kind of furniture a noble would be commissioning.

But that's why the baron sent the craftspeople off to work in the woods beyond his estate rather than in plain view on his grounds. The fact that it shortens the distance I needed to travel to stop by and make my assessment is a small but welcome side benefit.

The figures at this end of the clearing are manipulating the wood in a very different way. They're mostly dedicats to Creaden with gifts related to the godlen's knack for construction, although a few others have stepped up to lend talents that can be honed to our needs.

At a bark of an order from the head foreman, several of the workers spring into action. Their faces harden into masks of concentration as their hands rise to help direct their magic.

Pieces of wood lift from the ground and whirl toward each other. Interlocking joints snap together. Edges thump against one another. The slabs climb up above our heads—

A few of the boards smack into each other at the wrong angle. One wobbles and strikes another below. A worker grunts, another shuddering as he tries to maintain control, but it isn't enough.

The wooden pieces creak and strain, and the foreman shouts for them to be lowered. "We're not getting anywhere if you break them!"

The workers guide the partly constructed tower to the ground and let it tumble apart with a heavy patter against the uneven ground.

The foreman sighs. "Where did it go wrong this time? We need to be able to move fast, but we do actually have to build the thing properly."

I hold up my hand as I approach them. "Can we take a break from using gifts and put it together manually? I know it'll be slower, but I'd like to take a look at how the full structure is coming together. And I'd imagine everyone could use a chance to rest their minds."

The foreman's mouth tightens, but he nods. I catch hints of relief in the exhaled breaths and shifting bodies of his underlings.

It does take longer for them to fit the slabs together when they're building by hand, and after some time, they have to clamber up the base of the tower to continue. But the wood workers have gotten quite a bit done already. While there are more pieces to come, the tower already rises about twice my height.

I study it, noting the impressions it stirs in me, and glance around at the rest of the yard. "This is a section of the obstacle course, isn't it? How are the moving parts coming together? Do we have any of the other challenges ready to go?"

One of the Creaden dedicats motions to me with a wave of her hand. "A bunch of it is over here. And the bits of the puzzle boxes are almost finished too."

With a couple of her fellow workers, she demonstrates

how a few of the obstacles in the sequence will operate. Others fit together what they have so far of what they called the puzzle box. I ask one of them to step inside the huge cube so I can picture what it'll be like in action.

The foreman comes up beside me. "What do you think?" he asks gruffly.

He's braced for criticism but craving approval.

I nod slowly. "I think we're on the right track. We're going to want to add as much color as we can in the time we have, spark more feelings with that. And I'd recommend adding metal pieces to the wheel rather than having the teeth be wood—the shine catching the sun will have even more impact."

The foreman frowns. "We don't want the queen getting *hurt.*"

I glance at him, unable to stop my smile from tightening. Doesn't he realize how much harm we'll all be risking when we pull this immense gambit together?

"The people need to see she's taking real risks," I remind him. "She wants to prove every trait she believes makes a good ruler, and that includes bravery and the willingness to face danger on behalf of her country."

He lets out a faint huff, but he doesn't argue the point. Instead, he calls out to one of the workers to bring the materials from a storeroom and another to summon a couple of Inganne dedicats from the estate who have a way with paint.

I dip my head in thanks. "Let me know when the artists get here. I'll consult with them on what color scheme would be most effective for each part."

The trials we're going to set up don't need to just show off Petra's prowess, both physical and mental. They need to stir the hopes and hungers of her audience. Create a story of how fiercely this woman will fight for their happiness.

Is it going to be enough?

After seeing how easily Lothar has been able to sway the people of Silana in his favor, I don't know.

He certainly seems to believe it won't. He must know by now of the pamphlets we distributed in Florian, promising that Princess Petra would be hosting her trials in the coming days, but the announcements in the nearby towns all still place Lothar's on the day of Creadenala.

Whether because he can't prepare it in time or because he doesn't want to appear uncertain, he hasn't moved his spectacle forward. He doesn't think *we* could truly challenge him.

And he could be right. I'm not sure how we're going to ensure Petra makes it through our trials without the scourge sorcerers finding a way to strike her down.

Those uncertainties are still twisted inside me when one of the baron's other employees approaches. I've only seen her briefly during our time staying at his summer home, but I recognize her flaxen hair and dainty features from my frequent socializing in the royal court.

She's someone high up in Baron Cyris's retinue—a chief of staff of sorts, a go-between who ensures everything at the lower levels of his various estates is running smoothly. Nasha, if I remember her name correctly.

I don't believe we've ever spoken before, and I've never gotten much of an impression of her one way or another. But something in her face as she looks me up and down puts me on guard.

She clicks her tongue. "It's Casimir, isn't it?"

I hide the apprehension I don't totally understand behind a warm smile. "Yes. The queen asked me to—"

"I know why you're here." Nasha glances around the clearing. "Have you already surveyed the preparations so far?"

"Yes. I'm waiting to advise on some additions the craftspeople will be making once a few more workers have arrived."

"Then you can spare a little time."

I do my best to study her surreptitiously. "I'm at your disposal. What is it you need?"

She flicks her hand toward the trees. "It's better discussed in private."

I let her lead the way, tension creeping through my limbs. For all the authority she exudes, she's a slight thing, slimmer even than Ivy was when she first arrived at the college and a good head shorter than me. I'm not afraid she'd manage to physically harm me as long as I stay alert for weapons.

But I don't know what gifts she has. I don't know what she wants.

I shouldn't be thinking like this at all.

I wouldn't be, if her employer hadn't set himself up as the enemy of the woman I love.

We tramp between the trees in the direction that takes us farther from the baron's residence. The sounds of the construction fade swiftly, swallowed up by the magical protections around the clearing.

Nasha keeps walking, her head turning as she scans the forest. I'm not sure what she's looking for, but after a few minutes, she appears to find it. She stops in a small glade where the sun streaks past the leaves and over a patch of pale grass.

She pivots to face me. Her gaze rakes over me before I can speak, as if it's cutting through the woolen tunic and trousers I'm wearing.

Either my focus on the queen's plans clouded my usual awareness or Nasha was being more subtle before, because I recognize the intent that gleams in her eyes now. It's one I've seen dozens of times before.

There's no hostility, only a glimmer of lust.

"I heard so many stories about your prowess in court," she says. "I never thought I'd be able to afford you."

My gut lurches. "I'm not currently selling my services." Nor do I expect to any time in the foreseeable future.

She strolls closer, forcing me to back up a step before she can stroke her hand down my chest. She pauses with her lifted arm hovering between us. "You can't be serious. Already hailed as the most skilled courtesan under King Konram's reign before you'd even finished your education, and you're abandoning your career?"

I keep my voice carefully steady. "I see it more as adjusting my focus. Ardone celebrates more than just carnal pleasures."

Nasha hums to herself. "You're still showing off those gaudy teeth. You were on your way to being the most renowned courtesan in history. Always bringing your patrons every pleasure they could have asked for."

The rejection of that statement wells up inside me so fast I have to bite my tongue to keep from blurting out a simple, *No!* As I master my reaction, a rush of certainty follows like a gust of fresh air.

"No," I say more calmly. "That was my mother's legacy. I'm setting out on my own path, one that's more suitable for me."

Nasha takes another step forward, holding my gaze. "Then I'm asking you to make an exception. Because I *can* pay you now, in a currency that I'd imagine matters more than gold or silver to you at the moment. Give me a half hour with Casimir the courtesan—right here, as we are—and I'll see that you and your friends, including the riven sorcerer, are allowed to return to the safety of the baron's residence."

A rough laugh sputters out of me.

She hasn't judged completely wrong. That offer would matter to me more than money. But it sounds ridiculous to say that the baron's residence is *safe* when I have a predator from it here in front of me. And—

"The queen herself hasn't been able to convince him," I point out. "I think you may be offering a payment you don't actually have in hand."

"He's known me for years. He only just met her. He trusts me with nearly every aspect of his business. If anyone can persuade him, it's me."

She eases even nearer with a confidence that suggests she's sure of her success. When I retreat once more, her brow knits.

I pitch my voice as gentle as possible. "We're happy and secure enough where we are. And *I'm* happy with the present state of my career. I won't be taking any new patrons."

Nasha's eyes flash. She peers up at me with a sudden air of menace. "What if I put it this way, then: I'll pay you by *not* seeing that the Order finds out exactly where that monster of a woman is hiding."

A chill prickles over my skin. Truth rings through every harsh word.

She means her threat.

I study her even more warily. "That could be disastrous for your employer too."

"I can make sure the information is delivered without any ties to him." She tilts her head with a coyness that clashes with her attempt at blackmail. "Would it really be so horrible for you to tap into your talents with me, just this once?"

She isn't an unattractive woman. Months ago, before I met Ivy, I wouldn't have hesitated in the first place.

But now, the answer that peals through every particle of my body is yes. Yes, it would be horrible.

Not only because I'd be betraying the loyalty I've offered Ivy. My lover has never demanded that I abandon my trade.

No, I'd be betraying *myself*.

I am happy with who I am now, with how I'm conducting myself. With the ways I've used my talents and my devotion to my godlen that haven't required me sharing the bodily intimacy I once did with anyone other than the woman who's claimed my heart.

But what else can I do?

In a flare of desperation, I clench my teeth and push forward my gift. It feels like a hopeless gambit—Nasha has already told me very clearly what would make her happy, and it is technically something I can do—but I touch the side of my fist to my godlen brand and send a silent prayer to Ardone at the same time.

Show me a way through this.

A stream of imagery washes over me, and it isn't the lascivious tableau I was expecting.

Oh, a few flickers of my body twined with hers brush past me—she does desire that quite a bit. But shining through them come other glimpses: of Petra crowned and beaming down at Nasha while I stand at the queen's side, of Nasha looking down at a Melchiorek crest pinned to her vest.

Even more than she wants the pleasure I could offer her, she wants to please her future queen. To win Petra's favor and maybe even join her chosen staff.

She just hasn't considered that I could accomplish that much for her.

That doesn't mean I would, not to the extent she dreams. I'm not saying anything on her behalf to Petra without mentioning the threats and the blackmail.

It simply gives me a point of leverage that never occurred to me either.

I pull my posture a little straighter, aiming for

authoritative airs of my own. "Is that what you really want to risk everything on—a brief tumble in the forest? You're clearly ambitious and clever. The queen trusts *my* judgment, you know. I could see that you found yourself in a position your former colleagues would covet for the rest of your life."

There's no mistaking the greedy glint that comes back into Nasha's gaze. She wets her lips, the aggression ebbing from her stance. "Is that what you'd rather trade for?"

I let a smile play across my face. "I suspect it's what you'd rather trade for as well. Why shouldn't we both be happier with this encounter?"

"You would tell her—I give every task I'm assigned my all. I've never failed Baron Cyris. She could count on me for —for anything."

The words rush out of her breathlessly, and then a hint of a blush touches her cheeks. She's more embarrassed by her enthusiasm than how she attempted to force herself on me just moments ago.

"I'll speak to her," I say, picking my words carefully, "and she'll speak with you about the possibilities within the day."

Petra would agree. And Petra would retract those mentioned possibilities as soon as Ivy is safe from Lothar's retribution.

My future queen trusts me, and I trust her as well.

Nasha clasps her hands together, looking abruptly, bizarrely girlish in her apparent delight. Her voice only darkens for a second. "I'll expect you to hold to that. Oh, to really talk with her—to prepare her reign…"

She wanders back toward the clearing without another word to me, lost in her visions of grandeur.

As I watch her go, my pulse gradually smoothing out from its panicked rhythm, a flare of insight lights in my mind.

Ivy said we needed to show Petra to the world. To shine a light on her and let the people see who she really is.

How many of Silana's citizens have longed for the royal family's recognition of their struggles and contributions? How many of them have turned to the Order of the Wild because the scourge sorcerers pretended to care where King Konram didn't?

How happy would they be if they realized their queen needs them… and isn't afraid to tell them so. To extend her trust to them too.

Few things can engender loyalty more than having it freely offered back. Perhaps we can sway them back to our side so simply.

With a genuine smile touching my lips, I hurry over to the clearing myself. I still have more work to do, and I need to reach out to Petra to make more than one arrangement.

Ardone has shone on me and lit up the truth. There are so many ways other than those my mother wished that I can spread joy and love through this world.

Thirty-Six

Ivy

The cart thumps along the uneven country road, jostling me where I'm leaning against one of the walls. The rectangular space feels oddly empty with nothing in it except the four of us passengers while Casimir steers the horses.

But the afternoon air breezes over me with the fresh, tart scents of new growth, speaking of the spring that has almost reached us. It settles my nerves, though just a little.

I'm far too aware of the glass vials tucked into the pouch on my belt. The vials I asked Petra to obtain if she could, that she handed me shortly before we set out.

I have to talk to my men about them and everything else they need to be prepared for. I just haven't been able to bring myself to yet.

There's plenty of time still. Hours left in the day.

But with each passing minute, my stomach clenches a bit tighter.

Stavros sits all the way at the back of the cart, craning his

neck one way and the other to scan our surroundings for potential threats. I suspect the former general would be happier on horseback, able to control his own movements, but he hasn't complained.

We want to look as innocuous as possible. Just a simple band of travelers bearing cargo. The magic Tinom impressed into the cart before we left should divert anyone who isn't specifically looking for us.

Of course, there are quite a few people out there who are specifically looking for us. Or rather, for me.

Just in the past two days as Petra's growing assembly of allies scrambled to prepare everything we need for the kingship trials, two small delegations sent by nearby counts arrived at the baron's residence supposedly to "check in" and see how the baron and his people are faring. From what I heard, they were snooping as much as they could get away with, watching for anything suspicious.

It's annoying that the baron might have been a little right to remove me from the premises, but mostly I'm glad that no one picked up on Petra's presence there.

There's been more activity on the lands around our patch of forest as well, packs of riders trotting by at random intervals. We haven't ventured out of the forest to greet them, so I have no idea what they'd have said their purpose was, but whenever one of my men mentioned noticing the passersby, my skin crawled.

Pretty much all of Silana hates the riven—far more than they hate the scourge sorcerers they only have the vaguest of ideas about. Plenty of civilians would have been unnerved by the accusations we made against Lothar but uncertain of what to believe and what to do about it. Now he's given them a target for their apprehension that has nothing to do with his Order.

And an opportunity to take action while earning the tyrant's favor at the same time.

If all goes well, we can end the chaos he's created tomorrow.

I close my eyes for a few minutes, simply absorbing the spring scents and the rhythmic creak of the wheels. My nerves are too jumpy for me to fully relax.

"Are you sure the message will have gotten to your parents—and they'll have followed through?" I ask Alek, who's got his legs sprawled out across from me.

The scholar's expression turns pensive, but he nods. "They've delivered on every other request Petra's made. We indicated that this would be the last one and that she was pleased with their service. I can't imagine them letting the opportunity to become the royal weapons suppliers slip through their fingers when it's almost in their grasp."

"Even if that means associating with someone who allies with riven sorcerers?"

He meets my eyes more firmly then. "They'll only have gotten that news by hearsay—and they're already committed to Petra. At this point, I'd be incredibly surprised if they did anything other than dismiss it as negative propaganda and focus on what lines their coffers."

He sounds so certain that a little of the tension in me unwinds. Alek may not get along with his parents, but he does know them. He wouldn't have set us on this course if he thought there was any chance it'd put me in danger.

Well, more danger than I'm already in, which seems to be a bit much even by typical standards.

Stavros lets out a rough breath. "I'm still not convinced this is the wisest idea. We don't need to make it *easier* for our opponents to cut us to pieces."

"We're ensuring they won't be opponents," Casimir pipes up from the front of the cart. I can't see his face, but there's a smile in his voice. "And then they can cut up anyone who does decide to play that role."

Stavros makes a noncommittal sound. He's been the most doubtful about the courtesan's plan since Casimir first suggested it.

I stretch out my foot to give his knee a teasing tap. "It's not as if we won't want arms for our confirmed allies to defend the trials. We don't need to make a final decision until people start gathering and we can gauge their mood."

The massive man lowers his head in acknowledgment. "Sometimes you can't know the best strategy until you're in the thick of the battle."

I'm not sure I'll get a better opening.

I hesitate for a few seconds, partly hoping one of the others will add something else. But saying this isn't going to get any easier.

"There's something else we should talk about," I blurt out, and pause to collect myself so my next words come out more calmly. "Lothar and his followers are going to do whatever they can to tear down Petra tomorrow. You all must realize that there's a good chance I'll have to use a lot of magic to ensure we see the trials through. I don't know how it'll affect me."

Casimir reins in the horses and turns on his seat to face the rest of us. A shadow has crossed his face. "What are you saying, Ivy?"

I think he already knows.

Stavros's expression has hardened with resolve. "We'll have all our supporters there from every source we could draw from. It won't come down to you."

I force myself to meet his gaze, as painful as this conversation is for both of us. "Not necessarily. But it very well could. I'm the final line of defense, and there's no reason to assume Lothar won't manage to push that far. If it comes to that and I start to lose control, you need to act *immediately*—whoever's closest, whoever can do what needs to be done."

"Ivy," Alek starts in a rough voice.

I shake my head before he can fully protest and pull out the vials to show them. The milky liquid inside gleams in the sun. "Petra was able to get these for me. It's a strong sedative. Put me to sleep if you can manage to safely, to see what can be done for me later. But if you can't get the drug into me… I'd rather die than destroy anything we've worked for. Please."

My gaze slides across the faces of the men I love. Stavros has tensed so much he might as well have become a statue. Rheave's beautiful face has sallowed, his lips pressed together as if against the urge to vomit. Alek is simply staring, and Casimir works his jaw in silence.

"Please," I say again. "If I'm far enough gone that I can't restrain myself, ending my life is the kindest thing you could do for me. I'm trusting you not to let me become the sort of riven sorcerer they tell horror stories about."

Stavros's throat bobs with a thick swallow, but he nods, his hand on his sword as if echoing his promise. His voice comes out hoarse. "You couldn't be, Ivy. You're proving you're not simply by asking this."

He leans forward to accept one of the vials.

As Rheave watches it pass between our hands, a shudder ripples through his body.

I catch the daimon-man's gaze. "I know you don't want to lose me, but if my magic completely breaks my mind, I'll already be lost."

He considers me, his eerie eyes gone solemn. "If there's any other way, I'll take it. But I won't let you become something horrible."

Alek opens his mouth and closes it again. He presses his hand to his forehead. "I—I don't want to think about it. I understand that we have to, though. I won't let you down, Ivy."

Casimir pushes toward me to hold out his hand. "I might have the best chance of getting the sedative into you, by judging your mood."

I hand the second vial over and firm my voice. "If you can't, if I won't let you—"

He dips his head. "I know. I can do that kindness for you if there's no other choice."

Stavros opens his mouth to speak again, but at the same moment, Rheave jerks straighter in the corner where he was lounging. "I hear something. Other horses… coming this way."

Casimir swivels to grab the reins. We're just coming up on a low hill—it's impossible to see what's on the other side.

As soon as we all fall silent, a faint clopping reaches my ears, getting louder in the several seconds while my pulse hammers at my ribs.

Then a voice lifts, also distant but still audible. "That tree over there looks kind of strange, huh? You think a riven could've done that?"

My spine goes rigid.

Casimir's head whips around, scanning our surroundings. He nudges our horses off the road.

While it's mostly open fields on our side of the hill, there's a small patch of trees off to our right. It's too densely clustered for us to pull the cart between them, but Casimir steers us in that direction.

The grassy terrain partly muffles the hoofbeats of our own animals. Tinom's enchantment should divert attention from the noise too, at least a little.

I duck low, hoping the riven hunters are deep enough in their conversation that they don't notice any sound that filters through the spell.

With an intent expression, Rheave picks up the bow he had tipped against the cart wall next to him and fits an arrow into it. I wince inwardly at his obvious intention.

How much more will the world hate me if we leave a trail of bodies in our wake? These people searching for me might not have done anything worse than believing what the Order said—which wasn't entirely a lie—and wanting to protect their country.

The magic that's made me a target squirms in my chest and shoots out through my limbs. It could cloak us from view completely like it did so many times when we were chasing the Order's army weeks ago. It could send the hunters riding off in the opposite direction absolutely sure of their new destination.

It could erase them from existence so there were no bodies to be found at all. Like the guards at the palace in Regica. Like Lothar wanted me to do to the king and queen, to Petra and her siblings.

My hands clench against the boards beneath me at the memory.

I have to keep us safe to serve Petra now. But if I turn to my riven power for this, then what? More imaginary voices in my head, more delusions that even my allies are out to hurt me?

The mental effects of all the magic I expended earlier in our various journeys have faded as I've refused to use more, but I remember the viciousness of the worst panic with nerve-shuddering clarity. I need to save all the sanity I have left for our greatest challenge tomorrow.

I wind my imagined vine tight around me, holding my power in.

Casimir is urging the horses around the patch of trees. Soon the trunks will hide us from the road. As long as the hunters don't spot the cart's tracks and come over to investigate, we'll be fine.

My breaths remain shallow as the courtesan brings the cart to a halt. Rheave stays poised with his bow even though we can barely make out the road from here, let alone get a clear shot.

Stavros unsheathes his sword. He shoots me a glance as if to reassure me that they're prepared to defend me, whatever it takes.

As if the thought of my lovers getting hurt on my behalf makes me feel any better.

The hunters have stopped talking, but the hooves of their horses drum ever louder. It seems like no time at all before I catch a glimpse of the three of them cresting the hill.

It's hard to focus on them when seeing them only through the tiny gaps between the trees. I make out one head of dark hair and another covered by a bright blue cap, cloaks wrapped around them in varying shades of brown, a speckled gray horse, one dark bay, and the third ruddy chestnut.

From what I can tell, their clothes and mounts are of good quality and in good condition. Not extravagant, but I'd guess they're middle-class types, maybe merchants or craftsmen, taking a break from their regular work to chase the possible reward.

As we wait, crouched and silent, they continue by. Then the one on the bay draws his horse to a slower walk.

My heart skips a beat, and my magic flings itself at the barriers I've constructed against it.

They're going to find us—I have to act *now*—I can picture them charging toward our hiding spot—

I squeeze my jaw and my hands tight, resisting the wrenching of my power's demands with all my will.

Whatever the man slowed to look at, it hasn't caught his

attention for long. He kicks his steed back to a trot, and he and his companions ride off down the road.

I have only a matter of seconds for relief to trickle into me before a spear of pain stabs through my middle.

I manage to clamp my lips against a gasp, but a faint whine seeps from my throat. I wrap my arm around my gut as if the external pressure can offset the agony inside.

My magic sears through me from chest to gut, sending a familiar series of jabs into my lungs and stomach. It's pissed off at me, all right—getting impatient that I won't let it loose like I've been willing to so recently.

It took a lot more time before it hurt me this badly in the past… but that was before it had a real taste of freedom. That was before I'd already pushed it to the brink of its patience.

I sag to the side. Alek darts across the cart to catch me before I slump right onto the floor.

A ragged breath catches in my throat. I muffle a sputter of a cough as well as I can—and stare at the red flecks that dabble my palm.

Oh. So we're all the way back to this point, are we?

My power is literally tearing into my flesh.

Alek's arm squeezes around me. As the pain finally ebbs, I become aware of Rheave staring over at us, his face taut with worry, his knuckles white where he's gripping his bow.

His voice comes out in a strained whisper. "Did they do something to her?"

Alek shakes his head and helps me sit back up. "That looked like the fits she used to have at the college…" He peers into my eyes. "Your magic attacked you again?"

I nod, taking a moment before I'm sure I can speak steadily. I can barely hear the retreating hoofbeats now, but I keep my voice low to be safe. "It *really* wanted to protect us from those hunters. It's lashed out a couple of times recently, but not this badly. I was hoping I'd have more time before I got to this point."

A shadow has crossed Stavros's face. "You'll have even more reason to worry about protecting us—and Petra—during the trials. It could hurt you worse then if it gets riled up when you don't need to step in."

A flare of rebellion sparks in my chest in spite of everything. "If you're trying to tell me I should hang back out of the way and not even—"

He holds up his hand in surrender, an echo of our earlier conversation lingering in his solemn tone. "I know you wouldn't accept that. But you could end up more vulnerable if your magic is attacking you right in the midst of the danger."

Casimir has swiveled in his seat to join the conversation. "Isn't that part of what your training with Sulla was about? Finding ways to avoid the backlash from holding the magic in?"

The thought of those early days, back before I'd experienced the other types of harm my magic could inflict on me, sends a pang like homesickness through my chest. "Yes. But the idea was that we extend just a little magic here and there to appease it, not enough that the madness would start to take hold. I'm past that point."

Alek strokes his hand over my hair. "You've turned to it a couple of times since then for something small, and it doesn't seem to have affected you too badly. If you followed the typical regimen, it might still work to keep you at status quo. No worse than otherwise, and without it lashing out."

I wet my lips. "I guess I should probably give it a shot. At least to take the edge off before the trials."

Petra needs me tomorrow. If I'm ever going to use my magic again in a major way, it'll be to see her through our final stand against the scourge sorcerers. I can't risk being incapacitated when it's time to act.

It's the only way *I* can prove to all the allies who've watched me with trepidation and fear whose side I'm really on. The only way I can make up for the damage I've done to her reputation.

The best way I can possibly serve her, whatever it does to me.

But as I look down at myself and around the cart, every part of my body balks. I've spent so long tamping down on my power, and I have even more reason to fear it now than I did before.

No possibility that flits through my mind feels right. All I'm left with is a knot in my gut.

"I don't know what to do," I admit quietly. "I don't know what would be too much."

Stavros's expression softens. He takes one more glance over his shoulder toward the long-gone hunters and sheathes his sword before shifting closer to me.

When I raise an eyebrow at him in question, he rubs the scruff on his cheek with his hooked prosthetic. "I've been neglecting the razor since we changed accommodations. Removing a little hair seems like an awfully small act. You could give me a shave."

I stare at him for a second, my thoughts whirling.

He's accepted me as I am, he's accepted my magic enough to let me bring him back from the edge of death, but somehow this small offer cracks open something inside me.

"Are—are you sure?" I have to ask.

The former general gives me his usual cocky grin. "I'm trusting that you like my face enough to avoid wrecking it."

I can't suppress a snort, even as my stomach twists tighter. But somehow having his permission—his request, even—makes the decision easier.

I scoot closer and rest my hand on the side of his face. The bristles of a few days' growth of beard prickle against my palm.

Stavros watches me without a hint of hesitation or regret over his offer.

My gaze slides beyond the cart to the nearby trees and then the stretch of grassy field on the other side.

That should do. Take a fraction of an inch of growth from his face, send a patch of grass a fraction taller at the same time. A simple trade.

Inhaling deeply, I concentrate on both sides of the equation. I picture the tiny hairs shrinking down to his skin as the blades poke a little higher from the soil, gradually across his entire face.

When I lower my hand, Stavros's jaw gleams clean-shaven. He touches it with his own fingers, and his grin returns.

"I don't know why I ever bothered with a blade," he says teasingly.

His casual warmth relaxes me even more. I crack a smile of my own and consider the simmer of magic inside me. "I think that should be enough."

Casimir climbs into the base of the cart and sits next to me. "We should be sure, so you'll be completely safe tomorrow." He rests his hands gently on my lap, palms up. "The reins have left a little grit on my hands, and I've got nothing to wash it off with."

A laugh tumbles out of me. It's the tiniest of efforts he's requesting. If he wants to be a part of protecting me too, I don't see how it can hurt to humor him.

With a moment of concentration, I flick the dirt that's dug into his palms with a whiff of breeze that's echoed by an opposite puff up in the tree branches.

Alek hums and sidles close to me again. "I gave myself a

papercut on my thumb yesterday. Only a shallow one, but it still stings a bit. If you'd be kind enough to seal it for me…"

A tickle of heat flows over my skin both at the increasing attention and the nearness of my lovers all around me. I take Alek's hand in mine and find the tiny pink nick next to his thumbnail. "One more little thing. Just to be sure my magic is satisfied."

I focus on his thumb and one of the boards forming the wall of the cart. As the skin smooths, the smallest crack forms along the grain of the wood.

That's it. It's done.

I hold myself still, alert for any disorienting thoughts or hallucinated sounds, but my mind stays quiet.

Watching me, Rheave gives a bit of a growl, but all I can hear in it is sorrow. "It's sad that you can't use your magic all the time like I can. When you do, when it's to help someone, it lights you up."

His tone is so tender in its frustration that it makes my heart skip a beat. I aim a smile at him and then around at the other three men who've given so much to stay by my side. "*You* light me up. All of you, just by being with me. I love you. No matter what happens to me tomorrow, I want you to always know that."

If worse comes to worst tomorrow, which seems more likely than not, I may very well go mad. One of them might need to end my life before I destroy more than even Lothar has.

But it's not tomorrow yet. We have at least this one last day together.

Rheave answers my statement first, dropping his bow and pushing across the cart to meet me. He cups my cheek and draws me into an emphatic kiss.

When our lips part, he nuzzles his nose against mine. His voice drops even lower with a heated edge that makes me shiver. "I want to see if *my* magic can make you happy."

A tingle shoots straight to my groin. "What do you mean?"

Rheave trails his fingers down my arm, and a more concrete tingling races through my flesh. My breath catches.

He's sent just the softest pulse of his conjured lightning into me.

A heated chuckle escapes Stavros. "I think our lady thief approves."

Rheave beams and ducks his head to claim another kiss. As he does, his hand travels farther down to my hip.

A sizzling shiver darts from the warmth of his hand to the liquid heat pooling between my thighs.

As I kiss him back hard, I can't hold back a whimper. It's undeniably thrilling to become a vessel for his daimon energy, especially when he uses it to such skillful effect.

And there's something wonderful in general about taking in magic that I don't have to fear, that won't bring me anything but pleasure.

When Rheave relinquishes my mouth to chart a scorching path down my neck, Casimir is waiting to capture my lips. Alek leans in to tug aside my cloak and press a kiss to my shoulder.

Stavros tangles his fingers in my hair and nips the back of my neck. "We have time for a little joy before the rest of the hard work."

The daimon-man lets out an encouraging rumble. "To show our little vine how much we love her too."

Casimir eases back and runs his thumb over my lips in a gesture that's almost as provocative as his kiss. "Because we do love you, no matter what happens, no matter where we end up."

Alek slings his arm around my waist to hug me tight. "Being with you will always have been worth it."

Our strange makeshift family has survived so much. I can't say I have any regrets either, not when I can't be sure we'd all still be here if I'd made different choices to begin with.

And it's getting awfully hard to think of anything at all other than enjoying their company with their mouths and hands moving over my body.

Casimir edges up my skirt, and Rheave slips his hand between my legs to set off another spark right at my core. I gasp and almost bite Alek's lip, but he simply groans and kisses me harder.

Stavros dips his hand beneath the fabric of the plain bodice to fondle my breast skin to skin. Then he yanks at the lacing so he can drag the cloth down and expose the nipple to his seeking mouth.

The swipe of his tongue sets off another pulse of pleasure. I'm quivering with all sorts of sparks now, both magical and the kind any passionate caress can provoke.

I look after my men, and they look after me—in every possible way.

As Casimir teases my other breast, Rheave yanks at my underskirt and drawers. He grazes my sex with a series of tantalising tingles and makes a guttural sound low in his throat. "I want to be inside you, Ivy."

Alek pulls away so I can yank my newest lover to me for an answering kiss. Rheave's tongue darts over mine in a heady dance, and then he's yanking at his trousers.

Stavros gives a rumble that thrums from his chest into mine. "I think she deserves another joint effort. You've never seen her doubly filled."

A giddy jolt of anticipation shoots through my veins, and then he's sweeping me onto his lap. As I help him wrench down his own pants, Casimir glides his hand over my ass and between my thighs.

The courtesan dips his fingers between my folds, setting off another rush of heady sensation. At my eager gasp, he spreads the slickness he gathered around my back opening.

"You want to make sure she's ready for you," he explains to Rheave in a honeyed tone, and delves a finger inside me to delightful effect. "Our bodies are capable of providing so much more enjoyment than the most obvious."

Rheave's voice is full of need. "I never realized— Do you want me like this too, Ivy?"

"Yes," I mumble, my own desire burning through my limbs as Stavros rocks his rigid cock against my clit. "I want all of you, everywhere, always."

With a choked chuckle, the daimon-man presses closer to me. I sink down over Stavros's cock, and Rheave lines his up from behind.

I hold perfectly still as he slides into me. My nerves sing with the flood of mingling pleasures.

Stavros guides me up and down over his thick shaft. "You always feel so fucking good, Ivy. You can have it all, whenever you want. Just take it."

I do, swaying between them. With him before me and Rheave behind me, I've never felt so full. So encompassed.

Then Alek dips his hand between me and Stavros. As the other two men rock with the blissful rhythm we're building, the scholar swivels his thumb over my clit.

I whimper, the swell of pleasure drowning out every urge other than the need to buck to my release and clutch at the men around me. Only two are penetrating me, but all four of my lovers are part of this act, moving in concert.

Rheave and Stavros thrust home in tandem, and Casimir swallows my cry with a demanding kiss. I rock and grind between my men, caught up in wave after wave of bliss coursing through my body.

"That's right," Stavros murmurs into my ear with a brush of his lips. "Take it all the way, Lady Thief. We're here to catch you when you careen over the edge."

In their joint embrace, I do feel as if I'm flying wild.

Rheave plunges deeper, and Stavros drives into me at the perfect angle.

Alek's thumb flicks faster. Casimir applies his teeth to my nipple.

The shock of so much pleasure crackles through me. I'm lit up from the inside out.

Then the daimon-man pours one more stream of his giddying power through my nerves, and I shatter apart.

My breath hitches, and my body quakes. I grip the arms around me and lock my legs against Stavros's hips.

The former general slams into me with the shudder of his own climax. It only takes a few seconds more before Rheave gasps harshly and sways to a stop, bowing against my back.

He dapples my scars with the tenderest of kisses. "No one will ever hurt you like this again. Not while we're here, and we always will be."

We slowly sag together in a messy and rather sweaty heap. A warm glow of affection spreads through every inch of my sated body.

I love so much, and I'm loved in return. For who I am now, for what I'm doing now.

I've moved past the mistakes I made before. I can do something better, something *good*.

This is all the happiness I ever could have asked for, even if it ends tomorrow.

HISTORIA
TOTOP

THIRTY-SEVEN

Alek

Wooden thumps and metallic clinks resonate through the night. The structures our allies hurriedly designed and fashioned the pieces for are coming together all across the field far beyond Florian's walls.

The builders are working by only the faintest lanternlight in an attempt to avoid drawing too much attention to ourselves. The dim glow gives the scene a ghostly atmosphere.

I stand back from the enormous platform that'll allow our eventual audience to view the trials, watching it spread out piece by piece across the grass. The wind licks under my cloak, and a shiver travels down my spine, but it's not only due to the lingering winter chill.

I've spent most of my life immersing myself in historical records, chasing down the details of what the world was like

and how people lived centuries ago. Now, for the first time, it's hit me that in this one instance I'm part of real, living history in the making.

The knowledge is terrifying and yet also incredible.

At the rustle of footsteps over the grass, I turn. The few lights still glinting behind the capital city's walls at this dark hour gleam in the distance, about a mile away.

No aggressive shouts have broken the sounds of construction around me yet, but I know they're coming.

Ivy stops beside me and studies the terrain between us and the city with a pensive expression. "If we can't get everything ready quickly enough…"

I grasp her hand. "Don't even think that. We're going to make this work, whatever we have to do."

It's either that or let Lothar crush Petra with whatever he had planned during *his* swiftly approaching version of kingship trials. Perhaps we'll get lucky and he'll be off supervising his own preparations someplace far from here.

I don't actually have the slightest hope that'll be the case. And in some ways, our plans require him to be here, to play his role in the production we're creating.

Ivy swipes a strand of windblown hair from her face and squints across the flat plain. "People are coming. I can't tell if it's the right ones yet."

I tense up, but a moment later, a messenger rides up ahead of the crowd of shadowy forms.

"The Black Talons are fulfilling their duty," he announces with a salute. "We're bringing the daimon who agreed to help. And you've already got some spectators on the way."

Ivy's shoulders relax just a smidgeon. "What happened at the gate?"

The man's grin sharpens. "The guards are temporarily knocked out thanks to one of my friends and her very useful gift. It won't last more than a few hours, but that'll buy you a decent head start. When we spread the message on your signal, we included a mention that people should leave the city that way."

I drag in a breath. "We can't hope that no one loyal to the Order of the Wild will catch the message. We might not have very long at all before they try to interfere."

The messenger lets out a dismissive huff. "We'll be ready to keep them off your backs. It's about time those pricks got knocked down from their high horse. I'd even take King Konram and the old Crown's Watch over the wildness worshippers."

With a shake of his head in consternation, he wheels his horse. "Where can I find Princess Petra? My boss wanted me to speak directly to her."

Ivy motions to the mass of carts and wagons beyond the growing platform—the vehicles we used to bring us and all the equipment we needed out here. "She's staying well-guarded for the time being, but someone will let her know you're here so she can see you."

The crowd from the city is already drawing closer. I find myself resting my hand on the knife sheathed at my hip, even though I'm not particularly more confident using it than I was after Stavros's initial lessons weeks ago.

We know the gang is on our side, and presumably the daimon are too. But what can we expect from the first regular citizens who've come to witness the start of the trials?

Are they here to support Petra's attempt to reclaim her throne or to condemn it?

Ivy tugs her hood over her head, low enough to shadow her face. We don't know how the ordinary people will react if they recognize her from Lothar's accusatory announcements.

A wooden creak brings my head snapping around, but it's just Casimir leading the cart we arrived in. He gives us a good-humored wave and yanks the canvas back from the heap of daggers, swords, crossbows, and shields my parents' assistant supplied us with.

"The first wave of our most important allies is on the way," he says with perfect assurance. "It's time for us to show them how very important they are."

I'm relieved that Ivy studies the assortment of weaponry with a similar wariness to what I'm feeling.

"Do you really think we should bring out the blades right away?" she asks.

Casimir offers her a crooked smile. "Anyone who's coming to hurt us will have brought their own weaponry. As far as I can imagine, we'll only be arming those who are willing to take Petra's side but haven't had the means."

I restrain a grimace. "Let's at least hear what the Black Talons who've been walking with them have to say about their conduct first."

The courtesan dips his head in easy acceptance. I don't know how he can seem so calm about the momentous and precarious gambit we're trying to pull off in the coming day.

It doesn't take long for the new arrivals to reach us. Several figures with an air of criminal confidence push to the fore of the crowd, prodding a few dozen men and women who look rather dazed along with them.

Rheave leaps forward to welcome his fellow daimon. His urgent instructions reach my ears. "We need to keep watch all around this platform. We can use our magic if we have to. No one should be allowed to hurt the people conducting or participating in the trials, especially Princess Petra."

As some of the captured spirit creatures speak up in a clash of voices, Ivy strides over to an older man with patterns carved in his shaved head. "Glad to see you, Garom. How has our audience been behaving so far?"

She nods to the cluster of some fifty spectators who've

stopped farther back from the construction area. They're mostly wearing plain or even shabby clothes, their hair unartfully cut and their stances nervous.

I suppose that makes sense. The outer-warders would have been closest to the gates once the message went out.

The Black Talons' boss grunts. "There've been a lot of questions, mostly about whether the queen will really be here and what the Order might do about it. But they seem more stunned that they're actually going to see the trials in action than anything else."

"Perfect." Casimir grabs one of the dim lanterns.

As he clambers onto the edge of the platform, I scan the land between us and the city again. More figures on foot are trickling from the gate that faces this direction and heading our way. None of them are moving in a way that strikes me as threatening, but I'm hardly an expert on identifying potential combatants.

Ivy bumps her elbow against mine. "Stavros and our sort-of troops are keeping a careful eye on the spectators. They won't ignore anyone who looks like a real threat."

On his perch with the lantern at his feet to light him, Casimir claps his hands for attention. He pitches his voice to carry over the gathered gang members and daimon.

"People of Florian, thank you for joining us for the trials that will prove who deserves to rule our country. Our rightful queen, Princess Petra, needs your support now more than ever. It's only a matter of time before the Order of the Wild tries to murder her as they did her parents and so many others."

To my surprise, the princess herself approaches from the far side of the platform. She's flanked by two soldiers, and I catch a faint shimmer of magic around her that suggests there's some sort of barrier protecting her from an immediate attack.

She stops a few paces back from Casimir and holds up her own lantern. A new, simple crown one of our allies crafted for her gleams gold on her dark hair. "I intend to test myself today to show in every way possible that I will lead this kingdom fairly and well. Will you help give me that chance? Will you stand with me against those who would try to force the gods' hands?"

Casimir motions to a couple of workers who've come to lead the cart even farther forward, past the Black Talons members and daimon. "We've brought weapons for all those who are willing to stand with us against the traitors who want to tear Silana apart. We know you'll only use them to protect our country."

Petra offers a soft smile. "I don't *have* a country without all of you in it, living the lives you're meant to enjoy. Together, we can put an end to the horror of the scourge sorcery that's swept across our realm."

As uncertain as I was about Casimir's idea, the civilians appear to respond well. A few and then several more approach the cart to pick out a weapon and in a few cases a shield.

I can't help noticing that as soon as each is holding a blade or a bow, their stances draw up a little straighter with a newfound sense of purpose.

Well, the courtesan does understand human emotions in a way I'm not sure I ever will.

As more onlookers arrive, Casimir and Petra repeat their message—and I catch voices from amid the crowd enthusing about the special duty the princess has given them. A hint of a smile touches my lips despite my continued apprehension.

A lot of things might have been ruined during the scourge sorcerers' brief reign, but they haven't stopped Silana's people from recognizing a truly righteous cause.

Most of the spectators, realizing the trials aren't anywhere near ready to begin, turn to face the city with weapons at the ready. They greet their fellow citizens as they arrive.

But one voice hollers over the heads of the daimon toward the platform. "When are we going to see the proof?"

Tinom appears next to Petra, lending the answer an air of divine authority in his cleric-like robe. "All the tools for our tests are being assembled before your eyes. And of course we will wait for any competitors who wish to stake their own claim to arrive. We believe in a fair opportunity for all. We expect to be able to commence shortly after sunrise."

A gruff sound of warning reverberates from the far side of the platform, where I realize Stavros has been standing in the darkness. At his signal, a significant portion of our combat-trained allies hurry forward to join the gathered gang members.

Ivy tugs me farther behind our defensive line and glances over to where Sulla is standing on the other side of the platform. The older woman shakes her head as if to say she hasn't sensed any trouble.

Soon enough, the thunder of racing hoofbeats and the glimpses of red tunics beneath the moonlight reveal the reason for Stavros's concern. Our first Order representatives are charging over to confront us.

The Black Talons' bosses, thank the gods, have enough sense not to leave the regular civilians as our first line of defense. With a few brisk gestures, they send half of their force ahead of the growing crowd of spectators. The others and the daimon remain between the onlookers and the rest of us.

Petra holds her position in the middle of the platform, but her stance has gone slightly rigid. Stavros shifts position to stand closer to her, and Rheave moves so he's directly in front of her on the ground, ready to intercept a magical attack as best he can.

Ivy's hands have balled at her sides. She's prepared to use her own magic if there's no other choice.

The image of her fiercely determined expression yesterday in the cart lingers in my memory, along with the firmness of her voice.

There's a good chance I'll have to use a lot of magic making sure we see these trials through. I don't know how it'll affect me... If I start to lose control, you need to act immediately—whoever's closest, whoever can do what needs to be done.

My stomach starts to churn. It's not likely the final act would come down to me. And even if it did… letting her become the monster she's feared so much would be a worse betrayal than killing her.

But, Great God help me, let us avoid that fate.

"I'd better vanish," she murmurs to me now, and pulls out the charm that's the one kindness Tinom left her with.

"Stay safe," I tell her, my voice gone hoarse, and then she blinks out of sight before my eyes.

The several riders in red rein in their steeds a few paces shy of the first line of armed men. One scowls before bellowing at all of us. "Do you really think you'll get away with this treachery?"

Tinom replies in a tone thick with derision. "Treachery? The rightful queen is simply commencing the kingship trials your leader demanded. She wasn't willing to wait for his perverted version of them. Who could be more qualified to run the trials than those of us who've faithfully served the only royal family Silana has known since the Darium empire was overthrown?"

"The false royals who lead us all astray. Look at you, deluding these people over again." He aims his glower at the crowd. "Are you really going to fight those of us who've given so much to win our freedom? They're trying to chain you up again."

"What are you calling freedom?" Stavros retorts, stepping into the light. "The freedom to be murdered for daring to criticize you? I don't recall King Konram treating his people so brutally."

The riders ignore him, the one who appears to be their leader focusing all his attention on our audience. "They're hypnotizing you with riven magic. Turning you into criminals. This is your chance to stop them and carry out the justice they deserve!"

The crowd stirs uneasily. Is one of the Order members using a gift to rattle their conviction? Or sway it in Lothar's favor?

Petra lifts her voice, clear and steady. "These trials will provide justice and show who is worthy of the people's faith."

An anxious voice rises from the midst of the onlookers. "Where *is* the riven sorcerer you've let help you? Are you going to arrest her?"

Another civilian echoes the first's nervous tone. "How can we trust anything when you let one of those monsters walk free and work her magic on us?"

I wince inwardly, knowing Ivy is hearing these questions. She shouldn't have to.

She's fought so hard for these people, and still they want to heap so much blame on her.

Petra holds up her hands in a quelling gesture. "Lothar Riosemek has lied to you and encouraged your fears to stop you from taking him to task for his own misdeeds. He and his followers are the only ones who've been inflicting dangerous magic on you."

"He's not riven," another voice calls out. "He sacrificed his whole arm to the gods. That's an honest gift."

"Honest gifts can still be corrupted by—"

A woman cuts in. "You're trying to confuse us. We know the riven are fiends. Why would you have anything to do with that kind of magic? The gods would never support that!"

The lead rider from the Order nods. "Very true. This woman has no right to participate in the kingship trials, let alone determine how they should be run. What does she know about worthiness?"

What do the scourge sorcerers know? If they were following their history, they'd never have gone down their dark path of sacrificing the livelihoods of others in the first place.

The rider points toward the platform. "Lothar will conduct the *real* trials, the way they should be done. All of this ought to be torn apart."

He isn't outright telling our audience to do that for him, but several figures surge forward regardless. When the Black Talons move to block them, blades clang together.

More of the onlookers push in as if roused by the apparent aggression, even though their companions were the ones who provoked it.

My stomach sinks. Our soldiers and guards shift on their feet, poised but uncertain.

Casimir was right about one thing: Petra does need the support of the common people. We can't prove her worthiness for the throne in front of grass stained with the blood of Florian's citizens.

No one knows how the kingship trials are meant to be, I want to shout. *Barely any record of them exists. And the one sure thing is that the gods judged them, not any kind of man or woman.*

What good would it do to say that, though? Why would any of these people take *my* word for it?

They don't know me. It isn't as if we can ask the godlen to come down and weigh in—

As my gaze sweeps over the increasingly tumultuous

crowd, it snags on the row of daimon standing near the platform. Their faces are taut with confusion—they know they're meant to fend off scourge sorcerers, but they wouldn't have been prepared for this kind of "attack" from ordinary civilians.

An unnatural glow shimmers in their eyes with the inhuman magic they're prepared to send out.

We don't have godlen right here among us, but we do have the creatures that are closest to them.

The pieces of a plan crash together in my head so swiftly the breath spills from my lungs.

I don't have time to study every detail of it, to pick it apart for flaws. Someone has to act *now*, before the weapons my parents forged for us become our undoing.

I sprint over to where Rheave stands and grasp his arm. "I need your help with the other daimon. When I ask for it, I want you all to show off the unearthly energy you have. If you can bring even more daimon here, ones that aren't captured, to show their support, that would be even better."

He gives the briefest sound of acknowledgment, and I heft myself onto the platform. I yank my spine up straight there at the edge next to Casimir.

The courtesan steps back from his lantern as if giving me the stage. The crowd quiets for a moment, peering at me past the figures standing in their way. Waiting to see what's about to happen.

My face prickles all across my scarred skin, knowing they'll make note of it before anything else. I shove that thought aside and square my shoulders as if I don't care.

"I've studied the history of Silana all the way back to the times before the Darium empire invaded," I declare in as forceful a voice as I can summon. "There aren't many records about the kingship trials, but it's clear they were put before the godlen to judge who was worthy, not any mortal. It's time to seek out divine opinions. And we have the representatives of the gods right here with us, the creatures who are far closer to the godlen than any of us humans."

As I brandish my arm toward the gathered daimon, Rheave takes his cue. He says something to his fellow captured creatures.

In an instant, a glow jitters over their skin. It quivers over their heads and down their arms like lightning in slow motion.

They must have been able to summon other wandering spirits too. A few sparks flit through the air and beam into brighter spots of light above the daimon in human form. More streak across the fields and swarm to join them.

The supernatural glow spreads out in front of the platform, shining over us all. I can feel its warmth glancing off the ridges on my face, and suddenly I don't care anymore.

These scars show I'm not just some pampered college student. I've fucked up. I've worked to rectify my mistakes and deserve the life I've built.

I've been through trials of my own and come out the other side, and I know my chosen godlen smiles down on me.

I lift my voice again with renewed confidence. "Lothar and his scourge sorcerers can't deny what you're seeing with your own eyes. The trials we're assembling have the support of the spirit world. The divine energies we mortals can barely grasp will decide who is most likely to bring the All-Giver back to these realms."

The next chorus of murmurs that passes through our audience sounds awed, not hostile. A few keep staring, dazed, but most swing back to face the riders from the Order.

The lead rider sets his mouth in a tight line, but he doesn't seem to know how to argue against this very vivid demonstration.

Petra speaks into his silence. "The Order can have a place in these trials too. You were already preparing for your own, and we've been sending out word that ours are approaching for days. I'm sure you've picked your champions. Send them forth at dawn, and we'll see who the gods bless with their favor."

Thirty-Eight

Ivy

The fine chain of the concealment charm itches at my neck. I try to scratch surreptitiously, not that anyone can see me anyway.

It's been chafing against my skin all night.

Now the dawn glow is creeping across our hastily erected stage. The sunlight enriches the deep purples and blues and brilliant yellows and oranges that Casimir recommended. They give the wood an otherworldly quality, like a glow of enlightened energy shining out of the darkness. Looking up at the platform and the various painted structures rising from it, I could almost believe they were formed out of divine energy rather than human effort.

Hopefully our audience will take away the same impression. We need them to see this spectacle as definitive proof of the gods' approval.

Beyond the ring of daimon, Black Talons members, and guards poised behind me around the platform, the crowd of spectators has swelled. I can't count them all, but

I have to think thousands are craning their necks or sprawling on the grass, waiting for the spectacle of the trials to begin. And more are arriving in droves as the word has spread.

It won't be long now. All nine of the independent clerics we invited to oversee the different trials have arrived. Shortly after the last bell, the Order of the Wild brought forth a large carriage that supposedly holds three challengers to the throne who'll compete with Petra.

They haven't shown their faces yet, though a few different Order members have ducked into the carriage, presumably to discuss strategy.

There's been no sign of Lothar so far, but his representatives assured us that the former magic advisor intends to be here to ensure every step of the trials is carried out "fairly." By which I'd imagine he means, "in some way that'll let us win."

If he tries anything too obvious, there are thousands of witnesses to observe his villainy. But we have to stay on the alert for more subtle tricks.

I don't expect him to back down easily.

Tinom has set himself up as a sort of master of ceremonies, which suits me just fine. I can't even show my face, let alone run the most important event that's happened in Silana in decades. He eases down from the stage at a summons and goes to speak with a couple of Order representatives within a careful cluster of protective gang members.

A group of about a dozen riders catches my eye from the north, riding toward us at a canter. I wouldn't think much of the new arrivals, but it's unusual to see so many together on horseback.

I slip around the stage for a closer look, and a smile springs to my lips. The warming light catches off Voleska's sandy blond hair, swinging with her steed's strides in its usual ponytail.

We sent a message to Pima to let her and Emor know the trials were impending, but we hadn't known if either of them would make the trip in time.

The riders approach at the back of the platform by the spread of carts and wagons. A few of the people who came with us from Pima break from their ranks to greet Voleska and their colleagues, and Stavros and Casimir head over as well.

I slip between the carts to follow them, getting enough shelter to remove my charm.

When I step forward to meet Voleska and her gaze meets mine, I can't help hesitating. Something flickers through her expression in her initial pause, and it occurs to me that we never discussed the source of my magic, even though I assume she's caught wind of the real source and extent of my power by now.

Lothar has spread his tales about my murderous ways far and wide. Maybe she isn't enthusiastic about counting me as an ally any longer.

But the pause is only the space of a heartbeat. Then Voleska marches forward with a grin and grabs me in a brief but eager hug, topped off with a clap on the back. "Look at this production you've pulled together. We've come a long way from brandishing stolen shields, huh?"

A laugh that releases some of my bottled tension tumbles out of me. "I guess we have. I can't take much credit for this. I'm just making sure it all goes off without a hitch."

Voleska nods. "I'll let you get back to that, then. And I brought a few more friends to do our part."

Stavros taps my arm, peering toward the city. "Lothar is on his way. We'd better get into position."

He touches my cheek in a brief caress. We set off for the

stage together, me vanishing with another yank of the chain over my head.

Most of the structures on the platform are meant to serve a purpose in the trials themselves, but there's a semi-circle of boards just a little taller than Stavros off to one side. Slats cut between the boards give anyone standing in that alcove a view of both the rest of the platform and the audience.

Sulla, Casimir, and Rheave are already waiting for us there, their stances tensed. Stavros will be employing his gift at what seems like the most crucial moments in the hopes of preventing attacks before they happen. Casimir is judging the emotional atmosphere of the crowd.

The other three of us are staying braced to use our magic to solve any problems that arise.

As I settle into place, the crowd parts in front of the stage. Lothar strides between the watching figures, his posture as haughty as always. His velvet cloak drapes unevenly across his one-armed form.

Tinom makes a gesture, and our defensive force gives way to let his former colleague through. My teeth set on edge.

"We're letting him walk right up here?" I murmur.

Casimir smiles tightly. "It was negotiated. Tinom and Lothar are going to look over each of the candidates to confirm there are no signs of hidden magical advantages."

A chill rushes through me. "He's going to get that close to Petra?"

"I don't like it either, but it's supposed to be a show of trust. The other clerics will be right there, along with her guards."

That doesn't feel like enough. Without another word, I ease away from the wall and slink across the brightly painted boards amid the looming equipment.

Petra stands in the open center, now joined by the other three candidates: a lean man with a sharply pointed beard who I think I recognize as a count, a bulky fellow with flinty eyes who I wouldn't be surprised to discover was once in military service, and a sinewy-limbed woman with elegantly braided hair who's probably a minor noblewoman of some sort.

They've all dressed in the agreed-upon outfits of a simple short tunic and slacks. The single layer of fabric leaves little opportunity to disguise even small blades or magical trinkets, and their tight shoes offer no room to conceal a weapon.

As Lothar ascends the steps to the right of the stage to stand next to Tinom, I dart over behind him. The towering, lopsided man wafts a smoky cologne that makes my nose wrinkle. It reminds me too much of the late-night rituals his scourge sorcerer colleagues conducted.

I don't sense any magic in it, though. Even when I lean as close to him as I dare, I can't pick up the faintest vibration of magic on or around his body.

He could be holding his gift in reserve until he's right in front of Petra. Or maybe whatever his talent is, it wouldn't help him sabotage her, so he's counting on someone else's help.

At least I know he isn't carrying an enchanted object on him that could harm her.

My magic reverberates through my torso. My fingers curl into my palms, holding back the urge to harm *him* quite permanently now that he's finally right in front of me.

But he knows the audience works in his favor to some extent as well as ours. If Petra's allies murder the leader of the Order seemingly unprovoked, it'll appear to prove all his claims true.

Even if it looks like an accident, his people will blame it on treachery.

We need to treat him as an equal rather than a criminal until he exposes his true colors.

Restraining my power deep within me despite its frantic burn, I lurk nearby as he moves down the row of candidates. He gives each of his own only a cursory examination, already familiar with them. Any stealthy advantages they're concealing, he's approved.

When he stops in front of Petra, I tense even more, focusing all my senses on every minute movement of his body. Petra stands rigidly, her eyes fierce as she gazes back at the man she watched slaughter her parents. Her guards step forward to shadow her more closely.

Lothar skims his hands through the air around her body as if testing her, but I still can't pick up on any magic emanating from him. From his grimly satisfied expression, I think maybe he's just hoping to intimidate her.

Well, it would look awfully suspicious if she experienced any ill effects while he's standing right in front of her. Any sabotage he's planning, it'd be easier for him to get away with it once the trials have begun.

I don't completely let out my breath until he moves away from her. Tinom finishes studying the last of the Order's candidates and steps to the front of the stage.

Magical amplification sends his voice ringing over the crowd. "Now each of the candidates will swear before the All-Giver and all the godlen that they will not use their own or any other's gifts to assist their performance in these trials. They come to these tests with no foreknowledge of the correct answers or approach. They accept their judgment based on their own mortal skills."

As the candidates swear in one by one, I duck back into the spy alcove. I've only just returned when Filip hustles over to our part of the platform.

The Order defector faces us with an uncertain expression. "The three sacrificial accomplices who came with us in case we needed them to speak—they want to stay near Ivy and Sulla."

Sulla turns and asks the obvious question for me. "Why?"

He seems to grope for his words. "I'm not sure—I—"

"We think we can help." One of those accomplices is hobbling along the base of the platform to come up beside us, supported by a man from Pima. Poltus's voice comes out thick and the long cloak and loose pants he's wearing only hide some of the deformities inflicted on him, but we weren't going to put them back in their shrouds.

The eyeless, noseless man turns his mutilated face toward us. "The scourge sorcerers drew on our power before with the wrong intentions. You're trying to set things right. And the more of your own power you use, the harder it'll be on your minds. Isn't that right? If we lend you what we can of our gifts, you can make a small amount of your riven magic stretch farther."

A sharp ache pierces through my heart. Because it doesn't matter that I'm concealed when Poltus can't see anyway, I don't hold myself back from speaking. "We'd never ask to use you the way they did."

The man makes a dismissive sound. "You're not asking. We're offering. There isn't much we're capable of contributing in our current state… Please, let us do what we can to see Silana restored to peace."

I don't know how to argue with that request.

Sulla bobs her head respectfully with a rustle of her dress. "We appreciate your support more than you can imagine. Thank you."

Poltus sinks down on the grass next to the platform, tucked out of the way and I hope decently comfortable. His two companions limp to join him.

"I wish we could see the trials for ourselves," the one

woman murmurs to the others, and the ache in my chest expands through my ribs.

The scourge sorcerers have inflicted so much destruction and pain on the people they claimed to be raising up. I have to do everything in my power to ensure their reign ends today.

Tinom is calling forth the clerics he summoned from nine nearby temples. "A cleric of each godlen will set their own task to fit with the equipment we've assembled and to score by their own judgment with divine guidance," he announces to the crowd. "The leader of Silana should have strengths in every area our deities consider important. The Order of the Wild has been granted the opportunity to provide their own clerics to assess the candidates if they disagree with the outcome."

I grimace. No doubt we can expect plenty of disagreement.

The magic advisor spreads his hands as if in welcome. "The sequence of trials has been determined through random selection. We're beginning with Prospira, our godlen of prosperity and growth."

He taps the gesture of the divinities down his front, and it's echoed throughout our audience.

A man in the yellow robes of Prospira climbs onto the platform, motioning a few devouts in plainer clothes with him. "We've brought our own trial with us to ensure none of the candidates could have prepared in advance. My devouts and I were inspired by the call."

The devouts each unveil an identical miniature tree carved completely of wood. Fruits the size of my thumbpad poke from between joined leaves.

The cleric sets a statue before each of the candidates. "Please examine your tree. You will find that any part you wish may detach. Give it careful thought, considering the principles Prospira holds dear, and select what you feel is the most important aspect of the plant while preparing your explanation."

He turns to Tinom. "Can you use your gift with illusions to amplify the image for the crowd as you have our voices?"

Tinom rubs his hands together. "An excellent suggestion."

As the candidates bend down to examine their trees, each about waist height, the air shimmers in front of them. Tinom projects a single image of a tree, this one twice as tall as any person, with overlapping movements of ghostly hands as it accounts for all four of the people studying their own.

Well, it doesn't seem as though Petra is likely to face any danger with this trial, although I don't know how her answer will compare to the others. How much time has she spent thinking about trees?

I focus on the people beyond the platform, stretching my senses, staying on guard for the slightest hint of an attack. Next to me, Stavros scans the crowd as well, with a quiver in the air that tells me he's concentrating on his gift.

All at once, an impression of a sharper tingling hits me from above. Some sort of spell is plummeting toward the platform—hurled up there to disguise its source?

My pulse lurches, and I snatch Rheave's arm. "Magic above them!"

He doesn't need me to say more than that. The daimon-man whips his arm upward, and a thin crackle of his supernatural energy ripples through the air.

His defensive effort splits into a dozen tiny bolts—and one sizzles as it catches the advancing spell before it can crash down on Petra.

I whirl around to peer at the crowd. My gaze flicks left and right before catching on a woman a few bodies back from the front of the crowd just lifting her hand with a determined expression.

Rheave can't blast her from here. My heart skips another beat, but the words Sulla told me echo up from my memory.

Even very small acts can have a large impact.

My mind leaps to an appropriate counterbalance. I release a spurt of my magic to push down a patch of dirt beneath the platform—and thrust up an equivalent patch beneath the scourge sorcerer's feet.

She stumbles, knocking shoulders with the man next to her, and whatever attack she was going to send out next falters.

Another stream of magic courses past me, but this one moves from the huddled sacrificial accomplices toward Sulla. With a swell of heightened power, she aims her own attention at the woman I targeted.

The scourge sorcerer's body lights up with a glow stark enough to cut through the strengthening sunlight. The people around her glance over and stare.

With a harried expression, she pushes off through the crowd away from us, maybe afraid some worse punishment is coming.

While we've been fending off magic attacks, it seems the candidates have made their choices. They've all straightened up with their piece hidden in their clasped hands.

The Prospira cleric starts at the far end of the row from Petra. He beckons to the bearded count. "What did you pick?"

The count holds up a chunk of wood that's basically just a rectangular slab. Tinom amplifies that image too, so there's a second giant man looming like an immense ghost above his actual self.

"The wood of the tree is most important," he says. "It allows people to build their houses and warm them with fire.

To make carts to carry goods to market and bring new purchases back again. And it provides a home to animals as well."

The cleric hums, and a murmur spreads through the crowd. It sounds like a reasonable answer to me.

Without giving any judgment, the cleric strolls on to the bulky man with soldier airs. "And you?"

As Tinom's illusion shifts to him, the soldier holds up one of the wooden fruits. "The fruit of the tree feeds both people and animals. You can't build much if you're starving."

"True enough," the cleric says agreeably, and continues on to the sinewy noblewoman. "What do you think?"

She holds up a piece identical to the count's. "I also chose wood, for the same reasons—and it can also be used to build bridges, barns, fences, temples—everything a society needs to grow."

"Many excellent thoughts." The cleric's tone stays even. He reaches Petra and bobs his head to her. "Do you have anything new to say?"

"I do, actually."

Petra opens her hands. It takes me a second to realize she's holding one of the fruits—but only half of it, the inner side showing several seeds carved within.

She traces the tiny ovals. "The seeds are more important than anything else, because they allow more trees to sprout. One tree can't build much of a house or a fence, or offer enough food to feed a family for more than a few days. The more you can grow, the more you can provide."

A smile touches my lips. Yes, that's exactly it.

A ruler needs to think not just of the present moment but how the whole country can thrive together.

A sudden round of applause, punctuated by a few cheers, sweeps through the crowd. Petra keeps her composure but brightens a little.

The cleric smiles too. "Spoken like one who truly understands Prospira's hopes for us all. That is the answer I was seeking."

A man in the red tunic of the Order stomps his foot near the front of the crowd. "Hold on! How do we know you didn't give the false princess her answer beforehand?"

The cleric knits his brow. "I wouldn't dishonor my godlen by cheating her of a proper trial. But if you don't trust my answer, I suppose we could ask the daimon whether Princess Petra's answer felt genuine."

The captured daimon must give an invisible nudge, or maybe the spirits could understand. A streak of sparks lights up, flowing around Petra's body, as if giving their approval.

"But—" the man starts.

Lothar holds up his hand to stop him. "Let it stand."

I study him through the gaps in the wall. Why isn't he fighting every verdict tooth and nail? Is he worried about how he'll come across and waiting for a better chance?

Or does he *know* he'll get the opportunity he needs later?

The green-robed cleric for Estera comes forward next, holding a crate with several glossy balls about the size of the candidates' heads. She hands a ball to each of the candidates. "I'll light the globes with each correct answer. A ruler Estera can support will understand the history that brought us to this place and the countries that surround us as well as our own. You have ten chances to prove your knowledge."

She runs through the questions at a steady pace, touching on the effects of Darium rule, the overthrowing of the empire, past relations with our neighboring countries, and ending with three questions asked respectively in Veldunian, Bryfesh, and Icarian.

With each correct answer Petra gives, her orb glows brighter—and her fellow candidates stumble more. Whatever their existing education and the hasty studying Lothar will have put them through, it doesn't match that of a woman raised since birth as the heir to the throne.

I suspect Petra could have answered any of these questions nearly as well at ten years old as she does now.

None of the other candidates speaks enough of all three of the other languages to respond to all of those questions. By the end of the series, they're standing stiffly, the soldier ruddy-faced with frustration, the noblewoman pursing her lips unhappily.

I haven't spotted any incoming attacks, but before the cleric can announce her verdict, Lothar lifts his voice. "You were selected by the princess's allies, Your Holiness. I'd like to have a cleric the Order of the Wild chose test her with a few questions she can't be expecting."

Our cleric steps back. As a man in green robes takes the stage, my body tenses. But he keeps a careful distance from Petra as if to avoid any idea of threat.

He asks her another series of questions in each of the same three languages, throwing in one in Woudish and another in Darium after—long questions that I know at least in the tongues I can speak myself are much more convoluted than what the first cleric asked. But Petra answers each steadily enough, without a hint of being thrown off.

The cleric indicates his approval, but there's a hint of a sneer to his tone. "One last thing. The Battle of Raclawnem —how did your great grandmother's forces win the day?"

My skin prickles with the sense that this is some sort of trap, but Petra doesn't hesitate. "There was no Battle of Raclawnem. Raclawnem is a small valley town not far from the Pinch. The nearest significant battles I'm aware of that were fought in that area were in Mevild county during the rebellion against the empire, and outside the city of Accia under my grandfather's rule."

My gaze flicks to the cleric. Apparently he was hoping to

catch her in a lie of confusion or make her look inept. Instead, he's done the opposite.

He lets out a short chuckle and bows his head. "My questions are finished."

As he descends the platform, I think I see him shoot a brief apologetic grimace Lothar's way. Another round of applause rises up.

A gray-robed cleric for my self-appointed patron godlen takes over next, ushering the candidates into the large, intricate boxes constructed by the baron's craftspeople. Casimir contributed his insight to those too. They're painted an ominous thundercloud hue to enhance the sense of a threat, with a silvery sheen on the entwined parts so it'll be easy to spot when each segment is released on the way to freedom.

As the cleric explains to the candidates and the audience that these are identical puzzle boxes designed to test cleverness and ingenuity, I notice a slim man moving along the edge of the crowd.

He bends to place something on the ground several paces from the corner of the platform. Then he ventures farther where the mass of spectators has fanned out around the sides of the stage and sets another object down there.

There's nothing overtly threatening about his movements. The guards haven't moved to stop him. But something about his meticulousness sends a jangle of warning through me.

I nudge Casimir and point out the man. "What do you think of his intentions?"

Casimir studies him for a moment as the man meanders on along the side of the platform. "He doesn't care about the outcome of the current test. I suspect that's because he's planning to alter it. If I…"

A wisp of magic tickles past me, and the courtesan sucks in a breath. "What would make him happiest is if I looked the other way and pretended I never noticed him. He's definitely attempting some kind of sabotage."

My mind leaps through several possibilities even as my chest tightens at the thought of releasing more of my magic already. But I do have the sacrificial accomplices below me, waiting to play the one part they can.

Ignoring a twinge of queasiness, I touch Stavros's hand. "Signal the guards to be on the alert."

Then I extend my concentration toward not just my target and a couple of scraps of wood lying at the base of the platform, but the mutilated accomplices as well.

A waft of energy rushes through me, propelling my own magic out of me faster. Even with only a small intent in mind, I have to yank at my power to rein some of it in.

The two pieces of wood shift and nestle together—and the buttons on the man's trousers snap apart. The loose fabric drops to his ankles in an instant.

He stumbles and pitches forward. Several more of the objects he was holding spill from his arms.

In an instant, the guards Stavros alerted rush forward to restrain the guy and confiscate his cargo for examination.

"That was nicely done," Sulla says softly. "One more challenge down."

I can't manage more than a tight grin. "Who knows how many more to go."

Thirty-Nine

Ivy

It seems the count Lothar chose is quite clever himself. He bests Petra's speed at unraveling the puzzle box, though only by a matter of seconds.

That isn't anywhere near enough to shake her confidence. She tackles the next two trials with the same cool determination she's brought to the previous.

And without any significant interference from the scourge sorcerers. Sulla upends one more figure who tries to aim a spell toward the stage, and then there's nothing further.

My shoulders are starting to ache from the tension I'm holding in them. My gaze keeps flitting over the crowd, stretching ever farther as more and more spectators arrive from beyond the city.

Then the red-robed cleric for Sabrelle strides onto the platform, and my stomach knots. Her challenge is what the largest portion of our construction efforts went into, and it offers plenty of danger of its own.

Several workers push the apparatus fully together with a

rasp of wood against wood. A few devouts to Sabrelle step forward and add their magic, making the wheel of blades spin and the fragmented bridge ripple where it looms high above our heads. The streaks of crimson Casimir had the builders add give the impression of lurking brutality.

The cleric sweeps her hand toward the massive structure. "Each of the candidates will complete this course of physical challenges. Sabrelle wishes to see bravery, physical might, and logistical strategy in a ruler. Any candidate who fails to complete the course will be disqualified."

Lothar breaks in with a loud demand. "The princess should go first. She's had the advantage of seeing the course built—the other candidates should have the advantage of watching her handle it."

I scowl. The truth is that Petra avoided the construction area and insisted she not be told any details of the trials ahead of time—she has no more idea how to handle the various obstacles than the other candidates seeing it now do.

But we have no simple way of proving that to the audience.

Before I can think of a solid argument to offer, Petra bobs her head in acceptance. "I'll go first."

She steps toward the starting ramp with its tiny, irregular handholds. It's hard to keep my attention on the crowd while she's about to face a series of death-defying perils.

I scan the swarm of figures beyond the platform until my vision blurs. The cleric announces the start of the challenge. Petra's feet thud up the wooden surface.

And Stavros lets out a grunt of warning. "Something's going to happen in less than a minute to startle Petra and make her stumble. The way everyone reacts, I think it's a loud sound. I couldn't see where it'll come from."

He leaps to the side of the stage to pass specific instructions on to the guards. Dozens push into the crowd, but I can already tell there's no way they'll be able to check everyone in the matter of seconds we have.

I risk slipping out of our alcove too, hurrying to the front of the platform in my invisible state. My gaze sweeps over the crowd again, squinting toward the farther reaches—

There. A woman some twenty bodies back from the front lines is raising a slim, metallic object to her lips—a kind of instrument?

I don't have time to point the guards to her. I tap into the trickle of magic between me and the sacrificial accomplices and let it launch my power.

The clasp on my cloak expands, and the neck of the horn squashes inward, just as the woman blows. A squeak of a sound reaches my ears, so faint I might not have made it out if I hadn't been listening so hard.

I squeeze the windpipe even tighter for good measure.

Stavros has spotted her now. As he calls to the guards to point her out for arrest, I duck back into the shelter with no one the wiser.

In the midst of our panic, Petra has scrambled across half of the course. When I let myself glance up at her, I can see the military training she insisted on enduring at the college has paid off.

She leaps across the disjointed boards of the bridge so fast their jerking motions don't make her more than wobble. She pauses for just a second to judge the speed of the whirling blades and then dashes forward, ducking and weaving between them.

A gasp of pain reaches my ears, and I wince, yanking my gaze to the crowd again. But I don't think that was sabotage, only the difficulty of the course.

When Petra finally squeezes through the snare of ropes to emerge at the far end, a scratch on her upper arm is dribbling blood.

"Two minutes, thirty-seven seconds," the cleric announces. "Second candidate!"

Despite his advantage of having witnessed a run-through and his muscular strength, the soldier seems to find the nimbler areas difficult to navigate. He struggles through the ropes and arrives with a time only slightly faster than Petra's.

The noblewoman has to pause several times out of caution and takes more than four minutes.

The count hurtles into the course with an arrogant air, which proves to be over-confidence. Halfway across the bridge, he slips, fumbles, and falls between the slats.

He hits the platform with a crunch of broken bone and a pained cry. The workers and a healer who was standing by rush over.

From the way his limbs are twisted, I think he's broken his leg.

The cleric of Sabrelle appears totally unconcerned. "The fourth candidate is eliminated from the trials."

The audience doesn't seem bothered either. With each trial that ends with Petra showing her prowess, the cheers for her get louder.

She's won most of them and taken a close second place in the other two. It's obvious who the forerunner is.

My future queen's victories continue through the final few trials. By the time we reach the last—for Creaden, the godlen most concerned with leadership and authority—applause carries through the crowd whenever Petra's name is mentioned.

It's been a long morning, but the faces taking in the spectacle glow with avid anticipation.

The purple-robed cleric guides three smooth wooden towers forward and assembles a trio of his devouts at the base of each. He points to the seat fixed to the top of each tower, shining a golden yellow above the whirls of violet and midnight blue on the base. "You will each work together with your underlings to reach your throne. You will be judged by more than just speed."

Before he can give the order to begin, a tingle of magic courses over my skin. My head twitches toward it, but an instant later, another current touches me, and another—as if spells are being cast from all around the platform.

Next to me, Sulla stiffens. "What in the realms is *that?*"

I swivel, trying to navigate the swarm of impressions. "There's magic coming from all over the place," I say for our companions' benefit. "None of it very strong... Nothing's actually *happening* yet..."

Sulla's eyes widen. "It's a distraction. They know we picked up on their previous attempts, so they're trying to overwhelm us rather than being sneaky about it."

Casimir speaks up in a low voice. "Lothar looks as if he's preparing for something. He's walking around the far side of the platform like he means to go right around the back."

"We have to—" Stavros cuts himself off with a hiss of breath. "I got a glimpse—someone's going to appear at the front of the stage out of nowhere. They must be using concealment magic like your charm, Ivy."

"Do you know which direction they're coming from?" I ask.

He shakes his head in a jerk.

If it's a matter of physically getting in an attacker's way, I'm far more equipped for that duty than my older companion.

I set my jaw. "They'll be coming for Petra. I'll just have to get in their way."

I bolt across the front of the platform, dodging the cleric and staying clear of the towers set several paces back from the edge.

No one reacts; no one can see me through the charm's

magic. They're all gaping at the spectacle of three candidates trying to assemble their human helpers into some kind of ladder to get them up the tower.

Word of an impending threat must be passing through the guards and the daimon both, because the rows of them in front of me stir warily, a few drawing their weapons. Rheave has jumped down to join his fellow captured spirit creatures, his gaze darting around us. But they obviously can't make out the would-be attacker any more clearly than I can.

I station myself directly in front of Petra's tower and narrow my focus onto the thrum of magic resonating through the air.

Someone is going to attack. Someone who's concealed through magic like I am.

I should be able to sense them when they get close, even with the wafting eddies drifting by.

The back of my neck prickles at the thought of Lothar prowling around behind me, but Stavros will have warned the guards to watch for any threatening behavior from him too—and he said the attacker his gift showed him appeared at the front of the stage. I need to stay here.

Grunts and rough breaths carry from the towers behind me. The cleric strolls by, examining the candidates' progress with a casual air, totally unaware of the potential catastrophe.

Then I feel it: a thicker current of magic streaming almost straight toward me.

It's passing over the heads of the guards in front of the platform—using flight as well as invisibility to avoid notice. But they can't avoid me.

I adjust my stance to follow the impression I'm picking up and unsheathe the knife at my hip. My pulse thunders in my ears.

My riven power churns inside me, urging me to blast the intruder right out of the air.

No. I don't need to pick away at my sanity any more than I already have.

And the less this confrontation distracts from Petra's likely victory, the better.

The sensation of approaching magic blares louder and then seems to stop, right at the edge of the stage. Without letting myself hesitate, I launch myself at the presence I can feel in front of me.

Our bodies collide, and a woman in a cloak blinks into my view as she heaves herself to the side to avoid toppling off the platform. I clutch her tunic, forcing her to haul me with her.

She curses and lashes out with a blade of her own. I manage to jerk my head out of the way and wrench my hand up to try to force her surrender with my knife at her throat.

At the last second, she squirms partly out from under me. As I lunge after her, she swipes out with her knife again. Her boot slams into my gut when I dodge.

I reel backward, and a chorus of gasps rises up from the audience. When I glance around, most of the onlookers are staring at *me* rather than the trial.

My hand darts to my neck and finds nothing. The attacker must have snapped the chain holding my charm with one of those slashes I dodged.

She's still invisible, but the hum of the magic wafts off her. There's no time to worry about my exposure. I throw myself in the direction she's scrambling.

I collide with her hard enough to knock a grunt from her lungs. We tumble over again, my elbow jarring against the platform floor.

A cry rings out behind me. I yank my head around just in time to see a blaze of magic hurtling straight toward me—and Sulla sprinting out across the stage.

She flings herself right in front of the searing projectile

with a burst of her own magic. I don't know why she didn't try to deflect it from farther away—maybe she didn't trust her focus when she's never used her magic in combat or on this scale before.

The blaze rams into her. Her body crumples, spasming as it hits the floor.

A cry of my own lodges in my throat. But I can't run over to help her, because the would-be assassin is flailing at me like a wild cat.

I'm too distracted, and my opponent's dagger catches me across the jaw. A stinging line opens up in my flesh.

I shove her backward, driving her between two of the towers.

I have to get her away from Petra. Away from view. Stop this assault from becoming a total disaster.

The woman is clearly skilled in combat, but she didn't get the training I did on the streets. I dodge her next kick and dive in low, knocking her off her feet again. Rolling to the side, I jab my elbow into her nose.

My magic writhes alongside my limbs, rattling against my hold. I just need to subdue her—the guards will want to question her—if she can reveal that she isn't acting alone, we'll have proof to call for Lothar's arrest...

An urgent yell blares from the back of the platform. In the second I glance up, the woman seizes the opening. She stabs her blade straight at my neck.

My body reacts on instinct. I flinch, and my hand is already swinging.

Driving my own blade into her heart.

Her body sags, her knife only nicking my throat. Bitterness taints the relief that sweeps through me, but I don't have time to think about that.

Because the next thing I hear is Stavros's voice, taut and angry. "Ivy, we need you here."

When I step away from the body, the woman I just killed fades before my eyes. Whatever magic she had on her, it must require some kind of trigger to remove it.

The only evidence of her existence right now is the blood slowly staining the floorboards as it seeps far enough away from her slumped form.

I look up and realize several guards and a few daimon have gathered nearby, all of them braced and ready to leap in.

"She had a dagger—she was heading for Petra," I say quickly. "I stopped her."

Stavros's voice carries from farther back, in the shadows of the arching obstacle course. "Good. Now we need to deal with this traitor."

As I push myself forward, Casimir's soothing tones reach my ears from the front of the stage. He's speaking to the audience. "Our guards are dealing with the security problem. We'll ensure any threat to the candidates is subdued."

I have no idea how my sudden appearance and the confusing fight the onlookers witnessed has affected the trial, but that can't even be my second priority right now. As I hurry over, I'm already saying, "Sulla was hit by some kind of magic. She looked badly hurt. We'll need a healer—"

One of the guards interjects. "A couple of Elox dedicats have already gone over to see if there's anything they can do for her."

His tone doesn't give me any clue as to whether she was still even alive. I swallow thickly and then stall in my tracks at the sight of the man at the other end of Stavros's sword.

The former general has Lothar partly cornered against the underside of the arch. Three armed men form a semi-circle behind the leader of the Order, but they're on our side, their own weapons braced to come to bear if he makes a sudden move. A few more of our soldiers flank Stavros.

Everyone's expressions are stony, but none so much as

Stavros's. "Take the magic off the attacker we all know *you* sent," he snarls. "Let's see what we find."

Lothar glares back at him. "I don't know what you're talking about."

"You were sneaking around back here for some vile purpose. It's obviously all connected."

The former advisor doesn't stir. He's got an excellent bluffing face, I'll give him that.

I guess he'd have to for him to have fooled King Konram and the king before him all those years.

Footsteps creak across the platform. Tinom joins us with a sigh. "I should be able to do it. Where is this attacker?"

I point to the spot where the blood stain is spreading. He wrinkles his nose but bends down and spreads his hands.

My heart thuds a few times more, and then the cloaked woman materializes before our eyes.

"I've never seen her before in my life," Lothar announces.

Stavros lets out a scoffing sound. "You can barely see her now with that hood up. Someone pull it back."

I killed her, so I figure that really should be my job. I crouch down and tug away the swath of fabric that shaded the woman's head.

Then all I can do is stare.

Light blond hair spills around the woman's pale face, turned slightly reddish with the sort of tint that I've seen from the juice dyes the outer-warders sometimes use. She's taller than me but nearly as thin, with a narrow face and a knob of a chin much like mine.

She's hardly my twin, but the similarities send a shiver down my spine.

Stavros's jaw works. I don't think the details are lost on him either.

It's Alek who puts the pieces together completely. I hadn't

heard the scholar approaching, but his taut voice lifts from a few paces away where he's gazing down at the figure.

"After she murdered Petra, you were going to say it was Ivy attacking. That the riven sorcerer had turned on the princess who'd allied with her."

The moment the words leave his mouth, I can see the horrific beauty of the plan. Lothar could have eliminated Petra while displacing any hint of blame from himself and his scourge sorcerers.

Of course the audience would have been all too eager to believe that a monstrous riven could have behaved so abominably. I heard the way they talked when we were setting up last night.

My magic flails to be let out at him, but I keep it tightly contained and fold my arms over my chest. "What were you doing skulking around back here at the same time?"

Stavros scowls. "One of our people found a knife in his pocket. Maybe he was going to jump in and take down the assassin to reinforce the absurd idea that he's the hero in this scenario."

Lothar scoffs. "All I hear is a lot of blathering. You can't prove any part of this incredible story. Now let me return to my place so I can oversee the end of the trials."

As if we want him setting so much as his eyes on Petra after he's attempted this scheme. We still don't even know what *his* magic is capable of.

I stalk closer and prod his armless side with a swift finger. Maybe I can provoke some kind of reaction out of him. "This seems like a much better place for you. Or we can send you over to sit with your sacrificial accomplices, since you all gave up *so* much."

I let sarcasm taint my last words, but Lothar's face twitches as if he's restrained a flinch. I pause.

Why would that specific statement bother him more than the accusations we've tossed around?

Not the slightest hint of magic drifts off him even when I'm standing this close. That doesn't mean anything much—I can only pick up on threads of energy being cast out.

But it occurs to me that in all the time I was around Lothar, even when he had me under his control in close quarters, I've *never* felt even a trace of magic coming from him. Never seen him make use of the theoretically impressive gift he should have.

A suspicion trickles through my thoughts that I can't shake.

I ease even closer, studying Lothar's face. "Do you even *have* a gift, or did you give that arm away for nothing?"

Tinom sputters a disbelieving laugh, but Lothar tenses at the same time. Enough to take me from suspicious to sure.

I whirl toward Tinom, who worked more closely with the former magic advisor than anyone else still living. "In all the years you were colleagues, did you ever see him use his gift? Did he ever say exactly what it is?"

Tinom halts, and his forehead furrows. "It was something to do with potions…"

Stavros's eyebrows rise. "Potions don't need a gift for a person to make them right, only knowledge of the ingredients and processes. Were any of his potions things no one could have made without some kind of magical intervention?"

"This is absurd," Lothar snaps.

Tinom ignores him, his gaze gone distant in thought before it sharpens on the other man. "You know, I can't think of any specifically that fit that criteria. I always took it for granted—but I can't say I wasn't wrong."

My stomach twists. How awful must Lothar's intentions have been all the way back when he was a twelve-year-old boy for his chosen godlen to reject a sacrifice so huge?

How awful would he have felt? How much more would his sense of morality have soured after such an immense and permanent rejection?

"Prove it, then," I say in a terse voice that barely sounds like my own. "Tell us what your gift is and use it in front of us. There must be something you could direct it at."

Lothar lifts his head to look down his nose at us. "I shouldn't have to honor that ridiculous request with a response."

Tinom shakes his head, some of the color drained from his face. "All those years… You lied to the king about *everything* about who you are. That job never should have been yours in the first place."

"The job never should have been Hessild's," Lothar growls with a sudden flash of his eyes as he mentions the woman he had murdered. The woman who was once the chief magic advisor. "What was so wonderful about her power? What amazing things had *she* done? She and her whole family of snakes—the position should have been my father's back in his day, but the Melchioreks always liked the Korinyas best—they fawned over them, they were *nice*."

He bites off the last word with an acidic edge and then a clamping of his lips. But he's already said enough.

Tinom chokes out a laugh. "You let bitterness infect you, and it cost you the gift you could have gained. At least Hessild honestly had magic."

"I worked harder than you can possibly imagine for everything I've gained."

"Yes," I retort. "You've lied and manipulated children and murdered all kinds of people including the man you swore to serve. And you try to call me a monster."

He spins toward me, his face reddening. "Why should a

no one like *you* have limitless power because of some fluke of fate? You never even had to sacrifice."

Anger flares in my chest alongside a lash of my magic. "You have no idea what I've lost. I never asked to be riven."

Now his hostility toward me makes even more sense. It wasn't just the standard hatred of the riven but bone-deep, venomous jealousy.

Tinom nudges me backward to step between us, his face hardened into a solemn mask. "None of this matters. No matter who wins the trials, you're going to be arrested. This psychotic charade is over."

Alek glances toward the front of the platform. "And it's going to be Petra who wins. The final cleric just gave her his approval. All those people you tried to sway to your sick cause are rejoicing."

The cheers and whoops of celebration filter past the jumble of equipment to reach our ears. I don't doubt that Alek is right, even if I couldn't see the declaration myself.

Petra has proven herself again and again—not just to be a strong, steady ruler, but to care about ensuring every person she rules over feels like a valued part of the kingdom.

Lothar will have made all the same observations I have. He was counting on Petra being dead and no longer an option, not on her actual failure.

I wouldn't be surprised if he *knows* she'd be a better ruler than anyone he could put forth. He simply doesn't care as long as the Melchioreks fall.

A strangled sound escapes him, and he barrels forward faster than I'd have expected a man of his size could move. With his single hand, he snatches the small crossbow one of the guards was carrying and whips it under his arm to brace it so he can fire.

Fire the loaded bolt at Petra where she's standing at the front of the stage, unaware.

Stavros hurtles after him even faster. A guttural "No" bursts from his lips, and he heaves his sword through Lothar's back.

Lothar staggers, the crossbow slipping from his grasp. "Fucking pompous prick," he spits out with a gurgle of blood.

Stavros bears his teeth. "It's nothing less than the vengeance my king deserved."

He moves to yank out the blade—and perhaps stab the man a few more times, which I certainly would not object to —but Lothar manages to hurl himself a couple of steps farther. He grasps the edge of one of the discarded puzzle boxes and shoves it aside while heaving himself forward.

Out into view of the audience with a sword jutting from his back.

FORTY

Ivy

Lothar collapses into a heap, blood spreading across the floorboards beneath him, but the audience got a clear look at his face. They know the leader of the Order of the Wild has been quite literally stabbed in the back.

And they weren't privy to any of the revelations or acts that led up to this moment.

Stavros races forward to retrieve his sword. He holds up his other arm, his prosthetic flashing in the mid-day sun. "Lothar Riosemek attempted to murder Princess Petra. I did what I had to do to defend her."

For a second, the muttering in the crowd fades, and I think that might be all the explanation they need.

But even with Lothar dead, his underlings aren't ready to give up.

No doubt they know what fate awaits them if their full wrongdoings are uncovered.

One of the Order members in a red tunic hollers toward

the stage. "Lothar would never stoop so low. I hear nothing but lies. We all saw that woman who stumbled around on the stage and ran back there. Were you defending the riven sorcerer?"

I don't know whether he actually recognized me in the brief time I was grappling with the assassin or if he's riffing off the original plan and hoping the false version of me can still come into play. It doesn't really matter.

The audience erupts into an angry furor.

Accusing shouts meld together into a thunderous cacophony. Amid them I make out other voices amplified over the rest, probably from more scourge sorcerers, egging the crowd on.

"This was a set-up from the start. They duped us and killed the one man who was standing up for Silana!"

"The riven sorcerer was helping the false princess all along!"

"We can't let them get away with this! Silana deserves better."

Petra advances with her hands held up in a gesture for calm. "My people, let's talk about this. I saw Lothar murder my parents with my own eyes. He would have killed me then if he could have. My guards were only protecting me."

Her clear voice carries over the crowd, but I don't think it sinks in. The mass of bodies is already shoving toward the defensive lines of guards, gang members, and daimon that now looks far too thin.

Spectators are pushing each other as well as the figures standing between them and the platform. A stocky man throws a punch at one of the gang members, whose colleague wrenches the guy around with an arm pinned behind his back. But there are more angry citizens pressing forward all the while.

And they're not just coming at Petra physically. A bolt of

magic sizzles through the air and chars the boards inches from where Petra is standing. She retreats reluctantly and then dives to the side as another conjured attack shrieks toward her.

My hands fly up of their own accord. This is why I'm here—I'm on my own now that Sulla's been struck down.

With a hum of extra power thrumming into me from the sacrificial accomplices, I throw up a solid barrier of air between Petra and the rioting crowd.

A spurt of flame streaks toward her and shatters against my invisible shield. Someone yelps, and another chorus of Order voices mingle with the chaos.

"That must be riven magic right now!"

"The monster is there stopping justice from being done."

"Why would a true queen work with a woman who's been shunned by the gods themselves?"

I grit my teeth, willing the words to glance off me without stinging. I've heard similar sentiments so many times, but they still prick a little.

If only they knew how far from shunned I am… Where the fuck is Kosmel right now?

We were so close to ending the Order of the Wild and their scourge sorcery for good, and now they've turned the tide against us in one foul swoop.

I don't dare step closer where the crowd might actually see me. The bodies near the base of the platform are churning as the most aggressive members of the audience grapple with our guards.

Voleska's ponytail flashes in the sunlight as she and her people squeeze in to form another barrier between the attackers and our queen. I catch a glimpse of one daimon toppling a woman with a burst of scorching supernatural energy and a guard bringing the butt of his sword down on a man's head.

Our allies are going to start slaughtering them—the people Petra's been saying she wants to raise up with her. And then even more of the crowd will rage.

How in the realms do we come back from this?

Casimir and Stavros call out to the crowd in increasingly desperate voices. The shouts for justice, for riven blood, are only getting louder and more furious, drowning out most of my men's words.

There are at least a dozen times as many spectators as Petra has confirmed supporters. What are we supposed to do?

My magic flings itself against my ribs, providing its own, typical answer.

Knock them all to their knees. Steal their breaths to stop the yelling; break their arms to end the fighting.

These people want to execute me. Why shouldn't I return the favor?

But I don't want to. That's not who I fucking *am*.

I can't see what choice I have that's a good one, though. I don't have Sulla here to ask, if she'd even have an answer.

This is why she never wanted to come down from her mountain. Right now, I'm not sure I can blame her for her reluctance.

"Stop them but don't hurt them!" Petra calls out to the ring of figures around the platform, but there's only so much her protectors can do. More lightning crackles. Steel clangs against steel.

Another body and another falls—and not all of them from the audience.

The crowd surges farther forward. A crash from behind has me spinning toward the back of the stage.

The rioters have swarmed right around the platform to capture us in a sea of raging bodies. Now they're pulling apart the carts and wagons, ripping canvas and yanking off boards—in search of me?

Yes.

"Find the riven sorcerer!" someone hollers. "Destroy the monster!"

The blasted scourge sorcerers are still spewing out their toxic ideals. "We have to prove to the All-Giver that we embrace everything we're meant to be—and that we'll clean this country of everything we're not. Tear down the traitors who tried to trick us and lead us astray."

With a renewed roar, the audience heaves toward the platform. Grunts and groans warble through the air alongside the thump of collapsing bodies.

I can't calm them myself. To soften their anger, I'd have to stir up more to balance it out.

Soothing half of the people around us won't do any good if the other half rage even more furiously.

But I have to do *something*.

I reach for the boost in power the sacrificial accomplices have offered, but I can't sense them emanating their gifts anymore. My stomach flips over.

Have they been caught up in the riot too?

Clenching my jaw, I stretch out my arms and release a wave of magic that's all my own. It whips around the platform in a much larger shield than the one I created for Petra. More of the carts collapse, disintegrating as I shatter their wood in exchange for solidifying the air.

I haven't unleashed this much power in weeks. My thoughts seem to wobble in my head, and a spark of panic sears into my gut.

All these people want to carve me up and rip me to shreds. Even Tinom hates me, even Baron Cyris.

I can't trust *any* of them.

No. I squeeze my eyes shut for a second, pushing back against the rush of paranoia as forcefully as I can manage.

Hold strong, Ivy, Julita would have told me. *Don't let them break you now.*

It's not just our enemies threatening to tear me apart in this moment, though. The worst threat may be the power surging inside me.

A cry breaks through the tumult. It sounds like Rheave. Instinctively, I push the barrier farther, trying to protect all our allies from the onslaught.

They don't deserve my effort. What have all those guards and gangsters ever done for me other than glare at me with suspicion? Let them fall.

Shut up, shut up, shut up.

A clang sounds right behind me. I flinch, but when I wrench my head around, there's no one there.

Shudders pass through my body from limbs banging against my shield of solidified air. It's already wavering.

I'm going to need to feed the barrier even more power. And on and on—for how long?

How much will it take before they stop?

"The gods will want justice," someone is bellowing. "Let's set things right!"

It isn't even true. The gods want...

The gods wanted *me*.

Kosmel wanted me to stay alive so I could stand up to the scourge sorcerers. All the godlen wanted the riven souls they poured their magic through to end the horrors centuries ago.

They didn't curse us—they called on us as vessels for divine power.

Breaking us was an accident, not a condemnation.

If these people could just see... what really matters to me... what really matters to Petra...

What the gods have in their hearts, as much as they have those...

In the midst of my scrambled thoughts, a voice from my past rises up, but it's not Julita I'm imagining this time. It's my little sister, sprawled next to me as we stare up at the stars.

They're so beautiful, the way they sparkle. Do you think someday we could fly all the way there to see them up close?

I remember how I giggled before I answered, with a seven year old's unshakeable confidence. *Maybe they'll soar down to meet us. But we'll have to be careful we don't get burned.*

A sudden jolt of inspiration pierces through my muddled mind—or maybe it's more insanity. But it's something I can do.

Something only I can do.

The gods came down among us and used the riven to channel their magic, to stop what we humans couldn't on our own. But destroying the villains left even more destruction in its wake. It left the wildness and chaos the Order wants to breed.

If the godlen regret their stumble, why can't they balance the scales? I'm right here.

Yes, my powers were a mistake. They're also the only thing stopping this riot from turning into an outright slaughter.

I'm broken, but I could turn the tide toward peace if I just let myself break a little more.

Maybe it's time for *me* to step into the light and meet my fate. For the stars to fall down to shine through me.

Even if I get burned like Linzi's ribbon in Lothar's hand.

My innards turn to ice at the thought of what opening my soul up even farther might do to my tenuous grip on my sanity. But it isn't going to take much more of this before I've torn myself to shreds anyway.

I knew I might end up making my final sacrifice today. I'd better make it a good one.

Closing my eyes again, I pitch my inner voice as loud as I can, up toward the sky where I imagine the godlen might be watching.

Kosmel! You once told me you'd be there for me if I knew what I wanted. I'll only ask for one more thing. Send your power through me again, you and whatever other godlen care whether the realm falls into chaos. Use your divine will to show these people what really matters to the gods—and that it's not what the murdering scourge sorcerers say.

No voice answers, but a trickle of uncertainty winds through my thoughts that I don't think is my own. My conviction is holding perfectly steady.

I clench my jaw alongside my answer. *I know what it might mean for me. I don't care as long as we can calm the madness out there. Please. You set me on this journey. I need you now, just once more. Believe me. Believe* in *me.*

It's been a long time since I heard the overwhelming voice that floods all my senses a moment later. *I hear you, my wayward rogue. This isn't the fate I wanted for you. But maybe I can offer you something better.*

Before I can ask what that's supposed to mean, a torrent of power blares through the center of my body.

It's not like when I drew magic from the sacrificial accomplices. The boost they offered was a tiny creek compared to this roaring river.

And it shatters straight through me rather than welling up inside.

The divine magic explodes out of me, but not in a hail of fire like the stories of the Great Retribution. Even with my eyes closed, I see the brilliant glow that streams out across and above the platform, rising higher than the towers and the obstacle course, blazing brighter than the unclouded sky.

I hear it. I taste it. I feel it vibrating through my bones.

Symbols form across the expanding glow—the sigils of

each of the godlen, flaring into being one after the other until I count all nine. Distantly, I'm aware of the clamor of the crowd dwindling, the gasps of shock and awe.

We need more than this. More.

Show them!

You *are so much more than this*, Kosmel replies, in a tone that makes me want to sob, and then the glow shifts.

The divine light spreads even farther, rises higher, forming an image of a castle. Figures flit in and out of the doorways and along the road outside it.

They come together and embrace. They share pieces torn off a loaf of bread and gulps from a bottle of wine. They laugh and dance, nobles in fancy trimmings holding hands with urchins in scruffy clothes.

Peace. Happiness. Compassion. Cooperation.

A wave of emotion sweeps over me and out across the crowd. A collective sigh ripples from all around the platform.

Another figure appears, with a gleaming hole lit right in the middle of her. As if there's a crack in her soul.

As if it's been riven through.

The other people don't recoil. They gather around and embrace her too.

The light shines out of her and whirls away the palace into a farmland scene. Children clamber up trees to pick apples while adults offer food and water to the animals. Everything is bright and joyful.

The farmyard glimmers into a ballroom where lovers entangle themselves in intimate clasps. Then a squad of soldiers marching together, bumping fists and cheering each other on. A library where students huddle together to murmur insights from the books they're reading.

This is what life could be. This is what we should aim for.

Love and friendship and learning. Kindness and consideration.

The gods have spoken.

The energy leaves me all at once. My legs give; my knees smack the floor. Incoherent words sputter from my mouth.

And then I'm not there at all.

I'm floating in a mass of glowing light that shows no sign of the outside world. But it's warm, so warm, in the coziest possible way, like snuggling in bed under your favorite blanket.

Nine streaks of starker light materialize in a circle around me. Somehow I know where they all are even though some must be behind me.

Even though they're nothing more than a blurry glow, I also know the one directly in front of me is Kosmel.

"Hello, wayward rogue," he says in a voice that's somehow more *here* and also more *everywhere* both at the same time. Every particle of me, however much of me is present, quivers with it. "You served me well, didn't you?"

"I did my best for the kingdom and the people in it who needed help the most," I find myself saying.

What's going on here? Is this some side effect of all the magic I channeled?

Maybe this is the final stage of my riven madness, and he's not speaking to me at all. Maybe none of this is real.

As if he can hear my thoughts, the trickster godlen chuckles. "Oh, it's real in the most fundamental possible way. And I wanted to offer you an opportunity within this reality, as a reward for everything you've done."

I give his glowing form a puzzled look. "A reward?"

"Our mistakes left you with more than a lifetime's worth of guilt and pain. You've protected the realms despite that. I think you deserve just as much peace as the rest of those you fought so hard to save. What you're feeling right now, that can be yours always. You can linger here in the divine for as long as you wish until you're ready to release your soul."

I grapple with those words for a moment. "You're saying I'll be dead."

"You'll die eventually either way. I can't guarantee what awaits you down below, but it will definitely be more difficult and fraught than anything you'll experience among us."

My lips part, but no sound comes out.

He said I'd find only peace here. That I'd get to escape all the pain of my past existence. But a tiny ache has already bloomed in my heart.

What about Stavros and Casimir, Alek and Rheave? Am I really going to walk away from them without even a good-bye?

What about seeing Petra finally claim her throne? What about the promise I made to Julita to ensure her old county was in good hands?

What about all that life I've only just started really living rather than lurking on the fringes like a shadow?

Kosmel's voice gentles. "All those desires would quickly melt away in this place. You might not satisfy any of them if you return. Even we don't know what effect your last act will have on your mind."

I might be absolutely crazed if he returns me to my body, he means. I might have a few more minutes of agonized existence and then fade away into the nothingness of death.

Do I really want to trade this comforting warmth for that possibility?

Even as I ask the question, my certainty about my answer grows.

There are so many other possibilities ahead of me now. There's so much else I want to accomplish.

There will be pain and guilt and sadness along the way. It might be all I have left.

But it might not.

Even a slim chance at having more of the loving joy I found is worth all the rest.

I haven't spoken, but I get the impression of Kosmel nodding. "I see your resolve. I won't argue with you, and I hope your decision brings you more happiness than anguish."

I suck in one more breath of the glowing air, contentment rushing through my veins, and then I'm plummeting.

I slam back into my body with a heaved breath and more gibberish tumbling from my mouth.

An arm is wrapped around me, a hand cupping my cheek. A vial tips against my lips with a spill of cool, bitter liquid.

"We've got you," Casimir says tenderly, with a hint of a rasp. "And this is where we'll stay—right here, with you."

FORTY-ONE

Several months later

Ivy

A crowd of several dozen has gathered in the graveyard beyond the Laonek estate. As I stand next to Casimir, ready to give my eulogy, I can't help eyeing the mourners warily.

"When we talked to Hanie during the rebellion, she said the Order of the Wild people had murdered most of the family's staff," I murmur to the courtesan.

He shrugs, beaming at the latest arrivals. "From what I've gathered, these are mostly people who knew Julita from her jaunts into town. And of course there's the few school friends who made the trek all the way from Florian." He tips his head toward a cluster of young noblewomen who are standing off to the side, apart from the more modest provincial folk.

I consider those four with even more skepticism. I only vaguely recognize them from my time at Sovereign College—certainly none of them took note that I'd said I was Julita's friend and sought me out to ask what had happened to her. "They must be hoping that showing up will make them look good in the eyes of the queen now that Julita's been named a national hero."

Stavros comes up behind me with a teasing click of his tongue. "And our other national hero still has a few prejudices to work through."

I aim a light jab backward of my elbow at him. "Well-earned prejudices, thank you very much."

The abruptness of the small movement sends a brief jolt through my nerves. I go still, inhaling more deeply and focusing on my imagined vine holding my body together in the way that's become automatic now.

Casimir notices the shift in my attitude in an instant. He touches my arm. "Are you all right? If this is a little too much for you—you were closer to Julita than anyone in the end."

I shake my head carefully. No strange sounds blare in my ears; no frantic thoughts flit through my mind. "That's why I need to speak for her at least a little. I'm fine."

Fine, of course, is relative. I'm leagues more fine than I was in the first days after I collapsed in a fit of babbling and shudders after the godlen poured their magic through me.

My men sedated me before I could gather enough intent to do any significant harm, and I spent most of the next two months in a partly drugged daze at the Temple of Tranquil Skies, with Delfis and his devouts drawing on all their healing talents to soothe my nerves and restore my broken mind.

Some of the scourge sorcerers' former sacrificial accomplices assisted as well. Many of those we've rescued are now stationed at temples across the country to amplify the magical work the clerics are overseeing. A few are on the royal staff.

As Poltus, one of those who's stayed with the queen, told me the day of the trials, it's the one way they're most capable of contributing. For all their sacrifices, I can tell they're happier with their new sense of purpose.

I'm not sure Delfis's people could have mended my nerves without the boost those resilient souls provided.

Gradually I've recovered my wits and my self-control. The taint of madness hasn't totally left me, but I'm sharp enough now to recognize the minor flickers of hallucinations and delusional ideas when they arise.

My body has odd reactions at times as well, like the jolt I just experienced. Since I'm no longer facing off against psychotic sorcerers or surviving through stealth, I can tolerate that side effect for as long as it lasts.

My soul is still cracked, presumably even more than it was before. My magic flows and churns through my torso, always niggling at me for more freedom. But I've taken up Sulla's regimen of one small magical act per day, and that keeps it happy enough not to savage me.

And if I should ever need to defend queen and kingdom again, gods save me, I have all the power I need at my fingertips.

The cleric of the All-Giver from the main temple in Pima intones the standard blessing of the dead and then says a few words about Julita's contributions to freeing the county of Nikodi from the Order of the Wild. No one except my closest companions knows the full story of how Julita took her stand, but it's common knowledge now that she was the first to identify the scourge sorcery threat and that she lost her life taking down her brother, one of the leaders of their army.

When the cleric finishes, he motions for me to take his

place in front of her marble monument. The figure it depicts was carved by a sculptor from Florian with input from Casimir, Stavros, and Alek's memories of the living woman, but I used a few weeks of magical acts to carve a simple vine design along the base.

I give the etching a private smile, imagining how Julita would have responded to it, before I turn to face the crowd of mourners. My throat feels suddenly dry.

She can't hear me right now the way she followed every moment of my life for the few months we shared my body. Her consciousness will have drifted away into the embrace of her godlen.

I want to do her justice all the same.

I swallow hard and gather myself. "Julita and I met under strange circumstances, two people who couldn't be more different in position or temperament. But despite all those differences, she became the best friend I'd ever had. She could bolster my spirits when I had doubts and find something to laugh about in the darkest situations. Her fierce devotion to both Nikodi and Silana were awe-inspiring. Keeping all of us safe from the horrors she'd experienced firsthand mattered more to her than her own life."

A murmur of appreciation flows through the crowd.

My voice catches for a second before I can go on. "The last thing Julita ever asked from me was for me to see that Nikodi came under good rulership once she was gone as the last of her family line. Even when she knew she didn't have much time left in this world, she was thinking of the people she'd dreamed about taking care of someday. And her final act against the scourge sorcerers not only stopped the invasion of Regica but saved my life."

With a shaky breath, I bow my head. "I will forever remember Julita and the many ways she touched my life and earned my admiration. I hope her soul moved swiftly into the embrace of her godlen, and that generations to come see this monument as a symbol of leadership and courage."

I step back to a respectful smattering of applause. Rheave loops his arm around my back and tips his head close to mine. "That sounded very good to me."

I lean into his embrace. "I think you might be a little biased, but thank you."

One of the kitchen staff who survived the Order's massacre goes up to say a little about Julita's early life living on the estate, and Stavros comments on her commitment as a student and dedication to her classmates. Then we all stand in silence while the cleric offers the final blessing.

When the mourners move away from the grave at the end of the burial ceremony, I spot Voleska standing at the outskirts of the cemetery. As I head over to her, she offers a sympathetic smile that pulls at the scar on her cheek.

"I thought I should pay my respects to the woman who was meant to be in my position," she says. "They're big shoes to fill. I wish I'd had the chance to actually meet her rather than simply knowing of her family."

She doesn't realize that in a way she did meet Julita, while I was harboring the other woman's soul. I'd bet my ghostly friend would have approved of my choice of countess. Throughout the uprising, Voleska proved herself just as devoted to her country and this county as Julita was, with leadership skills to spare.

I give her arm a quick squeeze. "From what I hear, you and Emor are already doing a fantastic job." Her former co-leader has joined her as her chief of staff, without any resentment about the main title going to her.

"She can wear the fancy clothes and do the public appearances," he said with a laugh when he first heard about the appointment. "I'm happiest behind the scenes anyway."

Proving my point, Voleska leads the whole gathering

back to the estate to enjoy refreshments and music in Julita's honor—exactly the way I'd expect my noblewoman passenger would have wanted it.

As the wine flows, more stories emerge about Julita's escapades around town and at the college, with all her usual spirited charm. By the time we call it a night, I feel as if I know her even better than while she was sharing my head.

There, I can almost hear her say. *Now everything's as it should be.*

It's a long trek back to the capital, but at least it's more comfortable now that we're traveling as respected members of Queen Petra's inner circle rather than fugitives. Our two carriages with their softly cushioned benches rattle along the roads with an escort of half a dozen guards around us.

Some people still have hostile feelings toward the riven, unsurprising when the hatred was so entrenched. Technically I could topple any foe faster than those guards if I needed to, but Petra has made it clear that she never wants to put me in a situation where I feel I have to defend myself or the people I care about with magic, not again.

As we approach Florian, Rheave leans out the window for a gulp of fresh autumn air and to grin at the guard riding next to us, who's one of his fellow captured daimon. "It's an interesting thing, being perched up on an animal, isn't it?"

The guard chuckles in return. "Not like anything I knew before. I'm glad I listened to you and stayed to find out more about this side of the world."

Only about half of the daimon whose animated clay bodies survived the various battles decided to hold on to those bodies rather than returning to their former existence as purely spiritual creatures. As far as we can tell so far, the magically animated bodies are aging the same way regular ones do, so they can have close to normal lives for as long as any regular human being.

Quite a few of the daimon who remained opted to serve the new queen. Rheave has become a sort of captain of the guard for that specific segment.

He's still delighting in every aspect of his new physical existence, from the breeze to the sway of the carriage to the butterfly that swoops through the window and lands on his sleeve. Rheave laughs and holds it up to show me before it flits off across the fields again.

At the moment, my other companion in this carriage is Alek. The scholar has managed to open a map, a textbook, and a pad of notes on his lap all at once while also consulting a language reference he's spread out on the bench beside him.

The tension on his face echoes the worry coiled in my gut. I grimace around the question. "Do you think there's any chance the Darium delegation has *good* intentions?"

Alek snorts in a not particularly Alek-like way, which only highlights how absurd the idea is. "If there is, it's so small you couldn't make it out with a magnifying glass. I'm sure this trip is mainly about the emperor's people feeling out Petra—with an eye to identifying weaknesses they could exploit to drag Silana back under his control."

The idea of *that* ever happening makes me guffaw. "I expect they'll be sorely disappointed then. I wish we could tell them to stuff their delegation up Emperor Tarquin's ass."

"So do I," Alek says dryly. "But Petra can't simply throw the offer of negotiating a peace accord in their faces when so many people would benefit from an end to the constant conflict with Dariu. I suppose it'll give her a chance to feel out the emperor's representatives too."

Rheave hums. "Casimir will be able to sense what they're really after quickly enough."

Technically the courtesan has been appointed Petra's arts and entertainments advisor, but she often ensures he's on hand for any particularly uncertain meetings so he can make use of his gift on her behalf.

I clasp my hands together on my lap. "They'll be wondering about her entire cabinet of advisors. Do you think word has spread about my magic?"

Alek hesitates, his gaze softening with compassion. "I think it's unlikely that not a single spy has brought back word of the divine spectacle at the end of the trials. But they'll also be reporting that Silana has ended capital punishment for the riven and started a new habilitation and training program for any who are identified. And Petra will be introducing you as one of her magic advisors, after all— it'll be obvious she stands with you."

So they might think nasty things in their heads, but they'll probably refrain from saying them out loud. I guess that's a small comfort.

I'll have all of my men by my side as well. Petra appointed Stavros her lead military advisor and put Alek in charge of overseeing royal scholarship while he finishes his own studies. Rheave will tag along in the guise of a regular guard for additional protection.

I sigh and slump back in my seat. "Well, we've got until tomorrow before we *really* have to worry about it."

A small, sly smile touches Alek's lips. "The only part I'm looking forward to is seeing the emperor's representatives come face to face with our new Signy. They don't know what they're up against."

I scoff, but a warm glow spreads through my chest at the same time.

Maybe, just maybe, I've truly earned that comparison now.

Immediately outside the city, the recently constructed

stone mansion where Sulla is taking in riven pupils comes into view near the bank of the river. Seeing it gives me another whiff of relief despite my worries about tomorrow.

My mentor had nearly as long a recovery time as I did after the violence at the kingship trials, though her injuries were mostly physical. But she's nearly as hale as she was before, simply needing a cane to reduce the strain on her weakened legs if she's on her feet for long stretches.

I've stopped by at least once a week to help however I can with the training. So far she only has two students—a girl of eight whose magic only just showed itself, and a boy of fifteen who traveled all the way from Icar after hearing of Silana's new policies.

I'm not sure how many other riven who've escaped execution there are in the world, other than us. But if any are hiding in the shadows like I once did, I hope they find the faith to give a real life a chance.

Within the main city walls, all signs of the Order's presence have been eliminated. Banners with the Melchiorek family crest stream from flag poles, and we travel through a square where a new statue of Queen Petra has just been erected—perched on a throne at the top of a tower alongside the three helpers she managed to pull up with her, as she did during her final trial for Creaden.

I'm glad most people remember that moment of cooperation and camaraderie more than the chaos that followed.

The royal army Petra has reconstructed has spent a significant part of the past several months rounding up the remaining scourge sorcerers and vocal Order members. The former don't pose much of a threat without their accomplices to draw power from.

Quite a few of even the true believers of their cause swore themselves over to Petra's service after witnessing the message of amity and peace the godlen projected through me. The Order's pockets of influence have quickly dissolved.

Those whose destructive behavior couldn't be easily pardoned have been assigned to various types of enforced labor to the true betterment of the country. I believe a certain chief of staff who once worked for Baron Cyris has been sent to the mining camps near the Icarian border—far from my beloved courtesan, who she'll never get another chance to blackmail.

I can gaze out the window without fear of setting eyes on two other incredibly unwelcome faces. After I returned from my convalescence, Petra offered to extend a similar punishment to my parents for contributing to Lothar's campaign against me. She told me I could even confront them myself along with the arresting officers.

But presented with the opportunity, I found that more than anything I wanted to never again have to see the people who scarred me in so many ways.

So our queen came up with a suitable reprisal of her own. My mother and father have been ordered to travel from town to town with an escort of royal guards, sharing their shame for failing their riven daughter and counselling all of Silana to avoid their mistakes—to help rather than harm any children who show signs of the wildest of magic.

Thinking of it brings a bittersweet smile to my lips. May their story save at least one child from the same misery they inflicted on me.

At the edge of the middle wards, we pass several workers pulling apart the remains of the old city walls that so starkly divided the elite from the rest of the city. Petra has been working on expanding the throughways and hiring outer-ward citizens for various building and clean-up projects around the city's fringes, and the atmosphere across the city has already become brighter.

When we disembark from our carriages in front of the restored Capital Palace, the queen herself comes out onto the front steps to meet us.

"It's good to have you back," she says in her brisk but warm way. "Now let's finalize our plans for handling the Darium delegation."

Simply standing in the audience room with the members of the delegation feels like a subtle dance no one's taught me all the moves of.

How many guards can Petra employ, to match those our long-time enemies have brought for their own protection but not come across as overly threatening? How close should we position ourselves; how loudly should we talk?

Which subjects will we address, and which will we tiptoe around as if the empire hasn't been trying to crush Silana back into submission for the past eighty or so years?

Thankfully, I've got a lot of practice at adapting on the spot.

Petra is doing most of the talking anyway, with Tinom—who's serving as her main overall advisor while she's settling into her new royal role—occasionally interjecting. The old magic advisor's attitude toward me has taken quite a shift since he watched the godlen he worships channel their divine power through me. To my shock, I returned from the Temple of Tranquil Skies to find him outright respectful. He apologized so fervently I couldn't see the use in staying angry.

Both he and our queen are taking a polite but cautious approach with the head of the delegation, a sturdy-looking man with a soldier's bearing but the ornate clothes of a nobleman, fitted and heavily trimmed in the Darium fashion. Since we're meeting in Silana, Admiral Varus has conceded to speaking in the local tongue. But while he's said a lot of fancy words about how our countries might eventually cooperate, he hasn't produced anything remotely concrete.

I think he's paying more attention to Petra's movements and her interactions with the rest of us than to what she's saying. So far he hasn't shown any signs of casting magic toward her, though.

Possibly word has also gotten out that Petra's loyal riven sorcerer has a knack for sensing supernatural power. I can protect her simply by existing.

It does make for a welcome change.

Since Petra and Tinom are already focusing on him, I let my gaze wander over the rest of the delegation. As well as his four guards, Admiral Varus brought along a young man he calls his assistant, a woman who's a devout of Creaden, and one of the princes of Cotea.

The delegation leader only gave a brief explanation for the latter's presence, but from what I understand, Prince Bastien has some role in Emperor Tarquin's court. He came with the delegation to speak to how any agreements made will be reflected in the actions of our nearest neighbor among the empire's conquered countries.

The slim, almost gaunt fellow looks a year or two younger than me. He stands straight but lets his shaggy auburn hair fall forward to shadow his eyes, his mouth set in a tight line.

He's trying to hide it, but I don't think he wants to be here at all.

He's definitely the most intriguing member of the party. And infinitely more so after Petra cuts off the aimless blathering to suggest we walk along the palace's upper parapet for some fresh air.

It's two floors up from the audience room. At the base of

the first staircase, a couple of the Darium guards prod Prince Bastien.

"Let's see you really march for once, huh?" one says, and the other laughs.

The prince's lips flatten even more, but he strides up the stairs at the same pace as the apparent jokesters. By halfway up the second flight, his legs have started to wobble and his breath comes out of him in a wheeze.

The first of the guards shakes his head. "Shouldn't have given up that lung if you couldn't keep up without it."

He uses a teasing tone, but I pick up on an edge of a jeer. How harshly would he speak if he didn't have an audience?

Then what he said sinks in. I stare at Prince Bastien for a second before jerking my gaze away, not wanting my interest to be obvious.

He sacrificed an entire lung to his godlen? What kind of gift would you get for that?

Or, like Lothar, did he reach for too much out of the wrong reasons and get nothing at all?

I can't tell from the guards' heckling. The prince hasn't shown any signs of magic since he arrived, but then, Admiral Varus could have cautioned him against it. At least while I'm around.

As we amble along the front parapet overlooking the sprawl of the city, the rooftops gleam under the bright afternoon sun. I contrive to place myself next to Prince Bastien. I have to constrain my pace, because his own strides are still a little unsteady from the climb.

Petra, Varus, and the others pull ahead of us, Stavros shooting a quick glance back at me with a subtle tip of his head in approval. When they stop to resume their conversation near the corner of the walkway, I come to a halt several paces away.

I set my hands on the ridges of stone as if I simply want

to sightsee, blocking the prince from strolling straight onward too.

He pauses beside me rather than walking around. I wouldn't be surprised if he appreciates the break.

"It's a long way from Cotea's capital to Dariu's," I remark. "Do you see your family often?"

Bastien's voice comes out terse. "No."

I turn to lean against the wall sideways and decide to take a gamble. "Do you really think your emperor's soldiers are going to set down their arms and walk away?"

I manage to startle him with my bluntness. He blinks at me, a flash of emotion crossing his face and vanishing before I can decipher it. Then he turns to glower at the rest of Florian.

His answer sounds rehearsed. "That's not for me to say. I'm sure if negotiations proceed that way, my family will respect the empire's treaties."

"I wouldn't imply otherwise. It's only that Dariu has been awfully stubborn, emperor after emperor, for rather a lot of decades."

I think my wry tone earns me a twitch of his lips, though it's so brief I might have imagined it. For a moment, his eyes darken. "Everything changes, and nothing lasts forever. It just takes the right moment."

He could be talking about a moment of peace-making and negotiation, but his expression suggests otherwise. And right then, I catch the tiniest quiver of magic, as if his gift tried to flex itself and he yanked it back.

Oh, he has magic all right. And surely it's a lot with a sacrifice like that.

What kind of immense gift would the Darium emperor allow right under his own roof?

Before I can figure out how to wheedle that information out of Bastien, Varus clears his throat and makes a beckoning gesture. "Come on, young prince. You're meant to be part of this discussion as well."

Schooling his face into perfect blankness, the prince stalks over to join his colleagues.

Late that night, I only manage to make it until just after the doors have closed behind the delegates before my mouth gapes in a jaw-creaking yawn. I swipe my hand across my mouth and glance over at Petra. "Did you get anywhere at all with that puffed up lout?"

The queen lets out a low chuckle. "He talked in a lot of circles, certainly. I told him I'd like to see a formal proposal in writing, and he promised to speak to Emperor Tarquin to decide on their required terms, but I suspect we won't be seeing that."

Stavros drains the last of his wine from the cup he's carried with him to the front hall. "He got what he wanted, which was to examine the new ruler of Silana."

Tinom lets out a huff. "And now the emperor will know she's no one to be trifled with and that she's got the full strength of her people supporting her."

Casimir offers a crooked smile. "It'd have made him very happy if I'd informed him of the few minor points of emotional pressure I'm aware would affect you. He was definitely searching for weaknesses."

"Darium will keep trying us regardless," Stavros says, and then adds in a more optimistic tone, "but perhaps they'll spend a little less time on it now that we've got riven magic on our side along with everything else."

He aims his familiar cocky grin at me, and my heart skips a beat even after all this time.

"The Cotean prince," I begin, feeling it's important to

mention. "I think he could be a weakness to the empire. If they ever let him get involved with anything important."

Petra tilts her head to the side. "I'm not sure how that could come into play in protecting our borders, but it's best to consider every angle."

I stifle another yawn, and Rheave comes over to slip his hand around my elbow. "I think our favorite riven sorcerer needs her sleep now."

I mutter some sort of argument, but Petra laughs and waves us off. "I should fill in my siblings on today's minor results."

All four of my men draw in around me as we head through the halls to the quarters we've been assigned at the back of the palace.

As advisors of various sorts, we're considered members of the court. Even Alek has his own private quarters, though he still spends many of his nights in his dorm at the college for ease of access to the library.

None of us can complain about the accommodations, but my room is my favorite. When I step past the door, the large window at the far side shows a view over the sprawling back grounds. This season's crops poke from the soil in even rows where a section of the hunting woods has been cleared to make way for a garden Filip has been overseeing. Moonlight streams down over the treetops beyond.

The thick rug embraces my feet as I pull off my shoes. The built-in shelves that fill nearly all of one wall contain even books to keep me occupied in my less busy moments for many years to come.

And Petra, without comment, supplied me with an absolutely massive bed.

It's very fine for sprawling out on my own, but the best nights are those when I share it. Now, through unspoken agreement, all four of my men follow me into the room.

I strip down to my underclothes and allow myself to crash into the middle of the mattress. Casimir laughs and tugs the covers out from under me. "Looks like we need to tuck our Kindness in."

I make a disgruntled sound that peters into a happy sigh as the men clamber onto the immense bed around me. I'm too exhausted from the intense, hours-long parlay with the Darium delegation to be up for any of the other thrilling activities we've frequently enjoyed here, but it's a special kind of delight just falling asleep with my lovers around me—all of us safe and sound.

Alek has sprawled out near my head. As I start to doze, he caresses his fingers over my hair.

"Ivy," he says, sounding rather dreamy himself but maintaining his air of academic curiosity, "do you ever wish you'd taken Kosmel up on his offer? Floated around in total contentment for years on end?"

Once I was recovered enough from the trials to pull coherent sentences together, I told all of them about the moments after I opened myself to the gods' magic and what Kosmel said to me. We've never discussed it in much detail, though.

I guess I thought the facts went without saying. I certainly don't need to think for even a second before I answer, with total honesty.

"No. I couldn't possibly have been as content as I am in this life I've built with you."

Rheave lets out a rough sound of agreement and kisses my shoulder. Stavros loops his arm around my waist.

The five of us drift off together, ready to face whatever else the world throws at us as one.

The Gods of the Abandoned Realms

THE ALL-GIVER (the Great God, the One) - overseer of all existence, creator of the godlen

THE GODLEN OF THE SKY

Estera - wisdom, knowledge, and education

Inganne - creativity, play, childhood, and dreams

Kosmel - luck, trickery, and rebellion

THE GODLEN OF THE EARTH

Creaden - royalty, leadership, justice, and construction

Prospira - fertility, wealth, harvest, and parenthood

Sabrelle - warfare, sports, and hunting

THE GODLEN OF THE SEA

Ardone - love, beauty, and bodily pleasures

Elox - health, medicine, and peace

Jurnus - communication, travel, and weather

About the Author

Eva Chase lives in Canada with her family. She loves stories both swoony and supernatural, and strong women and the men who appreciate them.

Along with the Rites of Possession series, she is the author of the Shadowblood Souls series, the Heart of a Monster series, the Gang of Ghouls series, the Bound to the Fae series, the Flirting with Monsters series, the Cursed Studies trilogy, the Royals of Villain Academy series, the Moriarty's Men series, the Looking Glass Curse trilogy, the Their Dark Valkyrie series, the Witch's Consorts series, the Dragon Shifter's Mates series, the Demons of Fame series, and the Legends Reborn trilogy.

Connect with Eva online:
www.evachase.com
eva@evachase.com